DEADLY ENCOUNTER

The windows were fifty feet high, bisected into arches that created the effect of an enormous cathedral. Through the glass, Alivet could see the expanse of the city below: a sprawl of alleys and rookeries reaching as far as the fens. Latent Emanation's sun had already boiled away over the edge of the world, and the city was hazy in the damp evening air. Alivet knew that if she stepped across to the window and looked down, she would see the building curving like a carapace below her: a maze of fume bars and restaurants, dance halls and penitentials.

The complex was popular, though mercifully not with the Lords themselves. Alivet noted all manner of patrons from elsewhere in the fens: Hepsborough genuflexives waving their dining implements in animated conversation; Moderated Wives beneath a group veil and a single person reading an illegal political newspaper. Alivet's eyes widened; very few people dared to openly criticize the Lords and their Unpriests, and to sit reading such material in plain view seemed utter folly.

Alivet knew that she should avert her gaze and have nothing to do with this dangerous individual, but her curiosity was piqued and she stared. She saw two long pale hands at the edges of the paper. Then, as if realizing that he was being watched, the person lowered the paper and smiled up at her.

Alivet saw a narrow, handsome face, not quite human: ivory as a polished skull beneath sleek blue-black hair. His eyes, deep set in hollows of bone, were as dark as garnets. His smile was mocking, beguiling, holding all manner of promises . . .

the POISON MASTER

Liz Williams

BANTAM BOOKS

THE POISON MASTER

A Bantam Spectra Book / January 2003

Published by
Bantam Dell
A Division of Random House, Inc.
New York, New York

ISBN 0-553-58498-7

Manufactured in the United States of America
Published simultaneously in Canada

OPM   10 9 8 7 6 5 4 3 2 1

To my mother for the Gothics
and my dad for the magic,
to Joanna for Wuthering Heights,
and to Charles

ACKNOWLEDGMENTS

- to Shawna McCarthy and Anne Groell,
  for all their help
- to everyone in the Montpellier Writing
  Group
- to Tanith Lee, for her encouragement
  and support
- to Gardner Dozois, for accepting the original
  story for *Asimov's*
- to Damh, for the four-faced angel
- to Bob and Jan, for all the tea
- to Storyville and Broaduniverse, listmembers
  extraordinaire
- to Jane Austen, William Burroughs,
  and Jack Vance

. . . it is the stars,
The stars above us, govern our condition.

SHAKESPEARE, *King Lear*

the
POISON MASTER

part I

PREPARATION

In [discussing] thaumaturgy and theatrical effects, [Dee] wrote: "And for these and such like marvellous Acts and Feats, Naturally, Mathematically, and Mechanically wrought and contrived: ought any honest Student and Modest Christian Philosopher be counted and called a Conjuror? . . . Shall that man be . . . condemned as a Companion of the Hellhounds, and a Caller, and Conjuror of Wicked and damned Spirits?"

The answer, he was about to discover, was "Yes."

— BENJAMIN WOOLLEY, *The Queen's Conjuror*

chapter I

A re you certain this unnatural device will not fail us?" Sir John Cheke's face was a study in apprehension. Beyond the windows of the college hall, the May twilight grew blue and dim. Cheke reached for a candle and lit it.

"Of course I am certain," Dee replied, swallowing his impatience. "I should not have proposed such a matter to you if I had not been entirely sure of my theorems." He pointed to a complex arrangement of levers, mirrors, and pulleys, concealed behind the pale stone arches.

"Nevertheless, if the theatrical player is actually intended to ride upon this contraption—" Cheke hesitated. "And though I believe you to be a prodigy in mathematics, you are youthful, sir, and prone to eagerness. Will the actor be safe?"

"He will be as safe as if he sat bestride an aged mule upon the Ely road." John Dee took care to maintain a tranquil countenance above his frayed ruff, belying a degree of inner doubt. It had taken several sleepless nights to work out the practical consequences of his plan and Dee was by no means sure that it would prove a success. But how else to test the theory? The expression that

Cheke wore now was a familiar one. It had often been seen to steal across his old tutor's features, like cat-ice upon the millponds of the Cam, when Dee had come up with some new notion, but he was also confident that Cheke could be persuaded to support the current proposal. After all, it was well known that Cheke would not set foot out of his house before examining the configuration of the stars, and frequently consulted Dee as to the more pressing astrological portents. Moreover, Cheke and his colleagues had already proved instrumental in encouraging Erasmus' new learning at the University. Arabic arithmetic, which Dee was currently engaged in teaching to a new generation of undergraduates, was now all the rage. So was Greek philosophy and that meant that Greek plays might also be popular, such as Aristophanes' *Peace*, which Dee was now currently attempting to stage.

Cheke prodded the thing that sat before him with a wary foot.

"But a mechanical beetle? I do wonder, John, at the chambers that your imagination must contain. Even at nineteen you manage to surpass the notions held by men twice your age!"

The beetle, some four feet in length and constructed of wood and metal at a local forge, rocked gently at the touch of Cheke's shoe.

"Take care! And I venture to remark that it is not *my* imagination," Dee hastened to say, "but that of Aristophanes himself, who was the first to conceive of such a scheme."

"One might suggest that the playwright's interest was allegorical rather than mechanical." Cheke gestured disapprovingly toward the copy of *Peace* that lay upon a nearby table. "That the hero of this play succeeds in reaching Olympus and the gods on the back of a giant dung beetle, rather than the winged steed of legend, gives Aristophanes license for a number of broad jests and references."

"Broad jests aside, it is the principle that counts."

"Indeed. Explain to me once more how you intend to persuade this monster to part company from the ground?"

"I am beginning work upon an 'art mathematical,' which I term 'thaumaturgy,'" Dee explained. He took a deep breath, willing himself not to launch into an explanation that would cause a glaze to appear across Cheke's eyes. Sometimes it was difficult to remember that other people did not seem to enjoy the same ease with mathematics as Dee himself. Sorting through the muddled pile of notes, he took up a scrap of parchment and began to read. " 'It giveth certain order to make strange works, of the sense to be perceived and of men greatly to be wondered at.' "

"Men will indeed greatly wonder," Cheke remarked acidly, "if a gigantic flying dung beetle should hurtle across the college dining room and flatten the unhappy audience. I want details, sir, not idle speculation such as one may hear in any tavern in the town. *How* is it going to fly?"

"It is based on the principles explored by the Greek mathematician Archytas. He demonstrated it by means of a wooden dove, which was able to fly unaided," Dee explained. "In Nuremberg, too, an artificer succeeded in constructing an iron fly that soared about the room and returned safely to his hand. And an artificial eagle was also produced, with similar results. I myself have conducted experiments with a metal insect of my own, this time fashioned of bronze, and have achieved a measure of success. However, I am reluctant to do the same with an object of these proportions"—Dee nudged the beetle—"and hence I have arranged this purely mechanical sequence of pulleys, operated by the elements of air and water, which are intended to move the device between the rafters. Both methods involve the application of mathematics and if we are successful in this more material exercise, I will attempt to produce true *unaided* flight in the beetle itself. Imagine," he went on, "if we could devise a flying machine that could transport a man clear across the country. With the present condition of our English roads, a man could make a fortune with such an engine."

Cheke's round face embodied skepticism. "First things first, John. Let's get the beetle to the lofty peak of the Trinity ceiling before we start to muse about crossing the country."

"A wise plan," Dee agreed. Cheke was the Chancellor, when everything was said and done, and it would not do to be too insistent. He was fortunate that Cheke was allowing him to stage the play at all.

To the detriment of his students, Dee spent the next few days in a haze of mathematical speculation, distracted only by the imploring questions of the leading theatrical player.

"What if I fall off the device?" Will Grey pleaded, kneading his cap between his hands. "Are you certain that this is safe?"

With an inward sigh, Dee gave the same reassurances to Grey that he had previously made to Sir John Cheke.

"All you have to do is to maintain a steady hold upon the scarab's shell. The ropes and pulleys will do the rest of the work. Now, my Trygaeus, be brave, as befits a true hero approaching the Olympian heights!"

"All very well for you to say," Grey muttered. "Since your part is merely to skulk in the wings like a curber's warp."

"Exactly." Dee clapped Grey on the shoulder. "Where I shall be taking good care that everything goes according to plan."

Once the disconsolate actor had gone, Dee went back into his rooms and sat down at the desk. Spring rain streaked the leaded windows, turning the bleached stones of Trinity as gray as bone. An east wind, cold as the forests of Muscovy from which it had come, roared across the fens and rattled the doors. Somewhere in the building Dee could hear the drift of a lute. Footsteps clattered on the wooden staircase, accompanied by a sudden babble of voices. Ignoring these distractions, Dee riffled the parchments that covered the desk until he located the letter that had arrived that morning from Roger Ascham at Louvain. Reading the letter once more, Dee marveled at the prospect of living in such an age as this, when a new discovery seemed to spring forth every day like wisdom from the head of Jupiter...

He wondered whether there was any truth in this latest theory. He had come across it before in an account of Rheticius', but now it seemed that someone had published it in a book. It would be worth his while to hunt down a copy of this *De Revolutionibus*, Dee thought. An intriguing notion: that the Earth journeyed about the sun rather than the other way about, a return to most ancient principles.

Idly, Dee began to speculate and soon became engrossed in the half-visionary, half-mathematical dreaming that had proved the hallmark of his success to date. Despite Cheke's skepticism, he felt sure the principles that had led to the flight of the little bronze bee could be harnessed to lift a much larger object, and he pictured himself soaring above the woods and patchwork fields of England.

In his mind's eye, the Thames lay below, a silver thread snaking toward a glistening sea, and all the roofs and gables of London spread out beneath him like children's toys. It would be akin to the view from the spire of St. Mary's in Cambridge, the highest that Dee had ever stood above a town, yet surely from a greater height everything would look even more remote. Imagination took Dee sailing across London, over the black-and-white whimsy of Nonsuch Palace, over the turrets of Oxford and the green hills of Gloucestershire, as far as the borders of Wales and then up through the rainy skies into the heavens until he could see the Earth itself, hanging like an orb against a field of stars and suns.

It was the very image of an astrolabe: he could almost see the roads traveled by each and every world around the sun. And Dee thought: *If only my device could reach the realms of the sublunary spheres. Then I could see for myself the truth of the matter, whether the world travels around the sun, or vice versa . . .*

Someone knocked sharply on the door, returning Dee to Earth. It proved to be Cheke, with yet another worry, leaving Dee no more time for interplanetary speculation.

Much to Cheke's surprise, and Dee's secret relief, the rehearsals for the performance of *Peace* passed with only a few hitches.

"It will all go ill on the night," Cheke said gloomily, when Dee pointed out that this proved the soundness of his calculations. From the wings, Will Grey could be heard vomiting into a bucket, whether with the sensation of the flight itself or relief at having survived it, Dee did not know.

"Nonsense," said Dee. "You must have more faith in mathematics."

"I can see why some folk call it no better than conjuring," Cheke muttered.

Dee winced. The accusation was a familiar one. "Calculation" still meant "conjuring" to more than a few folk, and Pythagoras himself was commonly supposed to have been a magus. As long as they kept to burning books and not people, Dee thought, he should be safe enough. Though if the political situation changed, it might be a different story. He remembered the troubles earlier in the year: the sudden Protestant upheaval at the succession of the young King Edward that had seen statues destroyed in

St. Paul's and other churches. Still, if Plato and Aristotle had managed to live through the dark days of political unrest, Dee would endeavor to prove worthy of them. The main matter was knowledge.

"Do not be anxious," he instructed Cheke. "You will see when the performance is over what a great wonder it has been, and what fame the college will glean as a result. I have heard that people are even traveling from the court."

At this a glitter of calculation began to light Cheke's eye, and Dee knew that there would be no more carping about money or the furnishings.

"Alas! How frightened I am—I have no heart for jests," Will Grey cried, as the beetle hurtled from one side of Trinity Hall to the other above a gaping crowd. A greasy smoke billowed up from the pitch torches surrounding the stage as the beetle sailed past. "Ah, machinist, take great care of me!"

"I do not recollect those last words in the script," Cheke murmured; he had joined Dee for a moment in the wings.

"He meant it, though." It was a great shame that he could only snatch glimpses of the beetle's wonderful flight, Dee thought. The rest of his attention was riveted on the men working the system of ropes and pulleys that powered the device, and in angling the mirror above the stage that gave the illusion of depth. But he could hear the astonished murmurs of the audience and that was almost as good. The hall was packed; not only with students and tutors, but also with courtiers, who for all their city sophistication were just as slack-mouthed as the merest youth.

"It is a triumph," Cheke whispered. "I have been listening. They really have no notion how it was done." He bestowed a nervous glance upon his colleague. "They are already talking about sorcery, you know. We shall have to be careful."

Absently, Dee nodded. Ropes and trickery were all very well, but the experiment had served to convince him of one thing. He now knew that the real work lay in the future: in making that visionary flying machine, in traveling to the Earth's limits, and beyond.

chapter II

CITY OF LEVANAH, MONTH OF DRAGONFLIES

The meeting that night was held at a stilt-farm near the village of Edgewhere, in the middle of Deadwife Marsh. The causeway was unlit, but marsh fire flickered beneath its rickety poles and insects traced a pale light across the path of Alivet Dee. It was late in the Month of Dragonflies; the iridescent swarms had already lifted from the waters of the marsh and sailed up into the skies, hanging on the rising winds. Alivet pulled her greatcoat closer to guard against the dampness and the chill. The hem of her long skirt was already soaked. She could smell moss, growing somewhere in the brackish waters below, combining with the odor of mud and marsh weed. You could make something of that, Alivet thought: mingled with velivey and myrrh, it would make an interesting musk, and quite possibly a narcotic one, too. But she had other things to think about besides perfume and alchemicals.

As she neared the end of the causeway, Alivet glanced uneasily over her shoulder. The city of Levanah rose above the fens, a crust of dark buildings starred with lamps. A scarab flier hissed low over the horizon, carrying Unpriests to some unknown assignation, and Alivet shivered. Far to the left, she could see the silhouetted shapes of the Towers of

Contemplation, phosphorus gleaming along their pylons. Up there, the anube mendicants sat, locked in prayer for the soul of the city. There were never more than three or four; the Unpriests would come sooner or later, and toss them down into the marsh. Alivet had seen such a thing once before: a twisting jackal-headed body, plummeting silently into the waters from the rickety heights of the tower. More would always come to take their place, as the Unpriests clearly knew. Alivet wondered why they did not simply have the towers removed, but perhaps it amused the Unpriests to have such a stationary target, or perhaps it was symbolic of the uneasy relationship that existed between anube and human.

At the center of Levanah she could see the shattered stump of Luce Vo, a sight that always sent a chill through her. It was there that the Lords of Night had first come to the world of Latent Emanation; spiraling down above the World River delta in a drift-boat with a hold of human captives. That had been many hundreds of years ago now, Alivet thought, conjuring up the image of those captives— her own ancestors—to give herself courage. If they had faced such trials, surely she could put up with what she herself had to bear. The anvil of the landing site towered above the city, its summit lost in darkness. Alivet shuddered once and hurried on.

This had never been her favorite time of year. She had grown up in Edgewhere, and was familiar with dank, dark days when the lamps smoldered and not even the best waterproofs dried out properly. It was not a healthy time, either. Last year there had been an outbreak of the typhe, and the year before that, dozens had been lost to river fever. And it had been in the Month of Dragonflies that the Unpriests had come for Inkirietta: five years ago now, her sister and herself no more than seventeen. With one of the paradoxes of grief, it seemed at once a hundred years before, and yet no more distant than last week. Inki's cries and their aunt's pleas still resounded in Alivet's head like the cries of spirits out across the marsh.

An ill time, full of sickness and disappointment, old sorrows...She would rather be at home, tending her plants, than traipsing across Deadwife Causeway to pay her devotions, but the summons had been slipped beneath her door that evening, only an hour before. She could not disobey; it was her turn to take the Search tonight. It was the duty of all chosen citizens to participate in the Searches, the one thing that united them against the Unchurch.

Alivet trod in a puddle of fen-rot, turned her ankle, and swore. Seven weeks ago, the ceremony had been held in the basement of one of the old buildings at the back of Luce Vo; a more salubrious location in the city's center. A cold and sudden raindrop snaked down the back of her neck and Alivet was relieved to see the outlines of the stilt-farm rising out of the waters of the marsh.

A guardian was standing at the door. In silence, Alivet held out her summons. The guardian took her hand.

"One moment." She felt a pinprick at the end of her finger, sending a single drop of blood to hiss into a crucible. The clear liquid within turned a glowing red as soon as the blood touched it. The guardian nodded.

"You're marked off. Thanks for coming. In through the left entrance. You know what to do."

Alivet followed these instructions and found herself in a long, low room. It was a barn; she could see the barrels of frogs and creek creeper, destined for Levanah's markets, stacked with untidy haste against the wall. She sat cross-legged on the floor, tucking her long dress beneath her and noting with annoyance that her top-skirt had a fresh burn. Around the hem, acid had eaten away the fabric until it resembled the skeleton of a leaf. How had that happened? But she remembered a drop spilt from a crucible the day before, sizzling to the floor as it fell. She had bought the skirt only a month ago and already it looked old, but it would have to wait another year before she could afford to replace it. All the money between now and next Memory Day was earmarked for Inki.

Wing cases crackled beneath Alivet as she settled herself. The farmer could have swept the place more thoroughly, but probably had not had time. News that this was the meeting place would have reached the farmer only a short while before Alivet received her own summons. The barn was filling up, people filing in behind Alivet and sitting down around her, all in silence. A seeker appeared at the front of the assembly, carrying a second crucible. Alivet's sensitive nose caught the odor of tonight's drug: dreaming menifew, combined with opium. It was to be one of the trusted psychopomps, then, nothing new and experimental.

Be thankful for small mercies, Alivet thought. She did not fancy staggering home across the causeway, nauseated and shaking from someone's experimental brew. She wondered briefly what the Search must be like for someone who had little knowledge of hallucinogens and alchemicals. As a professional drug-maker and apothecary, at least she herself was familiar with the substances involved.

Still no one spoke. The crucible was handed to a person in the front row, who hunched over it for a moment and took a long, unsteady breath. The crucible was passed on. Alivet watched impatiently as each participant breathed in the drug in turn. The sooner this was over and done with, the more quickly she could return home. She had work to do that night, a preparation for a client on the following day, and she was already tired.

Alivet took a deep breath of musty air and closed her eyes, reciting the five-year-old reminder. The harder she worked, the more she would earn. The more she earned, the quicker she could pay the unbonding fee and buy Inki back from the Unpriests and their masters. If she continued to work hard and all went to plan, Inki could be back home within the year. Then perhaps she could find her sister an apprenticeship, and they could rent a few rooms in a decent house...

It was an old dream, and this was not the place or time for it. The crucible was already at the end of her row. She needed to prepare for it, not spend her time in daydreams.

The people in the front row were starting to slump, lying huddled in their cloaks on the dusty, wing-sharded floor. At last, the crucible reached Alivet. She took its warm bulb in her hand, then hunched over the flute-hole and breathed in. The smoke filled her senses, murmured in her head. She did not remember passing the crucible on, but her hands were suddenly empty. She stared down at them: her fingers were calloused and stained with acid and ash, and they seemed suddenly magnified to incredible significance. She could feel the weight of her long braid, dragged down by the twelve rings of her apprenticeship. Her head was suddenly too heavy to bear.

Alivet pulled her hood over her face and curled up on the floor, staring into warm, sparkling darkness as the drug coursed through her. Dreaming menifew: green, chthonic, familiar. It was one of the companion plants, not an enemy that needed placation and the small sacrifices of vomiting or mania. She focused, conjuring up an image of the plant: a thick, sap-filled stem, fleshy leaves with a black-jade gloss, small crimson flowers like drops of blood. She sent the image within, calling up the spirit of the psychopomp.

All drugs had spirits attached to them; it was simply a matter of whether those allied beings were friendly or not. But Alivet had met those attached to menifew before. Obligingly, the drug's spirit whispered to her, promising visions. Last time, it had been vetony and she had had to fight it, driving it back as it threatened to swamp her rational mind, but all the menifews were a friend to the Search.

Images pulsed past: a marsh mome drawn to the ceremony, its blades wheeling and snapping; then a vision of her own small room as if viewed through the end of a telescope. Patiently, Alivet waited for the neural froth to subside. Her aunt's voice murmured in her head: *Don't ever be afraid. Even if the spirit of a drug is your enemy, you must trust it. If you fear it, it will snatch you into the world of the lost until it passes from your blood and you will come back with nothing except shakes and fever.* That had happened once or twice, of course, until Alivet learned how to steer and guide.

You must learn, Alivet. She could see her aunt Elitta standing before her, dressed in her customary long black skirt and red shawl, holding a bundle of knitting. *The women of our family have been apothecaries for generations, Searching like so many others, involved in the Long Dream. It is your duty to participate, to find out where we come from.*

Aunty? What are you doing here? Oh. Of course, you're not really here, are you? Why, for a moment I thought—

Stop babbling, Alivet, her rational mind instructed her kindly. *Attend. Concentrate.*

She still had occasional nightmares, of things glimpsed in a drugged depth, but that was common to everyone. At least she had not failed as a Searcher; a few did, every year. The Search was secret, but somehow everyone still knew, as though folk held the knowledge of that failure in their faces.

Alivet, unfearing now and acquiescent, slid down the green and growing paths of the drug, seeking lost answers. Nothing was there, only the conjurings of menifew: water dreams, the flick of a fishtail into deeper seas, a voice whispering at the edge of hearing. Alivet turned in to the susurrus, but it was only a rhyme, chanted over and over again as if to a child. *Here we go round the mulberry bush . . .*

What was a mulberry bush? Alivet wondered if it could be important, then dismissed it.

It was at that point that she thought she saw something on the horizons of her mind: something small and glittering against an abyss of night. She directed her gaze toward it; it grew rapidly larger. It was a drift-boat, hanging in the heavens against a skein of stars. Alivet sidled against it like a seal, peered through a porthole to the massed ranks of human captives: her ancestors, with the dancing form of a Night Lord moving between them.

They were all a little different, the Lords, as if their species had borrowed scraps and patches from all manner of creatures. This Lord had a narrow, inhuman face, sharp mandibles twisting at the base of the jaw, and long clawed hands. But the drift-boat was the means by which humans had come to Latent Emanation and she saw her world now, hanging over her shoulder like a great dark eye.

Only the boat? Alivet questioned the menifew. *I have seen this before; show me more. Show me where we come from, which world. Show me the Origin, the object of our long Search.* Her phantom fist hammered on the porthole of the boat, seeking to wake the rows of floating forms. Their limbs had become entangled, as though they lay in water, having recently and sweetly drowned. Her gaze fell on an elderly man: a sleeping figure in a plain black robe, with a forked beard and a narrow face. The man's face was closed and grim. Even in sleep, he looked angry. Alivet wondered why.

Who are you? My many times great-grandfather? What is your name?

But the unconscious man did not reply.

Alivet cried out into the void to her ancestors: *You knew! You knew where you, and therefore we, came from, but you did not speak. Why did you never speak?* For surely this was the greatest secret of all, concealed by even the most ancient texts. And in the midst of her drugged dreaming, Alivet thought that perhaps heresy was truth: that her ancestors had never known, or, worse, were the creations of the Night Lords themselves, golems of animated clay who shambled and shuffled out their days and had no secret to tell to the ones who came after.

Even as the thought sped out, she knew it was a mistake. With vegetable slowness, the scene seeped and changed. The boat was no longer there. She was standing in a long hall, ringed with lamps of unlight. A Lord stood before her, its shadowy carapace swathed in mottled robes. Beneath its arm, Alivet saw a girl with a pale, drawn face. She held a smoking brazier, offering it beseechingly up to the Lord's jaw. As she bent forward, Alivet saw that there was only a puckered pinprick hole where the girl's left eye had been, and in the same moment she recognized her sister.

"Inki!" she cried. "Inkirietta!"

The girl turned and her face twisted in puzzlement.

"Who are you?" she asked. "Do I know you?"

"It's me, Alivet..." and then as the girl's mutilated face still betrayed no recognition, she cried, "I'm your sister! Don't you know me?"

She sprang forward into the scene, like someone stepping into a picture, and gripped Inki by the shoulders. The Night Lord towered above them. Alivet saw its head swinging from side to side like an anube's muzzle. On each cheek, a slit opened to reveal a lining of bristling darkness. This Night Lord could not see, but it could smell.

"Inki," Alivet whispered. "Inki, run!"

But the dreaming menifew, with a psychopomp's unreasoning power, deemed that she had seen enough and snatched her away and out of its lure. Or perhaps, the thought came to her, the Lords of Night watched even this most secret dreaming and had flicked forth their power, casting her out.

She lay shivering on the floor of the barn. A guardian hastened over to help her up. The moment a person was free of the drug, the watchers wanted them gone, in case they disturbed the dreams of others. Alivet was tugged gently to her feet and into a small adjoining chamber full of grinding equipment. A recording device stood on a mangle and the person seated behind it spun the recorder's wheel so that the brass drum started to rotate. Alivet leaned forward and in a rapid, trembling whisper related her vision into the speaking-tube. She told it only of the drift-boat. She did not mention Inkirietta. When she was done, she was given a reviving cordial and shown through the door of the barn. The lights of the distant city gleamed at the edges of the marsh, and a haze of autumn stars hung above her head. Alivet, breathing cold fresh air, swallowed her despair and started on the long walk home.

She felt as though she had really stood next to her twin, that it had not just been a vision. But if it had been a true seeing, then her sister still remained in the grip of the Night Lords; half-blinded, not knowing those dearest to her. She should have tried to keep hold of Inki, she should have somehow done *something*—as though it would have been possible to pull a living person through the visionary barrier of a drug and into the world.

Alivet's eyes filled with tears of anger and frustration. She brushed them away and wiped her nose. This was foolish. The only thing that she could do to save Inki was to work as hard as she could and buy her sister back.

Her senses, stimulated by the drug, were still resonating. Lights danced at the edges of vision, and as she was halfway down the causeway, she heard a sudden sharp footfall behind her. Alivet whipped around. There was nothing there. She could see a little knot of people by the barn, illuminated by the sudden opening of a door. Then the door closed and they were gone. She looked toward Levanah. The lights of the city lay before her, glowing in the darkness.

Uncertain, Alivet looked back once more. A figure was standing behind her, eyes like hot red coals. Alivet cried out, stumbled away. The figure was abruptly gone, down into the marsh. Alivet stood shaking, with her hand pressed to her mouth, trying to make sense of what she had just seen. But the causeway was quiet and the surface of the marsh untroubled. It was the residue of the drug, she told herself, or some phantom or lich come to lure her from the causeway. Turning, she hurried toward the city and the light.

It took her another fifteen minutes to reach the end of the causeway. From here, she had the choice of returning via Fond Hope Hill, or taking the quicker route through the series of alleyways known as the Strangulations: a reflection upon their labyrinthine narrowness. Neither was safe. The neighborhood of Fond Hope Hill was known for footpads and garglers, whereas the alleys bordered on the Unpriests' districts, a place called Ettar Vo. At this time of night Alivet decided to chance the alleys: a deadlier risk, perhaps, but one more swiftly run. She set off in the direction of the Strangulations.

Alivet's luck held as far as the end of the alleys. She saw no one apart from a man and a child, whispering in a doorway, but then she turned a corner and came face-to-face with two Unpriests. Both wore the same garments—the long coats, the leather boots, the round rotating monocles—but one of them was a woman. It was the woman who veered toward Alivet.

"You! Show me your pass."

Alivet, reaching into the pocket of her skirts, complied.

"Name: Alivet Dee. Address: some slum somewhere. Profession?"

"I'm an alchemical apothecary." Alivet peeled off her left glove and held up her hand to show the trademark wheel tattooed upon her palm.

"Make perfumes and possets, do we? Yes"—she seized Alivet by the chin and turned her face to the lamp—"you've got the pinched face of a drug-maker. And where have you been this evening? Servicing some whore with cut-price odors or cheap hallucinogens?"

Since this was entirely likely, Alivet decided not to take offense.

"Actually, yes."

"Where does she live, this whore? Or is it a boy?"

"It's a woman," Alivet said, improvising madly. The Unpriest's monocle began to rotate, slowly unscrewing itself from the pale mask that was the Unpriest's face. Alivet remembered her aunt's early instructions: *Do not look them in the eyes. They will be able to see into your head and steal your thoughts away.*

Who knew if that was true? Yet she had no desire to seem shifty. She fixed her gaze on a point slightly to the right of the Unpriest's shoulder.

"And where does she live?" the Unpriest repeated.

"Back there somewhere. The place has a blue mark on the door; I don't know the address."

"You don't know."

"No. I could probably find it again, though, if you want to go back with me and look." She was risking a lot on their laziness, but if she cooperated as much as possible they might grow bored. Indeed, the male Unpriest tugged at his companion's sleeve.

"We have better things to do. Wasn't there a rumor of a game in the Trowels?"

His tone was filled with a suppressed urgency, suggesting an imminent relief would be required. Alivet decided that she'd prefer not to know what he was talking about. Whatever it was, sex and violence were probably on the agenda.

She saw the woman give a slow, cold smile.

"Can't we bring her along?" She tickled Alivet under the chin.

It was all Alivet could do not to bite the Unpriest's finger off.

Then the woman smacked Alivet so hard across the side of the head that she fell against the wall.

"Go away. I'm tired of you."

With pleasure, Alivet thought, and hastened away before the Unpriest changed her mind. After a few steps she realized that she had dropped her glove, but she had no intention of going back for it. Replacing the glove would cost money that should go toward Inki's unbonding, so she'd just have to keep her hands in her pockets if the weather grew cold.

She hurried through the Strangulations and did not look back until she turned the corner into Small Maim Street. The Unpriests had gone, and good riddance to them. Alivet was going home.

chapter III

CITY OF LEVANAH, MONTH OF DRAGONFLIES

Once home, Alivet adjusted her gauze mask and leaned over the swarm tank. The memory of the Search, and the red-eyed stranger, would have to wait; there was work to be done. With satisfaction, she noted that three more hatchlings had appeared since the previous night, making twelve altogether. She reached for the tongs and chased each squirming hatchling through tendrils of wire-weed and water-moss, catching them with care and drawing them from the tank to be placed in the celled saving jar. This done, she rotated the glass seal that kept the contents of the tank secure, and locked it. Then she carried the saving jar to the sink, and stood it in the smallest water-bath. Impelled by this soothing heat, the hatchlings would grow, and then she could take them to her booth in the public alchematorium and begin the first stages of extracting the narcotic fever from their cells.

It was a painstakingly delicate process and Alivet much preferred the plant-work—in addition to feeling sorry for the hatchlings—but river-fever dust was pricey and popular and she had little choice. Besides, Genever Thant had made the commission and since he was her principal employer, that was that.

Once the saving jar had been dealt with, Alivet made her way around the long, narrow room, methodically watering the skeins and veils of growing plants. She used a wooden pole to carry the watering can to the highest corners of the room, scattering velivey and flowering sor with cool droplets. The plants that required the most warmth had been placed on the highest ledges of the room, just beneath the ceiling, with the small mosses tucked away by the skirting board where it was cooler. Alivet had become accustomed to working in cramped conditions and this place was not much smaller than her aunt's stilt-house in Edgewhere: plants in every last corner, breathing greenness into the air. The velivey chimed and rang as the water touched it, as if in gratitude, and Alivet smiled.

When the watering was done, and the leaves of the delicate plants checked for fungus or rot, Alivet heard the chimes of her neighbor's water-clock. Only five o'clock, time enough to rest for a few minutes before she needed to prepare for the evening. She would be seeing a client tonight, one of Genever Thant's commissions. Alivet's thoughts turned to money. If the evening went well and the client was pleased, Genever might give her a bonus. It had happened before. The coins went into the pot beneath the floorboards and would then be sent back to her aunt, to be hoarded in Edgewhere for Inki's unbonding.

She poured herself a glass of thyme tea and carried it out onto the rickety balcony. The trees hummed with watermoths. Alivet laid her hands on the rail of the balcony, feeling burnished wood beneath her palms. Reaching out, she snapped a flower from the clematis that wandered up the walls of the rookery and tucked it into the last of the apprentice rings that banded her long plait. Thyme tea and a single blossom: a modest luxury, but Alivet was grateful.

From this height, through the fronded leaves of sootwood, she could see all the way to the spires of the city center. The structure called Port Tree rose above the city in a series of anomalous bulbous domes: the Lords' architecture clashing with human buildings. Most of these were rookeries for the workers. (Alivet wondered idly, and not for the first time, what the word actually meant. The only rooks she knew of were the little chess pieces, and what had a house for lots of people to do with chess?)

Beyond, too far away to be seen, lay the Lords' Quarter, the Isle of Silence, and the causeway that led to the western-most of the four Palaces of Night. From this distance, the spires of the city spun a lacy mesh across the sky, and the rising star that was neighboring Sephuri glittered on the horizon like a raindrop in a spider's web. She had been fortunate, Alivet thought, to find a room in this old rookery, with its staircases of antique wood and polished copper, its trailing veils of clematis. But while she was sipping thyme tea on this charming balcony, Inkirietta was somewhere in the depths of a Night Palace. Her twin's face turned to meet Alivet's mind's eye and Alivet bit her lip until she tasted blood.

All this is for Inki, Alivet reminded herself. It did not quell the guilt. Her friends had been astounded when she had announced her intention to move to the outskirts, the liminal lands between the city and the expanse of the fens.

"But what will you *do* out there?" Yzabet Spenser had cried, raising her hands in horror. "Darling, it's *miles* away. You might as well be dead! And what do Brother Genever and your other employers think about this mad plan?"

"Genever won't care," Alivet said, with truth. "As long as I turn up for work on time and make sure that his phials are in order, he couldn't care less where I was living. Anyway, it's cheaper, and it'll give me a bit of peace and quiet to work on the new fume formulations."

The money was, of course, the principal issue. The new rooms, which were only slightly cramped and damp, were half the cost of her dortoire fees in the city center. That meant more money to send back to her aunt every month, and more money meant that the time Inki would have to spend Enbonded would be diminished.

"You're just feeling guilty because the Lords of Night

didn't take you," Yzabet had said, with a toss of her head. "So *silly*. That's the way the system works. It's always the prettiest who get chosen." She glanced across at the portrait that stood on the dresser. Inki stared back: dark-eyed, oval-faced, smiling between the long braids of hair. Her face was Alivet's own. "Though I suppose that's not true in *your* case. Anyway, your sister will learn such a lot."

"Inki will learn, all right. About perversity."

"About *life*. She'll be associating with the highest levels of society. Who knows, perhaps she might catch some Unpriest's eye and become a mistress."

"That's what worries me." Alivet sighed. "If only I'd been past my apprenticeship when the Enbonders came. Then we might have been able to afford to unbond her right away. As it is, I'll just have to save until I've got enough." She did not add: *Why her? Why did they take Inki, and not me?* Yzabet was right, but she did not want to talk about the old guilt, of being the one left safely behind.

"I'm sure Inki will be all right," Yzabet assured her. "Whatever the Lords might be, look at all they've done for us. Helped us build our city, make sure law and order is maintained—and they protect us, too, from the beings of the worlds beyond. Without the Lords, what would happen to us? My father always used to say that taking a few hundred youngsters to be Enbonded was a small price to pay, really. And not *that* many Enbonded die."

"So they say. Maybe it's even true. But plenty wish they had. And the longer they're Enbonded, the worse they become. As for what the Lords do for us, I do not see it. It seems to me that the Lords rule the Nine Families, the Families govern the Unpriests, and the Unpriests control the rest of us. I even wonder how much the Lords would be able to achieve without human aid, rather than the other way round. And besides, I do not know why we should not all be permitted to make our own future, devise our own laws and principles. The ones espoused by the Unpriests don't seem very just to me."

"Hush, Alivet!" Yzabet had grown pale.

"And this 'protection' that they grant us. Who tells us that there are people of the worlds beyond, who wish us ill? Why, the Unpriests themselves. Has anyone seen such a being? It seems to me that the Lords and their creatures are the ones from whom we need to be kept safe, not some vague outside threat," Alivet said, but she lowered her voice all the same. "Anyway, what good has their justice done my sister? Inki was only seventeen. She's been incarcerated in a Night Palace for five years now. Whoever comes out at the end of the bonding, it won't be my twin."

Now, remembering this conversation, Alivet's hands tightened on the balcony rail. If Inki hadn't fallen prey to the Unpriests, Alivet might be standing on a veranda in Celestia or Shadow Town by now, a rising alchemical apothecary. She knew she was good at her work; she had only to look at the tattooed wheel on her palm to prove that. Most students took five years to make apprentice, not three. If she spent another few years with Genever and her other commissioning employers to pay off Inki's unbonding fees, then she could start saving for the rest of the family and herself. Set up shop in Shadow Town, perhaps; bring Inki and her aunt to a better place than Edgewhere.

Her thoughts turned to her principal employer. At least Genever Thant, peculiar though he might be, left her alone. She had heard some horror stories from other apprentices: tales of sexual deviancy and torment, whispers of nightmare. Just because apothecaries supplied drugs, people seemed to expect them to supply other services as well. Alivet supposed that it was the price one paid for working in a not-very-respectable profession.

But apart from the scientific and alchemical arts, there weren't all that many openings for lower-class girls, except prostitution and perhaps a bit of tutoring. Cooking and science, held to be similar in their methods and applications, were considered reasonable professions for young ladies of ungenteel birth. The higher-born, should they develop an aptitude for such things, would become physicians or surgeons, but this kind of work was not open to lower-class girls. She had been lucky to have a talent for drug-making. Inki's interest, on the other hand, had always been in cookery. If she had not been Enbonded—but there was no use thinking about that.

It was also fortunate that Genever was too jaded to take any pleasure in—well, anything much anymore. On the one hand, this was good, as it spared Alivet from his possible excesses, but on the other, he was almost incapable of appreciating anything she produced. One sniff of a painstakingly created new perfume, and it would be, *Very nice, Alivet. I'm sure they'll like it*, pronounced in a tone so lackluster that he might as well have died.

But sometimes she caught him staring at her and his gaze was no longer dry and old. Then she would wonder, uneasily, what he really felt.

Compared with her sister's plight, however, these were small frustrations. Alivet set down the tea glass and went back inside, to prepare for the evening's client.

chapter IV

CITY OF LEVANAH, MONTH OF DRAGONFLIES

The sorbet was as black as night and as delicate as air. Alivet watched as Genever Thant took a spoonful and fed it wearily into the waiting, eager mouth of his companion, who strained against her bonds.

"Can you taste it?" _How many times had he whispered this over the course of the last month?_ Alivet wondered. Jaded he might have been, but Genever's sardonic face was fashionably powdered and he wore a velvet suit that must have cost a fortune; small wonder that he wanted to get his money's worth out of their aristocratic client tonight.

She smiled encouragingly at the client, even though the blindfolded girl could not see her. Around them, the murmur of conversation rose and fell. Fellow diners cast surreptitious glances in the direction of Alivet and her companions. _Good publicity,_ thought Alivet, _if all goes well._

Genever went on, "All the way from the palace kitchens of the Night Lords themselves, smuggled in for your delectation alone. The lamps over the Straits of Sesh; splint-lily and night-spice in the evening airs of the forests of Fem...A confection softer than kisses and more subtle than a lie."

He had a way with words, Alivet had to admit. She recognized the place names from a recent and fashionable play.

The lips of Madimi Garland closed over the foaming dark froth. She gave a whimper of pleasure.

"Told you so," Genever said, with something close to satisfaction. "Well, my Lady, what's your wish now?" Alivet saw that a trace of sorbet was smeared across his palm. Fastidiously, Genever wiped his hands on a silken handkerchief. It had not been a rhetorical question, though at first glance Madimi Garland was hard-pressed to answer. Her hands were bound behind her with fronds of sup-briar, which had flowered in the heat of the restaurant and now put forth tiny, translucent blossoms, tinged with the Lady's blood. If she looked closely, Alivet knew, she would see each little thorn twisting around to prick the girl's flesh and drink. But Madimi squirmed with pleasure, chafing her hands to drive in the thorns. Her ankles, similarly bound, were crossed daintily beneath the tablecloth.

Prior to the beginning of the meal, Alivet had inserted nose-plugs, so that the Lady's sole sense would be that of taste. Thus far, she seemed impressed, and this gratified Alivet, who had spent considerable time poring over possible menus. It might not be particularly respectable, but she took her work seriously, and as a partner of one of the oldest Experience firms in the city, Genever also had a reputation to maintain, not to mention Alivet's fee to pay.

Alivet wondered again about the possibility of a bonus, and surveyed with professional detachment the edges of the Lady's metal corset: an intricate affair of rods and panels above her voluminous skirts. The sharp hem was digging into the girl's flesh and Alivet could see the reddening line across her breasts. Swiftly, and without warning, Genever leaned across and turned a small screw. The corset tightened and the Lady squeaked.

Alivet winced, thankful that she was wearing her own comfortable and modest attire. Whilst she possessed a formal corset—a present from her aunt when she reached the marriageable age of seventeen—it was a simple confection of boned velvet, not this engineered construction. Aunt Elitta had given a corset to Inki, too, but Inki had never had the chance to wear it. Alivet felt her lips tighten as she looked at Madimi's rich clothes and she forced herself to smile.

Genever dusted sugar-glaze from the narrow cuffs of his brocade jacket and sighed, evidently unmoved by the girl's sensual discomfort. Madimi Garland hardly presented a challenge, but at least the girl was prepared to pay. Alivet was well aware that as an expert in the palates of different senses for over thirty years, Genever preferred local clients who had long since become jaded by the many pleasures that the city of Levanah had to offer its aristocracy. She assumed that to stimulate such people—scions of the Nine Families, with the wealth to support their appetites, or Unpriests who made a fetish of hedonism—could occasionally lead to a flicker of feeling within himself. Sometimes Alivet could even see it, reflected in his sad black eyes like a lantern spark. Those who had devoted themselves to the Search could be interesting, too: the many folk who, like herself, had spent time and care on the sacramental use of the psychopompic drugs, seeking to travel into the world-soul to seek out humanity's lost origins.

But the Lady was very young and her upbringing with the Sisters of Restriction had been traditionally confined. Three years ago a piece of seeded cake would have thrilled her, and a glass of wine would have been the ultimate in decadence. Now—divorced after a short formal marriage and disgustingly wealthy—Madimi Garland was evidently making up for lost time.

Alivet understood that Genever himself had long since exhausted the possibilities of bondage: the tired politics of domination and submission. He found the corruption of purity to be merely clichéd, whereas Alivet found it distasteful. She would have taken more care in selecting her clientele if it had not been for Inki and the need for money. She wished that they could have interested the Lady in one of the paths of the Search, but Madimi Garland had informed them in no uncertain terms that she'd had quite enough of being preached at. All the Sisters of Restriction had ever talked about was the need to prepare oneself for devotion to the Night Lords, should one be so fortunate as to be selected for Enbonding. *More fool them*, Alivet thought, but she could not entirely blame Madimi. The sisters were a part of the Unchurch, after all, albeit a minor branch, and their allegiance was to their masters. Who knew what manner of lies they had passed on to their young acolytes, or what delights they might have promised once the chosen entered service? Not for the first time, Alivet wondered just what kind of mind-wash drugs could be employed by the Lords and those who served them. The thought that there might be those who entered that service of their own free will, however, was more unnerving yet.

When the selection—of twenty girls of various ages—had finally been made, Madimi had not been among them. Now, therefore, she was ready for some fun—which, she reminded Alivet with all the sophistry of the conventually educated, was itself one of the paths to self-discipline, once one had exhausted all the possibilities. Asceticism always produced such tediously predictable results. Next, Madimi Garland would want to move on to drugs, and then, most probably, sexual congress with partners of varied gender and inclination. At least that wasn't a service Alivet herself would be expected to provide.

Alivet was soon proved right. The Lady swallowed the last of her shadowy sorbet, and whispered with a vestige of primness, "Let's go into the fume room. Can we do that?"

"Of course we can," Genever said. "You, my Lady, can do anything you wish." *After all*, Alivet forbore to add, *you're the one who's paying*.

Quivering with barely suppressed excitement, Madimi Garland allowed them to help her rise. Her briar-bound feet took a tottering step forward. Genever put a hand on each shoulder and gently propelled her toward the fume room. No one looked up as they passed, but Alivet surveyed her fellow diners with interest. Mid-week, the restaurant was crowded and the best tables were full. Genever had chosen not to sit by the window, in order to concentrate on Madimi, but Alivet snatched a brief glance as they passed. Whenever she came into this building, the difference between human scales of architecture and those of the Lords always struck home. It was hard not to be awed, and Alivet could see why so many of her fellow citizens regarded the Lords and their Unpriest acolytes with such cringing envy and respect; why there were so many folk who wanted a piece of that power. But Alivet found it harder still not to hate.

The windows were fifty feet high, bisected into arches that created the effect of an enormous cathedral. Through the glass, she could see the expanse of the city below: a sprawl of alleys and rookeries reaching as far as the fens. Latent Emanation's sun had already boiled away over the edge of the world, and the city was hazy in the damp evening air. Alivet knew that if she stepped across to the window and looked down, she would see the building curving like a carapace below her: a maze of fume bars and restaurants, dance halls and penitentials.

The complex was popular, though mercifully not with the Lords themselves. Alivet noted all manner of patrons from elsewhere in the fens: Hepsborough genuflexives waving their dining implements in animated conversation; Moderated Wives beneath a group veil; and a single person reading an illegal political newspaper. Alivet's eyes widened: very few people dared to openly criticize the Lords and their Unpriests, and to sit reading such material in plain view seemed utter folly.

Alivet knew that she should avert her gaze and have nothing to do with this dangerous individual, but her curiosity was piqued and she stared. She saw two long pale hands at the edges of the paper. Then, as if realizing that he was being watched, the person lowered the paper and smiled up at her. Alivet saw a narrow, handsome face, not quite human: ivory as a polished skull beneath sleek blue-black hair. His eyes, deep set in hollows of bone, were as dark as garnets. Alivet, remembering the red-eyed figure on the causeway, gasped.

The smile was mocking, beguiling, holding all manner of promises. She took a step back. The man bowed his head in polite acknowledgment of her presence and disappeared behind his paper.

"Alivet?" Genever asked, puzzled. "What's the matter?"

"Nothing. I—" She could not simply march up to the fellow and demand to know if he had been stalking her. The figure on the causeway had borne all the marks of a dream or vision. Doubtless it had been nothing more than a remnant of the drug. But then what was this red-eyed person doing here? Who was he, and what?

Unnerved, Alivet followed Genever and Madimi toward the fume room.

"That person over there, the one reading the newspaper," she said. "Did you see him?"

To her relief Genever replied, "Yes. What strange eyes he had, hadn't he? They had no whites. Perhaps they were lenses."

"Have you seen anyone like him before?"

"Never. Maybe he is from somewhere deep in the fens. There are some curious folk in the backwaters, I believe. There are said to be people who follow anube practices, who erect poles in emulation of sacrificial pedestals. It's safer to have nothing to do with such people." Genever dismissed the man with a languid flick of the fingers, but his eyes met Alivet's in mutual understanding and she knew that he was thinking of the Search. No one spoke of the Search outside the confines of its practice. "You'd be wise to stay away from such a one."

"I've no quarrel with that," said Alivet.

By now they had reached the door of the fume room and Alivet only just remembered to remove Madimi's nose-plugs in time. The Lady gasped, assailed by a thousand odors. Alivet's careful nose dissected, selected, and considered. Lantium dust made a brief foray into her neural synapses, encountered recognition, and withdrew. Serenity powder served only to make her sneeze these days, but jherolie was as sweet and pungent as it had ever been. Alivet looked at the rapturous visage of Madimi Garland, besieged by a hundred hallucinogenic odors, and tried to glean a vicarious thrill. But she had long since ceased to be a pharmacological virgin.

She gave the girl a little push between the shoulder blades. Might as well get on with it.

"What can we try first?" the Lady breathed.

Alivet considered this question. Better not start her off on something too powerful, or too long-lasting. After all, this was supposed to be an introductory session. Her mind moved briskly through a number of possibilities. She drew Genever aside.

"How about sozoma? Mild enough to be a good introductory substance, brief enough for her to move onto something more potent."

"Sounds all right to me," Genever said, wearily.

"Try not to be *too* enthusiastic, Brother Thant."

Genever gave a small smile. "I was wondering whether there was any amusement to be gained in giving her a good heavy dose of rupe. That would be an introduction she'd never forget."

"You can't do that!" Alivet was scandalized, though she was almost certain he was joking. "I'd prefer it if clients came back from time to time. We could do with the money. Anyway, I don't fancy watching the poor girl sweat and shriek out the next few hours. It would be a cruel and pointless thing to do. And I'd like an early night."

Whatever Genever's current level of ennui, he could still be reminded of his responsibilities. "You're probably right," he said. "You brought some sozoma, of course?"

"It's in my bag."

"Let's get started, then," Genever said, guiding Madimi Garland to a nearby couch. "Now, you sit there for a moment. Don't worry, we won't start you off on anything very pungent to begin with. Your sensibilities need to become acclimatized to different psychosomatic inputs. We're going to give you a mildly hallucinogenic fume called sozoma."

The Lady gave a happy nod, but as they settled themselves on the couch, someone reached out and touched Genever's arm. Alivet glanced up.

"Good evening," someone purred. The woman had the florid tattoo of a voluptuary sect inscribed upon her left breast, which was barely restrained by a velvet mesh dress. "Remember me?" She gave Genever a sultry look, her gaze assessing Alivet and slanting past. "The Hessing's unbonding party, about two years ago. Do you still think about those peony bushes? I do."

It was clear from the look on his face that Genever hadn't the faintest idea who she was. Alivet remembered the Hessing's party, but not the woman. The event had been an affair of such unparalleled dullness that it would be no wonder if Genever had seduced a stranger in the shrubbery. However, it would be unthinkable to be rude and the woman had an aura of money, so Alivet was not surprised when Genever leaned across and whispered into the woman's jeweled ear, "How could I ever have forgotten?"

The woman undulated against him, so close that Alivet could see the dilation of her pupils. She looked away, not wanting to appear too interested. As she did so, she saw the red-eyed man appear in the door of the fume room and look about him. He caught his lip between his teeth, all amused anticipation, then stepped through the door and strolled in the direction of the bar. Alivet stared at him with intense and covert curiosity. He wore long robes of some dark, rich material, but there was nothing very unusual about the clothes, no ceremonial marks or badges. He was moderately tall, and had a gliding walk, but there was nothing to really mark him apart from his odd countenance. It was impossible to estimate his age. Alivet forced herself to concentrate on Madimi.

"If you'd like a repeat performance..." Alivet heard the voluptuary say.

"Alas, I can't. I'm working tonight." Genever sounded almost regretful. Alivet's glance slid back to the red-eyed man.

He was staring directly at Alivet and she turned quickly away. As she did so, she saw his mocking smile return.

"You poor man," Genever's unknown paramour teased. "I'd better let you get back to these . . . little girls, then. But here's my address, if you did by any chance want to get in touch." She spoke with a practiced seductiveness. Genever took the slip of paper and inserted it into one of the loops in his jacket. Kissing her on the cheek, he turned back to his client. Alivet pushed the long sleeves of her evening jacket out of the way, cast a last glance in the direction of the red-eyed man, then took the somoza from her bag and handed the little phial to her employer.

"Brother Thant? Are you ready?" Their bound and blind-folded protégé was sitting hopefully on the couch.

"Indeed we are, and I have your initial choice: a small quantity of sozoma. Now, set and setting are critical for a gratifying experience, and I suggest that you take a moment and think of some particularly favorite fantasy."

"What sort of fantasy?" Madimi Garland blushed beneath the blindfold. Obviously the Sisters of Restriction had been thorough in their asceticism, or her husband peculiarly inept. Genever reached out and touched her wrist with professional detachment.

"To be perfectly frank, the drug works best with sexual images. It is of course up to you, and you don't have to tell me what they are." Alivet was thankful for that. In this line of work, she had heard enough fumbling adolescent scenarios to last a lifetime. It was enough to put one off the practice, not that she had the time for that sort of thing anyway. She thought of the boys of Edgewhere and suppressed a smile. If her previous—and admittedly somewhat limited—experience was anything to go by, it wasn't as though she was missing a great deal.

"I'll try and think of something," Madimi Garland said, and now she sounded nervous. Telling her to relax would almost certainly have the opposite effect. Alivet patted the girl's thorn-ringed hand.

"Just remember," Alivet said soothingly, "there's really no wrong way to go about it." Sozoma had been the obvious choice. Madimi Garland took a deep breath and let it out again. She quivered.

"Are you thinking of something?" Genever inquired.

"Yes," the Lady whispered.

Oh dear, thought Alivet, with resignation.

"In that case, we can begin." Genever snapped the glass teat at the end of the phial and held it under Madimi's nose. "Simply inhale."

Madimi Garland did so. Alivet saw the sparkling drift of sozoma lift from the phial and into the Lady's arched nostrils. The Lady gave a shuddering gasp. What must it be like, Alivet wondered, to have such virginal synapses? She was unhappily certain that sozoma had never affected her so deeply. She looked back toward the bar. The red-eyed man was no longer there. His absence unnerved Alivet almost as much as his presence had done; it was like a spider in the room that suddenly vanishes. Yet his vanishing left a curious emotion in its wake, which after a moment Alivet identified as disappointment. She told herself to pay attention to Madimi.

Madimi Garland slid limply back against the couch and closed her eyes. Her breathing deepened into trance.

"Alivet?" Genever said, momentarily dropping the decadent facade. "I meant to tell you. I spoke to Hilliet Kightly just before you arrived. He says he's done the formulations you asked for."

"About time! I made the order up a week ago."

"He says he's had problems with the vetony—a bad batch, it seems."

"He said that last time. It's always the same old excuse." She looked at the slumped form of Madimi Garland. "She'll be out cold for an hour or so. Do you want me to pick up the formulations now?" Hilliet Kightly's office was upstairs, after all, and it would save her making a return appointment. Genever echoed her thoughts.

"Why not? It'll save time later."

Alivet wondered whether he might be trying to get rid of her, but it didn't matter. She looked covertly around for the red-eyed man, but he was nowhere to be seen.

At the door, Alivet glanced back. As she had expected, Genever's lady friend had returned and was now perched on the arm of the couch, above the prone body of Madimi Garland. Alivet smiled sourly. Clearly Genever was seeking yet another diversion.

The hallway that led to the private offices was hushed and dim, smelling of old incense and new polish; of wood varnished with gilt resin and amber, and thick sea-wool rugs brought all the way from the Isles of Mice. A dozen elevators stood at the far end, as ornamented as sarcophagi. Alivet fidgeted impatiently as the ancient lift rattled upward, then touched her tattooed palm to the office bell. After a moment, the door opened.

The formulator had evidently been working late. Plates littered the desk and a strong smell of fried samphire filtered throughout the suite. In the public alchematorium where Alivet had her own rented cubicle, a policy had been agreed that no food was to be allowed onto the premises in case it disrupted the careful balance of odors achieved in each apprentice's cupboard, but the Port Tree formulators clearly considered themselves to be above such protocols. Alivet frowned. Hilliet Kightly, not at all discomfited, gave her a greasy smile, embellished with flakes of crab.

"You've come for your formulations? Such dedication! And they say that the young today have no sense of responsibility. It is a pretty thing to see."

"My formulations, please."

Kightly slid from behind his desk, but Alivet snatched her hand back before he could slobber fish all over it.

"You won't stay and have a drink? It's getting late, after all."

"I'm working. Where are my formulations?"

"In the lab, on the desk. But I have a bottle of wine, a very fine vintage. Just let me find a couple of glasses, and—"

He stepped forward but his bulk slowed him down. Alivet

dodged past and was through the alchematorium door, quick as a snake in a garden. He had only enough time to snatch at her flying braid and tweak it. *Like an overgrown schoolboy, fat on his secret fish.* The pull on her braid had hurt, but Alivet kept her mouth shut. A tug of her hair was one thing; if the old bastard tried anything else she'd follow her aunty's advice and give him a good kick in the yarbles.

Once again, she thanked the Wheel that Genever did not make a habit of molesting his colleagues. She slammed the door of the alchematorium shut behind her, taking momentary pleasure in the familiar ambience of a hundred, layered odors. Crucibles and alembics lined the walls, connected by the usual array of pipes and wires to the athanor furnace. Smaller burners stood beneath them, caked with a filthy residue, and the stone worktops were stained. A cold cup of herb tea stood on one of them, ringed with mold. Alivet frowned. Did Kightly's people take no pride in their work? She had heard that he used male apprentices; perhaps that accounted for the squalor. Employing boys, indeed, and putting honest girls out of a job. She would believe anything of Kightly.

A phial of unfinished perfume stood on the workbench, redolent of spinet resin and old opium. And a faint undernote of fish, Alivet noted with displeasure, which she would love to stop and filter out. But there was no time. Damn Hilliet Kightly and his culinary flagrance.

The formulations stood on the desk. Alivet ran swiftly through the order form. There were substances here from all over the fens: a spiral of gland-wood from Arden, a crush of lamp seeds, a phial of dust from the Fragrant Mulch Cliffs, and the vetony. With care, Alivet made the formulations into a bundle, closed the safe, and unlocked the alchematorium door.

Kightly was waiting by the entrance. He stepped adroitly into her path as she came through.

"You locked the door," he remarked, archly. He clasped fat fingers, and rocked slightly upon his toes. She was reminded of a stout, unwholesome child's toy.

"Did I? Sorry. Must be habit." Foreseeing that if she dodged to one side, Kightly would move as well, Alivet stayed still. He took a step forward. She could smell him. And city folk had the gall to say that the women of the marshes smelled of fish. Her aunt had always made sure that they were well scrubbed, morning and night, yet here was Kightly reeking of carp and clearly thinking that Alivet was no better than she should be.

"Genever works you too hard. You're young, should be out enjoying yourself, having fun—a pretty little thing like you."

"I do go out and enjoy myself. But not tonight. I'm working."

"Well, hark at Little Miss Prim." Kightly was about to get nasty. She'd seen the same thing in her father when she was a child: the sudden shift from jovial aggression to genuine spite. Maybe Kightly would manage to drown himself, too, and do everyone a favor.

A well-aimed kick would probably sort him out, but then again, he was one of Genever's most useful contacts and since she actually had to work in this city, temporarily emasculating Kightly might not be the most helpful option. Besides, her long skirts were hampering; she wasn't wearing the fen-dweller's boots and trousers anymore. There had to be another way, and Kightly's personal fragrance provided an answer.

"Wheel!" she said suddenly, and clutched at her throat. "What's that *smell?*"

Kightly looked blank. "What smell?"

Alivet, gagging, pointed to a corner of the room. "Coming from there...Can't you smell it? Maybe only an apothecary would—oh, no. I'm going to—" She retched convincingly, and Kightly stepped hastily back.

"Sink," Alivet gasped, and bolted through the door. Once out into the hallway, she did not bother with the elevator, but took the stairs two at a time.

She came out onto the landing that led to the restaurant and the fume rooms. The landing was empty, but a murmur of voices came from the main hall. Alivet turned toward the doors of the fume room and nearly dropped the bundle of formulations as the red-eyed man slipped from the shadows to stand in her path.

"Who are you?" Alivet asked, and to her dismay found that her voice was rising. "Are you following me?" Even more dismaying was the unfamiliar sense of excitement that accompanied this thought, a world away from her revulsion at the prospect of Kightly's roving hands. However, the stranger gave her a blank, blood-colored stare.

"Madam?" he inquired, politely. "Do you happen to know where the lavatories might be?"

Mortified, Alivet pointed down the hallway.

"Thank you. I'm so sorry to have troubled you."

Without a second look, the man brushed past her in a flutter of brocaded robes and disappeared down the hall. Alivet hurried back into the fume bar, feeling that she had made a fool of herself. That worry, however, was instantly diminished by the crisis occurring in the bar.

Genever, accompanied by a small crowd of interested onlookers, was bending over the motionless form of Madimi Garland, and for the first time in Alivet's recollection, he looked alarmed.

"Brother Thant? What's wrong?"

"I don't know. She won't wake up. I tried to rouse her and she just—gargled."

"Maybe she choked," someone supplied, helpfully.

"On what?" Alivet asked. She dropped to her knees beside the girl and took Madimi's hand.

"Madimi? Can you hear me? Are you all right?" Sometimes people grew faint under the influence of fumes and it took a while for them to come out of it. She shook the girl by the shoulder.

"Alivet," Genever said, sharply. "We have to bring her round. Where are the reviving salts?"

Alivet fumbled in her bag.

"Here."

"Well, give them to her, then."

"All right," Alivet said. She had never heard Genever sound so impatient. "I'm working as fast as I can."

As she held the salts beneath Madimi's aristocratic nose, however, the girl grew rigid. Her mouth opened. She arched backward with such force that the briar-bonds snapped and fell to the floor. Then she toppled from the couch.

"Madimi!" Alivet cried. She crouched by the fallen figure and felt for a pulse. There was nothing. Alivet covered the girl's mouth with her own, breathed out and in, then out again. Madimi's lungs did not respond.

"The antiallergen, quickly!" Genever snapped, kneeling by her side. Alivet fumbled for a needle and slid it into the girl's vein, but Madimi lay as stiff and cold as a glass doll. Rigor should not set in so swiftly; what in the world was wrong? The girl had certainly undertaken a full medical check; it was a prerequisite for all clients.

"What's the matter with her?" a drunken voice asked.

"She's dead," someone said. There was an indrawn rush of breath as the crowd leaned avariciously forward.

"Call the Unpriests!" someone else snapped. "Can't you see she's killed her?"

Alivet sat swiftly upright, with the heiress' corpse stiffening at her employer's immaculately clad feet. Genever was staring down at her and she was startled by the expression on his face. His usually melancholic demeanor had been sloughed away, to be replaced with a chilly calculation.

"We didn't kill her," Alivet protested. "We've done no such thing!" But it was too late. The sound of running feet indicated that someone had already bolted to summon the most feared of Latent Emanation's human citizens.

Part II

DISSOLUTION

And is there care in heaven? And is there love
In heavenly spirits to these creatures base,
That may compassion of their evils move?
There is: else much more wretched were the case
Of men than beasts. But oh th'exceeding grace
Of highest God that loves his creatures so
And all his works with mercy does embrace,
That blessed angels he sends to and fro
To serve to wicked man, to serve his wicked foe.

— EDMUND SPENSER, *The Faerie Queene*

chapter I

Remarkable," Gerard Mercator remarked, as the metal bee hummed about the chamber. John Dee could tell from the cartographer's face that he was genuinely impressed, and felt a small glow of pride. It was as well that the bee had not been damaged by the voyage from England. The day of flying devices, Dee thought, would not come a day too soon. Even in the summer months the roads had been difficult, with Dee enduring the bouncing, jolting journey across the Low Countries as best he could, plagued by the fear that the equipment would arrive in a thousand pieces. The first thing that he had done on arriving in Louvain was to unpack the bee and it was this that now soared between the rings of Mercator's many astrolabes like a small, unruly moon.

"I heard about your scarab," Mercator murmured, scowling in sudden sympathy. "Rumor had it that there were accusations of sorcery."

"I prefer the term 'thaumaturgy,'" Dee said, dryly. "But it's true, the experiment did produce an unfortunate stirring of the blood among the more credulous. It was a system of ropes and pulleys, nothing more. This"—he indicated the bee—"this is true mathematics: the use of incantations and number theory to produce flight. There is nothing of the black art about it."

"Do you anticipate difficulties on your return to England?"

"I don't know. I trust not, but these are not quiet times." Dee stared at the bee, which had now alighted on the sill and was crawling up the window toward freedom and the garden, where its living companions were buzzing among the lavender. Dee stepped forward, narrowly avoiding a stack of cross-staffs and measuring rods, and rescued the bee before it could make its escape.

"It seeks sunlight," Mercator said.

"It seeks room to fly. I have only once let it outside, and that was within a walled garden. It moved from point to point, as if exploring."

"A cartographic bee," Mercator mused. "If it proves capable of lengthy flight, then perhaps those ardent explorers of our day need not worry about the expense of locating the north-west passage. They can send the bee instead."

Dee smiled. "I don't think it would be capable of such a long voyage. But it's no bad notion." Placing the bee back in its leather traveling case, he peered over Mercator's shoulder. The bee hummed angrily for a moment, then fell silent.

Mercator's maps of the world were like none that Dee had ever seen. They showed four continents, not three, and the familiar features of such maps—dragons and the Garden of Eden, for example—were entirely absent. Dee watched in fascination as Mercator painstakingly measured the panels for his latest globe and his thoughts once more returned to that curious vision of the world as it must appear from the sublunary realms. Dee closed his eyes for a moment and imagined this new representation of the Earth; its seas and landscapes, viewed from afar. He wished it could be possible to inhabit the bronze body of the bee and send it up into the heavens, to map the gardens of the Earth.

Then Dee's gaze slid past Mercator's preoccupied figure to where the theorick stood on its special table. The brass shone in the sun. *And so must the light of reason fall upon the universe.* The theorick was as revolutionary as Mercator's globes: ten rings for the spheres bearing the planets and stars instead of eight, including the sphere for the *primum mobile*, the engine that drove the universe. The sun stood firmly at the center: Dee and Mercator had discovered common Copernican ground. It was the sight of the theorick glowing so boldly in the sunshine that gave Dee the courage to ask the question that had been preoccupying him ever since the staging of the play at Cambridge.

"What is your opinion," he asked, "of the possibility of life beyond the Earth?"

Mercator's mouth curved in a thin, sour smile. "My opinion? That it is inadvisable to speak of such things beyond the confines of this study. The Church—whatever its disposition—will call you a heretic; the academies will simply laugh."

"And within the confines of your study?"

Mercator sighed. "My dear Dr. Dee, I would not have become a cartographer if I had not been so entranced by what might lie beyond the known world. I do not have a marvelous flying device, nor am I likely to set foot on one of the Muscovy Company's sailing ships and see these coasts, these mountains"—he gestured toward the globes that lined the paneled walls of the study—"for myself, and that is why I have become so occupied with the making of maps. And even during my thirty-six years on this sphere, so many discoveries have been made, of other lands and other peoples, that I am quite willing to countenance the notion of life elsewhere. After all, are there not spirits and angels, that the common run of folk do not see every day? Perhaps the universe is teeming with such beings like a millpond in spring."

"But how to *converse* with them?" Dee mused.

"You had best put some work to your wonderful flying craft, and I to my maps," Mercator said. He turned, smiling. "Together, Dee, we will be voyagers—what do you say? Travel the boundaries of the universe together, as far as starlight?"

"As you say," Dee answered, thoughtfully. "I will put some work to it."

chapter II

CITY OF LEVANAH, MONTH OF DRAGONFLIES

The crowds of revelers, including the woman who had pressed her address upon Genever, had vanished like magic. Alivet found herself staring at the girl's sprawled body with a kind of numb curiosity. In death, Madimi Garland's skin had attained a faint translucence, reminding Alivet that the aristocrat had been only a few years younger than she herself—a girl whose only offense (as far as anyone knew) had been to purchase a few daring experiences after a girlhood of closed doors and repression. However Madimi had died, that she would never now enjoy even the limited experiences that she had so craved seemed the saddest thing of all. Alivet thought of Inkirietta and jumped as a hand closed around her arm.

It was Genever Thant. His face was pale beneath its layer of powder; his black eyes burned. The laconic person he had been only an hour before was gone: mercurially transformed by the crucible of fear. Alivet found herself staring at a white-lipped stranger. He whispered, "They will take us both, Alivet. They will imprison us, take us to the torment chamber and be dissatisfied with every answer."

"We'll tell them the truth," Alivet said, but she knew as soon as the words were out of her mouth that it would not be enough. The Unpriests were like their masters: capricious and cruel. Alchemical metaphors dominated her imagination: in the hands of the Unpriests, they would undergo dissolution, personalities and spirits rendered down. She went on, "Besides, don't you have aristocratic friends?"

"They'll still blame us. I may have friends in the Nine Families, but not even the Families can save me from the Lords."

"Where are you going?" Alivet asked. Yet she already knew the answer.

"I'm getting out of here, Alivet. I suggest you do likewise. Madimi's dead. She's beyond any help we might be able to give her." He was already fastening his coat with shaking hands.

"You can't just go," Alivet said. The reality of the situation was only now beginning to dawn on her. "Where will you hide? And what about me?"

"There are people who might be prevailed upon to hide me," Genever said. He gave her a brief, wintry smile. "I'm sorry I can't take you with me, Alivet. But I don't want extra baggage at present. I'm sure you understand."

"Wait, I—" Alivet began, but with a brief, ironic bow Genever was already vanishing through the door. The future unscrolled through her imagination like clockwork. Genever fleeing through the halls of Port Tree; the Unpriests pounding up the stairs; herself a fen-born drug-maker standing over the body of one of Levanah's wealthiest aristocrats. She remembered Inki, how her sister had looked when the Unpriest Enbonders had come for her. If she were arrested, Inki would remain forever in a Palace of Night.

"Sorry, Madimi," she murmured to the dead girl. She snatched up her bag and the empty phial of sozoma, then ran back into the deserted hallway. The elevator was whirring in a ponderous manner and Alivet veered away, heading for the stairs. She hastened down the narrow, paneled staircase toward the street. She was not entirely sure if that was where the staircase even led, but almost anything was better than an Unpriest's cell.

Twelve flights below, she came out into a corridor adjoining the main atrium of Port Tree. Three figures were striding up the steps, dressed in velvet and metal and carrying strip-whips in their hands. Alivet dodged behind the elegant green fronds of a winter-fern and waited until they had stepped into the cage of the elevator. Then she fled out into the street.

She needed to escape as swiftly as possible, but where to go? She could not return home. Enough people had seen her with Madimi, and all they would need to do in order to track her down would be to check Genever's records and match her image with the girl who had been seen in the fume bar. Moreover, that image was also on her records as a licensed drug-maker in the Apothecaries and Alchemical Merchants Guild. Nor was she willing to return to Edgewhere. The thought of Unpriests once more tramping up the steps of the stilt-house to where her aunt Elitta sat, unsuspecting over her knitting, was an appalling one.

But she must warn her aunt nonetheless. With foreknowledge, Elitta would be able to vanish into the fens. The Unpriests were not popular in the backwaters. Alivet thought that she should do the same, but it would still be best to avoid Edgewhere. Her first priority, therefore, must be to reach the shore and send a message to Elitta. She winced at the thought of what her aunt would say when she discovered that her niece was about to be imprisoned for murder, but there was no helping it.

The notion that she would be found innocent entered her mind for a fleeting moment, quailed at what it found there, and hastily departed. It was utter foolishness to think that she would receive anything resembling justice at the hands of the Unpriests. Alivet ducked beneath the rain-sodden branches of the sootwood and fumbled in her pocket for chaise fare.

As she did so, she realized that there was something already in the pocket. Bewildered, Alivet drew it out and found that it was a curling slip of paper. She unfolded the note and read an elegant inscription:

Is it your wish to save your sister and yourself? I may be able to help you. You will find me in Shadow Town tomorrow evening. I shall be expecting you.

It was signed: *Arieth Mahedi Ghairen, Poison Master of Hathes.* To Alivet's wondering mind, there could be only one candidate for the title, and that was the garnet-eyed gentleman whom she had last seen in the fume bar of Port Tree. Who was he, and what was a Poison Master? And whereabouts in Shadow Town, which must surely be over a mile from end to end? The situation did not sound promising, but it was certainly more appealing than the thought of the Unpriests.

Now she had a purpose, albeit mysterious, and a destination, albeit vague. It was surprising how much better this made her feel. Alivet stepped out into the street and flagged down a chaise.

chapter III

City of Levanah, Month of Dragonflies

I t was starting to rain again. Fat drops spun down
through the sootwood fronds, dappling the dust into
mud. Port Tree curved behind her, its carapace glistening in the lamplight. Alivet tasted the rank aroma of the distant fens, mingling with the fresher fragrance of rainy
sootwood and fried fish from the stall opposite. The combination reminded her unpleasantly of Kightly. Her fingers
curled around the message in her pocket. *Poison Master*. It
was not a reassuring title. If Genever had not abandoned her
to the dubious mercies of the Unpriests, she could have asked
him what it might mean, but Genever was gone. Along with
all her business and the prospect of future earnings, though
Alivet was trying not to think about that.

And how did a Poison Master, all the way from wherever
Hathes might be, know about her sister? Even more baffling,
why should he care? The possibility of some cruel game was
not far from Alivet's thoughts, but it was the first hope she'd
ever had that someone other than herself might be able to do
something about rescuing Inki. She did not dare allow those
hopes to gain a hold.

At last she managed to wave down a chaise from the
midst of the trundling traffic. A wobbling wheeled shell

swerved toward her, pulled by a loping anube, and Alivet scrambled in.

"Little Swamp Street, please." She would head for the fen docks and find a boat to the stilt-villages. Not Edgewhere— though a message could be sent on one of the outgoing craft—but perhaps Hopeless or Salvation. From there, she could catch a boat to Shadow Town, which lay farther along the river. Why couldn't this Poison Master have suggested a more convenient location?

"Which end?" the anube asked, in its soft, moderated voice. She could see the brass cogs whirring in the implant in its throat, below the long bald jackal's jaw.

"Not the Luce Vo end—the Flee Storms area. Take the by-route through Glissen."

"It will cost less to travel via Woeborough. The toll will be less expensive there." The anube's callused hands flexed on the handles of the chaise.

"I know, but I'm in a hurry." There would be no boats to the villages beyond midnight, and it was close to that now.

"Then I recommend Whin Passage, which has a medium toll and will add only ten minutes to your journey." The anube's head sidled around to fix her with a gleaming dark eye. Its ears flattened.

"Just go through Glissen," Alivet snapped, cursing for the first time in her life the punctilious honesty of chaise drivers.

"It is your choice," the anube said sadly, and veered off into the traffic, its bulbous feet padding swiftly over the wet road. Alivet swallowed her frustration. The anubes, stubbornly and with quiet, unyielding insistence, carried out their work according to their own principles: transparent honesty and a melancholic attachment to fairness. Once the concept of money had been divulged to them, all those many years before, they had proved swift to reject it. Transportation was their sacred task, they explained, once they had been assisted in mastering human speech. For thousands of years they had ferried one another about on the endless pilgrimages which criss-crossed Latent Emanation's watery surface; they would do the same for the newcomers, too, even though humans remained baffled by the practice.

Their human employers had eventually succeeded in persuading the anubes to accept a minimal charge, but no more than that. As entrepreneurs, they were a disaster, but as exemplars of the dignity of labor, they had proved to be a considerable success. This, however, was little comfort to Alivet, whose thoughts were concentrated entirely upon flight.

Behind her, Alivet could see the multiple domes of Port Tree rising above the buildings of the Pleasure Quarter. The spires of the Quarter were lost in drifting cloud. Port Tree itself rose out of the rain like a nest of scarabs. They were drawing near to the public alchematorium; she could see the rain pouring down from the brass globes on either side of the awning. Was Genever now running like herself into the tangled nest of the city? But despite his protestations, Genever was friendly with the aristocracy: he was doubtless sitting in someone's comfortable parlor right now, sipping a glass of wine with his feet stretched out to the fire...

Self-pity, Alivet reminded herself sternly, would get her nowhere.

Impatiently, she watched the city roll by: Foeside, Voynich, Winterwood—all the marsh-edge districts—until they reached the outskirts of Glissen and rattled over the maze of bridges. One day, Alivet told herself firmly, when this was all over, she would visit more of the city, stroll through groves of gland-trees and seek inspiration for new fumes.

The chaise passed across Diabolo's Bridge and onto the Crossing of Limited Manifestation, where two of the city's main canals met and the causeway for the westernmost Night Palace began. Alivet peered impatiently from beneath the canopy, smelling tarry mud and waterweed, a trace of salt from the estuary, samphire sizzling in a pan on the raised and rickety sidewalk.

By the time they reached Little Swamp Street, the rain had eased to a slow trickle. This was some compensation, at least. Alivet did not like the Little Swamp area; it was too close to the Night Palace, a haunt of Unpriests and water-children. And her friend Yzabet swore that she had once seen a Lord itself stalking through the damp streets, its lantern head swinging from side to side like a clockwork vulture. The memory made Alivet feel even more unsafe, and the anube did not seem happy, either. It tucked its long head into its chest and padded faster, causing the wheels of the chaise to leave a small wake in the flooded street. Finally, the anube put down the handles of the chaise with a sigh.

"This is your destination."

"Thank you," Alivet said, scrambling down from the chaise and pressing a handful of coins into the anube's hand. "Listen, I need to send a message. If I've missed the last boat here, I won't be able to send it until morning, and it's urgent."

"If you have a message, best to send it by such as myself to the Shore of Moss: there are boats there throughout the night, but not to the villages. However, they will be able to relay it," the anube said.

"Can you take it for me? How much will it cost?"

The anube reluctantly named a small price. Alivet scribbled a hasty explanation on a piece of parchment and folded it into the anube's unhuman hand along with the coins. She had very little money left, but it would be worth it if Aunt Elitta was warned in time.

"The address is on the front of the paper. I'm sending it to the village hall. From there, it must go to the woman who slapped Drew Marchal's face when they were seventeen. I've written that down."

Anyone at the village hall would know who that was. She did not want to put the details of Elitta's house upon the paper, in case it fell into the wrong hands. Happily, the anubes were no friends to the Unpriests; the message would be safest with them.

The chaise turned and began to trundle away. Alivet looked about her. There was no one to be seen. The rain had become a torrent, pouring down roofs and copings, battering the dying leaves into submission. At the end of Little Swamp

Street, Alivet could see the curved prows of the pilgrimage boats, their oars piled onto high nests set on poles to deter thieves. With a sinking heart she ran down toward the dock and out onto the wharf. The boats were all safely secured. As Alivet stared out across the marsh, she saw a faint, wavering light flickering over the water. She strained her eyes, trying to see. The light winked once, and was gone.

"The last boat's gone for tonight," said a reedy voice behind her. Alivet turned to see an ancient person wrapped in waterproofs. The face was as wrinkled as the shore after a storm, the eyes narrowed against the rain. She could not even tell what gender it might be beneath the shapeless bundle. Dismayed, Alivet said, "The last boat? I've missed it, then. It must be after midnight."

"Gone midnight, fifteen minutes ago. Where are you heading?"

"The villages," Alivet said cautiously. "But I've got to send a message. It's urgent." Something held her back from telling the stranger that she was headed for Shadow Town. If the Poison Master meant her harm, the more people who knew where she was going, the better. But a small, insistent instinct tugged at her mind, telling her to keep silent.

Alivet heeded it and did so.

"In the morning, boats will go again, all along the river. To the villages, and farther. To Salvation, New Emden, Shadow Town. You will have plenty of choices tomorrow. Why must you travel now?"

The narrowed eyes were bright with curiosity. Again, warning plucked at Alivet.

"My mother's ill," she said. "Listen, is there anywhere I can spend the night? A guest house or something?"

"Very few that are not full. Pilgrims and passengers, you see, waiting for tomorrow's boats. There is a place along the wharf."

"Where?" Alivet asked, hoping that the person would not offer to show it to her. But the ancient only said, "Do you see that blue lantern? It is there. Tell them Marlay sent you."

"Thanks," Alivet said. Turning, she walked quickly down the wharf. When she reached the end, she looked back. Marlay was gone. Alivet drew her hood more tightly against the rain and slipped down the street toward the blue lantern. A crack of welcoming light showed around the corner of a blind and for a moment, Alivet was tempted to do as she had been instructed and knock on the front door. But that strange, small song of warning was still nudging her, so instead she slid under the walkway that led to the house and into an alley. Alivet hurried down it and found herself on a boardwalk that followed the line of the foreshore. She doubled back toward the wharf.

She needed to get out of the rain. Pulling the hood of her greatcoat over her head, she ducked beneath the boardwalk. Something touched her face and she nearly cried out, but it was only a shower of woodrot dislodged by the rain. Feeling foolish, Alivet hastened on and at last found herself back at the wharf. The boats were deserted, the marsh empty. From far away, out in the teeming dark, she heard the thin cry of a night bird. She looked back longingly to the gleam of lamps, but even as she did so she heard feet marching along the boardwalk. The sound echoed wetly through the gloom.

Very carefully, still with warning prickling at the back of her neck, Alivet peered up through the cracks of the boardwalk. Boots gleamed in the rain. A pencil of green light arced through the air like a lightning flash and Alivet knew that she had been right to be afraid. Unpriests stood above her. She heard them conferring, in whispers. Then, to her relief, they set off toward the scatter of houses. Alivet clambered along the rickety supports of the wharf until she was out over the water.

Beneath the wharf, a boat pole stood at an angle. Alivet caught it in both hands, swung off the wharf, and climbed awkwardly down, hindered by her skirts. There was a space at the base of the wharf, just above the waterline. She could hide there until morning, until the soft padding feet of the anubes betrayed their presence on the wharf above.

The hole was as black as pitch. Clinging to the pole,

Alivet tore off a handful of moss and threw it into the hollow. She waited for a moment, dreading the hiss of waterchildren or whisps—it was debatable which was worse: whisps or Unpriests—but there was nothing. Alivet went feetfirst into the hole.

It was no colder than the barn had been during the Search, and no damper than Edgewhere in the winter. Crouching in the moist dark, she thought furiously. Were the Unpriests after her, or were they pursuing some other unfortunate? If they were after her already, then how had they found her? Someone must have spotted her in the street; it was unlikely that an anube would have given her away. It was possible that she was simply falling prey to paranoia. But everyone she had ever known—even her father, who had given little other sign of caring about his daughters—had told her: *Have as little truck with the Unpriests as possible. They do not care if you are innocent or guilty. They're just looking for an excuse to torment you.*

Rather a night in the damp than a night in a cell, Alivet thought. That was the trouble with the Unpriesthood; they obeyed the decrees set down by the Lords, who were themselves creatures of utmost whim. Without the protection of powerful friends, one might be treated with kindness and magnanimity for rapine, or flogged to within an inch of one's life and hurled into the nearest bog for jaywalking. Or, indeed, vice versa. No one understood the Unpriests' methods, and there was a considerable body of covert opinion that held that they did not have any, unpredictability being their primary weapon.

Yet nor did anyone know why the Lords did as they did. Why, for instance, would beings as powerful as they bring a thousand or so captive humans to a swampy place like Latent Emanation and then let them go to build their own city, with only Enbonding to ensure a surely unsatisfactorily meager servant class? The Lords answered to no one; the Unpriests only to the Lords and, to some degree, to the web of aristocratic influence exerted by the Nine Families. And that was surely the real problem: the lack of unity between humans, the vested interests that lay in the complex tangle of their relationship with the Lords. That relationship should be subjected to alchemical principles: dissolution, followed by a new combination of elements. Otherwise, humanity would just remain in the early stages of the alchemical process: corruption, separation, stagnation.

Alivet's thoughts were becoming familiar and depressing. Tomorrow, at first light, she would get passage on a pilgrimage boat and head for Shadow Town. She did not expect to sleep, but it claimed her nonetheless.

chapter IV

When Alivet awoke, it was already close to dawn. She was cramped and stiff, her clothes mottled with damp. She half stood, crouching in the small space beneath the wharf, and peered out to find that the rain had passed, leaving a mild, milky morning in its wake. She could even see the sun, sailing behind the clouds on the horizon like a silver penny. Her stomach churned with hunger. Alivet tucked her braid with its telltale rings more securely into her hood. There was nothing she could do about the wheel tattooed on her palm; she would just have to make sure she kept her hand in her pocket. Otherwise, she thought, there was surely nothing to identify her as Alivet Dee: apothecary and perhaps wanted person. She inched out of the hole onto the ladder.

When she reached the wharf, she saw that Little Swamp Street was already starting to stir. Chaises trundled by, carrying factors and stewards; locals drew carts filled with produce for the markets. There was no sign of anyone resembling an Unpriest or the mysterious ancient, Marlay. The smell of fried shrimp, pungent and fishy, cut through the morning air. Alivet walked swiftly along the wharf and around the corner of the shrimp stand. The woman at the stand reminded

Alivet of her aunt. She had the same oval face and dark hair, the heavy folded lids and broad hands.

"What, then?" she greeted Alivet.

"The shrimp. With water-grass and samphire. And river-wheat bread—a double portion, please."

"Haven't seen you before. Come in on one of the boats?"

"No. I'm seeking passage. To the Estuary—Hemmen's Slide. Illness in the family." She hoped to throw as much mud over her tracks as possible; gossip flew around the marshes like fever.

"I don't know the Slides," the stall woman said, pursing her mouth and handing over a greasy packet of shrimp and hot bread. Alivet, dismissed as a foreigner, added a pinch of salt and turned away.

Her aunt's injunction always to eat a good breakfast echoed in her head. She carried the steaming parcel down to the wharf and crouched beneath a pole tree to eat. There was movement among the pilgrimage boats: anubes, bare-shouldered and clad in their customary wrapped skirts, moving without haste along the narrow decks. She wondered, not for the first time, why they lived as they did; forever sailing up and down the innumerable rivulets of the fens, worshiping their poles and the larvae that lived there, transporting folk from place to place as though it was some kind of moral duty. Yet for them it seemed that it was, just as the Search was the duty of all upright citizens.

From this distance, the anubes looked like masked men, the long skulls weaving above their sinuous bodies. Their flesh was dappled in the sunlight: indigo, ebony, a light and startling aquamarine. Their glossy skins merged with the colors of the swamp. Alivet looked down at her own hands. She was colored like almost every other human, sallow and pale, though there were a group of dark-skinned folk along the river who were highly regarded for their reed-boat making. She wondered again about the Origin as she swallowed the last of the shrimp and wadded the packet into a ball. She dropped it into the sluggish waters below the wharf and watched as the creepers seethed around it. Within moments, it was gone.

That will be me, perhaps, if the Unpriests find me, Alivet thought. She rose to her feet and made her way along the wharf, keeping to the lower deck and out of sight. The anubes continued their work as she approached. They would not notice her, she knew, until she spoke. One stood no more than a few feet away, hauling a length of rope through its hard hands.

"Good morning, Brother," Alivet ventured. She had heard some folk say that the anubes did not deserve the courtesy of a human title, but Alivet disagreed.

"Sister, good day." Politely, the anube looked up, so that she was staring into the well of its eyes. The long face was bland; their expressions were unfathomable to her.

"I'm seeking passage," she said. "To Shadow Town."

"It is acceptable. There is a place on the third boat." The anube gestured. "It leaves in one hour, for First Commensurate Celebration, and goes by way of Mirror Marsh in order that communicants may present offerings to the poles. The journey may take longer than you wish."

"I don't have a lot of time," Alivet said, knowing that it would be useless to protest.

"That is wisdom," the anube replied. "Who among us has the time they need? Do you have offerings? If not, you must procure them."

"I have these small things," Alivet said, displaying the little bundle of formulations.

"It is probable that they will be acceptable," the anube said, with what was to Alivet an irritating caution. If the spices proved not to be acceptable, what would they do? Leave her in the middle of the marsh, clinging to a pole like a failed puntsman? But caution and reserve were the watchwords of the anubes.

"When must pilgrims come back to the boat?"

"A short while before the boat is due to leave—ten minutes, perhaps. Do not be late. We cannot wait for you; the ceremony follows a strict timetable."

"I understand. I won't be late. Thank you," Alivet said. The anube inclined its head and said nothing more.

She went back along the lower deck and down to the shore. A narrow strip of mud, lined with salt-rush and thimble pine, led past ancient jetties. Alivet followed this rudimentary path, stepping over the detritus brought in upon infrequent eddies or cast from passing ships. Creepers scattered across the mud as she approached, causing the shore to writhe as if alive. It was hard to imagine the fastidious figure of an Unpriest here in this somnolent, grimy place, but she could not let down her guard. The edges of the fens were too much like limbo, or the no-sleep of her ancestors within the drift-boat. She felt she might wander the shore forever like a lich.

Alivet stopped to shake the thought from her head. She could feel the will draining out of her, like the seep of blood from a little, fatal wound. She turned to see a marsh whisp hovering out on the swamp. Its tapering tail was rooted in the mud; she could see the thick stem beneath the water. Its body flickered like a column of heat. Alivet stepped swiftly back and stumbled over a root. The thing must be hungry, to be out so long after sunrise. Salt-rush clumps shimmered behind it, distorted by its translucent membranes. The whisp swayed on its stem; Alivet felt clammy and hot.

The marsh whisp beckoned with small, pale hands. Alivet took a tottering step forward. Her mind was starting to empty, but as it did so, she remembered the recent Search and once more she saw Inki's face, that terrible pleated hole where her eye had been. She felt as though someone had doused her with ice water. She threw herself back, out of reach of the whisp's influence, and ran along the shore. She did not stop until she reached the edges of the mud, where the pilings of the tall houses rose out of the marsh.

chapter V

CITY OF LEVANAH, MONTH OF DRAGONFLIES

Once she reached the relative sanctuary of the shore, Alivet hid down among the thimble pines, perched upon the high bole of a root above the water. She stared unseeingly out across the marsh, thinking of Inki. Her twin's face, with that puckered hole, still haunted her. She should be working in the alchematorium, earning the money to free her sister, not squatting here in a marsh. Frustration pounded behind her eyes like a headache. She glanced up at the sun, filtering down through the needles of the pines. It was almost time to make her way back to the pilgrimage boat.

There were several passengers waiting on the wharf. One was a marsh wife with an empty basket balanced upon her hip, her mouth moving with the rhythmic cud of uth gum. Alivet wondered what the woman was seeing in the steady march of hypnagogic images. There were also two old men, clearly brothers, clad in the dull green robes of the deep fens. No one paid any attention to Alivet. She took a seat on the bench beneath the shadow of the boathouse and watched the anubes make their final preparations. Cargo was loaded and oars checked. An anube in the prow gestured for the passengers to step forward. Alivet took the anube's hand as it helped her into the boat; the flesh was cool and moist, like the skin of a frog. She seated herself near the stern, out of the way of the rowers, and drew her hood over her face in case anyone might be watching from the wharf. She breathed deeply, trying to calm herself.

The anube at the prow gave a booming cry like a bell, startling Alivet. She considered asking the marsh wife for a piece of the gum to steady her nerves, but thought it best not to draw attention to herself. The boat rocked as the hawser was untied. A shaft of sunlight, reaching down through the clouds, sent quick sparkles across the water. Alivet looked back as the boat was rowed swiftly out into the channel. The buildings of Little Swamp Street were silent in the morning light. No one was watching. Alivet gripped the sides of the boat more tightly and looked out across the fen. The pilgrimage boat darted through the reeds, disturbing a nesting attern that bolted up in a flurry of dark wings. *Unlucky*, Alivet thought, and dipped her hand in the water in the old gesture against ill fortune.

It was growing warmer: the air between the high rushes was stifling and stagnant. The distant outline of the city fell away. Ahead, lay the stilt-villages. In a couple of hours, Alivet would be able to recognize the channels: the humps and islets where the First Farms were located. At least if it all went sour she could hide out in the fens for a time; there was plenty to eat, as long as one avoided ochiles and whisps. And liches and water-children; all the monsters of the marshes. No wonder the anubes spent so much of their time trying to placate the local deities through their sacrificial practices. Alivet's spirits took a turn for the worse.

Sweat was starting to trickle down the back of her neck. Reaching up, Alivet loosened the collar of her dress and her fingers encountered a thin, slippery chain, reminding her to check that her pendant, her aunt's gift, was safe. Alivet tugged the pendant from its place in the neck of her dress and glanced down at it. The pendant was an ancient thing, or so she had been told.

"It goes to the eldest girl," her aunt had said. "And you are the eldest by thirteen minutes. My grandmother once told me that it must have come from the Origin with the ancestors, that it hung around the throat of your great-great-great grandmother even as she stepped from the bowels of the Night Lords' boat."

Looking now at the pendant, Alivet wondered again whether the old story was true. She preferred to believe that it was—and indeed, belief was not hard. The pendant was a curious thing: a cross of metal perhaps an inch long, studded with garnets and pearls. Upon it was bound the little figure of a man, each hand fixed to the arms of the cross. His head was bowed, drooping to one side like a flower that the sun has ceased to touch. It seemed likely that the piece had come from the deep fens, where the small pearls were spat from the murie shells and littered the shore like beads. But the more fanciful story had greater appeal for Alivet.

"Who is this man?" she had asked her aunt, when she had first been shown the pendant.

"I have no idea," Elitta had replied. "I do not know who he might be, nor why he should be so sadly bound. There are no stories about him. Perhaps he had some meaning back in the Origin." She smiled at Alivet. "Keep it safe. My grandmother said that it was a protection against evil."

Well, if ever she needed protection against that, it was surely now. But Alivet wondered, as she always did, whether the pendant had not been the reason why the Unpriests had taken Inki and not herself. It was a foolish, superstitious thought, but she had never been able to shake it off.

The rest of the journey passed in a reverie of worry and plans. The phial that had contained the sozoma was still safely in her pocket; it might be a good idea to get that analyzed if she could find an alchemist. One of the backstreet people would probably do it without asking awkward questions. The possibility that the red-eyed Poison Master was involved with Madimi Garland's death had not been far from her mind ever since the events of the previous night. She was wary of being drawn into some kind of trap, but why would anyone bother? She was nobody special. Perhaps the empty phial might supply a clue.

The boat was drawing to a halt. Alivet looked up. A collection of ceremonial poles towered above her: black and shiny, with clusters of russet marsh moss entwined about the wheels at the summits. The anube rowers and the steersman, some nine people in all, stood up smoothly. The steersman again gave his booming cry and it rang out across the marsh, seeming to splinter the afternoon light. There was a ripple in the black water ahead. Again the cry, and movement beneath the water: things sinuous and long, sidling up to the base of the poles.

Alivet felt the air grow thick and shivery, and she looked at the marsh wife with unease. Sometimes people felt the need to cast themselves into the water around the poles and when they did, they sank without a sound and did not rise. But the marsh wife sat placidly chewing. The anube at the prow dropped a tangled mass into the water. There was a brief thrashing.

Alivet drew quickly back from the side of the boat and took her seat on the opposite edge, away from the poles. She looked up across the marsh, in the direction from which they had come. The sky was beginning to darken along the eastern horizon: a thunderhead building up like an anvil over the fens. Alivet could see the swarms of insects beginning to rise from the rushes, conjured by the promise of rain. Then a glint of unnatural light caught her eye. Another boat was approaching. It moved swiftly through the channels and she heard the sound of a glide motor. It was not a pilgrimage boat. A figure stood erect in the prow; the profile was human. Perhaps it was nothing more than a farmer, returning from the markets of the city...

Alivet strained to see. The sky grew darker. A curtain of rain swept across the marsh, seeming to drive the boat before it. The figure in the prow turned. She saw a black circle in the pallid face; the gleam of a lens. The anube's cry echoed out once more across the fens: a long, melancholy wail. Alivet drew her hood close about her face and nudged the arm of the nearest rower. The anube did not respond. It was staring into the untidy nest at the crest of the poles, where something was starting to stir.

"Excuse me," Alivet said, in an urgent whisper. "But I think an Unpriest's boat is coming."

The anube was silent. Alivet had never heard of any penalty for interrupting a devotion, but perhaps she was about to set a precedent. The boat would be upon them in minutes. She could take a chance and sit it out; she knew that fugitives sometimes fled into the marshes and perhaps the Unpriests' presence had nothing to do with her. Or she could cut and run—but Alivet glanced at the writhing water on either side of the boat and dismissed that possibility almost as soon as it occurred to her. Then she realized that the anube at the prow had spotted the approaching boat. It gave a low hiss, perhaps of disapproval.

"Make your offerings!" it instructed the passengers. Fumbling for the pouch in her pocket, Alivet took out some of the lamp seeds and, with one eye on the approaching boat, held them out. The anube took them without comment and scattered them around the base of the poles. The glowing seeds seemed to burrow into the mud, as though twisting downward by their own volition.

The first heavy drops of rain began to fall. Alivet glanced anxiously at the boat, which had now cut its glide engines and was sailing smoothly up the channel. It was now some fifty yards from the pilgrimage boat. The Unpriest at its prow was wrapped in a waterproof greatcoat; its tails streamed out behind him like half-unfurled wings. The lens in his eye had spiraled inward, so that the socket seemed puckered and bruised. Behind him, a woman crouched in the stern of the boat, leather-gloved fingers skittering over the engine casing. Unhurriedly the anube took offerings from the two old men, who clucked and muttered at the sight of the Unpriests, and from the marsh wife, still chewing her narcotic gum with bovine contentment. Alivet turned her hooded face away from the Unpriest and tried to look small and unobtrusive.

A sudden flurry of rain drummed on the floor of the pilgrimage boat. The last echo of the anube's cry fluted across the marsh and the steersman turned the prow of the boat away from the poles. Alivet held her breath, her heart hammering. They were moving out into another channel beyond the poles, out of the path of the glide boat. The head of the Unpriest snapped sharply up; the lens flickered.

"Remain where you are! We wish to question your passengers." It was a reedy, sibilant voice, suggesting that the Unpriest's vocal cords had undergone modification. The anubes behaved as if they had not heard. The steersman adjusted the tiller and signaled to the rowers. They pulled on the oars. The pilgrimage boat shot forward.

"Stop!" The glide boat nudged the edge of the poles. Alivet saw the water beneath grow suddenly still. Cold rain scattered across her hood. She looked up and saw a livid edge of cloud, glaring with the light of the hidden sun and a crack of sky. Then the clouds drew together. A shadow swept across the marsh. The Unpriest in the prow raised a long-barreled thing to his shoulder; Alivet recognized a webgun. If they were after her, at least she was wanted alive—but if you spent too long under a web it would eat into the skin, cause lesions that could prove fatal if touched by the infected waters of the fens.

The Unpriest fired. The glistening strands of the web fell out like white flame across the water. The anube steersman whistled an order and the boat spun around. The web fell short, hissing into the marsh. The Unpriest raised the gun again, adjusted the range, and methodically fired. The edge of the web fell across the marsh wife, who uttered a shrill, startled cry as though she had only just realized that they were under attack. Glutinous, burning strands attached themselves to Alivet's hand, welding it to the side of the boat. The marsh wife fell against her, entangling her further in the web. Lightning cracked through the clouds and hissed into the marsh.

Alivet, knocked to the floor of the boat by the marsh wife's struggles, saw in the sudden light that the nest at the top of the poles was moving. An elongated, dark red body twisted out and up, and fell on top of the Unpriests. Alivet glimpsed a bristling underside and a series of mouths like the lenses of a camera. The female Unpriest gave a sudden shrill scream, but the weight of the fallen thing was enough to roll her boat over. The Unpriests were sucked down into the marsh. A few ripples corrugated the surface, then all was calm and silent.

The steersman heeled the pilgrimage boat around and drew it farther up the channel. The marsh wife was still uttering small, yipping cries as she struggled. Alivet felt as though nails had been driven through her hand. She gritted her teeth against the pain and snapped, "Stay still! You're just making it worse."

"Only itumin will dissolve that," one of the old men said, with something approaching satisfaction. "Never any good for anything else, but wonderful stuff for the fire nets. Wonder what the dredgers wanted? Nothing here for them, you'd have thought."

Alivet twisted round to look at him. "You wouldn't happen to have any itumin, by any chance?"

"Oh, not here, Sister. You need to keep it in a jar. Got a jar on my boat—it's at the next wharf." He made a sucking sound, as if remembering something. "Expensive stuff, too," he told Alivet, and fixed her with a rheumy eye.

"I can pay," Alivet said, with very bad grace.

"That you'll have to."

Eventually, she reached an accommodation with the marsh wife. At least they were not welded to one another; Alivet was learning to be thankful for small mercies. Half sitting, half crouching, they remained in the bottom of the pilgrimage boat as it sped up the channel. The poles receded into the distance, as the storm flattened the reeds and rushes and drenched the passengers of the boat into a dreary silence.

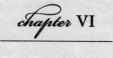

chapter VI

City of Levanah, Month of Dragonflies

By the time the pilgrimage boat came in sight of the Shadow Town docks, the storm had set in for the day. Alivet knew these torrents. Every autumn they boiled up from the south and rolled over the world, to drive the waters of the fens into a turbulent froth. But there was one good thing about the rain: it might keep the Unpriests from her path for a time. First, however, she was obliged to wait until the old man went to his boat and found the itumin. She was soon lighter of coin, but free from the Unpriests' web. She looked around, but there was no sign of the red-eyed Poison Master. Alivet swallowed bitterness. Perhaps he had no intention of meeting her here; perhaps it had been nothing more than some peculiar caprice. She could feel the note in her pocket, its presence heavy as lead. She wondered whether her message had reached Elitta, whether her aunt even now might be taking refuge.

Alivet swore under her breath. The thought of her poor aunt forced to flee into the fens flooded her with hot guilt. If she hadn't gone to Kightly's office to get the formulations, if she'd only stayed by her client and kept an eye on Madimi... But it was pointless to fret over what-might-have-beens.

The anube helmsman helped her from the boat, saying

nothing about what had occurred. Looking back, it seemed unreal: the pursuit, the attack, the vanishing of the Unpriests into the marsh. There was only a rope burn along her hand to remind her, but Alivet knew that it was not yet over. She had to get away from the wharf. Mumbling a hasty farewell to the marsh wife, she hurried along the dock.

Shadow Town was a far more prosperous area than the Little Swamp district. Here, the stilt-houses were tall, built of dark wood with plaster panels and bronze trim. Looking up, Alivet saw that each curved gable was ornamented with a gaping face: the stylized visages of whisps and momes, an old superstition designed to deter anything that might creep in from the fens. Even in the chancy storm light, Alivet could see through the gaps in the houses to the edges of the fens, and here there were no twisting trees or dank pools, but square upon square of riverwheat pasture.

Farther down the street lay a row of boardinghouses. Alivet looked longingly through the glowing windows, their lamps lit early against the storm, and thought of hot food and soft beds. But this part of town would be too expensive for her, quite apart from the risk of discovery. The Unpriests would surely be enraged at the loss of two of their number; they were proud to the point of madness and deeply resented humiliation. They were likely to double their efforts in tracking her down and someone would surely tell them that the boat had been heading for Shadow Town. Alivet fought despair. If she could find a pawnshop, she might be able to cash in her apprentice rings, but she shied away from the thought. It would be like selling herself. She still had a few coins left. She stopped at a stall and bought a bag of day-old bread.

"Are you from the city, then?" From the tone of the stall woman's voice, the people of Shadow Town clearly felt themselves a cut above those unfortunate enough to reside in other parts of Levanah. Alivet muttered noncommittally and turned to go, but as she stepped from beneath the awning, something soared overhead. She dodged back. It was one of the Unpriests' scarab fliers, coming in from over the marsh.

Its jade sides were slick with rain and the containment field crackled and spat like lightning. Beside Alivet, the stall woman craned her neck over the counter to get a better look. The flier veered low over a row of houses and disappeared.

"Wonder what they're looking for," the stall woman said. Her eyes narrowed with spite, her disapproval of Alivet was forgotten in the face of the common enemy. "Nothing for them here. You'd better get out of this rain, lovey. You'll catch your death."

Alivet, still staring in the direction of the flier, numbly agreed. Best find a place to hide. She stepped around the back of the stall and hastened down a side street. It was a wise, if inadvertent choice. Alivet found herself in a maze of small lanes, leading between tall houses. This must be the commercial district, for she could see signs for apothecaries and alchemists; ignatonic repair establishments; an Experience merchant's place with a grand gilt sign. It made her wonder how Genever might be faring. The narrow streets were crowded in spite of the rain. Alivet stepped under an overhang to avoid the rush. Everyone looked self-important and well dressed, as though they had somewhere to go and something urgent to attend to. Well, so did she. This would be a good place to get the phial analyzed, and it would get her off the street, too.

Alivet chose the seediest-looking apothecarium. She closed her fist to hide the betraying tattoo, and hoped that the apothecary would not recognize her for a fellow drugmaker. It was a frail hope, for a trained nose would be able to detect the perfumes that clung to her: sorivoy and tumerith ingrained into her skin and her hair still bearing traces of colote even after a night spent in the cold airs of the fens.

She could not smell herself, but whenever an apothecary stepped close to her in the streets around Port Tree or Heretic's Marsh, she could recognize a fellow worker from the accompanying melange of odors: subtle spices, drifts of astringency and sourness. If she lived through this, perhaps she would purchase a perfume to conceal her own betraying scent, but such things were unpopular among the apothecarial community, who claimed that they wrecked the delicate balance of the senses. Alivet was inclined to agree. She hesitated beneath the stranger's wheel before touching her palm to the frame of the door in respect and going inside.

Within, it was cool and dark, fragrant with a thousand odors. Alivet felt as though she had come home. She looked up at the plants that lined the shelves with as much relief as if she had stepped through the door of her own small chamber. At the end of the room, in the shadows, a voice said, "Yes? What do you want?"

"I need to get something analyzed. My sister had an allergic reaction to something last night. I'd like to get to the bottom of it."

Someone stepped out of the shadows, wiping his hands on a towel. Alivet saw a gangling man of middle age, with untidy wisps and drifts of hair above a thinning scalp. His overalls were stained. Evidently, she had interrupted his work.

He asked impatiently, "What was it, then? Jherolie? Tope? The number of people I've had in here this week, complaining about boils and wheezing—there must have been a bad batch. Not from here, I hasten to add. I only give out tope on prescription, and then only in the most modest doses. Tell your sister to use emollient cream and sleep with the window open. Should get better in a week or two."

"It wasn't tope. She took sozoma."

The apothecary snorted. "Wasn't an allergy, then. You might as well posit that she's allergic to air."

"Maybe it wasn't, but I'd like the phial analyzed anyway, just as a precaution. Also a—that is, my sister's handkerchief."

"Wise, wise," the apothecary mumbled. "Takes snuff, does she? Well, you never know. Bring them here and I'll run them both under the phonoscope. That'll be three fens and a penny."

In silence, careful not to stand too close, Alivet handed over the phial, the handkerchief, and the money. The apothecary, taking all three, ran a swab around the sides of the phial. He sniffed it once, quickly, then placed the swab in the phonoscope and set the dial. The phonoscope whirred.

"It'll take a few minutes," the apothecary said.

Alivet took a seat on a nearby stool to wait. Her thoughts drifted back to Genever. What if he had killed the girl? Yet even though he had abandoned her after Madimi's death, she couldn't see Genever slaying someone. Besides, he had seemed so concerned about Madimi: positively insisting on the application of the reviving salts. What if it had been the salts themselves that had poisoned the girl? But they were Alivet's own; Genever could have had no access to her bag and the last time she had occasion to use the salts on a client, all had been well. Anyway, what would Genever possibly have to gain from slaughtering a client? Or for implicating Alivet? He'd killed someone once, he had told her wearily, in one of the rented punishment booths, and the experience had not come up to expectations. Alivet shuddered. Was there anything Genever Thant had not done, in his thirty-odd years in the Experience trade? She hoped she'd still be able to get a thrill out of things when she reached fifty—if she lived. Perhaps the answer was to be born poor. At least then you appreciated little luxuries like thyme tea and breathing.

She was not even certain that whatever had killed Madimi Garland had been contained in the sozoma itself. It could have been in the sorbet. Or perhaps the voluptuary, leaning so suggestively over Genever, had released something into the air. Madimi Garland was an heiress, after all. There must be many people who would benefit from her death. And then there was the question of the Poison Master.

There was a faint gleam as the phonoscope finished its deliberations, then a scroll of paper slid out from the slot.

"What have we here? Nothing out of the ordinary. Sozoma, pure and simple. Not surprising. No one's allergic to sozoma, and for the record, it's surprisingly difficult to poison.

Put anything in it and the molecules just slide away. You'd know that if you'd had an apothecaric training."

"That's what I thought," Alivet said, accurately, but with no small degree of relief.

"Let's have a look at this handkerchief."

The apothecary tucked the silk square into the phonoscope. Alivet waited restlessly. The apothecary squinted at the results.

"How peculiar."

There was a long pause.

"What is it?" Alivet said. The apothecary gave her a sharp glance.

"Haven't a clue. Some kind of glistening residue. I've never seen anything like it before. What's your sis been up to?"

"I've no idea," Alivet said, with perfect truth.

"Indulging in a spot of experimental research, if you ask me. Has she been trying to make drugs? You know that's illegal without a license? Have the Unpriests down on you like a mud slide, that will. Your sister should be more careful."

"I'll go home right after work and have the truth out of the little creeper," Alivet said, aiming at hot indignation. It seemed to convince; the apothecary's frowning brow relaxed.

"You know what it smells like to me?" he said. "Darkness. Darkness and shadows, like the smell of evening. Imagine," he murmured, as if to himself, "if we could bottle light and atmosphere in the manner of the Lords. What delicacies of impression we might produce; what drugs and psychopomps to help us in our Search." His dreaming gaze met Alivet's, and held it for a moment with perfect understanding. "Take your results. Talk to your sister. Don't have any more crazy dreams than you have to."

"I won't," Alivet said. She slipped the papers into her pocket and turned to go.

"One more thing," the apothecary said. "I was listening to the wireless earlier. A girl died in Port Tree last night—a wealthy woman, taken up by an Experience merchant. The Unpriests are looking for an apothecary who was with him. For questioning. I thought I'd mention it." His face was carefully blank. A warning, or a threat? Alivet's fingers closed on the wheel upon her palm.

"That's interesting," she said. "I'll remember that." Then she was through the door and out into the evening, with a pocket half-full of answers. *Unpriests are looking for an apothecary.* But the man had not said that they were searching for the Experience merchant himself. Had the Unpriests caught up with Genever? Had he sought to blame her? She did not think he held her in any particular ill will, but a man might go a long way to save his skin, especially one as amoral as Genever Thant.

As soon as she came out into the street, she heard a humming sound, vibrating up through the wet stone beneath her feet. She glanced up between tall black walls. The scarab flier was hovering overhead. Alivet shrank back beneath the overhang and looked around her. There were people moving through the crowd, hooded like the rest beneath their greatcoats, but moving with heads down and hands clasped in pockets as if they did not wish to be noticed. Alivet knew that way of walking; indeed, she was practiced in it. They were people on their way to a Search, and the locations of a Search had been designed to be kept secret from the Unpriests...

A hooded figure paused, as if unsure of where to go, then set off again. Alivet followed it.

The searcher led her down a warren of streets: buildings with black glass windows and gold tracery across their facades. This must be a very old part of town, for the ornamentation signified circuit diagrams, stylized coils of arcane machinery, stars hidden in the lattices of wire. Perhaps these houses even dated from the years immediately after the Landing, when humanity still thought it could sail back to wherever it had come from, before the Nine Families gained ascendance and the Lords granted the Unpriests their full authority. She could still see the marks of chisels and sting-needles in the walls, where the ornamentation had been pried away and then replaced.

The figure before her stopped and glanced back. Alivet dived into a doorway and waited. As she did so, she took the chance to look behind her. No one appeared to be following. She had the sudden, eerie image of a dozen people reflected like the figures in an infinite mirror, all pursuing one another. And the one who led her: what might be leading this person? Dreams of a lost world... She could no longer hear the flier, but that might mean only that it had landed. Her head filled with images of Unpriests fanning out through the streets.

She followed the searcher into a street of steps, slippery with rain and dead leaves. At the top of the second flight, the figure disappeared. Alivet blinked, then hurried down the steps and saw a tall door, half hidden below the level of the street. Unless the searcher had been swallowed by the ground or flown up into the eaves, this was the only possibility. Cautiously, Alivet bent down and knocked. The door opened and Alivet was drawn into the entrance of a cellar.

"I've come for the Search," she told the man within. "I don't have my summons—I must have lost it." It had happened in truth, once before, and she was familiar with the drill. Moreover, the summonses were randomly distributed across the region; the Search kept no records.

"Take off your hood," the man told her. He motioned to someone deeper inside the cellar, a gesture of concealed alarm. Alivet did so. The man turned her head this way and that, and shone a light into her eyes. Alivet, trying not to twist away, had the impression of blue eyes in a narrow face, a widow's peak of hair.

"No scarring, no eye implants. You must understand, you could still be a spy." He sounded no more than faintly apologetic.

"I understand," Alivet said. It was no more than she had expected. The same held true for her: what if this should somehow be no more than an elaborate plot? But the Unpriests had no need of such complexity. The man reached down and took her hand, turning it over to peer at the wheel upon her palm.

"An apothecary's wheel, or a good copy . . . Place your palm on this."

He pressed her hand firmly down on a pad. Alivet felt warmth and a tingling in the palm as the scrying-glass read the delicate, hidden traces within the tattoo.

"Apprentice Alivet Dee. Your file is on record." He glanced up. "But even an apothecary's tattoo could be faked."

"Do you wish me to take Veracity, as a final precaution?"

"Might be a good idea," the man said, dryly. He held up a needle. She barely felt the sting as the drug entered her wrist. Then she heard herself say: "My name is Alivet Dee, Third Level Apprentice. I was born in Edgewhere; I have taken seventeen Searches since reaching my majority." Her voice seemed to come from a distance, as if she were speaking from the bottom of a well. The words rang and echoed in her head as the Veracity drug ebbed swiftly away.

"It's gone?" the man asked. Alivet nodded. "Such is the nature of truth," he told her, sadly. "Brief, and ill remembered. Go through."

Alivet went through a curtain into a long, dim room. It was almost full, and the crucible was already being passed around. This time, she thought, she would defy duty and only pretend to take the drug. She was wet, hungry, cold, and tired. If it was a minor psychopomp she would override it. And if not, it would only do her damage. She felt guilty—the Search was the principal duty of all responsible citizens and not to be taken lightly—but the Search could not now be her main concern. Besides, she reminded herself, she had not been summoned. Rationalizing did little good; the guilt remained.

She could see that this drug was something to be drunk. It was imone, perhaps, or one of the fungal alkaloids. Those in charge of the Search were evidently waiting until the room was full, for people were still slipping in through the door. Alivet shuffled up to make room for new neighbors, hooded and silent like herself. She waited patiently until the crucible was passed into her hands and raised it, pretending to take a sip. As the others had done, she rocked back with a sigh, and turned to her neighbor to pass on the crucible.

He was staring directly at her. She saw a pale, handsome face, ruby eyes in a fan of bone. Arieth Ghairen, the Poison Master, was sitting cross-legged, no more than a foot away, still smiling beguilingly.

Alivet's hands shook, jolting the crucible and spilling some of the substance onto the floor, where it hissed to a faint greasy smear. The Poison Master took the crucible carefully and sipped. She saw his pinprick pupils momentarily dilate, then slide into crescents, like small black moons against a sunset sky. Ghairen inclined his head and passed the crucible on.

Leaning closer to her, he murmured, "You had best pretend. The trance lasts for only a short while. We do not want to attract attention, do we? And you and I must have our wits with us when we leave." He patted the patch of ancient polished floor that lay between them. Alivet glanced around her, but there was no way out apart from the curtain. She could not simply get up and leave; it would make them suspicious.

How had Ghairen gotten in? The Search was supposed to be the best-kept secret in the city; she herself had been subjected to a scrying-glass and Veracity. Yet here he was, this unhuman person, sitting smiling beside her as though this was a commonplace for him. Had he followed her from the shore or from the center of Levanah? And if so, how? She had seen no sign of pursuit during her journey apart from the Unpriests' ill-fated boat, though there had been other craft in the marshes. And how could this strange man help her to free her sister?

Doubt filled her with a poison of its own. She sat silent and afraid, mimicking the dreaming souls around her and every so often stealing a glance at the Poison Master. His eyes were closed, his countenance serene. She found herself studying the planes and angles of his face. Sitting so close, she could smell him: a subtle combination of odors, oddly exciting to the senses, yet somehow familiar. He smelled, she realized, like an apothecary. The acridity of wormwood, cedar shavings, and charcoal, a faintness of spice. It was a reassuring smell and it served to calm her, but only a little.

chapter VII

CITY OF LEVANAH, MONTH OF DRAGONFLIES

The Search seemed to last for an eternity, leaving Alivet aching with impatience. When she saw that a few people had begun to emerge from their trance, she followed their lead, stretching and murmuring. A hand closed around her arm.

"Time to go," the Poison Master said into her ear.

Alivet struggled to her feet. Standing upright proved to be a mistake. The fumes from the drug, which now smoked about the room, were disorienting her, filling her head with paranoia. It had been a terrible idea to come here; she should have nothing to do with such a man. There was no way she could overpower him. She realized how much taller he was; she had to tilt her head to look into his face. If she could reach the front of the room, among the crowd, she might be able to evade him, but she was not even sure that she wanted to...

Stop this, she told herself, *it's only the fumes from the drug. You have to talk to Ghairen. What about Inki?*

"I'll have to tell them about my vision," she said, stalling.

"But you did not have a vision," Ghairen said, softly. "And I would not want to make a liar of you." His grip tightened. Her rational self told her that he was only trying to steady her, but the paranoia had a hold now and so, conversely, did an eager, unfamiliar voice that was instructing Alivet to follow him into the nearest dark corridor and comply with whatever happened next. That thought alarmed her so much that paranoia won.

"Let go of me," Alivet hissed. "I'm not going anywhere alone with you. If you want to talk, we can do it here."

Must be imone, her rational self said, with resignation. *It's a well-known delusion-bringer.*

The Poison Master did not reply. He drew her to the back of the crowd, as if they were moving to wait in line for the recording of their visions. Alivet tried to pull free, but his grip was too strong. She was steered behind a curtain into a narrow passage. Anticipation flooded through her. Here, however, the air was clearer and Alivet's unruly emotions began to ebb.

"Please," Ghairen said. "After you."

"You can go first," Alivet told him, breathing deeply. "I don't want you following me."

Rather to her surprise, he agreed. "I'm afraid I must insist that you don't try to run away," he told her with avuncular politeness, as if she were a willful child. Alivet bridled. "So…" She felt something cold tighten itself around her wrist and looked down to see a metal link snaking between them. Alivet tugged and the link tightened. "I realize it's an indignity," the Poison Master added, apologetically. "But I really am most keen to talk to you, and I'm sure you're equally eager." His eyes glinted with a return of mockery. "Now"—he drew her forward—"it isn't far."

The passages through which they passed smelled of dampness and age. The stone floor was slippery, and Alivet could see flood-marks traveling up the walls. The light from the Poison Master's lamp flickered over ancient carvings: gargoyles, momes, even a single representation of a Lord. Alivet stepped sharply back, startled. The long head, carapaced like that of an insect, showed sharp teeth and empty sockets. The head arched into the horned coil of the skull.

"I did not think that was permitted," Ghairen murmured. "They don't like to be represented, do they?"

"It isn't permitted. This place must be very old. And no, the Lords do not like to be represented. Statues, pictures—all that kind of thing is strictly forbidden. It can bring you the death penalty."

"Interesting. I'd heard that. Do you know why?"

"No."

"Perhaps the Lords are not entirely as they appear," Ghairen mused, "and wish to conceal any record of their various manifestations." His tone was bland and Alivet could not tell whether he was imparting information or simply musing aloud. He went on, "When did the Lords bring your people here? And when do you think this building dates from?"

"No one knows exactly when we came here. It could be as much as five hundred years old. There aren't many stone buildings before that—our ancestors didn't discover Godsbenediction Ridge until then."

"Discover where?" Ghairen's brows rose.

"The islands in the north of the fens, where most of our stone and metal comes from."

"I see." Ghairen paused before a door. "This place is a maze . . . but that's lucky for us." He motioned her through the door. "We're going up."

"There's nowhere else to go," Alivet observed.

"Ah, but there is. So many secret doors and passages, so many hiding holes. Your ancestors must have had a great many secrets. As you still do, hmmm?"

Alivet did not reply. Turning awkwardly in the passage, she followed Ghairen up the small, winding stairs.

The stairwell, it seemed, was more than merely a route from cellar to hall; it served the whole building. Alivet passed several doors and openings, which the Poison Master ignored. At last, when they could go no farther, he touched a panel in the wall and helped Alivet scramble through into a room.

"Now will you let me go?" Alivet demanded. It was disquieting, to be so close to him, and not unpleasant, which only contributed to her unease. She wondered, briefly, if this distillation of emotions was why people like Madimi got so enthusiastic about bondage. *Careful. Distillation leads to calcination, and corruption is swift to follow.* Alchemy did indeed have an answer to more subtle problems. Yet it was still only a question of chemistry, after all.

Ghairen did not reply, but the metal link fell away from her wrist and vanished into the pocket of his robe like a serpent. Freed, Alivet studied the room.

High windows looked out over the rooftops, gleaming with rain in the last of the light. Beyond, lay the misty expanse of the fens. The room was filled with plants: shelf upon shelf of fronded, ferny leaves. Alivet thought of her own rooms and closed her eyes, taking a breath of cool sweet air.

"Pleasant, isn't it?" the Poison Master said. "I was lucky to find such a place."

Alivet had no wish to waste time with small talk. "Perhaps so. But who are you? And what do you want with me? I'd like some answers."

"I've told you who I am. My name is Arieth Mahedi Ghairen. My—" there was the slightest hesitation "—friends call me Ari."

"And what should I call you?"

"You can call me Ari, too. *Brother* Ghairen sounds so formal, and since I don't come from Latent Emanation myself, it seems a touch presumptuous to adopt your mode of address."

"What?"

"I'm sorry?"

"What do you mean, you don't come from Latent Emanation?" Alivet asked blankly. The only folk who were known to travel into the heavens of the world were the Lords themselves, despite the threats and rumors of beings beyond. Perhaps he was mad—and yet the dark red eyes were like nothing she had seen before. She felt suddenly small and afraid and she turned to the window so that Ghairen could not see her face.

The Poison Master said equitably, "I am from elsewhere. From a world named Hathes, which orbits another sun. A very different planet to your own, yet not without its similarities. Folk marry, have children, grow old. They worry about their plants and if the weather will be fine."

He must be mad, surely, or from one of the strange places within the deep fens where folk spoke in riddles and metaphors. Alivet said carefully, "It sounds most interesting."

Ari Ghairen came to stand by Alivet's elbow. She could sense him behind her; his presence made her shiver. She twisted around and saw that he was still smiling. It occurred to her that it was not so much an expression of amusement or kindness as a form of habit, a simple configuration of the features as inexpressive as a mask. And she was alone with this madman in a small enclosed space. Not for the first time, Alivet cursed the Unpriests' prohibitions against carrying arms.

"What do you know of other worlds, Alivet?"

"I know only what the Lords allow us to know," Alivet said, with some bitterness. "And the little that we have discovered on our own. I know that our ancestors came from another world—that's what the Search is all about, after all. And I know that there are supposed to be other beings out there, who wish us harm and from whom the Lords are said to protect us. But there have never been more than rumors. No one I know has ever seen such a person. There are stories and legends, but it's hard to know what to believe. If anyone tried to make such a journey, I'd assume that the Lords would stop them."

"Then let me enlighten you. There are a number of other worlds, Alivet. Perhaps more than we know. Some of us are free to travel between them, as far as our technology and our purses allow. But the Lords and their human abettors keep you here, stagnating in your swamps. Even the deep fens are subject to Unpriest rule. And journeying to and from Latent Emanation is also prohibited by the Lords. I have taken a considerable risk in coming here."

Best to humor him, Alivet thought. Perhaps she could talk her way out of this.

"Then, *Brother* Ghairen," she said, "perhaps you'd like to tell me why you're here?"

"I told you. I'm a Poison Master," Ghairen said, as if this explained everything. "Fifth Grade, Scheduled Circle."

"I've never heard of such a thing," Alivet said.

Ghairen gave her an indulgent glance, as if she were a particularly promising pupil.

"Then I'll explain. My society is divided into many professions: diviners, engineers, linguists—and poisoners, to name but a few. My profession is similar to your own; I am basically an alchemical apothecary, although it is true that the focus of my work differs somewhat from the kind of thing with which you are engaged. I know something of hallucinogens and narcotics, but as my title suggests, my principal area of expertise involves the art of toxins."

"Why would anyone devote themselves to that?" Alivet asked. "For political reasons, or—?"

"Precisely. On Hathes, assassination is considered to be an accepted, if not acceptable, method of social climbing. My profession, you will doubtless be relieved to hear, is a relatively small one. There are not many Poison Masters."

Alivet was beginning to see why that might be so. Presumably they were all in the process of finishing one another off.

"But I don't wish to boast," Ghairen added. "The apothecaries of Latent Emanation know more about psychoceuticals and psychopomps, drugs and hallucinogens, than anyone else across the worlds. There is not so much of a call for drugs in my society. There is some private interest, naturally, but their use is not a form of socializing, as it is in yours, and we do not use drugs for spiritual purposes. Instead, we live, breathe, and work with toxins—and, indeed, with the healing of their effects. A Poison Master is both assassin and doctor. The Practical Examinations are legendary throughout Hathes." He gave a small, nostalgic sigh.

Alivet moved a little farther away. She said carefully, "I don't imagine that it's easy to get to the status of—what was it?—Fifth Grade, Scheduled Circle."

"That's very true," Ari Ghairen said. His pale face grew reflective. "So many of my colleagues . . . all fallen, taken by the years like autumn leaves."

"The years? Or your preparations?" Alivet's question was barbed.

The Poison Master glanced modestly at polished fingernails. "I'm very good at what I do," he murmured.

"Apparently so. I should like to know what a Poison Master—Fifth Grade, Scheduled Circle—is doing here," Alivet said. "And what do you know of my sister?"

"Your sister is an important part of this, it's true. But I've come for your help," Ari Ghairen said.

"My help? I thought *you* were offering to help *me*."

"Indeed I am. I have been staying here on Latent Emanation, disguised as an Imponderable, although I was obliged to take a risk back at Port Tree to attract your attention. I explored these lodgings thoroughly, so I know about the passages. And the room where the Search was held."

"How did you find me here in Shadow Town? I followed someone to the Search."

"Most certainly you did. You followed me. I saw you coming from the boat and rather than accosting you in a public place, I allowed myself to be found. It is the easiest thing in the world, to attract someone's attention."

"But you went into the Search. How did they let you in?"

"They didn't. You thought I went through the door, as you were intended to think. But I did not. I went upward, and you drew the obvious conclusion," the Poison Master said, with gentle reproach.

"Why did you offer to help my sister?" Alivet persisted. "And how did you know about her? Why does an—other-worlder take such an interest in local affairs?"

"Ah. Here we come to the nub of the question." Ghairen walked across to the window, where he stood staring out across the rooftops. "Come here."

Cautiously, Alivet went to stand beside him. The Poison Master murmured into her ear, "Tell me, Apothecary Dee, what do you see?"

Alivet followed his gaze. The world beyond seemed drowned, lost in a blue, rainy twilight. She could no longer see the fens. Below, the streetlights had been lit and as Alivet watched, a lamp smoldered in an opposite room. She saw a woman sink into a chair and ease off her shoes. Alivet envied the woman, wishing that she could share in the somber peace of that lamplight. She said as much to Ghairen.

"Why, do you envy her? Do you think she has an easier life than you?"

"Perhaps, perhaps not. She looks as though she might."

"But looks can deceive. I know that girl in the lamplit room. I took her for a drink a few days ago, in an inn along the street. I listened to her woes, and there is no shortage of them. She has lost a brother to the Unpriests. He serves in a Lord's palace; he has been there for years. She works as an artificer, to buy his freedom, but the taxes ensure that she is barely closer to the day of his release than when she began. She has inherited that tall house, and she rents out rooms to students at the Colleges of Shadow Town. The roof leaks, and the basement floods every winter. She spent Memory Day bailing out her cellar with a bucket instead of sitting down to steamed carp and samphire. She would envy you your lighter responsibilities, and greater wages."

"But my responsibilities are heavy, too, and there are unlikely to *be* any more wages, given that I seem to be wanted for murder," Alivet said. She did not think it was the right moment to ask if Ghairen had had a hand in Madimi's death, though given his proximity, it seemed all too probable. "You offered to help me. You keep evading my questions. Why?"

"You're a realist. I approve. So is the young woman across the way, and so are many folk on this little world, I find. Yet no one ever seems to address the central issue. If the Lords were gone, there would be no more Unpriests and no more Enbonding, and if there was no more Enbonding, people like you and the girl whom you envy would be free from such dogged slavery. Not to mention your Enbonded relatives. Tell me, how do you see the rule of the Lords and their creatures?"

"Some might call it a burden." Alivet spoke stiffly.

"Some, but not all?"

"You said it yourself. We are realists. And there are those of us who are more—pragmatic, than others. Those who gain advantage by allying themselves with the powerful, to whom cruelty is just another methodology." *Those like Yzabet, who believe the Lords protect us from beings from other worlds*. At that thought, Alivet felt a trickle of sweat run down the back of her neck.

"Is that just the voice of disappointment, Alivet? If you were given the opportunity, would you turn down the chance at power? Isn't it often the case that revolutionaries are simply the disgruntled?" He put his head on one side, studying her.

"I don't want that sort of power. And whatever I think about the way this world is ruled, there is little we can do about it." She had not intended to sound so frustrated.

"Indeed? I would have thought that disposing of the Lords of Night would have been a start."

"You know so little? There is no redress against the Lords. Do you think we are as meek as hatchlings, to take their governance for hundreds of years without protest? Many folk have tried to dispose of the Lords—years ago, a group discovered the making of gunpowder and tried to explode it in the cellars of a Night Palace. The Unpriests took them before they could set foot on the causeway and hung them on a gibbet. Others have tried arrows, fire, the use of the Unpriests' own weaponry. And poison, too. Nothing has worked. The Lords rarely set foot outside their palaces, and it's well nigh impossible to gain access. Many have tried, with terrible consequences. The Unpriests and the Families do their work for the Lords in the city and the fens."

"Do you understand the nature of the Lords?"

"What do you mean?"

"What kind of beings are they?"

Alivet thought for a moment. "I've always supposed that they are beings like humans and anubes, but much larger and more powerful. They are night creatures, we know that much. They are said to permit only dim lights in their palaces; they do not seem to like the day. But no one really knows. Those of the Enbonded who return are in no fit state to remember."

"Has anyone seen them during the hours of daylight?"

"I've never heard of such a thing. It's rare to see them in the city. They prefer the shadows, but they are not rumored to be like the lich-breed, who are said to burn at the first touch of the sun."

"There are no legends about what they are? No myths?"

"I have heard of none. But it's partly what the Search is concerned with—to discover why the Lords brought us here. And that could take us some distance toward discerning what kind of creatures they might be. Whatever they are, they seem impervious to harm."

"That is not true," Ari Ghairen said. Alivet stared at him. "They seem all-powerful only in comparison to yourselves. A way to defeat them can be found, if expertise can be pooled. I have researched you, Apothecary Dee. I have been studying you for some time now. I have seen your apothecarial records; read your reasons for wishing to enter the profession in your apprentice statement. I know all about Inki—how she was taken by the Lords and the steps you are taking to pay for her freedom. Now, I am prepared to help you free your sister, if you assist me in turn."

"Why do you need my help? I'm just an apothecary."

"Precisely. But you are a very good one. I told you, I've seen your records. You have an excellent reputation, and reason to be very angry over what has befallen your family. Plus, you are young, and thus do not have the caution and resignation that older people are prone to exhibit. And I need an apothecary."

Alivet sat back on the couch. "What for?"

"You make drugs. I make poisons. Together, it is my belief that we can pool our knowledge and create a substance that will bring down the Lords. For we share something else besides knowledge." He leaned confidingly toward her. "We both want the Lords gone."

"Why should you care about the Lords? Do they concern themselves with Hathes?"

"Not these days." Before she could ask him what he meant, he went on. "But Hathes is concerned with the Lords." He fixed her with an owlish eye. "There are grave violations of social justice on this world. Someone has to redress them."

"Don't patronize me," Alivet snapped. "I don't believe for a moment that you're motivated by questions of principle. By your own admission you're an assassin, not a social philanthropist."

"Well, maybe it doesn't sound too likely," Ghairen said after a moment. He smiled and she wondered whether he had been testing her gullibility. "Let's just say I have a number of vested interests in getting rid of the Lords."

"And are you going to tell me what these are?"

"No. Well, not yet, anyway."

That meant, Alivet thought, that she was unlikely to approve of those "vested interests." "So you're prepared to engage in—what? Assassination? War?"

"I'd prefer to think of it as the removal of a mutual problem." He was avoiding her gaze, Alivet noticed. His face had become shuttered, withdrawn. Yzabet's words echoed in her head: *And they protect us, too, from the beings of the worlds beyond. Without the Lords, what would happen to us?*

"Ask yourself this, Alivet. Do you want the Lords gone or don't you?"

Yzabet's fears—balanced against Inki's face, the blinded eye, the Unpriests' reign, hundreds of years of oppression and not knowing...A day or so ago, the choice would have seemed simple, but now, with Ari Ghairen standing smiling before her, Alivet was suddenly not so sure. Alchemical process: she separated her doubts from her desires.

"Yes," Alivet said slowly, "I want the Lords gone. But what

makes you think I'd be willing to embroil myself in treason? I know the penalties. The Unpriests would flay me over forty streets if the Lords ever found out."

"Alivet, I need your assistance, and I'm prepared to pay for it. I'll pay you enough to buy your sister out of Enbondment. I can take you to Hathes tonight. And it'll save your life, as well, not just Inki's."

"My life?" Alivet stared at him. "Are you talking about the Unpriests?" She was about to ask him whether he had been responsible for Madimi Garland's death. The thought that Ghairen was responsible for her most recent woes, that he had manipulated her into a position where she became dependent upon him, was appalling.

But just as she was about to accuse him, Ghairen said, "The Unpriests present an inconvenience. I'll happily help you to evade them. I promised Inki I wouldn't let any harm come to you."

"You've *spoken* to my sister? I don't believe you."

Ghairen sighed. "I thought that might be the case. It's like this. Some years ago now, I first came to Latent Emanation. I wanted to find out more about the Lords. And one of the things I discovered was that the Lords hold a banquet every year: a critical event, because it's the only time in the course of a year that the Lords are all in one place together.

"That first year, I tried to gain entrance into a Night Palace. I failed. A year later, I returned and tried again. That time, I managed to gain access. I introduced what I believed to be a lethal poison into the air of the palace, concealing it within a great perfumed fan. The Lords might as well have been breathing in the fragrant airs of the Mothlem mountains for all the effect it had.

"The last time—over a year ago now—I thought I had a chance of success. I was informed of an anube mendicant, living in the deep delta, who had once fought a Lord and defeated it. It was said that he knew of a method of killing them. I came back to Latent Emanation to search out the anube. But when I reached his pole-haunt, I found that the

Unpriests had got to him first. My informant had betrayed him. He was hanging from his own pole, for the larvae to feed upon. I narrowly escaped with my own life, but I dealt with the informant before he had a chance to betray me, too.

"It has taken me the last few months to find another option. But I have run into difficulties, and now the next banquet is only a week away. I do not want to lose another year. As soon as I could, I came to Latent Emanation, went back into a Night Palace, and skulked in the lower levels, looking for someone I might cultivate. I spied on kitchens and sculleries. At first I had little hope: the Enbonded were cowed, servile, vacant. The Lords use mind-washing drugs upon their servants. But some servants, the ones who perform the more complex tasks, are not so drugged. One day, a girl had an argument with the head chef over the preparation of a fondant." Ghairen smiled. "Actually, she threw a cake at him. The girl was confined to a cell for the night, which was where I visited her. I'm sure that you will not be surprised to learn that the girl's name was Inkirietta Dee."

The thought of her sister's defiance produced an uneasy mix of emotions in Alivet: pride at Inki's spirit, dismay at the risks she had run. And there was disquiet, too, at the notion of her sister in secret converse with the Poison Master.

"How is my sister?" she whispered.

"She's well enough. She's certainly retained her spirit. And she sends you her love."

Alivet turned back to the window. If she was going to cry, she did not want Ghairen as a witness. After a moment, she said, "Why did she talk to you?"

"I am neither Lord, Enbonded, nor Unpriest. Under the circumstances, I suspect that was good enough. Inki told me a great many things as she poured out her grievances over the Lords, and one was of particular interest to me. She told me that she had a twin sister in Levanah who had been planning to become an apothecary, and who had already demonstrated some considerable aptitude in the art. I didn't tell her a great deal about myself—if it comes to the point where she is interrogated," Ghairen said with careful neutrality, "I did not want her to have too much knowledge."

Alivet grew cold. "And how likely is interrogation?"

"Highly improbable. Inki need do nothing now except wait for you and me to come up with a solution."

"This plan," Alivet said, "have I got this right? You're intending to poison the Lords at their banquet, in one fell swoop."

"Precisely."

"Would it not be better to wait another year, plan things out? The Lords have been here for centuries, after all. Surely a year or so won't make much difference?"

Ghairen gave a thin smile. "I am an impatient man, Alivet."

She studied him. Nothing Ghairen had done so far had indicated a lack of patience. She was certain he was lying, but why?

"Do you have a suitable toxin in mind?"

"What I require—and what I believe I have now found after all these trying months of research"—frustration and strain were briefly visible in his face—"is a substance that is both a poison and a drug. But as I told you, I have run into difficulties. The substance I have in mind is highly unstable; I cannot work with it myself, and I could not bring it with me. That's why I need your expertise."

"But we don't have much time."

"I know. If the mendicant had not died—but such is life, plans fail. You're right, however—the clock is against us. We need to start out for Hathes as soon as possible."

"I still don't see why you can't wait."

"That won't be possible," Ghairen said and there was a raw edge below his words, like a wire in a bird-snare. Instinct told her not to press it further.

"Very well," Alivet said, cautiously. "But first, I want to know that you're not lying to me about Inki. How do I know that you've spoken to her? Everyone knows that I have an

Enbonded sister. You said you'd researched me—it wouldn't take a lot of investigation to find out about that."

"A good point and one that occurred to me. I asked Inki to tell me something that only a twin might know. And I hope you'll forgive me for embarrassing you, but I now know that you punched Nicholas Hakluyt when you were working in the marsh-hopper store, for suggesting that you sleep with him."

"Inki told you that?" Alivet said, outraged.

"She also told me that she dropped your aunt's wedding necklet through a crack in the boards when you were both seven and that you took the blame. Now are you convinced?"

"More or less," Alivet said grudgingly. "How do we get to Hathes?"

"There is," Ghairen seemed to be debating how much to tell her, "a means to reach a drift-boat. At Eleida Vo."

"Eleida Vo? That's the easternmost Palace of Night," Alivet said in horror.

"Quite."

"We're going back through a Night Palace?" Alivet was plunged back into doubt. Ghairen was a creature of the Lords: they had ransacked Inki's memory and this was some caprice of the Unpriests, a game within a cruel nest of games.

"There's a device—a portal—in the Night Palace which will take us onto a Hathanassi drift-boat. It's intended for the Lord's craft only, of course, but there is a way by which the coordinates can be altered for a short period. It's the only way to reach other worlds. The Lords take great care to keep you here, Alivet. They do not want your people to explore. The journey will be both difficult and dangerous."

"Difficult? To enter a Palace of Night is pure suicide!"

"It's the only way," Ghairen said, adding—not without irony—"Trust me."

Alivet could not bring herself to reply. Nonetheless, she waited impatiently in the hallway as the Poison Master, his face veiled, conducted some final transaction with the land-lady. She could feel the woman's curiosity and wondered

what the landlady thought. Did Ghairen often bring young
women back and forth his lodgings? Was he in the habit of
sleeping with them? She remembered the young woman in
the house opposite, slipping off her shoes in the lamplit room
and closing her eyes to think, perhaps, of her brother in the
depths of a Night Palace, just as Alivet thought of Inki. Had
Ari Ghairen made some bargain with that tired girl? Had he
merely bought her drinks and listened with sympathy in eyes
that were the color of poison? Or had he made love to her?
The thought aroused a curious sensation in Alivet: half
alarm, half envy. She thought of Ghairen's long fingers moving over someone's skin, brushing hair back from a face—
Alivet reined in her thoughts with a start. Enough of *that*.
There was no way of knowing. Yet if she lost sight of Ghairen
she, too, would be lost.

"You'll like Hathes." Ghairen spoke at her shoulder, making her jump. "A lovely world, full of wonders. Come on.
We'll go out the back way, just in case someone might be
watching."

"What if the Unpriests find us?" Alivet asked. "You know
that they're after me." The question trembled on her tongue:
Did you kill Madimi? She was suddenly very aware of Ghairen's
presence at her shoulder, of his moth-soft breath against her
neck. She should step away, she told herself, turn and face
him, and yet she could not move. *Stop being a fool. You've faced
Unpriests, bagmen, murderers before now and looked them
squarely in the eye. What is so different about this man?*

"Don't worry about the Unpriests. You're with me now."
Ghairen's hand brushed her shoulder. Clearly, he meant to be
reassuring, but condescension achieved what fear could not.
Alivet swung around.

"And what about Inki? If we're actually going into the
Night Palace, can I see her?"

"That wouldn't be wise."

"But—"

"We'll discuss it later."

The landlady, tucking a wad of money into the pockets of

her skirt, led them silently through a large, dank kitchen and out down a flight of steps. The wood was slippery; moss glowed green in the lights from the street. Wet fronds brushed Alivet's face as they made their way down the garden and out through a narrow gate.

Ghairen, moving swiftly, led Alivet along a maze of alleyways: she smelled rain-soaked earth, ripening marrows, and bitter cabbages. When she and Inki were children, Alivet had often imagined leaving Latent Emanation forever. But in those dreams, she had always been a princess or a pirate, rescued from the impostors who pretended to be her family and sailing up in a silver-winged ship surrounded by her devoted henchmen. The dreams of an eight-year-old did not encompass sidling through back gardens at night, led by a charming unhuman poisoner.

Alivet trod in a pothole and concluded that the dreams of eight years old were better.

"How are we getting to the Night Palace?" she hissed at Ghairen, now some strides ahead. He turned back.

"Well, we're not walking all the way."

"That's a relief."

"This is just a diversion. I don't think anyone was watching the house, but it never hurts to be sure. Tricky people, your Unpriests. Once we come out onto the main road, we'll take a chaise."

"What if the Unpriests have issued a description of me?"

"Do you think the anubes will hand you in? They did not do so out on the marsh."

"How do you know so much about what happened on the marsh? I didn't see you skulking in the rushes."

"I keep informed," Ghairen murmured. "The marsh wife, for example. A most helpful lady. Though the anubes keep their own counsel, you will be interested to hear. I have tried to co-opt them before but—apart from my poor mendicant— with a lamentable lack of success."

"I see," Alivet said sourly. How far did his network of informers extend? she wondered. Had Genever Thant been bought? The Poison Master had clearly been busy during his time in Levanah. Ghairen stepped over an irrigation channel, footsteps splashing in the thick wet moss, and pointed.

"There's the road that leads to the causeway. I've arranged transport for some of the way, then we'll need to be more covert."

Now that her eyes had adjusted to the shadows, Alivet saw that there was a chaise waiting. It was run-down and old, the canopy in tatters. The anube who waited so patiently between its shafts did not look up as they approached, nor did it turn its head as Ghairen extended a hand to help Alivet onto the seat.

Once they were both inside, the anube loped out into the road, still in silence. Numbly, Alivet watched the streets roll by and soon they were out near the causeway that led to the Night Palace.

"Not far now," Ghairen said. He gestured toward a ring of lights. "There's the entrance to the causeway." But as they neared the middle of the causeway, something swift and black darted overhead. Alivet gripped Ghairen's arm.

"That's the Unpriests' flier."

"I told you not to worry."

"Ghairen—"

"Just trust me, Alivet."

She looked back. There was no other traffic on the causeway. They were as visible as a bird on a lake. The flier veered once and turned. The causeway rose high above the marsh: if she sprang from the chaise and jumped, she would be killed.

"Almost there," Ghairen said, comfortingly. The vast gates of the causeway entrance rose before them. Ghairen tapped the anube on the shoulder. The chaise slowed to a halt.

"Now," Ghairen said, "walk slowly, and keep close to me. Keep your hood over your head and your hands in your pockets."

Alivet did so. She followed Ghairen to the gate, resisting the temptation to look up. This was the closest she had ever come to a Night Palace. It was Lord technology, far beyond a human scale. Both gates and walls were built of a dense, translucent substance, like columns of dark air. She could see the Palace of Night at the end of the causeway, glimmering as if glimpsed through water. An Unpriest stepped out of the gatehouse and stood before them, tapping a hand sheathed in rippling metal against her thigh.

"Entrance is forbidden. Where are your documents?"

"Here." Ghairen handed over a strip and the Unpriest held it beneath her mechanical eye. Alivet could see the lens dilating in and out as it processed the information.

"An Imponderable. You're a long way from home, aren't you? What about you?" She gestured to Alivet, who grew cold with the dismay of betrayal. Ghairen had given her nothing, had issued no instructions.

It was all a cruel and elaborate trap. He was employed by the Unpriests to bring her in. If she turned and ran, the woman would kill her. She stepped back and as she did so her eyes met Ghairen's own. He had cast aside the Imponderable's veil. The night ran around her, blurring in sudden heat. Her skin felt warm as summer and she stumbled. A skein of material was clapped over her face and she breathed something fresh and astringent, dispelling the faintness. Ghairen's hand was around her arm and he pulled her forward. Then they were through the gate, leaving the slumping figure of the Unpriest behind.

"Quickly, now. The toxin won't last forever." Ghairen pointed to the banked sides of the causeway. "We'll go along the bank, not the causeway. The Unpriest's forgotten that she ever set eyes on us, but I don't want to stroll down the causeway in plain view."

Alivet slithered down the bank after him, the back of her neck prickling with alarm. She could see the bulk of Eleida Vo rising before her now: dark and glittering against the sky. This was where Inki had been taken. The notion of seeing her sister made Alivet grow clammy with apprehension. Wild thoughts raced through her mind: of snatching Inki away, fleeing into the marsh . . .

Since Ghairen had spoken to her, it seemed that her mind

had not been her own, but subsumed under some alien presence. It occurred to her that perhaps this was his artistry as a master of poisons: the real toxin was his manipulation of the fears in her agitated mind. But it was too late now. The great gate of the causeway lay behind her, and the Night Palace was rising up like a black orchid out of the marsh. Alivet blinked. Ghairen, who had been striding before her, had gone.

"Ghairen?" Alivet whispered into the empty air. "Where are you?"

His voice floated up from the ground.

"Down here."

Crouching down, Alivet saw that a yawning hole lay between the clusters of rushes.

"It's quite safe."

Alivet doubted this, but even as she hesitated, the air began to hum as if struck like a bell. The flier was coming back. She could see its lights arcing out before it and the dragonfly bulb of its hull striped with rain. As it swung around, Alivet gathered her skirts around her and dived into the hole. It was a long drop and she landed in a heap. Ghairen pulled her to her feet.

"Ghairen, there's a flier out there."

"Then we must hurry."

To Alivet's surprise, the tunnel was high enough to stand upright, and its walls were dry.

"Where are we?" she asked, as Ghairen turned and began to walk swiftly along the tunnel.

"This is an anube passage, from the days before the Lords," Ghairen said over his shoulder. "The mendicant knew of it."

Alivet put out a hand to steady herself and encountered smooth, cool stone. They had reached the end of the tunnel. A round chamber arched above her head, made from blocks of interlocking rock. And there was a face looking at her from out of the darkness. Alivet gasped, then realized that the face was not that of a living thing.

"What's that?"

The visage was cut into a pillar: a head, unattached to a

body, but with four faces. The faces were human: beautiful and wild, with curling mouths. Alivet stepped around the pillar to see the fourth face and found that this one was serene. Its eyes were closed and the lips were curved into a faint, melancholic smile. She could not tell whether it was male or female.

"This surely wasn't made by the anubes," she said. "The faces are human—why would they bother?"

"Who knows?" Ghairen said. Alivet glanced at him. In the light of his torch, Ghairen's face was closed, the red eyes downcast and full of secrets. She was certain that he was lying. "This is the entrance to the Palace of Night," Ghairen added. "Follow me, as closely as you can. Do not speak and try not to look about you—I know the temptation will be great, and I know that you want to search for your sister. But if we are discovered, you will never see her—or anything—again. I will not condescend by asking if this is clear. I know that you understand me."

"Believe me," Alivet said with feeling, "I've no wish to do anything in a Night Palace which could draw attention to myself."

"Good."

He raised a hand to the wall. There was a gleam of light, a pattern against the stone. Alivet saw that it came from Ghairen's glove: a diagram of lights that flickered over his palm.

"What's that?" she whispered. Ghairen did not answer. The stones of the wall began to grow translucent, so that Alivet could see through them to a darkness beyond. Images slid across the transparent stones. She saw the face of an anube bearing a great golden crown, a procession of tiny figures crossing over a place that looked both high and cold, the fourfold face of the statue behind her with the eyes staring and fierce. The images marched through the stone, like dreams through the sleeping mind, and were gone. And the wall was gone with them, melted away and leaving an emptiness upon the air.

Beckoning, Ghairen stepped through. Alivet, following, found that the air in the space beyond was much colder. Her teeth snapped together and gooseflesh rose on her arms. Ghairen paused to fasten his coat more securely. Alivet rammed her hands into her pockets and walked on. The torchlight picked out a path along the wall. She stood in a winding red corridor, its walls glazed as if with frost. It reminded her of the meat-rack she and Inki had crept into as children, to gaze with wonder at row upon row of icy butchered carcasses, destined for the tables of the aristocracy. The meat-rack had smelled of chilled blood; this place was warm and fragrant, with undernotes of ginger and musk, resinous amber and living flesh. Alivet stopped and stared.

"Ghairen?"

"Just follow me."

She had always thought of the Night Palaces as being dead places, cold and somber, but the network of corridors through which they walked seemed horribly alive. Alivet felt eyes on her back, as though the walls were watching. The floor pulsed gently beneath her feet and she had the feeling that she had wandered into nightmare, that Ghairen was her dream-guide, her psychopomp, that she would never return.

Stop this, Alivet told herself. *Think of what Inki must have been through.*

It was a dreadful thought.

After Inki had been taken by the Unpriests, Alivet had spent long hours awake in the cold nights of the fens, imagining what might be happening to her sister. She had even dreamed of it: imagining that it had been she who had been taken, not Inki, that it was she who was walking through dead and ancient halls and serving the whims of the Lords of Night. She had never dreamed that their palaces would be anything like this. And with these thoughts came the old guilt: *It should have been me.*

Hate filled Alivet's heart. She fastened her gaze on the elegant figure of Ghairen, striding ahead. She would never have believed it possible an hour ago, but she was glad that he was here with her now. However sly and sidling Ghairen might be, he still seemed to be a part of her world rather than that of the Lords. If she could only see her sister, just once—but she was forced to admit that Ghairen might be right. It would not be wise, to risk all for the sake of a glimpse of Inki, yet reason and sense were at war with her instincts.

Eventually, the twists and turns of the corridor led them out into a hallway. It was on a massive scale; the Palace of Night seemed even larger from within than it did from without. Soft, thick rugs covered the floor, but it was impossible to see their pattern in this dimness. The ceiling lay far above Alivet's head, a narrow strip of wan light between the crimson buttresses. She could not tell where the illumination was coming from. It looked like reflected light rather than a direct source.

Then she cannoned into Ghairen. His hand snapped around her wrist and he drew her back behind an arch of stone. Alivet, remembering her instructions to keep silent, had to bite her tongue. Ghairen nudged her in the ribs. She turned to see a small procession of people coming down the hallway. One of them was a girl. The dark red walls of the hallway receded from Alivet's gaze; the ceiling grew dim and distant. She could hear only the roaring of the blood in her head.

"Inkirietta." The syllables crunched like ice. She did not realize that she had spoken aloud until Ghairen's hand clamped over her mouth.

"Alivet," he murmured into her ear. "Alivet, listen to me. That is *not* your sister." His arm was around her waist, all that was stopping Alivet from bolting out into the hall and seizing the girl by the hand.

As the procession drew nearer, however, she could see that he was right. It was not Inki. This girl was younger, the age that Inki had been when she was taken, and she had golden hair. Her face was pinched and wizened, and she was hunched over as if in pain. The two boys who accompanied her were older; they wore silk doublets and leather breeches, and their expressions held a cold vacancy. They looked like two stilted puppets, drawn along on a string. The third boy was even younger than the girl and he looked simply afraid. Each of them was carrying a platter, covered by a serving dish.

Alivet tapped Ghairen's hand, mutely requesting release. She thought of toxins crawling over his skin and worming through her clothes, but there was a warmth beneath the fear. Ghairen's arm remained firmly where it was, and then a Lord stepped through the doors at the far end of the hall.

Alivet watched, breathless. She had never been so close to one before. The Lord stood nine feet high, its armored head drifting from side to side. It seemed to be formed from a mass of shadows: planes of ebony, indigo, and storm-cloud gray, yet its face was more human than many of the Lords of Night: Alivet saw bulbous eyes and a pursed mouth. Its antennae exuded a faint and musty fragrance. Movement rustled beneath its robes; the Lord's body seemed to coil and shift. Alivet remembered Ghairen's remark: *Perhaps the Lords are not entirely as they appear . . .*

The Lord moved with ponderous, swinging slowness down the hall, and in its wake the air seemed suddenly thinner and darker, as though it breathed in health and light and gave out nothing. Another shadowy form followed through the double doors. Alivet caught sight of the long out-thrust jaw and the slotted vertebrae of its throat beneath its hood. It placed a delicately jointed foot on the thick carpet and teetered forward, past the Enbonded boys and girl.

The Lord brushed against one boy as it tottered by. He stepped back at once, but the platter that he carried fell to the floor. Alivet saw a black and glistening lump fall from beneath the cover and creep away. The Lord gave a whistling cry. A jointed hand flicked out and caught the boy by the shoulders. His mouth opened, but he made no sound. The Lord spun the boy around and Alivet saw a tiny hole open in the air. She could not see what was beyond it. Ghairen's arm was like steel around her waist. The girl and the other two boys continued on their stilted progress along the hall, as if nothing had happened.

The circle hovered, a disc of unlight, silhouetted against the velvet curtains that hung upon the opposite wall. The Lord, with pats and pinches, compelled the boy to look through. Alivet saw with horror that the boy's eyes were squeezed tightly shut, his face screwed into the citric sourness of terrified resolution. She could hear him panting and she tried to break free of Ghairen's arm.

Ghairen's response was to clasp her more firmly. The Lord's fingers crept around the sides of the boy's face and tapped once beneath his eyelids. The boy's eyes flew open. He stared into the circle of unlight and his face took on an expression of entranced numbness. He leaned forward, peering into the hole and angling his head to see more clearly. Alivet saw the expression drain out of his face like water, leaving it slack and blank. The circle was gone. The boy slumped to the floor and lay there, quivering. The Lord veered away, stepping over him and continuing on its unsteady journey. More Enbonded retainers rushed forward, picked up the boy, and carried him away through the curtains. Alivet saw a trickle of blood coming from the boy's right eye, and her heart grew heavy and cold.

"Wait until they have gone," Ghairen whispered into her ear. She could feel his breath on her face and thought of death, but she waited until the Lords and the Enbonded retainers had disappeared from view. She scanned the faces of the Enbonded; they were all male. Yet she knew that the Unpriests prized girls: what happened to them? Alivet believed she knew the answer to that, but it did not bear thinking about. She had reached that conclusion years before, when the thought of her sister in the clammy embrace of an Unpriest had been almost enough to drive her out into the city and knife the first one she came across. That, however, would have helped no one, and Inki least of all.

Ghairen stepped out from their hiding place and reached

out a beckoning hand to Alivet. Together, they crept along the hallway to the double doors at the end. Surely Ghairen was not planning to stroll through the doors themselves— but then Alivet saw a small chamber to her left. Ghairen slipped soundlessly through the entrance. Alivet followed and found that they were in a round room. Here, the walls were black and made of some smooth crystalline substance, yet crusty patches marred their surface, as though the walls had been wounded and scabbed. She reached up a hand to touch the wall, but Ghairen wheeled around and knocked her arm away. He shook his head, put a finger to his lips. Alivet nodded understanding. She gazed up at the curved ceiling of the chamber, and realized that she could see through it. Claws tapped on the ceiling, far above her head, and with a cold shock Alivet recognized a Lord, seen from below. She tugged at Ghairen's sleeve and pointed upward. Ghairen's eyes narrowed. He motioned Alivet to move to the edges of the room, mouthing, *"Slowly."* If the Lord should look down and see figures below . . . Perhaps it would assume they were Enbonded servants. Or perhaps not.

Ghairen was resting his gloved palm against the wall; she could see the glow of the lights on the glove. With excruciating slowness, the wall melted away. Ghairen and Alivet hurried through into a second long hallway. As she stepped through the wall, Alivet turned and looked up. Beyond the translucent ceiling of the chamber, there was a sudden flurry of robes, like watching a fish dive into the mud.

The Lord had seen them.

chapter VIII

THE PALACE OF NIGHT

Alivet seized Ghairen by the shoulder and pointed frantically back. The Poison Master's face registered alarm. He gestured to the end of the hallway. "*Run.*"

Alivet did not need prompting. Something was coming through the chamber behind her. There was a palpable wave of an inimical presence: emotions so powerful that they rushed over her like a sudden wave—anger, sorrow, and a sense of outrage, an all-encompassing incomprehension that anyone could enter the Palace, defy the Lords, act of their own free will. And after that came a refined, anticipatory cruelty; she saw what the Lord intended for her, a long slow draining of her mind that would leave her empty and mad. It was the only glimpse that Alivet had ever had into the mind of a Lord and it horrified her. She picked up her skirts and bolted down the hallway.

"Ghairen? Where are we going?"

"Not far now," Ghairen called back, but the hallway was spinning around her, dissolving into shards of red frost like the falling leaves in the Month of Dragonflies. She felt the touch of the Lord's mind on her own. A great cold whisper of air breathed down the hallway. Someone sprang into Alivet's path: a young man dressed in black, his face distorted with fury or fear. Alivet pushed him aside, but there were more of them—the hallway spun again and a hand gripped her wrist. Alivet realized that it was not the Lord who was creating the mental confusion, but Ghairen himself. She could taste poison, fizzing like metallic sherbet on her tongue. Ahead, a hole opened in the air. Alivet, remembering the Enbonded boy who had looked through such a hole not long before and been struck blind, pulled back, but Ghairen cried, "No! We're going through."

The hole grew wider, forming a portal of nothingness in the air. She could not see beyond it. Another young man sprang in front of her. He carried a weapon of brass from which a pale fire was flickering. Ghairen stepped forward and threw a handful of dust. The young man dropped the weapon and fell to his knees, clawing at his face. The hole widened like a pursing mouth.

"What is it?" Alivet cried, but hands were clasping at her, pulling her away from Ghairen. An Enbonded girl had seized her arm in both hands. Alivet looked down into a peaked face, the left eye puckered into a seamless scar beneath a fringe of dark hair. But the other eye widened with recognition.

"Inki!"

Inkirietta's mouth fell open. She took a swift glance over her shoulder and Alivet saw that the Lord was gliding up the hallway.

"Inki, come with me—"

But Ghairen cried, "Alivet! There's no time."

Alivet saw her sister swallow and nod.

"Just go," Inki said, and then she turned and pushed Alivet away, so hard that she stumbled against the edge of the hole in the air. Inki, the Enbonded, the Lord, and the Palace of Night: all were gone, whisked to a pinpoint vision, and Alivet was falling through nowhere.

part III

ASCENSION

How oft do they their silver bowers leave
To come to succour us that succour want;
How oft do they with golden pinions cleave
The flitting skies like flying pursuivant
Against foul fiends to aid us militant.
They for us fight, they watch and duly ward
And their bright squadrons round us plant;
And all for love and nothing for reward.
Oh, why should heavenly love to men have such regard?

— EDMUND SPENSER, *The Faerie Queene*

chapter I

LONDON ∽ 1555

T here is," the warder said, "a second charge, that
has recently been made."

Dee peered up at him through the bars of the
cell. The warder smelled of grease and old smoke, and the
reek of cheap ale. Still, the stink spoke of the outside
world, and as such, was an improvement upon dead rats.

"What, then?" Dee asked, warily. "Was not simple
witchcraft good reason enough for a necklace of gunpowder?"

"The charge is that you have endeavored by enchant-
ments to destroy Queen Mary."

Dee snorted. "Who told them that?"

"I cannot say," the warder said. He stared uneasily
down at Dee, who wondered if it was worth trying to in-
timidate the man. Almost certainly not. Bishop Bonner's
men might be mad, but they were neither cowards nor
fools.

"It was Pridaux, I would warrant—he's an informer of
yours, is he not? Or was it George Ferrers, the king of mis-
rule?" Ferrers had disliked him on sight, and Dee's un-
feigned mirth during Ferrers' Christmas entertainment at
court had not gone unnoticed by the lawyer. Unfortunately,

Dee's mirth had been for all the wrong reasons, since Ferrers was corpulent and remarkably unsuited to satin. It seemed little enough on which to notify the authorities that one's enemy had been practicing witchcraft, but little enough was sufficient, these days.

He should never have left the Low Countries, Dee reflected with bitterness, once the warder had gone and he was left alone to crouch in the rat-ridden cell. There, he'd had a position and prospects; here, he was nothing more than a heretic awaiting the fire. But all the mighty seemed swift to fall these days, beneath the fanatical scourge of Bishop "Bloody" Bonner.

Dee grimaced, reflecting on past glories. It had all been going so well. He had been the pearl in the oyster of Europe. There had been the packed lectures on geometry in Paris, the ambassadorial dinners in Brussels. There had been the friends whom now he might never set eyes on again—Mercator, that wise and clever man; Frisius and Ortelius, fellow cartographers and mathematicians; the celebrated navigator Núñez, whom Dee now counted among his closest colleagues. All planets in the firmament of Europe, spiraling around the world that was Dee himself.

And no less than five offers from the Christian emperors, court positions that Dee had turned down to come home to England, seeking a place closer to home. But unless he could talk his way out of it, England would repay his loyalty with the flames.

Dee shuffled back against the wall and closed his eyes. The chains were uncomfortable and the cell stank, but the worst thing of all was the tedium. He had not realized how much he had come to depend on his books for company—and when the men had come from the Court of Wards to arrest him, Dee had been right in the middle of a set of calculations that he could not now recapture without the aid of a parchment and quill, no matter how hard he tried. But even this was a trifle compared to the impact upon his family. His father had, of course, already been tried and escaped with financial ruin rather than loss of life, but the arrest of her son would surely send his mother into a further decline. At least his wife was there to look after them both, but her health had suffered in recent months; an excess of black bile that produced a melancholy, seeming to draw her deeper and deeper into herself. He had given her a necklace of garnets to keep the sorrow from her, but the remedy had failed.

Mercator had been right, Dee mused now. The Church had called him a heretic, but not because of any unwise speculation about life on other worlds or, indeed, as a result of his religious practices as such. No, what Bishop Bonner objected to was the dark art of mathematics. *Calculating, conjuring, and witchcraft.* Dee recited the dismal litany beneath his breath. Those were the charges, based upon the accusation that he had drawn up horoscopes for those in power and out of it: Mary the Queen, and the princess Elizabeth, and Philip. True enough, Dee reflected, ruefully. The rising sign at Mary's nuptials had been Libra, ruled by gentle Venus, and a good omen, one would have thought—but not for Dee.

Later, standing before the Bishop, Dee could almost smell death emanating from the man, as though the skeletal figure itself stood behind his shoulder with its antic grin. Bonner was a large man, meaty as a Smithfield hog. *But if Bonner has his way,* Dee reminded himself, *you'll be that hog, spitted on a Smithfield pyre.*

"Dr. Dee," Bonner said, beaming as though Dee had merely chanced by for a cup of wine and a chat. "Please, do sit down." He waved expansively at the nearest chair. Warily, Dee took it.

"You know," Bonner said, leaning forward and glancing toward the door, "I am most certain that your arrest has been nothing more than the grossest error, and I promise I mean you no more hurt than I do to my own person. But," and here Bonner sighed, "the court must need be satisfied that I have done my duty. I will, therefore, ask you no more than a few trifling questions."

Dee, who until now had been anxious, felt himself grow afraid. Bonner spoke sweet, mincing reason, but the light eyes, glittering in the florid expanse of the Bishop's face, looked upon Dee as a starving man looks upon a banquet. It did not need great sensitivity to realize that Bonner was a man requiring a daily feed of pain and blood.

"But you must be weary," Bonner said, and beckoned to the guard at the door. "Wine, for Dr. Dee."

The man came back with a glass of claret, gleaming thick and red in the firelight. Dee looked at it and thought immediately of poison, but in his estimation Bonner was both grosser and more subtle than that.

"Tell me," Bishop Bonner said, leaning back in his chair. "St. Cyprian informs us that there must be one high priest, whom the residue must obey. What do you say to this?"

A reference to the Pope, Dee thought, though one might argue that St. Cyprian was discussing his own position as patriarch of Africa. But one would have to be most careful how one argued theology with Bonner.

"St. Cyprian has these words: 'That upon Peter was builded the church, as upon the first beginning of unity.'" He did not add: *For myself, I believe in God and his angels, and all else is petty squabbling.* He remembered Elizabeth's words, uttered in his hearing only a week ago: "There is only one Jesus Christ, Dr. Dee. The rest is dispute over trifles."

And that is why he would continue to work for her, Dee told himself. For of them all save perhaps Francis Walsingham, Elizabeth took the longest view. She would make a good queen, if any of them lived to see it.

Meanwhile, however, it would be necessary to dissemble. If Bonner wanted to prove him a Catholic, then a Catholic he would be. He had work to do, here on Earth and in the wider spheres of the universe, but for now he could see only as far as the fires.

The theological cat-and-mouse continued for over an hour. Dee, watching the flames burn down, answered as glibly as he could, but his fears continued to grow. Bonner was a contradictory man: gross in appetite, refined in intellect—the opposite of the run of the aristocracy. Dee did not find it a reassuring combination. He felt as though a crowd pressed behind him, urging him to answer wisely for their sakes. It seemed to him that he could glimpse his mother's drawn face in the uncertain, flickering light; his father, defeated by recent woes. His wife's visage fluttered before his mind's eye and it was as though she already slipped toward the grave, veiled by her melancholy as with a shroud. But the face that returned with most frequency, that grave countenance with its cold, sad eyes, was that of Elizabeth.

"This small matter," Bonner said now, toying with a ragged quill and speaking idly, as a man might comment upon a passing shower of rain. "This trifling question of conjuration. Speak to me of this." He glanced up, eyes bright, lips pursed as if anticipating sweetmeats, and Dee realized that everything that had passed over the course of the previous hour was nothing more than a prelude to this apparently final question. Bonner wanted to see a sorcerer burn, bursting in the flames like a toy stuffed with gunpowder. And with the avidity of a child who has been denied, he would make sure that he got his wish. It would matter little what Dee now told him.

"I have no interest in witchcraft," Dee said. "It is a matter for old wives and cunning men, not for the learned. I have applied myself to the art of mathematics, which as you will well know, is taught in all the universities these days."

"Yes, I know this. And one such is the University of Louvain, is it not?"

"That is so."

"The Low Countries. I have heard that many theories

pass through the Low Countries upon a daily basis, as commonly as flocks of geese." The Bishop raised an eyebrow.

"That is also so. There is much intertraffic of the mind."

"And one might say that such a place is low not only in geography, but also in sympathies." Bonner grinned at his own wordplay. "Louvain is reputed to be a seat of Protestant fervency; the inhabitants of the University are said to have dangerous ideas. Gerardus Mercator echoes the Copernican heresy, I have heard, and Frisius himself is known for certain peculiar practices."

"I should hardly call trigonometry a peculiar practice," Dee said mildly. "It reflects God's work, nothing more."

"As do your own mathematical arts? Making dung beetles fly through the heavens?" Bonner leaned forward and the mask fell away. "For what purpose other than to mock God?"

"I did not—"

"And the making of waxen effigies? The lewd and vain practices of calculating and conjuring? You have been charged once already, Dr. Dee."

"In that instance Lord Broke concluded that the charges could not be substantiated and moreover—"

"I know of Lord Broke's conclusions. I am not of a similar mind, nor do I hedge and fret as Broke so clearly did, because you are close to Elizabeth. There are such charges; they still stand and substance will be given to them." Bonner still spoke courteously, but his gaze was a serpent's own. "What do you say, Dr. Dee?"

Dee knew that he could make no plea for clemency. If Bonner could not find evidence of heresy, he would manufacture it. And the Lord knew that there was plenty of material at Dee's house that could be used against him; Bonner would be a thousand times more thorough than the hedging, pragmatic Lord Broke. The bronze bee, the precious globes that Mercator had given to him and which were now hidden in the cellar. Thank God, thought Dee, that he had taken care not to commit to parchment any of the ideas about sublunary flight or his increasingly interesting investigations into the alchemical sciences.

"I am waiting, Dr. Dee."

Dee felt his skin grow clammy. This was it, then, the moment that the skeleton hand would first tap him upon the shoulder. The room grew icy and the fire hissed as if snow had fallen down the chimney. Then Dee caught sight of the Bishop's face and realized that it wasn't just fear that had caused such an effect. The room really was arctic, and Bonner was staring behind Dee's shoulder like a man who has glimpsed the Devil. After a startled moment, Dee turned.

Something was standing at the far end of the room. Dee, paralyzed with shock, only knew that it was an angel because its long hands were folded in front of it in an attitude of prayer. It did not have the bland face and the swan's wings of the Catholic statues. Its face was blank and cold as marble, and as Dee stared, it turned slowly on its own axis so that he could see that it had not one face, but four. Two of the faces were female, the lips set in an awful fixed smile. The other two faces were male. It wore robes and it was transparent, as if made of some vitreous substance. Its mouths stayed closed and it continued to revolve slowly, like a planetary orb.

"What—" Bonner's voice had risen by an octave. Dee himself was too astounded to speak. It did not occur to him to talk to the angel, any more than he would have thought to address one of Mercator's globes. The angel spun faster, and started to grow huge until it filled the whole room. Bonner started to scream then, and went on screaming until the angel burst the room apart and sent the midnight stars flying down around Dee's head.

chapter II

Drift-Boat, Orbit

"Where are we?" Alivet asked. She was somewhere dark and hot, with a complex smell of a thousand spices. She could not see an inch in front of her face. She reached out, trying to locate Ghairen.

"It's all right." The Poison Master's voice came from somewhere off to her left. "We're on the drift-boat. You're safe now."

Hardly, thought Alivet. Ghairen went on, "I must apologize. I thought I'd taken precautions not to be spotted. I didn't count on being seen from above."

"What precautions? That poison? And what is it, anyway?" She could still feel it, fizzing deep inside her mind.

"It's designed to disrupt the visual cortex. Can you see at all?"

"No. Isn't that because it's dark?"

"It isn't dark, Alivet. You've been temporarily blinded. Come and sit down."

First the Night Palace, now blindness. It was as though the world had stored up a collection of horrors, then released them all at once, a flock of black-winged birds.

"Don't worry," Ghairen said. "It won't last more than a few minutes. And the portal is sealed behind us, in case you're wondering. Nothing's going to follow from that direction." She felt his hand on her arm, guiding her forward. She sat down on something plushy and soft.

"I saw my sister," she told him, in a whisper.

There was a pause.

"Alivet, you don't know that. Your vision must have been affected."

"No. I know what I saw, Ghairen. And so do you. Don't lie to me." She did not know whether he was playing games, or trying to be kind. "It was Inkirietta. Her eye—" Alivet had to stop then, and collect herself—"her eye was gone, but she knew me. I saw it in her face—she remembered. And I left her there! I let her go again."

Ghairen touched her hand, but Alivet pulled it sharply away.

He said, "If you had not gone through the portal, then the Lords would have had you both. It's possible that the Lord could not see what was happening. For all you know, Inki may be rewarded for trying to stop the intruders."

"Yes, and she may be tortured inside a cell. I saw the Lord's mind, Ghairen. I know what it had planned for us."

Alivet was starting to notice sparks in the darkness: a skein of firecracker images, a dim red glow. She blinked, trying to clear her vision.

"We don't know. But remember—if they had caught us, even the slim threat that we represent would be gone. When we are successful in finding a substance that will put paid to the Lords, then you will realize that it was worth it."

"Even if I have to sacrifice my sister?"

If there really was a way to defeat the Lords, just what was she prepared to sacrifice? Her own life? Yes, if necessary, though it was hardly an attractive prospect. But what about Inkirietta's life? For the last few years, her goal had been to free her sister from Enbonding. The thought of failure was hard to bear.

The light around her was starting to grow.

"How's your sight now?" Ghairen asked.

"I can see," Alivet conceded. They were sitting in what

appeared to be the center of some vast machine. The floor and walls were made of some burnished metal; her own dim face looked out at her from a dozen different directions. She looked up and saw a lattice of wires, so intricately laced that it was impossible to tell how far upward it extended. Yet high in the lattice Alivet could see points of glittering lights: stars, or some mechanism of the drift-boat itself? There was an oval opening in the opposite wall, but she could see nothing reflected in it except a dark swirl that moved like a restless current.

"What's that?"

"The other end of the portal through which we traveled lies beyond that door." Ghairen indicated a metal panel at the far end of the room. "When we came through, you were disoriented and barely conscious, so I brought you here to recover."

"I've seen inside a drift-boat," Alivet told him. "And it seemed very different—just rows of unconscious people."

"Did you see such a thing during a Search?"

"Yes."

"What you glimpsed, then, may have been truth or it may not, as I'm sure you are aware. The Lords—as you'll also be aware—do things differently than us. They do not build on a human scale; they pay little attention to human comforts. We, on the other hand, believe that if one is to go to the considerable trouble of interworldly travel, then one might as well do so with a modicum of indulgence. Certainly we pay enough for it." Ghairen arranged his disordered robes in a more elegant manner and sat back in his chair, as if dismissing the subject.

"How is it that the—thing—in the Lords' Palace connects with this boat, then?"

"There are portals on all the worlds, but some are unstable. On Hathes, for example, the boat actually docks. There is a ruined landing site on Latent Emanation. Some worlds have only a few portals, like your own—and the Lords, as you now know, impose strict controls upon who enters and leaves Latent Emanation." Ghairen smiled. "There is usually a direct correlation between those who go in, and those who fail to come out."

"You're not the only one, then? I got the idea that you were a sole traveler."

"Did I give that impression? Well, there have been a few others. But generally the Lords prefer to keep a tight rein on their uninvited visitors. The portals are not the Lords' own technology, however."

"Who built them, then?"

"No one. They're a natural phenomenon. They can be harnessed, by means of special devices, and connected to craft such as the drift-boats. It is difficult, however, and Hathes has only one vessel, in which you are now sitting. It took us a considerable time to build. It's quite old."

"So where are we now?"

"Between worlds. Legend has it that it is possible to travel without the use of a craft, to move directly between portals, but I know of no one who has achieved such a thing." Ghairen glanced toward the dark opening. "The boat will soon be voyaging to Hathes. I must say, I'll be relieved to reach home."

"Unfortunately, I can't say the same."

"Don't worry, Alivet. You'll be home soon enough." His fingers brushed her hand.

Was that a threat or a promise? Alivet wondered. With the Poison Master, it was hard to tell.

"We'll have to stay here," Ghairen explained, "until the boat is on its way. Then I will show you the dormitory."

"The dormitory?"

"Our journey will take a single night. And I'm sure you must be tired."

No thanks to you, Alivet thought. She sank into her seat, and felt its warmth close around her. When she looked down, she saw that a thin mesh of tendrils had crept about her waist, holding her in. She was encased in bronze wire, ornamented with tiny metal leaves. Then the enormity of what she had embarked upon overtook her, and she closed her eyes. Memories of her sister kept returning in grim, cold waves. Far below, in the depths of the boat, she could hear a low hum, which intensified as she listened. She became aware of a curious and unfamiliar smell, which filled her head like a murmur of wasps. She tried to place it—metal? rain? a chemical?—but could not.

The smell grew stronger and more astringent, and Alivet felt a shudder beneath her feet. Moments later, the tendrils of mesh around her waist drew away, leaving her free to stand.

"Our journey has begun," Ghairen said. "The drift-boat's moving. Follow me."

He led her through into an adjoining passage; again, a dim, hushed place. The polished walls produced a faint glow. She turned, to see a dark, pale-faced girl with a hand to her mouth. A reflected sequence of Alivets marched into mirrored depths. Lights flickered beneath her feet, chasing one another across the floor like mice. The walls sparkled and a bloom spread across them as though they had been touched by a frosty wind. Alivet thought again of the drift-boat she had seen in the Search and how different it was. Compared to this, the Lords' drift-boat was nothing more than a hollow shell.

Ghairen stood aside to let other passengers go by. Alivet watched them curiously. All were men. Some resembled Ghairen with their hollowed eyes and sleek dark hair, others looked pinched and ancient. Their eyes were as black as winter-sloes, the whites clearly visible; why, then, were Ghairen's eyes red? Alivet wondered about the effects of a prolonged exposure to poisons. The men wore rustling, complex clothes and whispered together in soft voices. Alivet strained to overhear, but found that she could not understand them. They were not speaking her own language, nor did it sound like the Mooric tongue of the deep fens. Yet Ghairen was fluent enough.

"Where are these people from?" she whispered.

"They are traders, for the most part. The boat visits several worlds on each trip."

"Including mine?"

"Ah." Ghairen smiled. "Not usually. I persuaded them to make a detour. If we had been delayed in the Night Palace, the portal—well, let's just say that things might have been awkward. I'm afraid our fellow passengers might not be very pleased with me, if they suspect that I've been responsible for their wait."

"How long has the boat been within reach of Latent, then?"

"A couple of days—portal reach, that is, but outside the Lords' detection system, which is a little arcane. I gave the ship a rough time of arrival, but they wouldn't have waited forever."

So if the ship had gone, presumably she and Ghairen would have been stuck in the depths of the Palace of Night. Not a comforting thought. Alivet wrapped her arms around herself and leaned back against the wall.

Ghairen strode ahead to speak to an official-looking person at the far end of the passage and as he did so, a woman stepped from the shadows.

Alivet saw a small curved nose like a fen-hawk's beak. The woman's eyes were huge, a translucent, watery gray, and her mouth was melancholy and folded, as if hiding secrets. In common with the men she, too, wore a robe: a layered construction of loops of brocade beneath a high-necked bodice. Her hair was tightly braided and clasped close to her head. Alivet's hand stole up to touch her own long plait, banded by the apprentice rings. The woman glanced up, startled. Her eyes widened as she saw the wheel on Alivet's palm, she seemed about to speak, then she turned swiftly away and disappeared into the recesses of the drift-boat.

Alivet wanted to explore the boat but Ari Ghairen, smiling indulgently, would not allow her to do so and insisted that they remain seated in an alcove adjoining the main chamber of the ship. More lattices concealed the alcove, casting a dappled pattern of shadows across Ghairen's face. Alivet did not find the alcove comfortable. The seat was too hard and curiously shaped, and the table was very low, as if designed for people other than humans. Yet Ghairen had said that this was a drift-boat belonging to his own world. She wondered whether he had lied; perhaps this boat had been captured from some other race, or designed by them. Alivet was growing accustomed to mysteries, but she still did not enjoy them.

Other passengers drifted by, clustering in small groups and whispering conspiratorially. Ghairen ignored them. Alivet kept an eye out for the woman, but she was nowhere to be seen.

"Why won't you let me see the rest of the boat?" she asked.

"Much too dangerous," Ghairen informed her airily. "What if you were to stray into one of the toxic chambers?"

"Why would a drift-boat have toxic chambers? Do you practice your art on your passengers? And wouldn't such places be sealed off?" Alivet asked. He was surely lying to her, or perhaps this was nothing more than some whimsical game.

"Nothing is sealed. What is poison to one person may be nothing more than a light floral perfume to another." Ghairen waved a languid hand. "What is deadly to you is likely to be harmless to me. It depends on one's grade."

"So how do people know where they can and can't go? Are there warnings on the doors?"

"Usually. But most of the passengers are from Hathes, and have an understanding of such things, just as you know which drugs are safe to take, and in what dosage, and so forth. Other passengers may wander as they please throughout the boat, but whether they live to tell of what they have witnessed is entirely another matter. I suggest that you keep close to me. Would you like some tea?"

Alivet nearly declined, but the hot air of the drift-boat was making her thirsty and she could hardly refrain from touching food or drink over the course of her journey.

"Very well," she said, stiffly.

"Then tea we will have," Ari Ghairen agreed. He rose to his feet and summoned a floating servitor: a dull silver platform, whorled like a shell. Ghairen flicked his fingers and lights sparked over the surface of the servitor. Alivet watched with interest as it glided away. Then she turned her attention to the room beyond.

"How does this boat move?" she asked. "What propels it?"

"I've no idea." Ari Ghairen spoke with indifference.

"You must have *some* notion."

"No, none whatsoever. Why should I concern myself with such things? I am a Poison Master, not a mechanic or a pilot. I would no more expect an engineer to trouble herself with the details of my work than I would expect her to ask me to go down to the engine room and ratchet the wheel arch or add more hot coals to the furnace. Or whatever it is that they do."

"Aren't you interested in anyone else's profession, then? Don't you think that a little wider knowledge might come in useful?"

"Of course. I don't pride myself on my ignorance. For example, I am extremely interested in *your* profession, and I look forward to having many long and interesting conversations about it. Aha! Here is the tea."

Alivet, with a dubious glance, took the glass from the servitor and gave a cautious sniff. She smelled a dark array of spices: amber-flowering lavender, summer balsam.

"We have," Ari Ghairen remarked with seeming irrelevance, "seven hundred and thirty-two varieties of tea on Hathes. It is a veritable industry." He gave her a sidelong look and Alivet thought, *He's trying to make things up to me. He thinks I'll be interested.* To her annoyance, however, Ghairen was right. For the first time since her flight from the Unpriests, Alivet glimpsed the possibility of a future for herself. Perhaps an exclusive importer of otherworldly beverages might be a promising trade? In this fleeting vision, she saw Inki by her side, learning the business. She blinked, dispelling the image. They had a long way to travel before that came to pass.

"Has anyone tried them all?" she inquired of Ghairen.

"A few. The tea masters, of course. Some of them are very old; they've spent their lives in the tasting chambers."

"Can women be masters? Of poison, or of tea?"

"Of course. We are an equitable society, in many spheres."

"That's good to know," Alivet said, dryly. "And how soon can one attain mastery? At what age?" She looked at Ghairen, trying to assess him. It wasn't easy. The smooth countenance bore no betraying lines; the crimson eyes in their bone cradle were ageless. With reluctance, Alivet lowered her gaze, only to find it drawn back again. She should not stare at him so. Ghairen appeared not to have noticed.

"It depends. I myself was forty-three when I attained Fifth Grade."

"And how long do your people live?"

"Two hundred years, perhaps. If they are lucky. Almost no one reaches that age."

"But two hundred years is a natural life span?" Alivet pursued. Ghairen smiled, sipped tea.

"My dear young lady, there's no such thing as a natural life span on Hathes."

Well, that shut *her* up, Alivet thought. She drank her tea in silence, appreciating its depth of taste. When she had finished, Ghairen appeared to relent and suggested a tour of the boat, suggesting to Alivet that his talk of poisoned chambers had been nothing more than an unpleasant fable.

"You won't come to any harm if I'm with you."

Alivet forbore from comment and followed him from the observation lounge. They walked down silent passages, the walls concealed by etched metal panels. Whatever Alivet might think of the morals of the people of Hathes, she could not fault their sense of design. Yet there were no windows: no way of gazing out upon the passing stars.

"And in here," Ghairen said, drawing aside a tall, folded metal door, "is where we'll be sleeping."

Alivet looked at him. " 'We'?"

"Of course." He smiled at her and she saw a flicker in his eyes like a flame. She felt her mouth grow dry, a fluttering deep within.

"This is where everyone sleeps," he added. He ushered her through into an antechamber. Above her head rose row upon row of honeycomb cells, glistening golden-red. Each was approximately the length of a human being. Alivet peered into a nearby cell and saw that it was padded.

"Tell me when you wish to sleep, and I'll lock you in."

"You're going to lock me in. And why is that, exactly?"

"It's for your own protection," Ghairen said, solemnly. "We don't want someone getting ideas and deciding to test a preparation on you, do we?"

Alivet glared at him. "No, we do not. But why would they?"

"I do have enemies, Alivet." He seemed slightly hurt, as though she had expressed doubt that anyone might take him seriously. It was a most unpleasant thought that some unknown soul might seek to kill her purely because of her associate. From this perspective, Hathes seemed little better than her own society. And there were more immediate considerations.

"What happens if I need to visit the lavatory in the middle of the night? And where is it, anyway? Don't tell me that's out-of-bounds as well."

"The washing facilities are over there, behind that door. I will be in an adjoining cell. Knock on the wall and I'll let you out. Don't worry about waking me up."

"You don't normally sleep like this, do you? In cells such as these?"

"It's the usual arrangement, when voyaging. In case a member of the poison clans is on board."

"Don't you trust one another?"

She was speaking ironically, but Ghairen answered with an air of mild affront. "Of course not."

"What a horrible society yours must be, Ari Ghairen. And I thought we suffered with the Lords."

"I see that you have entirely misunderstood our culture," Ghairen said. "However, it is entirely forgivable, since you can know so little of it. You seem to see us as guided wholly by animosity, by continual attempts to gain the upper hand."

"And aren't you?"

"We would never have survived. Our current state is a function of our advanced civilization. Primitive tribes must trust one another, draw close. Yes, we play games, of life and death, health and sickness. The poison clans have their own way of doing things, but they are only one aspect of our society. Moreover, some things are sacred, and sleep is one of them. It must be protected. People must be permitted to sleep soundly, and therefore dream. After all, what is a life without dreams?—as I'm sure you know. What else is the Search, after all?"

"The Search seeks truth," Alivet said.

Ghairen frowned. "Let me ask you something. If the Search revealed the origins of your people, through someone's drugged vision, and this revelation was then corroborated by others—a chorus of voices, all clamoring that this was the reality for which you have been looking for so long—would that be held as truth?"

"I would think so, yes."

"Even if it was not open to any confirmation by evidence? Even if you still could not travel to that world, and see for yourselves? Would there not be a lingering doubt?"

"In the lack of evidence, truth must come from consensus."

"Is science based upon consensus, then?"

"Science is based upon agreement, that is so, and its ultimate goal is transformation. That is what the alchemical sciences are all about. We draw up theories to explain the world, and the more evidence that we find, the more the world becomes transformed. But first, we must agree as to what counts as evidence."

"Is that the goal of the Search, then? For all to agree upon what is real and what is not? Is that not an invention of the past rather than true discovery?"

"But perhaps," Alivet said, surprising herself, "it would be better if we could not travel to that world and see for ourselves. Perhaps invention itself, and consensus upon it, is the real goal."

Ari Ghairen became very still. The red gaze focused on her face. "And why is that?"

"Because the Search is already our shared dream. It is the secret which unites us—and yes, before you make some other clever remark, I know that there has been speculation that the Lords know of the Search and do nothing about it, holding the Unpriests back for their own reasons. I know that there are those who say that the Lords prefer us to waste our days in drugs and dreams than in an organized resistance which we have already realized to be futile. But whatever the truth behind the Search, I do believe that it is a unifying force."

The Poison Master looked at Alivet for a long moment. Then he said, "I hope you'll dream as well on Hathes, Alivet."

She did not know whether it was encouragement or a warning. In silence, she followed him back down the metal passageways.

They ate together. The other passengers kept their distance and Alivet noticed that there was much evidence of phials and potions at the beginning of the meal, with tests conducted in tiny bowls upon a rack. Glances were cast in the direction of Ari Ghairen. There was distant muttering. Ghairen followed the same methods: shaking a thin black powder over the surface of a bubbling broth, dipping a delicate pipette into the sauce that accompanied steamed greens.

"Is that why your people seem to like their food so hot?" Alivet said, eyes streaming after an incautious mouthful of the broth. "To fight poisons away, as spices are used to disguise bad meat?"

"It's one reason, yes. Also I think we just like it that way. They eat blander food in the southern parts." He regarded her solicitously as she took another gulp of water. "Is it too much for you? The galley could doubtless provide something less spicy."

"I'll be all right," Alivet said. Fen cuisine was fiery, to combat the chilling effects of marsh and rain and to sustain the choleric humors. She refused to be fed pap like a child. The broth was ferocious, but after a few cautious sips the pain subsided. She might keep the roof of her mouth, after all.

Ari Ghairen seemed approving. "We may make a gourmet of you yet."

"We've got a week. Better be quick."

"Don't be so pessimistic."

The other passengers conversed in low voices, forming a sibilant background to the meal. No one paid any attention to Alivet, for which she was grateful. Once the bowls were cleared away Ari Ghairen pronounced himself tired and suggested that they retire. Alivet was quick to agree. She did not relish the thought of making polite after-dinner conversation and it had been a long and exacting day. The image of Inki's face, with its sad missing eye, kept returning to haunt her. She returned with Ghairen to the dormitory. The washroom smelled clinical and clean. Ari Ghairen followed her in.

Alivet spun around. "Am I to have no privacy? Would you care to watch me while I wash?"

"This won't take a moment."

Ghairen took a small, flat wand from the pocket of his robes and drew it along the walls, above the sink, and across a small hole in the floor that Alivet deduced to be the lavatory. "All clear. Take your time. Here's something for your teeth—I bought it in Shadow Town and it's quite safe—and a cleanser. We do not have bathing facilities in the manner of your world; it's too easy to transmit toxins through the water supply. Instead, there is a hot-air system that transforms the cleanser into a fragrant dust. You'll find it entirely effective, I assure you."

"All right," Alivet said glumly. "You'd better leave me to get on with it."

Once he had gone, she stripped and applied the cleansing paste. It worked much as Ghairen had described, and though the process was hardly refreshing, she did at least feel cleaner. She rubbed the paste over her teeth and spat down the lavatory hole. Once she had finished, she went back out into the dormitory. Ghairen was sitting at the edge of the honeycomb cell, wearing what appeared to be a voluminous dressing gown. He gestured to the neighboring slot.

"In you go, and remember, just knock on the wall if you need anything. I do hope you sleep well."

Alivet levered herself into the cell and heard the door hiss shut behind her. She was encased in warm, red darkness. Thoughts circled her uneasy mind: dying alone on another world, her lungs constricting and collapsing, her nerves strung tighter and tighter, fraying against the touch of the drug. And Alivet thought, determined: *That's not how I'm going to die. Nor Inki. Whether Ghairen gets his results or not.*

 part IV

CRYSTALLIZATION

. . . the knowledge and experience which the wiser sort hath had of counsels, forces, persons, times, and practices may minister more certain guesses in this case than all the stars and planets of the firmament . . .

— LORD HENRY HOWARD, *A Defensative Against the Poison of Supposed Prophecies*, 1583

chapter I

LONDON, TWELFTH NIGHT ⟶ 1559

Beyond Dee's study the storm was raging, snatching at the tiles and whistling through the cracks in the eaves. Dee ignored the howling gusts as best he could and tried to concentrate on the astrological charts before him. Almost there... but the storm was distracting, as though Herne and his hounds coursed about the rooftops, chasing souls.

And Jupiter being in Aquarius, Dee thought, *denotes the qualities of statesmen: tolerance, impartiality, and justice, with Mars in Scorpio for passion.* He squinted down at the ephemeris. January 15th it would be, a cold coronation to the new Queen's reign, but an auspicious date nonetheless.

Auspicious for Dee himself, too. After the episode with the angel, Bonner had, with bitter irony, become a tacit convert to Dee's equally unspoken cause. In the aftermath of the angel's visit, looking through the shattered roof of his study to the cloud-raced heavens, Bonner had said shakily, "It appears I owe you an apology, Dr. Dee."

Dee, with what he later felt to be considerable presence of mind, said magnanimously, "God recognizes virtue, Bishop, in all its forms. No doubt He has sent his angels only to remind you of the fact." It could easily have gone the other way, with a panicked and stricken Bonner ordering Dee's summary execution, but the Bishop had evidently taken the manifestation as evidence of divine protection rather than demonic intervention. That, to Dee's mind, had been the real miracle. Bonner, perhaps feeling that someone in Dee's position would be better kept close, rounded off the evening by offering him a place.

Dee, who had entered the Bishop's study as a heretical conjuror bound for the stake, left it as Bonner's chaplain. He had taken care to keep Elizabeth informed, a wise precaution in these chancy times; once the political dust had finally settled, his reward had been to predict the most promising day for her coronation.

Grateful though he was, however, Dee knew that he was destined for better things than the casting of horoscopes, even if it was a task dedicated to queens. The appearance of the angel had acted upon Dee's mind like the alchemical process itself. All of Dee's scientific preoccupations—mathematics and mechanics, astrology and alchemy—had become dissolved, to crystallize in a different, and more potent, form. *In this age of exploration,* Dee thought, *I, too, will become an explorer. I will gather together a likely crew and venture out into the universe itself. I will draw charts of the stars, not as an astrologer here on Earth, but as a sailor upon the seas of space. I will seek out the very geography of heaven.*

It was a thought of utmost daring and heresy, and though Dee had neither committed it to paper nor voiced it to a single living soul, it had still given him a number of sleepless nights. Indeed, it had been swift to cross his mind that the angel had been no angel at all, but a star-demon sent to lead him into evil. A night on his knees before the altar had served to reassure him, but only a little.

Rising from the table, Dee swept the parchments into a rough pile and picked up the candle, intending to seek out his bed. The storm gave a last buffet of wind, as though a wave had broken over the rooftops, and fell silent. Dee turned and dropped the candle. The light went out, plunging the room into darkness, and Dee could hear himself crying out in terror. In the last moments of light, he had seen the angel standing in the corner, looking at him.

"Be still," a voice said, at once inside his head and all around him, filling the room. Dee clutched at the table's edge to stop himself from falling. He could hear his own harsh, panting breath. Little by little, a dim glow appeared at the far end of the room. The angel stood in a column of red light, silhouetted against the oak-paneled wall. Its faces were as expressionless as masks. Its curiously bulky robes billowed out, as if the angel stood in a breeze that Dee could neither feel nor see. Its hands were invisible.

"What are you? Are you angel or devil?"

"I am star-born."

"What does that *mean*?"

"I will show you."

Slowly, a map began to spread out from the being's feet, until it resembled those portraits of kings that stood upon the world. It was like no map that Dee had ever seen, however, for it was moving. He saw a great river, vaster by far than the Thames, with a great scattering of tributaries like arteries and veins. The map rose up, spilling out into additional dimensions until Dee was standing within it, at the very edge of a lip of stone that looked out across a marsh. The illusion was complete: he could hear the cries of night-birds in the swamp, and smell the rankness of weed and water, like the river after heavy rain had sluiced out the Fleet and all the other sewers of the city.

"See," the being's hissing voice said in his ear. "They are all that is here."

"Is this real?"

"It is an image, nothing more. To journey here will be difficult and dangerous."

And now Dee could see a huge gate, flanked by wooden columns, rising out of the waters of the marsh. A figure stood beside it, which Dee recognized: it was the jackal-headed god Anubis, the Egyptian Lord of the Dead. For a moment Dee thought that it was a statue, but then the long pointed head turned and the thing was staring at him. Dee stumbled backward and fell over the table. The illusion was abruptly gone.

"The world of the dead," Dee gasped. "I have visited hell."

"Not hell," the being said. It came to stand by him, and Dee, who usually found himself looking down on men, was compelled to stare up into the nearest of its faces. "Another world. A world that is ripe for the taking, for those brave enough to make the journey."

"You serve only to deceive," Dee said as boldly as he could, but found that his voice had retreated to a hoarse whisper.

"I do God's work, as we all must," the being said. There was no expression in its large, light eyes. Dee could not tell if it lied.

"God's work? Or Satan's?"

"I have come to you because you have knowledge. You understand science, mathematics, the first vestiges of star-craft. And you worship God, and understand the nature of His universe. The world that I have shown you," the being said smoothly, "is a world before a Fall. Here, in this new world, humanity has the chance to begin again, to remake society in heaven's image."

"What is the world called?" Dee asked, before he could stop himself.

"It has no name."

"A Meta Incognita, then, like the Terrae Incognitae of our own Earth."

"Think of this world, John Dee. It has the shape of

your dreams, if you only have the courage to follow where they lead."

"How am I to do that?"

"We will give you instructions—a set of codes by which you may open a gate between the worlds and travel through. We will show you a craft like the ships that sail the seas of your own world. You may bring others with you, a colony like those that are being formed in other lands on your world. But in the place to which I will lead you, there will be no persecution, no bonfires of human bones, no human jealousy and hate. Only peace and the chance for you to carry out God's work." Its voice was as smooth as a serpent's egg.

"How do I know that this is true?" Dee asked.

"Question your conscience. Pray to God."

Now the being was fading, becoming as transparent as a ghost.

"Wait!" Dee cried, but it was almost gone. Its perfect lips moved, but no sound emerged. Dee was alone in the study, in darkness.

Drift-Boat, Orbit

Alivet woke with a start, still encompassed in the cloying russet dark and with a memory of nightmares. But the dream was fading fast, slipping away from her, and the sounds outside her honeycomb coffin were real. Alivet lay still and listened. A deathwatch ticking echoed within the coffin, like a latent bomb. It grew steadily louder, then stopped. Alivet held her breath, trying to work out where the sound had been coming from. Then there was a hiss of released air and the hatch of her cell slid open. Alivet blinked.

"Ghairen? Is that you?" There was a sudden tightness in her chest. "Ari?" She struggled to sit up. A cool hand reached in and helped her from the cell. Alivet slid down to the floor, her heart pounding. The dormitory hive was quiet, with only a single lamp. The figure who stood before her was not Ghairen, but the woman Alivet had seen earlier. The woman laid a finger across her lips with exaggerated care, a parody of a human gesture. The long nail was lacquered black. The finger crooked: *Come with me*.

Alivet cast a doubtful look back at the cells to where Ghairen presumably lay sleeping. The woman stepped backward into the shadows. Alivet said, in a warning whisper, "If you have anything to say to me, you can say it here. I'm not going anywhere with you."

"Wise," a murmuring voice said, from the darkness. "The protégés of the poison clans learn quickly...But you shouldn't be afraid of me. I'm here to help you."

"I've heard *that* before. Who are you?"

"A friend. I came here to warn you." The words were melodramatic, but the woman's tone was cool and invested with a concern that sounded sincere.

"A friend? I've never seen you before today. Why should you be any friend of mine?"

"Ghairen's enemy, then."

That made more sense.

"I know what he's done to you," the woman said. "I can help."

"What do you mean, what he's done to me? Ghairen and I made a deal: I help him, he helps me. The details of that aren't any of your business. Who are you, anyway?"

"I am well aware of the details. Ghairen wants your help in defeating the Lords of Night; in exchange, he'll help to free your sister. What you do not know is that—whether or not Ghairen is successful—he does not want surviving evidence of his plots. And that includes you. He's poisoned you, Alivet."

"What do you mean, he's poisoned me?" Alivet whispered furiously. She felt a coldness spreading over her skin; she thought of winter-ice across the fens.

"It's a plant-based toxin called mayjen. It's cued to temporal markers and it enters through the pores of the skin. It's almost always fatal. How long has Ghairen given you to get a result?"

It was as though Alivet stood in a vast, empty space, where words echoed and made little sense.

"A week," she said, numbly. There was a hissing in her head. She recalled Ghairen's reluctance to wait another year: Did that have anything to do with his plans to dispose of her?

"Then that will be when the poison is due to strike."

"You said it was fatal," Alivet said. "What about anti-dotes?"

"There might be a way to save you, but it will not be easy. I will do my best."

"How do I know you're telling me the truth?"

"You don't. You have only my own word—the word of a stranger, and the actions of Ghairen himself. What do you consider to be the truth?"

"I don't know," Alivet said, but from what she had seen of the Poison Master, it seemed all too probable that he would prefer a plot without loose ends.

"I do not ask for your trust. Nor do I ask that you believe me. I only ask that you give me the opportunity to help you, once we reach Hathes." The voice was low, a verbal caress.

"All right," Alivet said, not knowing what to think. "But why should you go to such trouble for a stranger? I know you said you were Ghairen's enemy, but I can mean nothing to you."

"Perhaps that's true," the woman said. She stepped forward once more, her heels clicking on the metal floor; Alivet recognized the deathwatch sound that had awoken her. "I will be honest with you. My name is Iraguila Ust. My father was a Poison Master, too, Third Grade. He died from a dose of yth, administered to the leaves of a plant along the course of his daily walk. I know who administered that poison."

"And you want revenge," Alivet stated. Iraguila Ust's face floated before her in the pool of light cast by the lamp: small, pointed, and pale like a porcelain doll, the eyes lambent wells. "Well, I can understand that."

"Helping you takes me closer to that revenge," Iraguila murmured, and now Alivet could hear the hatred beneath the soft voice. "Any disruption to Ghairen's plans is a victory for me."

"Where can I get in touch with you?" Alivet had no intention of entering into a fruitless dialogue. There could also be no question of trusting the woman, if her limited experience of the people of Hathes was anything to go by, but she needed to make sure of as many options as she could. Iraguila represented one such option. Perhaps the woman was even telling the truth...

The thought of being poisoned, disposed of as soon as she had ceased to be of use, filled Alivet with a sick dismay and something strangely like betrayal.

"I will come to you. And now I must go."

Before Alivet could protest, Iraguila Ust had melted away.

"Iraguila?" she said, questioning the empty air. She waited, lingering in the silence of the dormitory, but there was no reply, only the name echoing back from the walls in a whispering hiss.

Alivet slid back into the cell and pulled the hatch shut behind her. Lying in the hot darkness, she made a quick mental inventory: *Do I feel nauseous? Is my pulse too high? Where do I hurt?* But everything seemed normal, except that her heart was racing and that might be caused by fright rather than a toxin.

There were two simple options. Either Iraguila was lying, or she was telling the truth. If the former, then Alivet needed to find out why one of Ghairen's enemies would go to the trouble of seeking her out and manipulating her. If Iraguila spoke the truth, then Alivet must find an antidote as swiftly as possible. She wondered whether to confront Ghairen and decided against it; best to lie low. If Ghairen believed that Alivet knew nothing, then there was the possibility that he might betray himself. Besides, if he knew that she was aware of his actions, he would simply keep a closer watch on her, and Alivet needed to be as free as possible. She was an alchemist, an apothecary. It was not a discipline that taught a person to act without due thought and care. Hasty decisions resulted in experimental collapse. A person could be injured or killed.

Alivet set her anger and her fear, simmering like a crucible, to the back of her mind. *And when the time is right, I'll let it bubble and boil. I'll transform it, into alchemical fire, and you, Ari Ghairen, will take the full force of that explosion.*

Tossing restlessly in the little cell, it also occurred to her to wonder just how secure the dormitory could be, if any enemy could open a cell and sip from the honey within. The ease with which Iraguila had gained access was at odds with what Ghairen had told her about security and paranoia. Alivet frowned into the darkness. She did not like anomalies. Whenever they cropped up during her alchemical preparations, they almost invariably presaged disaster. This situation was likely enough to blow up in her face or fizzle into dust without additional complications. She needed to think things through. But the heat from the walls of her cell lulled her into unsettled sleep, her head still full of contradictions and alarm.

chapter III

DRIFT-BOAT, ORBIT

In the morning, she wondered whether it had been a dream. The face at the entrance to her cell was Ghairen's: still smiling, still concerned. She watched him warily, trying not to let her confusion show.

"Alivet? Did you sleep well? Was the cell comfortable?"

"Well enough. I didn't wake in the night."

"That's good," Ghairen said, blandly. "I'll let you freshen up and then we must have you decontaminated."

The decontamination room lay close to the dormitory, but it took some time for Ghairen to make his preparations. Perched uncomfortably on a narrow bench, Alivet watched as the Poison Master ransacked racks of vials. She had protested in vain. Ghairen had been adamant that she would be unable to set foot on Hathes without these measures. He had asked her to remove her skirts and shirt, but Alivet had flatly refused. The memory of Ghairen's hands, and the occasional glitter in his eyes when he looked at her, would have been enough to make her unsettled, even without the possibility of the poisoning. She felt as though she was in the hands of some sinister uncle. Yet there had been that moment of late-night confusion when she had mistaken Iraguila for Ghairen, the sudden rush of heat at the thought of his presence...Alivet made a resolute decision to ignore these inconsistencies.

She said, "You're not going to examine me, are you? You have access to my tongue and the skin of my hands—that's usually enough to administer a potion."

"Normally, you see, you'd have been inoculated against all these things when you were a child, but as you're an off-worlder, we'll just have to start from scratch."

"What side effects can I expect?"

"Oh, a few, probably. Shouldn't be worse than the occasional rash, or double vision. Let me know if you start getting any peculiar symptoms and I'll see what I can do. I'll give you the basics now. Ready?"

Reluctantly, Alivet held out her arm. *Wait*, she told herself. *Do nothing yet.*

"Now, this is a general antivenin, good against orope, perganum hamala, hoama, and mang. Very comprehensive. Grit your teeth." Alivet felt a slight stinging sensation in her wrist. "Good girl." He touched the line of her jaw, impersonally gentle. Alivet raised her chin and Ghairen dabbed something cool at the base of her throat. "Es-asa. Once it penetrates the bloodstream, it'll reduce the effect of some of the major alkaloids."

But not, presumably, the ones that mattered.

"How many antidotes have *you* taken, Ghairen? How many does a Fifth Grade master need?"

"My dear young lady, I am positively *awash* with all manner of substances. I have been given fatal doses of poison some nine times. Or is it ten? No, I'm sure nine is correct. As you see, I am still here. I would estimate that I've had something in the region of a hundred and seventy major protectives, and many more minor ones. But don't worry. It's not so likely that anyone would try to poison you. Once we've reached home, that is. I have every confidence that we won't see you lying on the autopsist's slab when our week is up."

Alivet said nothing. She was taking careful note of the substances used by Ghairen. Still with that gentle touch, the

Poison Master lifted up her plait of hair. She felt a needle at the base of her neck. She pulled away.

"What are you doing now?"

"Just a final precaution against thrope. You never know. The spores get everywhere these days..." His hand brushed her plait. "You have lovely hair, Alivet. As black as a night-dove's wing, as we say on Hathes."

"Get on with it." If he began complimenting her, Alivet felt, she would only weaken, and she felt compromised enough already.

"All done." Ghairen stepped back, his head on one side. "We'd better find you some more suitable attire. You can't go around in those skimpy garments."

Thus far, the Poison Master had hardly seemed prudish. "What do you mean, skimpy? I'm covered from my neck to my boots."

"Nonsense. You have only two layers of skirts—and what are you wearing under that blouse? A shift? You might as well be naked. It's a matter of practicality, not morality. If you brush up against someone, or take an accidental spray hit, the results could be nasty. After all, you're not fully inoculated yet."

"Are you saying I need protective clothes?"

The Poison Master beamed at her. "Of course, but nothing too prosaic, don't worry. They will be the height of fashion. I've gone to a lot of trouble to get you here, Alivet. I've no intention of losing you now. Besides, it would be a sad thing for such a charming young lady to meet a painful end if she didn't have to."

Everything Ghairen said to her now seemed to contain a threat, wrapped in layers of meaning. He went to a tube on the wall and murmured into it. Alivet heard the sibilant syllables of what was presumably his own language.

"We're very close to Hathes. The drift-boat will dock at the landing site—no more portals, this time. I've asked the Journey Master to get you some clothes. I myself will check the garments thoroughly for toxins. I took the liberty of ordering black and red. I thought it would go with your hair."

"It'll do." The color of her clothes was the least of her worries, Alivet thought, but it was not lost on her that in that case, she would match Ghairen. Did he see her as some kind of accessory, perhaps? She felt her lips tighten.

"We'll head straight to the laboratory. I'm sure you understand the need to begin work. I'll arrange for you to have something to eat when we get there."

"I can eat on Hathes, can I? I won't drop dead at the first mouthful?"

Ghairen considered this. "Not unless you're *very* unfortunate. But my home—the Atoront Tower—is quite secure. Here are your clothes."

Taking them from a person at the door, he carried the bundle across the room. "A fumigation and a check, and then I'll let you get dressed."

Alivet watched as he performed various tests: dusting the heavy skirts with a powder and placing a drop of luminous blue fluid upon the hem. Then, handing her the clothes, he turned his back. Alivet examined the garments, trying to make sense of them. The clothes seemed complicated: a mass of buckles and straps, and she couldn't see how they fitted. Eventually, she worked it out and found that she was dressed in a high-necked, puff-shouldered blouse with many hooks and buttons, and long looped skirts that reached her ankles, all made from some stiff glazed fabric.

The skirts hobbled her and the blouse was tight. She felt constrained and constricted and wondered whether Ghairen had chosen such restrictive garments deliberately. His treatment of her seemed fraught with subtle humiliations, but she wasn't going to give him the satisfaction of asking for help. Did all the women of Hathes go around trussed like a festival hen? Then she remembered Iraguila Ust; it would seem that they did. She fastened the last buckle and said with some apprehension, "I'm ready." She did not want to look a fool in front of him.

Ghairen's mouth twitched slightly when he turned around, but he said nothing. He tweaked two of the buckles, and adjusted her collar. Alivet tried not to flinch.

Under the circumstances, she would never have admitted to Ghairen that she was entranced with the prospect of seeing another world. Like most people, she had seen relatively few places even on Latent Emanation and the prospect of experiencing a different planet, even with the threat of such dire consequences, was enthralling. The dreams of the eight-year-old Alivet, of flight and freedom, returned to haunt her.

She accompanied Ghairen back to the alcove chamber, where other passengers were meshing themselves in.

"How long before we dock?"

"Soon."

The drift-boat hummed beneath her feet and the whir of distant engines grew louder. The mesh grew tight against her waist and she felt a pressure behind her eyes. The drift-boat shuddered once and then was still.

"We're here," Ghairen said, rising from his seat. With the Poison Master, Alivet joined the queue of passengers filing along the corridor and passed out through a sequence of doors. She looked about her with interest as they left the drift-boat. Here were metal corridors: strange, glistening architecture like spun glass. The floor was pale and polished, disquietingly similar to the texture of Ghairen's skin. Alivet paused to run her palm over it; it was cool and smooth, like Ghairen's impersonal hands. She wondered whether the people of Hathes made their world in their own image and if so, what it would be like outside. There were, however, no windows.

As if he had caught her thought, Ghairen said over his shoulder, "This is the landing tower. We'll be coming to one of the land bridges soon. That'll give you a better view of the city and the boat."

"What's the city called?"

"The oldest name for it is Ukesh, though it is sometimes known as Mothlem," Ghairen said. "Freezing in winter, hot in summer—though it must be said that summer is short. We're on the edge of the arid lands, so there's always a wind, but you won't be going outside."

"Why not?"

But Ghairen did not seem to hear her. He led her down a gallery that overlooked a hall. Alivet looked down past pillars of crimson glass to see a throng of people below, moving across a patterned black floor. From this height, they looked no larger than insects. Alivet's head spun and she stepped back quickly. Ghairen's hand steadied her. Alivet did not pull away.

The gallery led to a platform, reached by a flight of steps. The platform itself appeared translucent, as though a solidified section of the air hung above her head. It reminded her of the Night Palace, and indeed, the landing tower was built on the same inhuman scale. Once again, Alivet could not help wondering how much of their technology the people of Hathes had inherited, or stolen, from the Lords. Or could there be other species like the Lords? That was yet another disquieting thought.

"It's quite safe," Ghairen said. "There's no way you can fall."

Nervously, Alivet followed him up the stairs, then forgot to be afraid. The platform overlooked a series of immense windows, each reaching hundreds of feet high. From here, a plain made jagged with rocks vanished into the shimmering distance. She saw a boiling red sun hanging low on the horizon, set in a sea of cloud, and the light was caught and reflected by a ziggurat towering up into the sky. As Alivet gazed, the sun dropped behind a bank of clouds and the gleaming walls of the ziggurat dimmed as though a light had been switched off. Alivet saw groves and forests inside the ziggurat, a plume of white water cascading from the heights.

"What is *that*?" she whispered, and Ghairen replied, "It's called Athes-efra. In your language—I suppose 'parc-verticale' is the closest translation."

"It's a park?"

"Park, sanctuary, and alchematorium. Most of all, it is a poison garden. It's where the botanical components of our most valuable toxins are grown, though refining and distillation are conducted elsewhere. I have"—Ghairen gave a modest cough—"a small garden of my own, as I will show you if we have time. But there is more to see here."

On the other side of the platform, a spine of glass extended into a second gallery. Alivet stepped onto it and glanced down. The ground lay far below; she felt as though she had ventured out into empty air. In a dizzying moment she saw a sweep of rock: twisted black pinnacles as tiny as spent matches. Ghairen had already reached the far end of the gallery. Alivet gritted her teeth and followed. The floor was slippery, coated with a gliding fluid. Now it was as though she walked on water rather than air. Alivet moved with care, imagining herself falling, the glass shattering so that she flew down to the rocks below. Ahead, Ghairen's footsteps were light and soundless; he stepped forward like a tightrope walker she had once seen at the World's End Fair. He waited for her to catch up.

"There," he said, pointing. "That is Ukesh."

Alivet looked out across a sea of spires that reached to the horizon. The base of each spire was broad, perhaps a half mile in width: from the foundation, the towers twisted up into the heavens like spirals of dark sugar-candy. Between them lay plazas, edged with trees as sharp as the shadows of needles.

"Hathanassi cypress," Ghairen said, following her gaze. "Little else will grow outside."

At first Alivet thought that roads snaked between the towers, but with a silver flash from the last of the sun Alivet realized that they were canals.

"Each tower houses a clan," the Poison Master informed her. "There"—he pointed to the nearest spiral—"is the home of the Weapon Makers. And in that tower, festooned with ignatonic tracery, live the Master Communicants. That one, etched with sigils, is the Tower of the Linguists, who collect and analyze every known tongue. And over there, you can see my home: Sehur, also called the Atoront Tower. It is the Tower of the Poison Clans, in which I was born and raised. In that tower is my alchematorium." He turned and pointed in the opposite direction. "And there is the boat on which we arrived."

The drift-boat, tethered above a platform, was like a collection of jade and black shells, a cluster of ammonites sliding unnaturally upon the winds. Clouds slipped past its sides. The umbilical that connected it to the platform—presumably the passage down which they had come—seemed too fragile to moor such a monster to the world. It was nothing like the boat that she had seen during the Search. It was like nothing she had ever seen.

"Impressed?" Ghairen asked, softly.

Alivet did not reply, embarrassed at feeling overwhelmed. She followed Ghairen back along the glass spur and down into the depths of what must surely be yet another tower. They crossed the vast hallway and went down through a series of passages. Here, staircases glided back and forth into a chasm.

"We'll take the next boat," Ghairen said over his shoulder. "Not so scenic as the vaporetter, perhaps, but quicker." Alivet peered past him and saw a gleam in the darkness below. After a long descent, they stepped out onto an obsidian dock.

"Watch your footing," Ghairen warned. He reached out and took her hand, tucking it firmly into the crook of his arm so that her hand was trapped against his side. "You don't want to slip," he murmured.

Now that she was able to see more clearly, Alivet realized that the substance glistening below the dock was not water but metal: something mercurial and quick, that glided and swelled around the hull of a long covered barge. "We have very little water on Hathes," said Ghairen. "We use what is available to us, but much of it is conserved for the plants in the parc-verticale. As one of the sources of our livelihood, they are precious."

"So what's in the canal?" She did not think it was mercury: this liquid flowed rather than moving in quicksilver droplets.

"A liquid called aqua-vistra. All the canals are based on a system of spirals; the boat has no propulsion mechanism. Instead, the pilot simply unchains the craft and away it goes on the current. A simple mode of transport, but quick and effective."

The thin note of a siren sounded throughout the docking area and Ghairen helped Alivet down the steps into the barge. "The boat is covered, but you'll be able to see out."

Stumbling over her heavy skirts, Alivet took a seat near the front of the barge. Gradually, the craft filled up: the now-familiar men in their neat dark robes; women dressed like herself in long skirts and concealing blouses, some with tight hoods drawn up over their hair. For the first time, Alivet saw a child, solemn and saucer-eyed, clinging to the hand of a wizened old man. Everyone assembled without fuss and in silence. Their gazes slid over Alivet and away. Their expressions did not change, but she was certain that she had been observed and noted by everyone.

When all the seats were filled, the siren sounded once more, mournful as a bird upon the marsh, and a heavy chain slipped down the side of the barge into the canal. The barge sailed out into the stream, gliding through great double doors that opened onto twilight. Alivet looked back as the barge was whisked through and saw a tower rising behind her, bathed in ruby light. The sun had gone, clouds massed on the western horizon, and she saw the glow of lamps in the passing towers. Alivet wondered once more about the origins of these people. Ukesh was like a forest of unnatural glass trees, leafless and blasted by the storm. She found herself longing for Latent Emanation: for crumbling wooden houses and the familiar, human odors of marsh and city. She turned her face from the great towers. Ari Ghairen touched her hand. Alivet jerked it away and rammed her fists into her pockets.

Darkness fell swiftly across the world. Alivet began to doze, lulled by the rocking motion of the boat. She awoke with a start as the barge knocked against a wharf. People were leaving: the old man with the child; several rustling, whispering women. As the old man reached the steps, the child turned and stared back at Alivet with a somber, considering gaze. The old man tugged at its hand. It climbed the steps, still looking back. Ghairen smiled.

"Curious, as always. Do you wish for children, Alivet?"

"One day, yes," Alivet replied shortly. *When I've got free of you and rescued my sister. And the Night Lords are gone from my world and gold falls from the sky.* The thought was self-pitying and it disgusted Alivet.

"Well, you're young yet," Ghairen remarked, indulgently. "I myself have three daughters."

Alivet stared at him. "You have children?" Ghairen still seemed so exotic a being that the notion of him having a family had never occurred to her. Nor had the possibility of a wife. Alivet felt herself grow small with sudden dismay. A voice inside her head said coldly: *You are a fool. He has poisoned you, perhaps. He cannot be trusted.* And another, less certain voice answered: *I know. And yet . . .*

"Indeed. One by my first wife, and the other two by— other people. The oldest is thirteen, the youngest is three, and the middle girl is eight. I'd ask you to meet them, but alas, they have to be kept safely secluded, away from my colleagues until they have been fully inoculated. The eldest is nearly at her final dosage, however—perhaps you can meet her."

Alivet's imagination conjured three pale doll-like girls, as similar as peas in a pod, each one slightly smaller than the last. She blinked.

"Will I meet their mothers?"

"Unlikely."

What did *that* mean? That they were no longer around to be met, or that Alivet, as the hired help, was not in a position to be presented to the lady of the house? This was a fruitless line of inquiry, Alivet reminded herself with some sternness.

"Your daughters. Do they have ambitions to enter the poison trade?"

Ari Ghairen beamed at her. He seemed pleased that she was taking an interest. "My eldest girl, Celana, has more of an interest in music. The middle girl, Ryma, has already shown some aptitude with the substances: she poisoned her tutor last year. We were all very proud."

"What! Did the tutor die?"

"No, no. He made a full recovery. It wasn't done from malice, after all. Purely in the spirit of scientific inquiry. As you said, the goal of alchemical science is transformation."

"Surely not from 'alive' to 'dead'?"

Ghairen leaned across Alivet and gestured. "And there it is. The Atoront Tower, home of the Poison Clans." He rose to his feet and held out a hand to Alivet. Ignoring it, Alivet stepped past him toward the dock. The other passengers covertly watched her; she saw disquiet in a woman's face, which swiftly schooled itself back to blandness as Ghairen turned. No one else was leaving the barge. Alivet and Ghairen climbed out onto an empty wharf. The barge glided away, borne quickly from sight on the current.

"You understand that there are procedures?" Ghairen asked. "We cannot simply stroll into the tower." He drew her through a round door, embellished with stylized leaves and branches. The trumpet head of a metal lily nodded from the door frame and delicate tendrils of bronze ivy entwined themselves around the lintel. "The tools of my trade, such plants," Ghairen said, evidently noting the direction of Alivet's gaze. "Indeed, of your own as well. I'm sure that you'll find much to interest you here."

The door rolled shut behind them, trapping them in a cylindrical walkway. The air was hot and humming, adding to Alivet's unease. It made her feel drowsy. She smelled something sweet, a honey in the air, passing between her lips and melting soft as sugar on her tongue. A sudden astringent mist brought her wide awake. A silver bee zoomed out from the trumpet of the metal lily and settled in Alivet's hair. She batted at it. Ghairen said quickly, "Don't move. It's only a de-contaminant carrier."

Alivet felt her scalp prickle and then the bee was gone.

"Are all your methodologies so whimsical?" she asked, crossly.

"The poison trade is a dark one, Alivet. We aim for beauty where we can."

At the far end of the room, a second round door rolled open. Alivet followed Ghairen into a farther chamber. This, too, sealed shut behind her and she was wrapped in darkness. Something was singing into her ear, faint and far away. There was an impression of many different voices, crowding in upon her. Her ears rang and a dim light appeared, glowing around her.

"Ghairen? What is it?" she asked.

"It's a linguistic device. It will be a little while before it starts to work properly, so you may have difficulty understanding people at first. Now, let's go up into the tower."

They passed through the round door into a passage. Like the boat, the walls were dark and silvered, but the air was cooler. Alivet and Ghairen climbed a staircase of wide, winding steps onto a high gallery. Alivet had a glimpse of a patterned floor far below and then the Poison Master was leading her through into an elevator.

"Where are we going?" Alivet asked.

"To show you your room, briefly, and then the alchematorium, if you're ready to begin some preliminary preparations?" The question was polite, but Alivet did not think he was offering her a choice. And indeed, she was eager to get on with whatever she had to do. The quicker she investigated the alchematorium, the more swiftly she could find out how real the threat of poisoning might be.

Ghairen went on, "This part of the tower is my own, by the way. There's no reason to fear anyone here."

Only you, Alivet thought. The doors of the elevator opened out into a narrow hallway, lined with panels of bronze. Again Alivet's reflection marched off into infinity, revealing many Alivets and many possibilities. But her reflection was blurred: a faceless specter, enveloped in her skirts.

Ghairen's reflection floated beside her like a ghost. As she followed him down the hallway, her footsteps muffled by a soft moss-colored carpet, she saw from the corner of her eye that one of the doors was open. An eye was peering through the crack. As Alivet whisked around, the door was hastily pulled shut.

"What was that?" Ghairen asked, frowning. He strode to the door and stepped through, drawing it shut behind him. Alivet could not see who was inside, but she could hear Ghairen's voice raised in exasperation.

"Celana, why aren't you in bed?"

A child, Alivet thought. Was this the one who had poisoned her tutor? Or was Celana the eldest girl? She resolved to give the invisible, mutinous Celana a wide berth, but the distraction gave her the chance to look around the hallway. She needed to get her bearings in case there was a chance of slipping out of here. The thought of passing back through those barriers and down to the dock was intimidating, but how else would she contact Iraguila Ust? Where was Ust to be found, anyway? She could hardly go wandering about the tower, querying strangers. She gazed around the hall, noting with slight surprise that the furniture was both elegant and comfortable. A tall jade jar stood on a lacquered cabinet; a nearby chair was padded with worn velvet cushions. It was bemusing to find herself essentially a captive in someone's family home.

At this point Ghairen stopped remonstrating with his off-spring and came back out into the hall. Alivet was glad to see that he appeared harassed.

"My eldest," he explained. "If you ever have children, you must make certain that you nail them to their beds every evening, otherwise they'll be up and about the moment you turn your back."

"What about her mother?" Alivet asked, before she could stop herself. "Doesn't she have any influence?"

"Her mother is dead," Ghairen said. His back was turned, so that Alivet could not see his face, but his voice held no expression. She wondered if Ghairen's had been the hand by which the woman had died, and if so, why.

"I'm sorry," she said, taking refuge in commonplaces.

"To each his monster," she thought she heard Ghairen say. The strangeness of the phrase took her aback. No wonder Celana seemed to present problems. Or were Ghairen's mistresses the cause of that?

"Through here," Ghairen said. He held open a door and Alivet passed into a narrow room. Windows occupied the whole of one wall. She could see the lights of Ukesh beyond, and then darkness. A bed was placed against one wall; there was a desk of dark wood, inlaid with gold wire, on which stood a jug and a bowl of fruit that were the color of garnets. A frieze of metal leaves ran along the wall, coiling outward. Ghairen touched a lamp and colors appeared: moss green, mahogany, chestnut. Forest colors, Alivet thought, strange in this world of black glass and mercuric silver. It occurred to her that this room might belong originally to one of Ghairen's daughters: it had a lived-in quality. Or—macabre thought—was it the dead wife's room? If that was the case, then its occupant could have no further use for it. It was far from being the cell that she had envisaged ever since she had learned of the poisoning. Ghairen was clearly taking pains to treat her as an honored guest, but his courtesies unnerved Alivet almost more than anything else.

"I hope you'll have everything you need," Ghairen said. "If not, let me know. Are you hungry?"

Alivet shook her head. "Not yet. Ghairen, as you remarked, the clock is moving on. I don't mind working at night. I do it often enough. Can I see the alchematorium?"

"Of course."

They went back into the hallway to where a second elevator was situated. Ghairen stood between Alivet and the panel, so she could not see the display, but she could tell that they were moving upward. She tried to count the floors, but it was difficult: one? two? Then the elevator slowed and the doors opened out onto another hallway, very different from the one downstairs: all black glass and burnished silver. She caught a whiff of something chemical and stinging as they stepped through the doors.

"Welcome to your workplace," Ghairen said.

It took Alivet's eyes a while to adjust to the darkness, then she saw that there were blinds covering the tall windows at the end of the room. Ghairen drifted down the alchematorium, flicking a hand at orb lamps, which began to glow. How did he do that? Alivet wondered. The lamps must be activated by physical presence. By their light she saw a low metal bench, arranged with instruments. An athanor furnace stood in the corner of the room, radiating residual heat. A tall container of fire-suppressant powder stood by the furnace; it was reassuring to see that Ghairen observed a few safety regulations, at least. Alembics and crucibles stood on racks, flanked by pelican vessels made of all kinds of glass: obsidian-dark, pearl-pale, configured in ridges and scales. Above, on a shelf, stood ash cupels and cementation boxes. To Alivet's professional eye, the equipment looked first-rate. Despite the circumstances, excitement rose within her at the thought of what she could accomplish in this laboratory. The air smelled pungent, like gunpowder: a familiar alchemical odor.

"Best to work in low light," Ghairen said into her ear, making her jump. "The preparations seem to prefer it."

"What am I to work on now?"

"I'll show you." Ghairen opened a cabinet and took out a rack containing a bowl. He carried it carefully across to Alivet. The bowl was filled with a black, crumbling substance, like resin. An acrid scent drifted upward. Ghairen pointed to the resinous powder.

"This is a substance called tabernanthe. Since my anube contact's demise, I've spent the last year testing all manner of carriers—regis, for example, and khairuvet—but tabernanthe seems to have most of the necessary properties as far as being a bearer for toxicity is concerned. But what I'm having trouble in ascertaining is its hallucinogenic qualities. Despite the solid appearance of the tabernanthe, for instance, it is subtle, unstable, mutable. Like many drugs, it does not entirely lie in this world, and it has a spirit, for want of a better word, that animates it."

"All drugs have such a spirit. If you want to work with the animating force of this substance, you'll have to get to know it. Talk to it, spend time with it, make it your ally."

Ghairen smiled at her. "That's where you come in."

She wanted to tell him that such a process could take longer than anticipated, that if he wanted to be certain, he should wait until next year's banquet and spend the time in preparation. But he seemed so reluctant to wait, and if Iraguila was to be believed, had already taken steps to eliminate Alivet from further equations. She said nothing.

"I don't have the training to assess this part of its nature, or to converse with the drug." She could hear the frustration in his voice. "But you—as an experienced apothecary—do. Watch."

He lit a thin taper and drew the ensuing column of smoke across the bowl. Immediately, the tabernanthe wavered and shook, as though on the point of vanishing. Alivet frowned. It was as though she saw the substance through a haze of heat, but the warmth produced by the little taper would never have been enough to create such an effect.

"If it isn't entirely in this world," Alivet said. "Then where is it?"

Ghairen smiled. "It is *between* worlds. It shifts. Like the Lords themselves, it does not entirely belong to this dimension. It lies between the living language of dreams, and the dead language of waking. And so we must interpret and translate—except that I don't have the skill."

Alivet nodded. "You say it shifts. Just as our consciousness shifts during the Search. If this is true, then yes, it does have the qualities of a drug. Where did you get it from?"

"I purchased it—at great expense, I might add, so don't waste it—from a colleague. Originally, it's the sap of a plant that grows high in the mountains to the very far south of Hathes, almost at the upper reaches of the atmosphere. It is thus a rarefied substance, and it's been treated so that it remains in this form at certain temperatures. It also responds very powerfully to light."

"You said it was a carrier for a poison, not the poison itself."

"That's correct."

"So what is the poison?"

"Light."

"I don't understand," Alivet said.

"Describe the Lords to me, Alivet," Ghairen said, as he had asked once before. "Describe their essence."

Alivet thought for a moment, seeking the right words. "The Lords are dark. They keep to the shadows of their palaces." She remembered the huge forms she had seen in the Palace of Night. "They seem made of shadow. They ban light from the surrounding area, allowing only enough for their human servants to work in."

"Has anyone sought to attack them with light? With lamps, for instance, or by letting daylight into a palace?"

"Not to my knowledge. But I told you back in Shadow Town, I have never heard that light would harm them, just that they dislike it. I saw two of them in the hallway, there in the palace. They did not seem to shy away from the lamps. Although it's true that the lamps were dim."

She shivered, still thinking of the Palace of Night and her sister's wan, wounded face.

"I see. And now describe your world."

"But you've been there."

"When you come from a place, Alivet, you take things for granted. You need to look at it with new eyes in order to consider things of importance. How does the light of Hathes differ from that of Latent Emanation, for instance?"

"Hathes is brighter," Alivet said slowly. "The light here seems more direct, somehow."

Ari Ghairen appeared pleased. "Exactly so. Latent Emanation—'Yesech' in my own language—is a twilight world. It is penumbral, as its name suggests. The Lords of Night prefer such places; they are creatures of darkness, after all. They come from a dark dimension." Alivet opened her mouth to ask him how he knew this, but he held up a hand and went on, "They abhor light—not the ordinary kind, otherwise we could merely flood their palaces with it, torment them with lamps and fires—but a sort that can be ingested, that will act as a poison upon them. If I can find a way to force them to ingest this light, then perhaps we will be free of them."

"What will it do? Kill them?"

"From the studies I have done, it could have a variety of effects. It might kill them, or change their form, or send them back where they come from. Any of those will serve our purposes. But the light needs a carrier, something that will allow it to work upon the Lords' other-dimensional nature. Because the tabernanthe is itself interdimensional, and because of its reaction to luminescence, I have selected it as such a carrier."

"Well, if it doesn't work," Alivet said, "you can surely do some more research and try something else."

He turned on her, saying sharply, "No! It has to work, Alivet. This time, I—" He broke off, adding in a more conciliatory manner, "You must forgive me. I'm a little edgy."

Was it the prospect of murdering her that was making him so uneasy, Alivet wondered. He was on his own admission a professional assassin. How far was he really capable of guilt?

"How much do you know about the Lords, Ghairen? How do you know where they come from? Do you know what they are?"

"My employers are the governing body of Hathes: the Soret." There was a flicker in his eyes; Alivet, watching narrowly, wondered what it meant, but the next moment his expression was once again unreadable. "They've been studying the Lords for some time—they know, for example, that the Lords were the ones who originally brought us to Hathes, thousands of years ago. At first, the Lords were benevolent, but over time they became corrupt. They were driven from Hathes and took refuge in their palaces on other worlds."

"How were they driven out?"

"We don't know. We had our own class of Unpriests then—a group which has since become a more chastened religious order. They fought to regain control, buildings were destroyed, records lost. It was a chaotic period."

"So are you saying that the Lords haven't always been evil?"

Ghairen grimaced. "I knew that talking about such things to you would open a floodgate of questions. I've told you all I know." *Unlikely*, thought Alivet. He pointed to the bowl of tabernanthe. "I want you to study that. Familiarize yourself with its structure. Conduct the same kinds of experiments that you would undergo with your fumes and psychotropics. I want you to find out the degree to which tabernanthe has hallucinogenic properties, whether its animating spirit can be persuaded to ally itself with us. And now I have duties to undertake." His mouth turned down. Alivet wondered if the duties were related to his offspring's discipline. "I'll be back later this evening. Good luck."

With a rustle of robes, he was gone, leaving Alivet to stare after him and wonder, not for the first time, whether the Poison Master was entirely in his right mind.

As the door closed behind him, she heard the hiss of the lock.

Many of the instruments in the alchematorium were unfamiliar, but Alivet found everything she needed in order to run preliminary tests, gathered together on a shelf. She made a quick inventory of alembics, crucibles, pestles, and votrices. The equipment was of excellent quality and must have been expensive. Clearly, mad or not, Ghairen knew what he was about.

Then she searched the alchematorium, seeking any books or pamphlets that might contain information on the poisons that Ghairen employed, but could find nothing. There were no books. The cupboards were filled with equipment only. Alivet, standing in the middle of the alchematorium, dusted off her hands and resolved to do what she had always been accustomed to doing in times of crisis: to work. She could do nothing about the hovering fear with which Iraguila Ust's pronouncements had imbued her, but threats of death would have to wait until she gathered more certain evidence.

She took a pinch of the tabernanthe, placed it in the alembic, and lit a burner. Then she watched as the resin began to bubble. The alchematorium began to fill with a fragrant smoke. Alivet poured a drop of the now-liquid substance into ten test tubes and reached for the pipettes. These contained the testing substances: first, the chemicals corresponding to the elements, and then the purifiers. Tested with sulphur, the tabernanthe shrank and smoldered. Rancid smoke drifted up from the test tube. When she introduced irachium, however, the tabernanthe expanded, coiling up the tube like a stroked cat. The test tube began to glow, then abruptly shattered. Alivet frowned. The next few tests yielded similarly extreme results. Two tubes melted over the workbench and a third crumbled into dust when Alivet's back was turned. She made a note: *Tabernanthe responds with excessive force to standard elementals, particularly those that generate heat.*

It was time to try some combinations. Over the course of the next hour, Alivet prepared, mixed, and measured different fumes and alchemicals: combining ambergris and copper; myrrh and mercury; camphor, alum, and sulphur. Alivet became so absorbed that she even forgot about her death sentence. The air of the alchematorium became thick and stifling. When Ari Ghairen next stepped through the door, he choked.

"I can tell you've been busy," he said, coughing.

Alivet blinked through the fumes. "Close the door; you'll disturb the balance."

Rather to her surprise, Ghairen did as he was told.

"What have you found?" he inquired, coming to peer over her shoulder.

"This tabernanthe is a volatile substance, certainly. It's not amenable to being mixed with other alchemicals—it has no 'sister,' as we say. It likes heat, phosphorescence, luminescence—rather too much. It becomes explosive." She gestured to the fragments of melted glass.

"How much have we got left?" Ghairen examined the bowl.

"I've been frugal," Alivet told him.

"So you don't think it would make a good carrier for latent light?"

"From what I've seen of its properties, it's a reactive. So no, it would not make a good carrier as it is. It would need a stabilizer. But I've only been working on this for a couple of hours, Ghairen. I'd need to do more work on it before I decide for certain what it can, and cannot, do. I haven't tested its psychotropic qualities, for instance. And I'd like to leave some of this material in the athanor overnight to anneal and crystallize." She suppressed a yawn, only then realizing how tired she was.

"Very well." Ghairen bestowed an encouraging smile upon her. "Make your preparations, then sleep. I'll take you back to your room."

He was, she thought, doing a thorough job of curtailing her movements, but now was not the time to protest. Under Ghairen's silent supervision, she placed the remaining substances in the little round vessel called the Philosopher's Egg, put that in the athanor, and set it on a slow, steady heat, then cleaned the workbench. There was some comfort to be found in the order of routine. Her tasks completed, she accompanied Ghairen to the rooms below.

"Alivet. I hope you'll sleep well. There's food there if you want it." He looked at her for an unfathomable moment, still with that slight and unsettling smile, and she thought of slow poison in her veins. She bit back frustration and anger, and something more that she was afraid to examine too closely. Then she bade him good night.

As soon as she heard the snick of the lock behind him, she ran to the window and looked out. The windows were sealed shut. When she craned her neck and looked down, she saw the gleam of silver a thousand feet below. The sheer glass wall of the tower raced away beneath the window. To her right, a metal spine like a dragon's back climbed upward from the ground, but between it and the window, the wall was featureless. Frustrated, Alivet explored the room thoroughly, but could find no other exit.

Instead, she turned her attention to the fruit that sat in a bowl on a low table. She did not like to think what it might contain, but she had eaten nothing all day, so she picked up one of the fruits and took a bite. It was as fresh and cold as water. Alivet ate it all, and spat out the shiny black pip. A moment later, she could hardly keep her eyes open. She splashed the contents of the water-jug over her face, but to no avail.

As she climbed into the bed, she spared a thought for Ghairen's daughters and their mothers: were they, too, shut away in this luxurious eyrie away from freedom and the sun? Perhaps they would be amenable to the notion of escape. In the fleeting moments before sleep claimed her, Alivet resolved to find out.

Part V

DIVISION

. . . I consider that by nature we are composed of earthly elements and governed by heavenly, and . . . I am not ignorant that our dispositions are caused in part by supernatural signs . . .

— QUEEN ELIZABETH, *writing to Mary Stuart,* 1568

ANTWERP ～ 1564

It seemed fitting that the first tavern that Dee came across should be called the Golden Angel; for one who had dedicated much of his life to the study of omens, its appropriacy was clear. Apart from its name, and its proximity to the center of Antwerp, however, the tavern had little to recommend it, being more alehouse than inn and even more verminous than most. But it was also cheap, and after his experiences in Bonner's prison, Dee found that he had grown accustomed to discomfort.

He stepped through the door and secured a small, shabby room that looked out onto an alley. This, he thought, would do well enough for his purposes. Besides, it was good to get out of the streaming rain of a February night; he had forgotten how cold and miserable this part of the world could become. Chilblains burned and gnawed at his toes and it brought back memories of winter in Louvain, of pissing on his feet to cure the cold. He laid his sodden hose and doublet over a nearby bench and rummaged in the bag for some dry garments. Then, ensuring that his bag was safely hidden beneath the bed, he went back down the stairs. A grimy boy was sitting glumly at the entrance to the kitchen.

"You," said Dee in his bad Flemish. "Would you like to earn a penny?"

The boy nodded eagerly. "What must I do, master?" The child's dialect was so thick as to be almost unintelligible and Dee wondered whether he was in error in entrusting the task to such a lad.

"I want you to take a message to a man. Can you read?"

"No."

"Then do you know where might be found the house of one Abraham Ortelius?" Ortelius was well known, after all, and Antwerp was not so large.

"Is he a man who makes maps?"

"That is he. Tell him that Dr. Dee has now arrived from England and is residing at the Golden Angel."

"I know the house. Give me the penny and I will take your message."

"Upon your return," Dee said, fixing the grubby child with a basilisk eye, "I shall surely do so."

The boy disappeared into the rain. Dee ordered a cup of Antwerp's strong sour ale and a meat pie and sat down at a bench to watch the usual panoply of whores and roaring boys. Dee had little interest in either. The tavern was stuffy and seemed steeped in the smell of salt cod; he might as well have taken up residence in a herring wherry. The spectacle would have been depressing had he not felt fortunate to be here at all. His spell in Bonner's prison had instilled in him a perpetual anxiety, disturbing his usually sanguine temperament.

As he waited for Ortelius to come, Dee listened idly to the conversations around him. He was accustomed to the atmosphere of taverns. There were certain constant elements—the apple-squires each with their gaggle of whores, the moon-men, light heels, and jark-men, all of them drunken and quarreling—but the inns of each city had their own particular tune, a descant to the principal melody, and in Antwerp, that descant was composed of printing and money.

"It is all in the stars," a man was protesting to Dee's left. Dee's ears pricked up. He turned, to see a thin, nervous face above a pickled beard of the kind that he himself wore. A fellow astrologer, Dee thought, but the man's next words dispelled this notion. "My years in the financial markets have taught me that future prices are divinely ordained, and discoverable through astrological observation. People buy when prices are at their highest, for the upper influences so blind the natural reason with affections or desires."

Dee smiled to himself behind the cup of ale. If only it was that simple. Then he could return to England and make a fortune on the back of the market. But such a theorem did not take into account the subtler influences: the effects of restriction and balance generated by the planetary orbs. He was about to engage the star-broker in conversation when Ortelius' shambling figure appeared at the tavern door, accompanied by the boy, whom Dee paid and dismissed.

"I have your books," Ortelius said, without preamble.

Dee felt a pang within his liver. "The *Steganographia*?"

"Not yet." Ortelius raised a woolly eyebrow. "You have let fond dreaming become fact."

It was hardly likely that Ortelius had hunted down the volume, Dee admitted. He had let his hopes run away with him. After all, Trithemius' famous book had been missing for sixty years; it would have been little short of miraculous if Ortelius had strolled through the door with the manuscript beneath his arm. But the thought of the knowledge contained in that book gnawed at him like a rat in a cellar, such wonders did Trithemius claim: a method of sending messages over great distances by means of fire, a way of teaching Latin in no more than two hours, communication that could be achieved without speech or signs ... But it was the book's rumored Cabalistic content that interested Dee the most; a system of scientific incantations by which the powers of the universe itself might be harnessed. Dee remembered the gateway of which the angel had spoken and felt excitement course through him.

And if it is no angel? his conscience queried him, *but a devil come to tempt you?* Dee sighed. It had become a familiar inner discourse.

"Birkmann is still searching," Ortelius informed him now. He eased himself stiffly onto the opposite bench and Dee winced. Ortelius was no older than he himself, not yet forty, but he moved like an ancient. The elements of water and air seemed to influence the humors to produce an unhappy effect upon the limbs. "I know this manuscript is the principal reason that you have come to Antwerp. But I should like you to meet a body of folk that will be of valuable acquaintance." Ortelius' English was as stiff as his joints but Dee paid careful attention. He had great respect for the mapmaker, and besides, Ortelius was almost as much a master of his craft as Gerardus Mercator.

"You have spoken of these people in your letters, have you not? And they are your own sect?"

"They are. We call ourselves 'Familists,' for we perceive ourselves to be one family. We invite all lovers of truth, of what nation and religion soever they be—Christian, Jews, Mahomites, or Turks or heathen—to become part of one learned brotherhood. And sisterhood," Ortelius added.

"It is a worthy cause," Dee said with approval. He felt a sudden spark of interest, as if Ortelius' words had touched a flint to tinder. *These people will be important.* A moment of precognition? It seemed that the sign of the Golden Angel was proving auspicious, despite its greasy surroundings.

"Then, if you are willing, we shall see them upon the morrow. There are only a few of them here in Antwerp at the present time; they were forced to leave Emden a few years ago and since then have been scattered."

"Will they welcome me, then?" Such sects were wary of strangers, with good reason.

Ortelius nodded. "If I am with you. Besides, they have heard of you. They are anxious to discuss your work."

When Ortelius had left, Dee took the books up to his room and examined them. Even if nothing else came of the sojourn in Antwerp, it would have been worth a visit for these volumes alone: books on cryptography and mathematics, and a single work on the Cabala—the subject which had led poor Trithemius to be accused of trafficking with demons. Slowly, Dee turned the pages, examining the familiar diagrams by which man could ascend the spheres of existence. All the worlds were here: the Earth itself, then Yesod, Hod, Netzach, and beyond, each with their own characteristics and descriptions.

All of the books had been published by Officina Plantiniana, Antwerp's foremost printing house. If the *Steganographia* was to be found anywhere, Dee believed, it would be here. And once he had found it, he could begin the work that would open up the spheres to his view: the summoning of angels. He slept, dreaming an uneasy dream that a star-demon had sailed down from the moon and was talking to him in a voice he did not understand.

Next day, the rain turned to snow and Dee went with Ortelius to meet the Familists, crunching through the drifts to the east of the city to where a member of the sect had rented a tall house. A wind was blowing from the sea, full of salt and heralding further cold. Members of the sect were clustered around a fire. Dee saw a tall man, with a pale, drawn face and a spark of fervor in his eyes, accompanied by two youths, another man of middle age and unremarkable appearance, and a third man who was clearly a Moor. Dee noted the dark, impassive countenance and saw, too, the man's stillness. Here was someone, it seemed to Dee, who would not easily be swayed by fools. Ortelius introduced them all: the tall man was Hendrick Niclaes, the founder of the sect. The Moor's name was Nabil. He inclined his head to Dee, but did not speak.

"Welcome," Niclaes said. He had a curious, flustered manner, quite unlike the smooth charlatans to whom Dee had become accustomed in London. "I am most glad to see that you have braved the snow. It is quite an honor, to have the famous Dr. Dee visit us."

"The honor, sir, is mine. My friend here has told me something of you; I am eager to learn more."

"Then sit." Niclaes fussed around him, drawing a chair closer to the fire and calling for wine. Not a sect of absteemers, then, thought Dee with secret approval, and some relief. Niclaes thrust a book into his hands.

"It is my own. It will tell you what we are about." The others stood about him, conversing in low voices about a manner of everyday subjects, while Dee perused the volume: *An Introduction to the Holy Understanding of the Glass of Righteousness*. The "glass," it seemed, was the spirit of Christ. The doctrine that Niclaes proposed was philanthropic, pantheistic, and antinomian. Members of the sect were baptized into it. It was, to Dee's mind, both open and tolerant, though somewhat eclectic.

This would suit his own purposes well, however. The commune-based hierarchy suggested by Niclaes was based upon the Catholic Church, but the doctrinal aspect of the work appeared to follow certain of the German mystics and placed the principles of divine love above all texts, including the Bible itself. The German element suggested to Dee that Niclaes and his followers were likely to be versed already in alchemical knowledge: that would make his work a little easier. He was interested to note that the doctrine of claimed impeccability was suggested, for both Niclaes and the hierarchy. Rendering oneself exempt from sinning was, Dee considered, a practical element of any religious practice, but he could not help wondering what Niclaes had in mind. Again, the doctrine could suit Dee's own purposes admirably.

"The principle of love, then, is foremost in your doctrines?" he said aloud.

"Indeed. We hold that it lies above all and that it is to be adhered to absolutely."

"Even if the rule beneath which one finds oneself

proves cruel?" Once a man had come close to the pyres of heresy, they singed him forever.

"Even in the face of oppression, one must remain peaceful."

Perhaps not the most realistic notion, Dee thought, but there was little doubt that Niclaes was sincere.

"The inward light cannot be extinguished by persecution," Niclaes hastened to explain. "It can only be put out by the actions of the self against love." He paused. "We permit ourselves to recant when faced with persecution, but we hold to our opinions."

So they were not so impractical, after all. There was a certain slipperiness there that made Dee smile.

"Tell me," he said. "What else do you believe?"

"That men and women might recapture on Earth the state of innocence which existed before the Fall. Our enemies say we claim to attain Christ's own perfection, but this is not so. We hold our property in common, believe that all things come by nature."

"A pretty doctrine," Dee said. "But a subtle one, that it is this life which is to be infused by spirit, and not a slavish adherence to the life to come."

"You understand perfectly." It was clear from the expression on Niclaes' face that he felt a need for a kindred spirit: this was not a man who sought unquestioning subservience from colleagues and followers, as did so many of the sect leaders with whom Dee had come into contact. Hendrick Niclaes sought soul mates.

"Tell me," said Dee, stretching his chilblained feet to the fire and taking another sip of wine, "you who know so much of the inner light—what do you know of alchemy?"

That night, in the cold, cheerless room of the Golden Angel, Dee sat staring into the snowy dark beyond the window and knew that he had found the people who would be his fellow travelers. He had made an arrangement with

Niclaes to meet on the following day, this time without the company of Ortelius. Despite his convictions, Dee knew that this was not yet the time to broach the subject of the Meta Incognita, the colony of another world, with the leader of the Family of Love; nonetheless, that time was not far away. Niclaes was coming to England, to London itself, and it would be London, Dee knew, that would prove the cradle of the new movement: not a sect, but an expedition, into the realms of the stars.

TOWER OF THE POISONERS, HATHES

That night, in her silk-sheeted bed in the Tower of the Poisoners, Alivet dreamed.

She was standing by the window, looking out over the panorama of Ukesh, but now the towers gleamed in a stormy sunlight and the windows were wide open, letting in winds that were alternatively scorching and frosty. Someone came up behind her and put two hands on her shoulders.

"Well?" a warm voice said in her ear. "Shall we fly?"

"Yes," Alivet said, gladness singing through her at the thought that Ghairen had come to seek her out. "I've always wanted to do that."

"Then take my hands and hold tight," the voice said. Alivet did so, and they soared out through the window and high above the city. The canals glittered in the light; Alivet tasted snow on the wind.

"Where are we going?" she cried. The wind snatched the words out of her mouth, but the voice in her ear replied, "To the portal, of course. You must know where it is, if you're ever going to come and visit me." Then they were sailing down toward the ziggurat that Alivet had seen on her arrival, that Ghairen had told her was called the parc-verticale. She could see the forests encased within its transparent walls and she closed her eyes as they hurtled toward the glass, but then the walls of the ziggurat parted and they were through.

Alivet's bare feet sank into moss. She breathed in the smells of mud and river and green growing things: honeysuckle and lilies, lotus and a drift of roses. The parc-verticale smelled of summer and heat, as if the world that it contained lay a thousand miles away from cold Hathes, and Alivet basked in the warmth.

"Where are you?" she called.

"Why, over here," the familiar voice said. Alivet looked up and saw that it was not Ari Ghairen at all, but a woman sitting among the creepers. Her flesh, mottled silver striped with dark bands, appeared slightly transparent. Alivet could see the shadow of bones beneath the skin. Her eyes were the color of jade and dark hair streamed down her back.

"Who are you?" Alivet asked, though she felt that she should know the answer to this question. The woman smiled.

"My name is Gulzhur Elaniel. One day, you're going to come and visit me."

"Do you live here?" Alivet asked, assailed by the logic of dreams.

"Oh no. Hathes is too cold a place for my kind, so *formal*, don't you think? All about the head, and not a scrap left for the heart or the body. No, I am from sweet Nethes."

"Where's that?" Alivet asked.

"You'll find out in time," the woman said. "The portal lies that way, in the great temple. See?" She pointed through the wall of the ziggurat. The distance seemed to close up, so that the city lay spread at Alivet's feet like a map. She saw two great pillars and a long sequence of steps leading up from a canal.

"Remember the way," the woman said. "You wouldn't want to get lost. You'd never find your way out of the woods."

Alivet opened her mouth to ask the woman what she was talking about, but at that moment she came abruptly awake. The room was filled with an uncertain light. Ari Ghairen was leaning over her, holding a metal cup.

"Alivet? Good morning. I'm glad to see you've been sleeping so well."

Alivet, pushing aside the sheets, realized that she was still fully dressed. The memory of the previous day and the threat of poison rushed back to meet her, like a cold tide.

"I'll leave the tea here. Don't be too long. Breakfast first, and then I think we'd best begin work. After all, it isn't as though we have all the time in the world, is it?"

When he had gone, Alivet sipped the tea and struggled out of her clothes in order to wash, fumbling at the hooks and buttons. The morning light brought no new comfort; the Atoront Tower seemed even more fortresslike than it had on the previous evening. Castles and turrets of frost formed a lacy border around the windows and Alivet's breath steamed the pane, but inside the room it was still warm. She looked out over fresh snowfall, covering the ground around the towers so that the spires resembled dragons sleeping beneath the drifts.

She still felt besieged by her dream, which wrapped itself around her in psychic tatters. The woman had seemed as real as Ghairen himself. And it was embarrassing to remember how, in her dream, she had welcomed Ghairen and his touch. Thoughtfully, Alivet dressed once more, picked up the teacup and tried to open the door. It was still locked. Alivet rapped on the door until it opened.

Ghairen was waiting in the hallway, looking elegant and precise in his dark robes. He was presumably unwilling to let Alivet wander around on her own. She had no chance of finding Iraguila Ust, she thought, if Ghairen kept her continually under his eye. Today, the doors that led from the hallway were all closed. There was no sound from any of the rooms and the place felt empty. Ghairen took her through into a room with a long table, on which sat fruit and bread.

"I don't really know what you like," he said, apologetically. "Perhaps if you could give me some ideas?"

"Don't worry about making me feel at home," Alivet told him grimly, adding before she could stop herself, "I'm hardly likely to do that."

Ghairen gave her a thoughtful glance. "I suppose not. But one might as well make the best of things. After all, we are trying to help one other, aren't we?"

Alivet chewed some of the bread and pushed the rest away. Ghairen said nothing. When she had finished a second cup of the thin, fragrant tea, he gestured toward the door.

"Shall we? Only if you're ready, of course."

"Let's get on with it," Alivet said.

The substances in the athanor had annealed well. Alivet removed them and prepared the workbench for a range of tests. Later, she told herself, she would go exploring. Perhaps if she could find Ghairen's own supplies...Surely he would have antidotes on the premises. And there must be a way of finding out whether she had been poisoned or not, some test she could run. She did not trust the word of Iraguila Ust, and she did not trust Ghairen, either.

The problem gnawed at her until it became a distraction, so Alivet set it firmly aside and concentrated on her tests. The world contracted down to the basic stages of the alchemical sequence: dissolution, evaporation, crystallization. Alivet lost track of the time, until Ghairen reappeared.

"I know you're busy and you want to get on, but would you like something to eat? I've asked the servants to prepare something."

Hungry though she was, Alivet would have preferred food to be brought into the alchematorium, but it was the first time that Ghairen had mentioned servants, and her interest was immediately engaged. Where there was an underclass— as she knew all too well—there were resentments, and those could be exploited.

"Very well," she said, and followed Ghairen out of the alchematorium and back down to the main rooms. The acid light of Hathes flooded through the dining room window, casting silvery shadows across the floor. Ghairen held out a chair for Alivet at the head of the long table. He spoke, but she did not understand him.

"I beg your pardon?"

Ghairen inclined his head in acknowledgment and spoke again. The language was sibilant and hissing, at first nothing more than a jumble of speech, until Alivet realized that fragments and odd words were known to her. Gradually, the confusion resolved.

". . . takes a little while before your linguistic implant starts to work," Ghairen said. "But my daughter, obviously, was not raised to speak your language."

"The voices in the elevator," Alivet said. "You told me they gave me language. Is that what this is?" She frowned. "But I'm speaking my own tongue."

"We will be able to understand one another," Ghairen assured her. "My eldest will be joining us—Celana, whom you saw last night. My other daughters, Ryma and Ladeiné, are elsewhere." Turning to the door, he nodded sharply to someone unseen. Two women entered the dining room. The youngest—evidently Celana—was tall and slender. She looked nothing like her father. The dark eyes were heavily lidded, provocative above the demure high collar and the long skirts, but her mouth was tight. It was a small, closed face. Beneath the long sleeves, her wrists were painfully thin, and the knuckles of her long fingers—she had evidently inherited her hands from her father—seemed to stretch the skin. She barely glanced at Alivet, but scraped a chair out from the table and slid into it.

"Hello," Alivet said encouragingly. The girl mumbled something in reply.

Alivet turned to the second woman and nearly gasped aloud. The woman's face was half hidden by a mask, reaching from cheeks to hairline. Her eyes were hidden behind black lenses, extending from her face like binoculars. At first Alivet thought of the Unpriests, but the mask was etched with a delicate pattern of leaves. The woman wore a stiff rubber bodice from hips to chin; silk sleeves fell past her wrists.

"Celana's governess," Ghairen explained. "Semilay, this is my guest, Alivet Dee."

"Welcome to Ukesh, Sister Dee," the woman murmured,

and as soon as she spoke, Alivet recognized her. It was Iraguila Ust. Well, that was one problem solved, and a hundred gained.

Iraguila's face was impassive as she took her seat at the table. Ghairen struck a small bell and a creature glided through the door, carrying a platter. Alivet saw a narrow, bald head with eyes like ball bearings and small scaled hands. The thing was the size of a ten-year-old child. It moved as though it ran on wheels, its legs concealed beneath a long, drifting dress.

"A shiffrey," Ghairen explained. "Native to Hathes. They're analogous to your anubes."

"Are they all servants?" Alivet asked.

"By no means. Some are farmers; they own smallholdings in the hills beyond the towers. The land may look barren, but it's amazing what they manage to produce from it. These salty tubers, for instance, and the small green fruit by the side of your plate."

The shiffrey glided away. Celana stared after it, her face creased with resentment. The household seemed to seethe with tensions of which Alivet had no understanding. She did not dare look at Iraguila Ust, who was engaged in serving the food brought in by the shiffrey. Later, Alivet decided, she would seek the woman out. Hopefully, Ghairen would leave her alone in the afternoon and then perhaps she could find a way to get out of the alchematorium. She watched as Ust's gloved hands sliced the thick bread, diced fruit, and poured a glistening wine into frosted glasses.

Alivet immediately noticed that Ust sampled a portion of each type of food before passing the plates; the woman was a taster as well as a governess. The thought of placing someone else in such danger horrified Alivet, who had been raised to believe that one should run the risks of one's profession oneself. How long had Ust been in this position? And why, if she was the household's taster, had she not simply found a way to poison Ghairen herself and exact her revenge? Perhaps that vengeance was aimed at Celana, to deprive Ghairen of his daughter just as Ust's father had been taken from her.

Alivet glanced at the girl and saw that she was staring sulkily into her plate. Celana had barely touched her food. Occasionally she gave it a disdainful push with the end of her fork. Alivet could see that growing up in a poisoner's household might have a less than encouraging effect on the appetite and Celana did indeed seem very thin. The girl looked up, as if conscious of Alivet's scrutiny. Alivet smiled. Celana gave her an impassive stare, as though Alivet were some form of insect life that had disgraced itself upon the tablecloth.

Alivet restrained the impulse to lean across the table and give the girl a good sharp smack. She looked at the uncharacteristically silent Ghairen and saw that he was busying himself with his wineglass. She wondered whether he had witnessed her exchange with his daughter, whether he was subtly encouraging the tensions that ebbed and flowed around the dining table.

Finally the strained silence grew too much for Alivet. Turning back to Celana, she said, "Tell me about your studies, Celana. What is your governess teaching you?" She did not want to refer to the woman directly, in case she stumbled over Ust's assumed name. Celana's mouth grew even thinner. She stared at her plate and did not answer.

"Alivet asked you a question, Celana," Ghairen said sharply.

"Why should she have any interest in what I'm doing?" Celana snapped. "She doesn't give a flick of her fingers what I'm studying."

"That's not the point, Celana," Iraguila Ust whispered.

"What is the point, then?" Celana cried. "To be polite? To someone like *her*?" Her lip curled as she looked at Alivet, who was too astonished by the outburst to speak. "A drugged junkie from a world of peasants? If my mother were alive, she'd—"

"She'd box your ears and send you to your room," Ghairen

said, rising. He took his daughter by the arm and marched her through the door. Alivet could hear her protests as they receded down the hallway. Iraguila Ust leaned across the table and spoke quickly, the words tumbling over one another.

"You must not think poorly of her, it is all feigned to give us a moment alone. I know about the work that you are doing. We must take you to someone who can help you—it is vital that Ghairen should lose his hold over you."

"I don't want to help Ghairen any more than I can," Alivet hissed. "Look, we have to talk. Can you come and see me later? In the alchematorium, or my room?"

"The doors are self-keyed, I—" Iraguila began, but at that point Ghairen stepped into the room, looking ruffled.

"I must apologize," he said to Alivet, ignoring the governess. "Celana has been a troubled child ever since her mother's death, and I'm afraid I do not have the time to discipline her myself. That is a task for Semilay." He glanced at the governess, who once more sat with head bowed, the picture of dreary compliance.

Alivet wanted to ask more about the two younger girls and their mothers, but decided that this, too, was a question for Iraguila Ust. She muttered something noncommittal and turned her attention back to her neglected food. Ust, murmuring an excuse, slipped from the room. Ghairen watched her go without expression. Then he said, as if nothing had happened, "I'm sure you're eager to return to the alchematorium, Alivet. Shall we go?"

After the meal the dim, vaporous atmosphere of the alchematorium came as a relief. Ghairen perched himself on a high stool by the workbench, the folds of his robes settling around him like dark wings. She could feel him staring at her. Deciding that the best thing to do would be to pretend he wasn't there, Alivet ignored him and devoted herself instead to a thorough investigation of elemental preparations. Nothing worked. Whatever she tried, the tabernanthe still fractured and shattered, exploding into wafts of noxious smoke.

By the end of the afternoon, Alivet's hands were covered with a dozen tiny burns and scratches, but even under the strained circumstances, it was good to be doing what she knew best. Eventually she ran out of ideas and turned to the Poison Master.

"I can't get a result with this," she told him impatiently, running her hand over her hair. Her fingers were smudged with ash and there was a burn on the side of her thumb, but these were familiar nuisances.

"You need a break," Ghairen said at once, all solicitude. "Perhaps you'd like to see the garden?"

"I thought I couldn't go outside."

"In this world our gardens are covered, as you saw in the case of the parc-verticale." Alivet started at this, as though he had somehow managed to penetrate her dreams. Ghairen went on, "My own garden is not nearly so extensive, naturally, but it has attracted much favorable comment."

"How nice," Alivet said. It seemed that Ghairen did not appreciate the irony, for he beamed.

"Yes, I think so. Gardening is a great interest of mine and one likes one's efforts to be appreciated."

He indicated a door at the far end of the alchematorium.

"It's through here. You'll find it refreshing," Ghairen said, reaching for the door panel. "The winds are simulated, of course. The air is filtered, and quite safe."

Alivet stepped out onto a high, bright platform and was almost lifted off her feet by a sudden gust. Ghairen had not lied: the air was fresh and sweet. She leaned back against the lintel and took a deep breath as her eyes adjusted to the light. The roof of the platform shimmered a little in the late-afternoon sun, otherwise Alivet might have thought it entirely open to the elements. The coiled, twisted peak of the tower hovered above her like a horn.

Ahead stretched the garden. Ferns coiled from walls of black rock; fronds and skeins of vines obscured a delicate arch of ceiling. Light filtered down to cast an underwater glow over the scene. As Alivet wandered out, guided by the watchful Ghairen, she saw that small plants and lichens grew between the ferns: ocher cushions of anemone, patches of viridian moss, a honey-colored fungus exuding clouds of spores that caught the light like sparks.

"So this is where they come from," Alivet said. "Your toxins."

Ghairen nodded.

"This is my poison garden, yes. Don't step too close to that fungus—it's my best source of immanita."

"This must have cost a fortune," Alivet mused. "How long did it take you to gather all these plants?"

"Almost twenty years. I have been diligent in my approach, and also disciplined." Ghairen's dark robes fluttered across a carpet of moss as he stepped forward. "Nothing but the best quality. And organically grown—one doesn't want one's preparations contaminated by chemicals, after all. These plants contain the poisons in their latent form—the live material is over there, behind the glass wall. You need protective clothing to venture in there."

"Can I see?" Alivet asked.

"But of course."

She followed him across the garden to the partition and peered in at a toxic jungle. Harnify creeper snaked along the wall, its blooms extending their raw red tongues; Fatal Orchis curled fleshy leaves above a small pool. Alivet did not recognize many of the species and said as much.

"Many are combinations and grafts. I am constantly refining and mixing the genes. There are even animal crossbreeds. That lily contains scorpion venom, for instance, and the soke—a common household bloom, entirely innocuous—contains the exudations of the shriek-bat. Some of my developments have been described as revolutionary. I've had a lot of papers published."

"You must be very proud," Alivet said.

"One does what one can," Ari Ghairen murmured modestly. "Come and take a look out of the main windows. I often come up here at sunset. The view is really quite spectacular." His hand hovered around her waist, guiding her toward the windows.

Despite the distraction of his touch, Alivet was obliged to agree. From this high vantage point, she could look out across all Ukesh. Some of the more distant spiral towers seemed no bigger than the tendrils of the poisonous creeper; others rocketed into the heavens, too immense for the eye to absorb. A high pile of cumulus was massing on the far horizon, its anvil head promising more snow. To her right, Alivet could see the parc-verticale and she thought again of the woman of her dream, beckoning from a tangle of vines.

"Do you let your children come up here?" she asked.

Ghairen smiled. "No. But Celana comes anyway. She sneaks out from her lessons or her bed when she thinks I'm not looking, to steal and secrete away poisons. Her main talent is for music, but she still takes after me. Though not, I feel obliged to add, in the manner of her rudeness."

"With so many poisons around," Alivet said with careful nonchalance, "and your children taking such an interest in the family business, I hope you have plenty of antidotes."

"I keep antidotes for everything here"—Ghairen glanced at her sidelong and indicated a tall metal case—"all safely locked away. There's another cabinet at the back of the alchematorium. You might have noticed it yesterday."

"You keep duplicates?"

"If someone was exposed to something up here, they could die in the time it took to fetch an antidote from downstairs."

Alivet took careful note of the case and decided to change the subject. "Celana," she ventured, "does not seem happy."

"There is no 'seeming' about it. She isn't happy. She blames me for her mother's death. But she'll get over it. She'll be an heiress one day; that goes a long way to sweeten a bitter pill."

"What happened to her mother? How did she die?"

"She was poisoned," Ghairen said evenly.

"Why does that not surprise me? Did you poison her?"

"Alivet, I don't go around poisoning *everyone*. I don't

have the time. But so that you don't get some crusading impulse into your head and start asking awkward questions at the dinner table, no, I did not poison my late wife, and I don't know who did. I deeply regretted her demise, as a matter of fact." He paused, then added, "If you really want details, her name was Arylde. She died in a place called Loviti, on the Small Sea. I sent her there for a holiday, with Celana. She was dead within a day." He looked somewhat surprised, as if he had not intended to impart such a relative wealth of information.

"You must miss her very much," Alivet said, taking advantage of the moment to probe. But then there were the mistresses...

"I owed her many pleasures and many sorrows. Arylde was not an easy woman." He fell silent for a moment. She could not read his expression. "Shall we return to the alchematorium?" He offered her his arm, which, after a moment, Alivet took. Whatever might have befallen Celana's mother, Alivet thought, she did not believe Ghairen's explanation for a second.

chapter III

TOWER OF THE POISONERS, HATHES

Neither Celana nor Iraguila Ust appeared at dinner that evening. Alivet dined alone, thankful to be spared her host's attentions but with a head full of plans. The shiffrey servant glided silently in and out, bearing a selection of broth and wine.

"So," Alivet said to it, when it next entered, "can you speak? What's your name?"

The shiffrey stopped dead and stared at Alivet out of its ball-bearing eyes. The small hands were closer to claws: thin twig fingers ending in a bulbous pad. At first, she had thought that the thing lacked a mouth, then realized that there was a narrow hole tucked away beneath its pointed chin. Its skin had the smooth pallor of wax. She was unable to read its expression.

"Who are you?" Alivet said again. "Talk to me." She reached out and patted one of the little hands.

The shiffrey became agitated. It emitted a low hooting noise and spun about, its skirts whirling. Alivet caught a glimpse of two tiny feet, clawed balls like the casters of a chair. Ghairen had told her that they were a native life form, but there was something almost mechanical about the creature.

"It's all right," she said hastily. "I won't hurt you. You can go."

The shiffrey shot away through the door. It did not return. Alivet put down her knife, took a final fortifying swig of wine, and went out after it. Ghairen rose smoothly from the armchair in the hall.

"Did you enjoy your meal? Was everything all right?"

"Fine, thank you," Alivet muttered. Evidently she was still being kept beneath Ghairen's watchful eye. She thought of spending the evening with him and was filled with sudden nerves. "I'm a little tired." She put a hand to her brow, as if feeling faint. "I'd like an early night."

"Naturally. A strange day in a strange place and you've been working so hard . . . You're looking quite pale." Ghairen put a steadying hand on her arm. "I've taken the liberty of putting some books in your room. I thought you might like some reading matter."

"That's very kind," Alivet said. Actually, it was a relief. The prospect of spending hours in her room, brooding on her possible death sentence, had not been appealing. But then, she did not plan to spend all that much time in her room if she could possibly help it. Ghairen walked her the short distance to her door, then left her mercifully in peace.

Alivet closed the door behind her and leaned against it. This constant attention was getting on her nerves; it would have been less alarming if she had been kept in a cell. Ghairen's presence was so—unsettling. She wondered whether this was what her sister must feel, a mouse in a gilded cage. At least Ghairen wasn't in the same league as the Lords of Night. Or was he? If Iraguila was to be believed, he'd poisoned her, and she had no doubt that he was prepared to see her die if he didn't get what he wanted. And what was that, exactly? Iraguila Ust had been emphatic; Ghairen must not be allowed to succeed in his preparations. Was he really trying to find a way to dispatch the Lords? Or had that simply been a convenient explanation, to further engage Alivet's help and insert a level of ambiguity into their relationship? A relationship, she felt, that possessed enough ambiguity already.

The books sat in a neat pile by the side of the bed. Alivet

wanted to make sure that Ghairen was out of the way before she started trying to open the door, so she sat down on the bed and began to peruse the Poison Master's idea of reading material. Two of the books were from her own world: classics relating to an old man's pilgrimage into the fens and a girl growing up in a privileged family in Shadow Town. It seemed remarkable to Alivet that she had been standing in those very streets only a few days before. She felt as though she had been incarcerated in Ghairen's household for months.

But her aunt had drilled these books, and other classics, into Alivet and Inki when they were still children and the novels had not become Alivet's favorites. She put them aside and turned to the other books. First on the pile was a tome entitled *A Guide to Hathes and Its Customs*. Much more interesting, Alivet thought. She flicked through it. There were pictures of the towers and the canals, and an illustration of a shiffrey in a peculiar, crenellated hat, brandishing something that looked like a kitchen spatula. The caption read, *Shiffrey in war bonnet, with ceremonial spear*. Alivet couldn't help feeling sorry for the shiffrey; they seemed such a pathetic, inoffensive species.

It also had a section on the language of Hathes: a complex alphabet that reminded Alivet of a row of rushes or reeds. She read some of the accompanying text, which was written in an elaborate, archaic form of her own tongue, but the print required the aid of a magnifying glass.

Alivet put down *A Guide to Hathes* and picked up the last two books. They looked ancient: the leather covers cracked and peeling, the pages wafer-thin. Alivet puzzled out the name on a spine: *Jerusalem*. She opened the book and tried to read a passage, but although the alphabet and some of the words were familiar, she could make little sense of it. The book told of places that Alivet had never heard of, and the names were strange.

The last book seemed even older; the pages were stained. Alivet held it under the light and managed to make out the words on the frontispiece: *A Most Ancient and Secret History of the Cabala*. The name of the author was missing. Alivet turned the pages and found a diagram; a symmetrical pattern of circles, joined together by lines. As with the other book, the print was tiny and she strained her eyes trying to read it. She could not even tell what it might be about.

She wondered how Ari Ghairen had made this somewhat eclectic selection. The fat guide to Hathes was the most promising so far, but Alivet had little time for reading. She stacked the books on the side table and went over to the window. It was close to dark. What time was Ghairen likely to go to bed? Did he even sleep? She wouldn't have put it past him to sit perched on the top of the tower like a leech-bird, awaiting passing victims.

Crossing to the door, she put her ear to it, but could hear nothing. Very carefully, she tried the door handle. It was still locked, no surprises there. What had Iraguila said? The door was self-keyed, whatever that meant. Alivet frowned. The lock was made of metal: an elaborate confection of swirls and leaves. She knelt down and examined it. At the center of the lock was a little hole, no wider than a pin. Alivet cast about for something that might be used as a key. The bedroom was devoid of anything useful, but as she bent to look beneath the bed, her uncomfortable corset creaked and that gave Alivet an idea. She tore off the corset. Then, standing in her shift, she tugged at the side stitches of the garment until they gave way. A slender wire protruded. Alivet pulled the wire out and snapped it by trapping it under the bed leg. She knelt down at the door and inserted the wire, jiggling it inside the lock. Nothing happened.

Grimacing with frustration, Alivet withdrew the wire and inserted the other end. Still nothing. Perhaps the wire was too wide: it had taken a certain degree of pushing to get it into the hole. She pulled the wire out and picked at it, but without result. She sat down on the bed and eventually managed to detach a thin strand from the wire. She was just about to apply this to the lock when the door swung open of its own accord. Alivet saw a gleaming eye through the crack.

"Iraguila? Is that you?"

The figure turned and bolted. Alivet sprang for the door and peered out. A thin shape was disappearing along the hall in the direction of the alchematorium: not Iraguila, but the girl in her charge. Perhaps Celana had intended to spy upon her father's guest, thinking that Alivet was asleep—whatever the reason, the door was open.

Still in her shift, Alivet put her head cautiously around the door and looked out. The hallway was empty. A lamp glowed in a far corner, casting a pool of light upon the floor, but otherwise the hallway was dark. Alivet slipped back into the room, picked up the thinnest book—one of the childhood classics—and wedged it in the frame of the door so that it would not swing shut behind her. But if Ghairen or anyone else took it into their heads to go prowling around, she did not want it to look wide open, either.

She studied the door. Then, satisfied, she took her bearings. The alchematorium lay upstairs. To her right was the dining room, her own room, and a third, unknown, door. Across the hall, another two doors were visible. Alivet crept over and put her ear to one of them. It was silent within. There was no sound or movement anywhere in the apartment. She gave the door an experimental push, but it did not move. Ghairen, she felt sure, would have taken the utmost precautions to protect himself and his family and she was certain that the other doors, too, would be locked. She tried them and found that this was indeed the case. Frustrated, Alivet retraced her steps to the hallway, wondering with uneasy fancy if either of Ghairen's absent mistresses might be found behind these bolted doors.

She had to find Iraguila Ust, or seek out Ghairen's antidotes for herself. The latter option was more appealing. She did not trust the murmuring governess, sensing plots within plots.

As she was about to try the elevator, she heard footsteps—measured, but muffled—inside one of the inner rooms. Alivet stepped quickly back into the shadows and crouched down behind the high wings of the armchair. A door opened—third on the left, Alivet noted—and Iraguila slipped through it, wearing a silk nightgown. Her feet were bare. Before Alivet could call to her she ran swiftly and silently through the hall and disappeared. Alivet rose quickly to her feet. At the end of the long hallway, far beyond the lamplight, she saw a small door. It was ajar. Brimming with curiosity, Alivet ducked through the door and found herself on a spiral iron staircase, leading up past paneled walls. Footsteps echoed distantly down the stairwell: Celana had gone up, toward the alchematorium and the poison garden. As quietly as she could, Alivet followed.

Soon, she reached the landing. Ahead, lay two more doors. One, possibly leading to a further staircase, was barred, but the other stood open. A wan, frosty light streamed through into the stairwell and Alivet realized that she had reached the garden. She stepped through the door, keeping close to the shadows by the wall.

Above, through the glass ceiling, she could see only darkness. But light was coming from somewhere: a dim, intermittent glow. It took Alivet a moment to realize that the illumination was coming from the rocks themselves. In daylight, they had been obsidian black, but now they gleamed silver, casting wavering shadows across the garden floor. The ferns fronded outward, as if courting darkness. Celana stood by the window, hands pressed against the glass. Her shoulders were shaking. Suddenly, Alivet felt very sorry for her—how must it be, to live in this stifling place and have Ghairen as a father? To put up with the sinister kindness, the threats veiled by oppressive concern?

It wasn't only Inki who needed rescuing, Alivet thought. She might not be able to help everyone—perhaps she would not even be able to save herself—but Alivet decided then and there that Celana was another one whose name was now on the list. Celana's hands were banging soundlessly against the glass and for a terrible moment Alivet feared that she might be trying to break through and fall down the side of the great black tower, tiny as the ghost of a leaf. She was about to step forward, but Celana turned abruptly and stood quivering, with her back to the window.

"You!" she cried. "Why have you followed me up here? Why are you always following me? Why can't you just leave me alone?"

Alivet was about to step forth and say that Celana had been the one to seek her out, but realized just in time that the girl had been speaking to someone else.

"Now, Celana," Ghairen said, gliding out of the shadows. He wore his usual robes. Alivet thought immediately of the door of her bedroom, still ajar. And where had Iraguila Ust vanished to? "There's no need to be upset. We're simply worried about you, that's all. Now be a good girl and come back to bed." Something in his tone suggested unspeakable possibilities to Alivet. Could Ghairen be sleeping with his daughter? It would explain Celana's erratic behavior.

"Go away!" Celana cried. She spun back to the window. Ghairen strode swiftly across the garden and tapped her on the shoulder. Celana grew rigid. Then she crumpled into her father's arms. Ghairen picked her up as though she were weightless and with her head dangling bonelessly over the crook of his elbow, carried her back through the poisonous, dreaming ferns and into the elevator. The doors hummed shut and Ghairen and his daughter were gone. Alivet stepped out into the garden and a hand gripped her arm. She leaped, turning her ankle on the moss, and lashed out. Iraguila Ust hovered at her shoulder like a large dragonfly. The lenses that had concealed her eyes had been removed. Her eyes glowed in the pale light like moons.

"What are you doing up here?" the governess whispered.

"Celana opened the door of my room. What about you?"

"I sleep next door to Celana; I heard her leave her bed. She's done it before. She walks in her sleep."

Alivet did not believe this. Celana's movements had seemed all too purposeful. "How did Ghairen know she was wandering about?"

"I don't know," Iraguila said. "He seems to know things . . ."

"Then it's not such a wonderful idea for us to be standing up here, is it? I left my bedroom door open."

"It's too late now," Iraguila said, nervously. "And at least it's private up here. Alivet, we have to take you to an alchemist—to someone who can give you an antidote. I know of someone who may help. Can you meet me here tomorrow, around this time?"

"I'll try," Alivet said. "How am I going to open my door?"

"The lock is genetically keyed. Do you know what that means?"

Alivet shook her head.

"You need some of Ghairen's blood, or saliva, to open the door."

"How in the world am I going to get that?"

"I don't know. You won't need much—just a smear will do. You'll have to insert it into the lock; it will read the blood. I'll do my best to help you, but you'll have to try, too."

"I'll see what I can do," Alivet promised, dubiously.

Iraguila seemed to feel that this was enough. She bobbed her head and, with a quick lizardlike glance through the door, left the garden. Alivet waited for a moment as Iraguila vanished into the depths of the stairwell, then she headed into the glowing garden.

The first place she tried was the antidote case. To her dismay, though not to her surprise, it was securely sealed. It did not even seem to possess a lock, but appeared to be nothing more than an ornamented box. At last Alivet gave up and turned back to the garden itself.

There were some plants here that she recognized, plants that could prove useful. Taking care not to touch anything with her bare hands, she gathered a selection of leaves and berries into a fold of her dress. Her heart was pounding, as though at any moment Ari Ghairen might glide out of the shadows and place a toxic hand upon her shoulder. But the garden remained still and silent.

Clasping her precious cargo of poisons, Alivet made her way back down the stairs. When she reached the landing level with the hallway, she could hardly bring herself to step through. She did not want to look up and see her bedroom door closed against her, Ghairen standing accusingly in the hall... But the hallway was empty. The single lamp glowed, her bedroom door was ajar, just as she had left it twenty minutes before.

Alivet listened. She could hear voices in one of the adjoining rooms: someone—Celana?—cried out, but the sound was abruptly stifled. Then came a lower, male voice, speaking in a cold, measured way that nevertheless caused a chill to run down Alivet's spine. The voice clearly belonged to Ghairen and Alivet thought with a pang of Celana, facing her father's wrath. She saw herself rushing to the door, hammering upon it, forcing Ghairen to leave his daughter alone.

But such thoughts were nothing more than fantasies. Celana was not Alivet's responsibility. And yet Alivet could not help but feel that she must do something to help the girl. Battling frustration and anger, she crept across the hallway to her bedroom, Ghairen's icy voice still echoing through the shadows.

Once inside the illusory sanctuary of her own room, Alivet leaned against the door and closed her eyes for a moment in sheer relief. Then she spread her hoard of stolen poisons across the bed and made a quick inventory. Paralysis; blindness; flowers to freeze the voice and cause the breath to stop in the throat. She had an array of latent weapons at her disposal, and an alchematorium in which to distill them. She still had no antidote, but for the first time since her fatal meeting with Ghairen, Alivet felt that she finally possessed a means of defense.

What now remained was a decision about how, and when, to deploy that means. If she simply killed Ghairen, she would be disposing of the Night Lords' enemy—assuming that Ghairen had been telling her the truth. And she still had no way of ascertaining whether Iraguila, too, had been lying. But then she thought: *There might be a way*. The Search had taught her to travel within, using a drug as her guide. Though she had no drug to hand, perhaps she could still travel inside her own mind, see if she could get a hint of the true state of her health.

Alivet lay back on the bed and closed her eyes.

She pretended to herself that she had indeed ingested some substance: menifew, perhaps, a friendly ally. She focused on the symptoms generated by menifew, imagining herself in the grip of the drug, and very slowly the pathways of her mind began to open up before her. She traveled along them, picturing herself walking a road and noting what she saw upon it. There was a darkness upon the horizon: clouds of fear, storms of anxiety. The imagery was simple, but effective. If she looked up, she could see the neurons of her brain arching over the road like the branches of trees, pulsing with lights. She passed a figure with its back turned to her: from the black robe and the silky hair, she recognized Ari Ghairen. A mixture of emotions swarmed around him: fear, anger, resentment, hope—and something complicated and arousing, from which Alivet shied away.

Take me to that part of my mind that tells me about my own body, she instructed herself. *Let me see if I am well.* And gradually, slowly, the scene changed. She was in a room, surrounded by plants. Some were green and thriving, but many of them were already brittle and dry. In the corner, a small fern trailed dead from its pot. Alivet's hand crept to her throat. The room was icy cold, then burning with heat. If this was her health, then something was clearly wrong. Her eyes snapped open, bringing her out of her head. She lay consumed with worry.

Even if Iraguila's contact could cure her, if Ghairen were gone, her chances of getting home and rescuing Inki were slim. She closed her eyes once more, wrestling with possibilities. *Am I dying? Or is this just a fancy, brought about by fright and stress? Let's see what Iraguila can do for me.* And then, *If and when I'm cured, I'll find a way to deal with the Poison Master.*

part VI

CORRUPTION

Elizabeth gave Dee warrant . . . "to do what I would in philosophy and alchemy, and none should check, control or molest me . . ."

— DR. JOHN DEE, *diary*

chapter I

MORTLAKE ⟶ 1564

Summer was drawing to a close now, and the September sunlight lay low over rosemary and henbane, parsley and hellebore and rue. Dee regarded the garden with satisfaction: it had taken most of the spring to set in order, patiently following moon to moon to ensure that the most auspicious planting times were achieved. The parsley seeds that he had put in on the eve of Good Friday had produced a particularly fine crop.

As it is with my garden, Dee thought, *so it is with my life*. The last few years had been turbulant ones, akin to sailing a small ship upon uncharted seas, with many changes in season and climate. Dee had been lucky to navigate through such inclement political weather. It still seemed miraculous that he was standing here in this silent summer garden, listening to the humming of the bees and the lapping of the Thames against the water-stairs, rather than reduced to a pile of ash and bones in the flames of Smithfield.

But Dee's compromises had left a stain, nonetheless. Dee might be the Royal Astrologer, called upon to advise on such matters as the wax effigy of the Queen, bristling with hog hairs and found in Lincoln's Inn Fields, or the blazing star that had recently appeared in the heavens, but there had been no ensuing promotion as Court Philosopher. In a way, this was no bad thing. It left Dee a poorer man, but with more time to study those most burning questions: the issue of the colony, of taking Niclaes and his Family of Love to the new world of Meta Incognita.

"John!" He could hear Katherine crying out from the kitchen, and turned. His wife came flying up the path, her skirts flapping around her like wings. Immediately, Dee feared the worst.

"Is it my mother?" The old lady had already fallen once, tumbling down the long staircase. Fortunately, she had broken no more than her wrist, but it was an ill precedent.

"No. It's the Queen."

"She's dead?" The garden spun around him, the sound of the bees a roaring in his head.

"No, John," Katherine said, losing patience. "Really, you are the most morbid man—the Queen is *here*. She's come to see you."

After a gaping moment, Dee followed his wife down the path to the house with all speed. As he pushed open the twisted oak slab of the front door, the sun slid behind a cloud. Yet Elizabeth, standing among the lavender bushes in Dee's garden, seemed to shine with a light of her own. No doubt this was a function of the pearl-stitched cloth-of-gold of her gown, but the effect was dazzling. Dee bowed.

"Your Majesty," he said, "is indeed the sun around which all else turns." Flattery never went amiss, but the strange thing was that he could not help but mean it; the Queen had that effect on people. Elizabeth's Spanish dwarf, Thomasina, hovered at her side like a stray moon.

"Indeed," the Queen replied and Dee could hear the chilly amusement in her voice, "but do I not represent the Earth the universal center of which your Copernicus would deprive me?"

When discoursing with queens, Dee had discovered, the ground could very often open up and swallow you whole, like Jonah's whale. Elizabeth could be a stimulating woman and Dee would have enjoyed the verbal fencing if only she had not been the Queen, and had held so much power in those small gloved hands.

"The sun is the greater body, and thus more fitting," he ventured. He saw the dwarf Thomasina hide a smile; her intelligent dark eyes rested on Dee for a moment. As Elizabeth's toy, she no doubt had an understanding of her mistress' whims.

"Well, and that is kind, but I am here not to talk of suns, but of moons and their reflected light," the Queen remarked.

What was she talking about? Dee wondered, panicking. The trouble with Elizabeth, as opposed to duller monarchs, was that she frequently honed the sharpness of her wit upon her subjects and left them bleeding. He ransacked his thoughts for an answer and found it.

"Your Majesty wishes to inspect the mirror?" If he had half the powers of prediction that his neighbors attributed to him, he should have foreseen this. He glimpsed Katherine's face as she hovered in the hallway and her face became momentarily blank with shock. He knew what she was thinking as clearly as if she had spoken aloud: *Will she be coming in? And the house in such a state* . . . But the Queen must have been used to such reactions. He saw the faintest trace of a smile across her mouth as she said, "We will not trouble you to entertain us, Dr. Dee. We shall inspect the mirror here, among the loveliness of your garden."

Relieved, Dee said, "I shall be happy to bring it to you."

The Queen nodded in brief dismissal. Dee hurried up the stairs, past the gaping servants, and into the study where he kept the most precious of his books and artifacts. He had hidden the mirror, wrapped in a soft cloth and a leather case, beneath the floorboards. Perhaps he had been unwise to tell others about the device, but there was little he could do about that now. He pushed the board aside and retrieved the case containing the mirror, then carried it carefully downstairs.

He half feared that the Queen's visit might yet prove to be nothing more than some waking phantasm, that would splinter and fracture in the noonday sun, but he told himself to stop being a fool. It was not such an extraordinary thing that the Queen should ride out this way. Walsingham lived only a short distance from Dee's own house. Besides, did she not value Dee's own counsel and his astrological expertise? Yet Dee was always conscious of not being quite within the Royal inner sanctum, and that meant that he was not entirely trusted.

Elizabeth stood where he had left her in the golden September sunlight. "Will it work upon so bright a day?" she asked as Dee panted up the path.

"Noon or midnight should make no difference," Dee told her.

He unwrapped the mirror and held it out to her. The mirror filled his hands like a pool of darkness. It was made of some black polished substance, perhaps glass or obsidian, which seemed to swallow the light.

"Sir William Pickering gave you this, I believe, during your sojourn in the Low Countries?"

"That is so. A most valuable gift, for which I am permanently indebted." That was true enough. Pickering had picked up the thing as a curiosity, having no idea of its value.

"Explain to me what it does, and how it functions," the Queen instructed.

"It is my own belief that every object emits a kind of light, that delineates its shape and form. We cannot see such a light with our eyes, but certain substances attract it, as a lodestone draws iron to its very self. And once the light has been attracted, the mirror retains it, thus allowing us to witness objects from afar."

"And how," Elizabeth said, frowning, "does the mirror choose its subjects?"

"The mirror does not choose. Rather, the one who looks into the mirror must apply their mind to the purpose and settle upon one or another place or object. This attention helps the mirror to focus, the light being filtered through the concentration of the mind as if through a colored glass."

"So if I should wish to see a thing, I need only think upon it?"

"That is so." Dee added, quickly, "It is usual to enlist a trained scryer for the task, such a one whose mind is used to this process of 'tuning.'" He would, he thought, spare the Queen an account of how troublesome it had been to find a scryer who was neither a rogue nor mad and how he was at present without a man who could provide such a service. If he embarked upon such a recitation, they would be there until sunset.

He felt, rather than saw, the Queen's basilisk gaze. Beside her, Thomasina shifted restlessly.

"We do not," the Queen said, "require the services of such. We will do it ourselves." Noting the shift into the Royal plural, Dee was swift to concur. The Queen frowned down into the mirror. The sunlight around her seemed to glow more brightly, as if she willed it into her own essence. Dee held his breath. It would not work; he would be cast from her orbit into the outer dark and never see the rarefied light of the court again... And then Elizabeth's cold eyes opened in wonder. She said, "I can see it!"

Dee took the liberty of peering over her shoulder and saw that an image had appeared in the black opacity of the glass: a tiny ship, tossed on a storming sea.

"The Muscovy Company," the Queen said slowly. "I recognize the ship. I saw it set sail from Tilbury not more than a month ago."

"Was this what you wished to see?" Dee asked.

"Yes." Her glance this time was oblique, half concealed by the heavy lids, and Dee realized that she had refrained from seeking something of political sensitivity, in case the glass had worked and he had seen. He swallowed a brief bitterness, for the Queen was smiling.

"My Lord Walsingham will be most intrigued," she said, and it was Dee's turn to smile. Ever since the spymaster had had word of the mirror, he had pestered Dee until he had been shown the device in operation. The mirror accounted for most of Walsingham's visits to Dee's household; Dee supposed that it was good of the man to bother, when he could simply have had the thing impounded. However, the mirror was not always wholly reliable when Walsingham consulted it. There were long periods when it remained dark, or when a cataract like the bloom of a plum appeared over it, and then it was useless. This, Dee reflected, was true of most of the wonders in his possession: they worked erratically, if at all. It was as though the universe occasionally condescended to confirm his theories, but most of the time was unwilling to play fair.

"Well," the Queen remarked, "it is indeed a great delight." She ran a gloved finger across the surface of the mirror, dispelling seas and ship alike. "You had some interest in the voyage to Cathay, I recollect."

"Richard Chancellor was well beloved of me," Dee replied. "When the Cathay expedition was first conceived of, he came to me with his instruments and we prepared charts for his voyage, of the northern seas."

"And that voyage was to result in the establishment of the Muscovy Company," the Queen mused. "He did not reach Cathay, but he did us no small service nonetheless. Did he speak to you of the voyage?"

"Indeed he did, and a most arduous time he had of it. He spoke of the far north, beyond the uncharted world, where he found no night at all but a continual light and brightness of the sun shining clearly upon the sea."

"I have heard it spoken of as Meta Incognita," the Queen said.

Dee smiled. "Much of this world could be named as such."

"It would," the Queen said, "be good to learn more of it." For a brief, disconcerting moment, Dee met Elizabeth's gaze. "If you see any such unknown or foreign places, you will tell me of them, will you not?"

For a moment Dee was afraid that she somehow knew of the spirit, the star-demon, and what it had promised him. The thought chilled him, despite the summer warmth of the day.

"I will tell you first among all," he said, and the Queen's cold eyes looked past him for a moment, into some unimaginable future. For a moment Dee was afraid that she might insist on taking the mirror with her, but then she handed it back to him, saying, "Keep it safe for me."

"I shall, Your Majesty."

When Elizabeth and her retinue—her dwarf, her maidservants, her carriage, the whole glittering procession—had swept away, Dee went slowly back inside the house and returned the mirror to its hiding place. Then he sat down at the desk and stared unseeingly at the manuscripts scattered across it. The Queen had been delighted by the mirror, but she saw it, as a monarch must, principally as a means to establish her own security. Walsingham was the same, and as Elizabeth's spymaster, his concerns would reflect her own as surely as the black mirror reflected the sun.

As a satellite of the outer court, Dee was sufficiently trusted in neither the political nor the intellectual sphere for the Queen to take the action that mattered most: the endowment of money. Without money, Dee's research would be kept to a minimum, tinkering about with small devices such as the bronze bee. His most valuable possessions had been given to him by others. Even the house belonged to his mother. With the debts left by his father's financial ruin, and the deprivation of his own living at Upton during the course of his imprisonment, Dee was entirely too dependent on charity for his own liking. Perhaps the expeditions mounted by the Muscovy Company, the search for that elusive north-west passage, might prove lucrative—but Dee wanted to explore so much farther than that, to break these bounds of Earth and head for the unknown.

The study seemed suddenly to hem him in, the wide garden beyond no more than yet another cell. Dee stared into the glare of the sun and slowly, gradually, the thought began to emerge into the daylight like an uncoiling seed. The star-demon, with its four stark faces, had come to Dee twice, and twice only. But it had come nonetheless and this meant that it could come again. Dee had never sought to challenge heaven, but he knew that mechanical means were increasingly becoming more remote due to his lack of funds. The Family of Love, now firmly installed in London under Hendrick Niclaes' guidance, were already preparing for their voyage to the new world. If he could not go forth into the universe, Dee resolved, then he would have to bring the universe to him. He would summon the star-demon. And for that, he needed a scryer.

Tower of the Poisoners, Hathes

Alivet spent the next day in the alchematorium, working on a variety of substances. Toward the end of the afternoon Ghairen came to watch, perching on the stool and making light conversation with which Alivet found herself incapable of engaging. She could barely bring herself to look at him, consumed by frustration, fury, and fear that the previous night's wanderings were somehow inscribed across her face: a map of the landscape of guilt. At least he was present in the alchematorium; if she was to collect a sample of his blood, then it must be done here. She wondered whether saliva might be easier, if she could trap Ghairen into kissing her. The thought was both unnerving and enticing, and opened the prospect of further intimacies. Was that really what she wanted; to sleep with a professional poisoner who might be molesting his daughter? To her horror, Alivet realized that she did not know.

Blood, she decided, would be easier. She began to formulate a plan.

Ghairen seemed at first to suspect nothing of her night's activities. He treated her with the same unsettling solicitude that was the hallmark of his manner toward her, commenting upon the weather, the chemicals that she was using, the neatness of her preparations. But there was a nervous edge to his conversation that she found hard to define: was it simply stress, over the little progress they had made, or was there some deeper concern which she could not fathom? Mindful once more of the issues of conscience that might face a professional murderer, Alivet buried herself in her work and answered in monosyllables. Then it occurred to her that she did, in fact, have a question.

"Those books you gave me," she said, glancing up at last from the workbench. "Where do they come from?"

"You're not familiar with *The Days of the Delta*? I felt sure that it was a much loved classic on your world."

"Not the ones from Latent—the other books. *Jerusalem*, or whatever it's called. And the one with all the diagrams."

"Ah," Ghairen said, looking vaguely pleased with himself. "I felt sure that you'd find those of interest. They're from another of the human worlds. A place called Malkuth."

Alivet frowned. "Never heard of it." But then, she had never heard of anywhere until Ghairen had appeared.

"A strange place. Some people claim it to be of interest. Most, however, feel that it's a backward world, with little to offer the casual visitor."

"Have you been there? What's it like?"

"Oh, I've never been there, I'm afraid. The books might repay your attention, however."

Something about his tone caught Alivet's interest; he spoke with studied indifference, as though delivering some hint that lay beyond her current understanding. His eyes were fixed on a spot just above her head. Doubtless yet another game, thought Alivet with annoyance. As though she didn't have enough to fret over without reading books about a place she'd never heard of.

At that thought, she remembered her planned meeting with Iraguila. Her hands grew clammy with nerves and she wiped them hastily on a nearby rag. What if the blood trick didn't work? What if she couldn't get free of her room and Iraguila concluded that she was simply too scared to take the risk and lost patience? Alivet took a deep breath of acrid air and steered her thought away from this dangerous channel. Life was already too congested with "what ifs." She turned to face Ghairen.

"That's everything for now. I need to put the next batch of samples in the athanor."

"You might as well eat while you're waiting. I won't join you; I have an appointment."

"I just need to rinse these beakers." Alivet picked up one of the delicate glass containers, making covertly sure that it was still wet from its previous immersion. It slipped through her fingers and shattered on the floor. Ghairen swooped and Alivet knelt to help him.

"Be careful," Ghairen said, raising a finger to his mouth. His hand was smeared with dark blood. Relief clashed with an unexpected impulse to reach out and comfort him. Instead, Alivet fetched a cloth and retrieved the shattered fragments.

"Make sure you find all of them," Ghairen said, sharply. "I don't want splinters of glass lying around."

Alivet collected the fragments onto a piece of paper, but as she was straightening up she saw a gleam from beneath the workbench. It was a sliver of glass, stained with blood.

"Is that all?" Ghairen asked.

"Yes." Alivet glanced up. "Are there any pieces on the workbench?" Ghairen was gazing around him, searching for stray fragments. As he turned his head, her hand shot out and snatched up the bloodstained splinter.

"I can see none," he said.

"Good," Alivet remarked, standing up. "I think we found all of them." She tucked the splinter loosely into the palm of her hand as she threw the rest of the fragments away. "Sorry," she added. "That was clumsy."

"Happens to us all," Ghairen remarked, magnanimously.

To her relief, Ghairen vanished to his unnamed appointment and Alivet was once more left alone at the meal. She picked at her food, too fraught to eat more than a few mouthfuls of the pungent broth. When the shiffrey came in, gliding along the floor in its unnatural manner, Alivet told it to take the plates away, then went to her room.

Just as she reached the door, Ghairen came back along the hallway.

"Good evening," she said. He murmured something in response. His face was drawn and tense; she wondered just whom his appointment had been with. The mysterious Soret, his masters, or one of his two-too-many mistresses? Alivet wished him a hasty good night and ducked into her room.

She felt strange: light-headed and unreal, as though she were drifting through a dream. Was it simply anxiety, the prospect of once more breaking out of her room and skulking up the stairs to her host's poisonous fern-fronded garden, or was the toxin with which Ghairen had allegedly infected her beginning to work? What if he had misjudged the dose, or built in some fail-safe so that exertion or unwarranted anxiety would trigger the poison? She pictured herself falling down the dark stairwell, spinning to the mercuric waters of the canal and disappearing beneath them without a sound, or folding down among the dangerous ferns just as Celana would have fallen, had her father not caught her . . .

Alivet ran a hand over her face. The metal water-jug that stood on the table had been filled in her absence. She poured a glass and drank it slowly, beginning to feel a little better. Beyond the window, it was growing dark. To pass the time, Alivet picked up the book on symbolism and studied it, but it made no more sense than last time. The diagrams were baffling: the pillars of severity and mercy, what were they? She frowned over the lists of correspondences.

> *The creature of Yesod is the jackal, who waits at the gates of the moon . . . Its order of angels are the Kherubim, called the Strong. It grants the Vision of the Machinery of the Universe.*

It meant nothing to Alivet, but as she read farther, she saw a name that she recognized:

*And I have passed through the gates of the moon, and
looked upon Levanah . . .*

Levanah. The city in which Alivet had been born, in which
she lived. Alivet stared at the book. What was a "moon"?
And what were its gates? She wondered how old the book
might be.

Glancing up, she saw that it was now quite dark. The lamps
were going out across Ukesh. Alivet rose to her feet. Then she
inserted the splinter into the lock of her opulent cell, and after a nerve-racking moment, the door swung open.

Once again, the hallway was silent. Alivet thought of all
those locked doors and shivered. The lamp cast a pool of
light across the floor. Alivet slunk across the hall and up the
stairs to the poison garden. At first, she thought that Iraguila
Ust was not there, but then the governess crept forth.

"Alivet? I thought you weren't coming." Iraguila was not
wearing her lenses and her eyes were sparks in the dim light.
A prickle ran up the length of Alivet's spine.

"It is not too late. But we have to leave now," Iraguila
whispered.

"Where are we going?"

"To see someone who can help you." Iraguila turned, but
instead of moving back onto the landing as Alivet had anticipated, she glided out into the poison garden. "This way."

Alivet followed, taking care not to tread on anything
thorny. Iraguila led her to the far side of the garden, where a
round window looked out over the side of the tower.

"We go through here."

Alivet stood on tiptoe and craned her neck. She could see
one of the spines that ran up the side of the tower, like a row of
shining glass teeth. There was no sign of a ladder, or footholds.
She said to Iraguila Ust, "You're mad. We can't go out there!"

Iraguila smiled. "But we must, Alivet. There is no other
way. The apartment is sealed; there are wards on the elevators that would betray the presence of anyone traveling into
the lower depths. Don't be afraid. It can be done."

She put a gloved finger to her lips and licked the tip, just once. Then she rubbed her wet finger along the frame of the window. It opened with a hiss.

"Wait!" Alivet said, frantic.

"What is the matter now?"

"The air—Ghairen told me that I could not set foot outside. I thought the atmosphere was contaminated."

"Not so, it is just cold. Do you believe all that Ghairen tells you?"

"Of course not," Alivet said, feeling foolish.

Iraguila, moving with serpent swiftness despite her heavy skirts, hoisted herself upward and out of the window. Alivet hesitated. There was no further sign of Iraguila. It was as though she had vanished into an abyss. Alivet thought of Ghairen, infecting her with death and smiling as he did so. It was pure resentment that made her jump for the windowsill, cling on by her fingertips, and haul herself up.

A blast of cold air smacked her in the face, snatching her breath away. She glanced down and saw the sides of the tower sheering away to the base, far below. Alivet rocked backward and closed her eyes. Her fingers would not move from the sides of the sill.

"Alivet?" Iraguila asked, reprovingly. Alivet looked up. Iraguila stood on a narrow ledge, no more than a couple of feet wide. Her chin was tucked in against the arctic air, her gloved hands were folded primly in front of her. She looked like a governess waiting for a recalcitrant child to enter the schoolroom. "Come along, quickly. If you do not, the garden thermometer will register the change in temperature. The plants will start to wilt. Ghairen may be alerted."

Slowly, Alivet willed her fingers away from the sill. Iraguila reached down and with sudden alarming strength pulled her out onto the ledge.

"Be careful," she said, with what Alivet felt to be unnecessary caution. "The ledge is frosty."

Then she disappeared. Alivet gaped after her, before the realization dawned that Iraguila had not plummeted into the depths, but had simply stepped around the corner. Alivet forced herself to follow. The ledge was as slippery as a skating rink. She took tiny, mincing steps, packing the frost down beneath the heels of her boots as she did so and flattening her hands against the wall. She did not repeat the mistake of looking down. Eventually, her groping fingers encountered a sharp edge; she had reached the corner. Alivet inched around it and gasped.

The ledge widened to an immense shelf. She was standing at the very summit of the tower, looking out over a glittering expanse of icy roof. The roof raced away, falling perhaps fifty feet to a narrow chasm before it rose once more in a frozen wave above the tower. The architecture was inherently inhuman, all strange angles and veering plateaus, and seemingly at odds from the dark, organic interiors. Alivet wondered fleetingly what this said about the people of Hathes, but she was too glad to be away from the awful edge to care greatly.

"Come," Iraguila said again. She was standing at the far end of the shelf, holding a chain in one hand.

"What's that?" Alivet asked.

"We have to get to the other side of the roof. There's a way down from there." She tugged on the chain and Alivet saw that it was attached to a narrow curve of metal: lacy with frost like a frozen wave. "A roof-runner. They use them for maintenance."

As she drew closer, Alivet saw that the runner was attached to thin rails, which extended over the edge of the shelf and away over the roof. The chain presumably attached the runner to some form of support. Iraguila Ust settled herself at the front end of the runner. "Sit behind me," she instructed. "Hold on to me and do not let go. We will be moving swiftly."

Alivet sat gingerly on the narrow seat at the back of the runner and clasped Iraguila around the waist. She could feel the lower rim of Iraguila's corsets digging into her arms. The woman's body was hard and unyielding and Alivet felt as though she were embracing a large beetle.

"Hold tight," Iraguila said, and let go of the chain. It rattled into the runner, which shot forward like a cork from a bottle. Alivet opened her mouth to cry out and received a lungful of freezing air. They went over the side of the shelf and down, rocketing across the roof. If anyone was in the rooms beneath, Alivet reflected, they would think a crowd of folk must be stampeding about up here. But perhaps they were used to it—Iraguila had said that the device was used for maintenance. The icy slopes flew by. They were traveling upward again, propelled by the momentum of the runner. Iraguila slung the chain deftly forward and the runner slid to a halt. Alivet tumbled onto a second shelf and looked back. She could see the windows where the poison garden lay.

"How many times have you made this journey?" she asked Iraguila, curiously. "Do others use the same route?" The governess did not reply. She was marching along the shelf, her boot-heels clicking on the frozen metal. Alivet stumbled after her, wishing that she had managed to keep hold of her usual clothes. If Ghairen wanted to keep control over his womenfolk, he was certainly aided by fashion. She found Iraguila standing by a circular object, made of metal and resembling a large seedpod.

"This is how we shall reach the ground," Iraguila informed her, impatiently.

"What is it?"

"It is a maintenance device, like the runner. The shiffrey use them." She touched the pod and the door slid open to reveal a cavity with a sling seat. "You may take the seat. I will stand."

Alivet climbed into the pod. Iraguila followed, closing the door behind her. Alivet was so intent on working out the configuration of the seat, which was ridiculously small, that it was a moment before she could look through the round window set into the side of the pod and see where she was. She wished she hadn't. Looking up, she could see that the pod hung from what appeared to be a fragile thread, dangling from a girder arching out from the main tower. She was reminded of a pea hanging from a spider's web: the thread looked far too frail to support anything the size of the pod.

"Going down," Iraguila whispered. She touched a lever and braced herself against the wall of the pod, which described a graceful roll until it was lying on its side. Alivet, to her horror, found that she was staring down the side of the tower, all the way down to the ground. The pod shuddered once, and fell. Alivet—fists clenched, eyes squeezed grimly closed—felt her heart sail up to her throat and lodge there. She was not sure whether the roaring in her head was the sound of air rushing past the pod, or simply the panicking surge of her own blood.

And then there was silence, and stillness. The pod had stopped, rocking gently a few feet above the ground. Twisting her head, Alivet saw that Iraguila Ust, spread-eagled like a spider, was still clinging to the walls above her. Gently, the pod turned right side up. Iraguila activated the door mechanism and dropped three feet to the ground.

"Where now?" Alivet asked, extricating herself from the seat. Iraguila gave her a long, measured look, entirely ambiguous.

"You're outside," she said. "How do you find it?"

Alivet took a deep breath. "Cold."

"We will go," Iraguila said serenely, and turned away. The woman was almost as bad as Ghairen, Alivet thought, with her oblique conversation and seeming irrelevancies. Grudgingly, she followed Iraguila across the frosty space between the towers. Apart from a black line of cypress, the ground was barren; the stones rimed with ice. There was no sign of life. Perhaps it wasn't just the snow, she thought, perhaps the very ground beneath the towers was poisoned and little could grow there except the ominous spines of the trees.

The parc-verticale loomed on the horizon, so immense that it appeared curiously insubstantial. Alivet found it hard to judge the distance. Was it close, or far away? It seemed to shift whenever she looked at it. She was growing colder, too. Suddenly the oppressive warmth of Ghairen's apartment was almost appealing. She trudged on, rubbing her hands, and caught up with Iraguila.

"Are we going to walk all the way?"

"No," Iraguila said shortly. "We go through here."

They were nearing the base of one of the towers, to a point where the spines spiraled down into the snow like a gigantic corkscrew. Iraguila slipped between the spines. Alivet, following, saw that there was a crack in the wall through which the governess had gone. She thought again of insects.

Once inside, however, she found that they were in a cavernous, echoing space. A drift of cold air through the crack was swallowed by sudden warmth. The cavern was heated: from somewhere far below, she could hear the hum of machinery. Pillars marched off into the distance, seemingly made of plain polished stone, but when Alivet looked at them from the corner of her eye she saw faces springing out at her, lost among traceries of carved leaves. Her steps faltered, she felt as though she were falling.

"Iraguila?" she whispered. "What is this place?"

"It is a Memory Hall," Iraguila replied. She turned and looked back, a tiny figure between the towering figures. "Don't be afraid, Alivet. Just follow me. But I would advise you not to look at the pillars."

That, thought Alivet as she walked with her head down, was easier said than done. The pillars seemed to summon her attention. She had the impression that they were calling out to her in voices like distant bells, pulling her back into an unimaginable past. She remembered the ancient book and its diagrams. What did it mean, and why had it spoken of Levanah? As she thought of the name, it echoed through the hall like a sigh and something moved far above her. Alivet glanced up and saw her sister Inkirietta's face gazing down upon her.

"Inki!" she cried. Iraguila Ust spun around. Inki's features were struggling forth from the stone, as if it imprisoned her. Her mouth was open. Alivet stood beneath her, transfixed with horror.

"Who is this?" Iraguila Ust sounded annoyed. "It is not real, Alivet. Pay no attention."

"It's my sister," Alivet cried. "Inkirietta! Can you hear me?"

"Alivet, we must go. My contact won't wait all night and we're already late."

"But I can't leave her!" Alivet ran to the pillar and pressed her hands against it. It was as smooth as glass or ice, impossible to climb.

"I told you, Alivet—it isn't real. The pillars feast on the memories of the living. They are trees, not stone. They are parasitic, they will leech your dearest thoughts from your head."

"Then why aren't they affecting you?" Momentarily distracted, Alivet saw that Inki's face was fading, her expression becoming closed and bland and merging back into the pillar.

"I am protected," Iraguila said curtly. "I would have secured such protection for you, but there was not time. Now we must hurry."

Inki's face had now entirely gone. The pillar rippled, like water after a cast stone. Alivet shivered, but followed Iraguila through the Memory Hall. She could not help feeling that she had abandoned Inki yet again: left her to suffer, encased in stone. And if that was only a conjured memory, what was happening to the real Inkirietta? The thought of her sister's missing eye, that small scrunched hole in her flesh, haunted Alivet. *It should have been me*, she thought dismally. *If only the Lords of Night had taken me. At least I would have known that Aunt Elitta and Inki were safe*. But she had not been so fortunate—or so unlucky. Now she must deal with whatever the universe had given her, even if it took the form of Ghairen and his poisonous household.

When they reached the end of the Memory Hall, Alivet felt that she could breathe once more. The pillars lay behind her and a series of steps led down to a rippling canal where a barge was waiting.

"Get in," Iraguila said. Alivet did so. There was no sign of a pilot. Iraguila unchained the barge and they were carried away.

"You're going to a lot of trouble to help me," Alivet said dubiously.

"I told you—helping you will diminish Ghairen." Iraguila patted her hand, not unkindly.

"But you're living in his house. You're his daughter's tutor. You seem to come and go from his poison garden as you please. Surely you're ideally placed to exact whatever vengeance you wish? Why don't you just poison him?"

"It isn't that easy."

"Isn't it? I would." *I may yet*, Alivet thought, but it was best not to give voice to that particular notion.

"Ghairen is a Poison Master. The toxins found in his gardens are simples compared to what he is capable of distilling. He contains within himself the possibility of a thousand antidotes."

"Well, it doesn't have to be poison, does it? Can't you just stick a knife in his ribs?"

"I could not get close enough," Iraguila said, bitterly. "He is armored, you know, beneath his robes. His rooms are warded. Besides, he can withstand a high level of injury: his immune system has been reengineered by the alchemists of Hathes so that he is barely human."

This raised an entirely different question.

"Your people," Alivet said. "Are you human? Are you like us?"

"We are human enough. We all come from the same place."

"And where is that?" Alivet asked, her heart starting to pound.

"Who can say?" Iraguila replied blandly. "Somewhere lost in far history."

"But you have the Memory Hall. Can't you visit it and seek the place of our origin? We believe that it lies within the human form, locked somewhere in the unconscious mind." *If I were to undertake a Search in the Memory Hall*, Alivet thought, *what would it reveal?*

Iraguila smiled. "We have no interest in such questions. We are concerned only with the future, not with the past. We do not care where we are from—it's where we are going that matters."

"Then why is the Memory Hall there at all?"

"It grew, and it would take time and effort to eradicate. No one visits it. That is why we took this route. This is the oldest tower of Ukesh and it is not populated. I do not want us to be seen."

The barge was moving swiftly now, down a labyrinth of narrow streams. Gleaming liquid slapped against ruined wharves as they passed.

"The other reason why it is not yet the time to take my full revenge on Ghairen is because of Celana," Iraguila said abruptly, surprising Alivet. "Once she's free of the household, then I'll make my move."

"What about the other two girls?"

"They are in less danger. Ghairen will simply have them removed when the time is right—to other schooling," she added, seeing Alivet's look of horror. "But I am afraid for Celana. I'm afraid she will try to kill her father, and fail. If she does, he may decide to put her out of the way. If I can persuade him to send her to another tower—or elsewhere— then she will be safer and I can see to Ghairen."

"I thought he was intending to send her to study music?"

Iraguila glanced at her. "Is that what he's told you?"

"Isn't it true?"

Iraguila did not reply, but fell into a brooding silence. She certainly seemed sincere in her hatred of the Poison Master, and yet her reasoning did not seem to add up. If she was so concerned about Celana, why was she taking what must be a considerable risk in assisting Alivet herself, who was nothing more than an alien stranger? Perhaps she was hoping that Alivet might be persuaded to take Celana back to Latent Emanation. Alivet would be quite willing to do that, if it got the girl from out of her father's clutches, but first she herself would have to get free of Ghairen. And then there was the issue of the work she was undertaking for the Poison Master, which Iraguila seemed to feel was so dangerous.

Iraguila stood in the prow of the barge and threw the chain deftly around a mooring post. The barge drifted to a halt.

"Here is where we get off," Iraguila said. "We are now beneath the parc-verticale."

Alivet feared that they would have to enter another maintenance pod, but instead Iraguila led her to the base of a moving staircase.

"The parc is not protected," she explained over her shoulder. "It is a public place."

"But we're not supposed to be here in the middle of the night, is that right?"

"No. But people do come here—illicit lovers and the like. There are heavy penalties if one is caught, but it is often said that the parc is the only place on Hathes where one can be free for a time. As such," she added dryly, "it's popular."

The lower levels of the parc seemed old: water-worn stone was skeined with vines like some ancient ruin. Faces peered from the masonry, making Alivet jump, before she realized that they were nothing more than carvings. Even so, after her experience in the Memory Hall, she found herself reluctant to turn her back on them. There was a smell of rotten growth, a steamy greenness. Her apothecary's training held true: Alivet found herself matching this new odor to other possibilities, combining it with the memory of a dark musk, or the damp scents of Levanah at evening. She longed to be back in the public alchematorium at home, combining perfumes. What she could bring back from Hathes, she thought, if only she was allowed to live.

Something feather-soft brushed against her face. Alivet gasped and struck out, but the thing was gone. She saw it soaring into the green distance; it was a huge moth. She could see more of them now, clustering around the dim glow of the windows and hanging from the girders. Alivet thought of caterpillars and shuddered. The parc was becoming more ornate, more formal. Garlands of trumpet blossoms, as pale as silk and each with a long golden tongue, spat pollen into the welcoming air. Alivet saw rows of what might have been roses, but each stem was weighed down by great night-black blooms that she could not have held in her two cupped hands. The petals looked soft and dense, as though covered with fur. Orchids entwined around the girders.

Alivet sensed a wan sweetness drifting out across the air, conjured forth by darkness. A moth settled upon a flower: tongue sipped from tongue. The orchid shrank back into itself, rolling up into a tight parasol. The moth, dusted with pollen, sailed drunkenly away. Alivet was unable now to see the limits of the parc-verticale. Occasionally she caught a glimpse of crimson glass through the labyrinth of blooms, but now they were ascending into the higher levels and the jungle grew all around her. She heard voices, a sudden peal of laughter that was abruptly curtailed. Iraguila's back was stiffly eloquent in its disapproval. Flicking her fingers to Alivet in a cursory summons, she vanished beneath a bower of vines. Alivet followed.

Here, the parc was barely lit. It was hard to see the ground in front of her and Alivet had to take care not to stumble. Iraguila Ust moved with swift assuredness, as though she had passed this way many times before. Alivet followed her, brushing aside the scented, clinging vines and clambering over shattered masonry. How old was this place? she wondered. Was it even an original part of the parc-verticale, or had the parc grown up around it, replacing earlier structures? There was a smell of age and mold, like an unlocked room. Peering through the shadows, Alivet glimpsed a faint glow ahead.

"What's that?" she whispered.

"That is the alchemist's haunt," Iraguila replied. She reached out a hand and before Alivet could protest, hooked Alivet's fingers with her own in a tight, painful grip. "Do not speak, unless I tell you to. The alchemist is old, has little patience, and will not want to answer foolish questions."

"But will the alchemist be able to cure me?" Alivet asked, wondering if the alchemist might not simply be some self-termed shaman, and she the victim of Iraguila's superstitions. She knew so little about the woman, after all.

"She will cure you," Iraguila said firmly, as if there was no doubt about the matter. "But you will have to do exactly as she says." She drew aside a veil of vines that hung above a small, dark entrance.

"We are here," she called.

Alivet expected a crabbed old voice to answer, a querulous inquiry about who might be bothering the alchemist at this late hour. But there was no sound from within the doorway and Alivet suddenly smelled blood: a stale, rank odor. Paranoia at once overwhelmed her. It was Ghairen; he had divined her purpose and reached the alchemist before her, he would be waiting inside, still smiling . . . Then she saw that an eye was peering at her from inside the doorway.

"This is the human girl?" a whispering voice said.

"Yes." Iraguila's clasp of Alivet's hand tightened and Alivet winced. Iraguila was gripping her fingers with such force that she imagined the bones crumbling within, scattering into dust.

"Bring her here. I can't see her." The voice did not sound old, but it had a curiously sibilant, whistling quality that grated on the ear.

"Alivet, step forward," Iraguila commanded. Alivet did so, ducking beneath the lintel, which seemed designed for a child. Perhaps folk had been smaller when this level was built. But when she stood before the alchemist, crouching down to avoid knocking her head on the low ceiling, she realized why the place was so small. The alchemist was a shiffrey.

The shiffrey sat, bundled up in rags, upon a stool. Her face was a pointed mask, reminiscent of the muzzle of one of the little white foxes that haunted Latent's marshes like stray spirits. The round, mercurial eyes were opaque with cataract.

"Come here. I cannot see. I must smell you." She reached

out with a clawed hand. Iraguila gave Alivet an encouraging push. She knelt in front of the shiffrey, and it was clear now where the scent of old blood was coming from. The shiffrey's tattered robes seemed to have been soaked in the stuff. Used as she was to noxious aromas, Alivet had to try hard not to gag. The shiffrey's small hand, the fingers as gnarled and twisted as twigs, poked at her face. They entered her mouth and Alivet jerked her head away. The fingers tasted foul.

"Stay still!" the shiffrey hissed. She rubbed Alivet's gums, making her mouth flood with saliva. Alivet, choking, cried out. The shiffrey's fingers withdrew. She placed them in the small hole beneath the sharp muzzle. Alivet heard a sucking sound. Then the shiffrey was sniffing Alivet's face: a stiff fringe of whiskers rustling along its jaw. The whiskers scratched, drew blood.

"That's enough!" Alivet stood up and banged her head on the ceiling.

"Yes, that is enough," the shiffrey agreed, as though Alivet had been wholly cooperative. Iraguila touched Alivet's shoulder and gave her a warning shake, but Alivet thought she had obeyed the governess for too long already.

"Just tell me if you can help me," she snapped at the shiffrey. "And then let me be gone."

The shiffrey withdrew into her rags, hissing to herself. Alivet heard Iraguila give an exasperated sigh, but then the shiffrey said, "Yes, I know this thing, this substance with which you are infected. Mayjen, distilled from one of the oldest plants, the mayjen ivy that used to fill the world before humankind ever came to Hathes."

"Can you do anything about it?" Alivet demanded.

"I can sing to the spirit of the substance. I can coax it from your veins—but only if it wants to be free of you."

"What do you mean, if it wants to be free?" Alivet rounded on Iraguila Ust. "You said you were certain she could cure me!"

"I did not want you to entertain more doubts than you already did," Iraguila said flatly.

"The mayjen is an old ally, an older enemy. It may not wish to be free: you are its carrier, its eyes-upon-the-world," the shiffrey informed her.

Alivet was beginning to understand. "It is not just a poison, is it? It's a drug."

"That is so. Used correctly, it can bring true visions. Used unwisely, it can kill."

"It seems likely to kill me," Alivet said, "unless you can convince it to do otherwise."

"Then sit," the shiffrey said, indicating the ground before it. Alivet looked at Iraguila Ust, but the woman's face was expressionless. Alivet sat gingerly down in front of the shiffrey. The sharp fox's muzzle arrowed above her head. From this angle, it could have been a skull, with the lines etched along the bone, the eyes gliding within their sockets. There was something mechanical about the shiffrey, something unnatural, yet the creature had that sour, organic reek. Alivet looked down and saw a curling claw protruding from beneath the shiffrey's robes. She thought of a witch in a fairy tale, the devourer of small children.

"Close your eyes," the shiffrey commanded, "and bow your head."

Neither option was appealing. Alivet leaned forward, but kept her eyes half-open. She could still see the shiffrey's muzzle weaving above her.

The shiffrey began to hum beneath its breath, a high, eerie note. Against her will, Alivet's eyes snapped shut, as though a bright light had flashed to blind her. There was a ringing darkness inside her head; the sound made by the shiffrey seemed to fill it, reverberating against the sides of her skull. Her head felt as though it was about to burst.

Through a veil of pain, she imagined it splitting into a thousand petals and falling to the ground. She remembered the strange black flowers that grew in the heights of the parc-verticale, seemed to see faces within their depths, knew them for the minds of the captured. Her veins sang like taut wire. It was with a distant surprise that she realized she was hallucinating, deep beneath the pull of an unknown drug. Slowly, harshly, the shiffrey's consciousness began to invade her own and Alivet gasped. It was intrusive, with no regard for her feelings or her will. She tried to fight back, but the shiffrey was stronger, battering her way into Alivet's mind, ramming along human nerves. Alivet had a sudden impression of something utterly alien: emotions that she could not comprehend, thoughts and preoccupations that she was incapable of grasping.

And now there was something else, rising up inside her head, a shining presence. She glimpsed a dark double face above a serpent's body, gazing in opposite directions. This must be the mayjen, the spirit ally that embodied the drug. And now the voice of the shiffrey was addressing it, wheedling and obsequious, flattering the mayjen and beckoning it to a better place, a higher mind. The double faces of the mayjen frowned. It turned first one countenance, then another, and Alivet saw that it was both male and female.

It asked a question, the terms of which Alivet did not understand. The shiffrey replied, softly and glibly. Alivet retreated to the depths of her own head and watched them from a distance. She could see the inner presence of the shiffrey now, and it looked nothing like the creature's outward form. The shiffrey was slender and beautiful, with a fine-boned face and a fall of pale hair. Only the round silver eyes were the same, anomalously repellent in the perfect face. The shiffrey put its head on one side, cajoling and seductive. Slowly, cautiously, the mayjen began to glide toward it, scales rasping against the surface of Alivet's mind and causing ripples of pain to run through her.

"Come with me," the shiffrey said to the drug. "Your brothers and sisters await you; I can show you many things. Do not be afraid, do not be wary. I speak only truth."

Alivet would never have believed such an appeal, but the mayjen was the spirit of a drug and not a human being. It had different concerns. It glided forward, following the retreating figure of the shiffrey. This time, there was no harshness, no pain. The shiffrey left Alivet's consciousness so gently that it was a moment before she realized that she was gone.

"There," the shiffrey said. A twiglike hand was placed beneath Alivet's chin, lifting up her head. "Now you are healed. It is gone."

Alivet took a long, shaking breath. The splitting headache was receding, yet she felt no different. She said so.

"The mayjen is a subtle poison, a cautious drug. It prefers to have little effect until it strikes. That is why it is a good threat: it renders the victim still capable of action, yet it will kill them. But you need not worry now. I have subsumed it, drawn it from you."

"Where is it now?"

"It is within me. Once its spirit is gone, so is its efficacy. I can contain such spirits inside myself, safe and enclosed, until the time comes to send them forth, back to the plants from which they came."

"Thank you," Alivet said, shakily. The thought of being free from Ghairen's yoke was exhilarating, a relief so great that she almost crumpled against the shiffrey's side. "I'm very grateful."

"There is something else. Something you must know about your tormentor."

"About the mayjen? Or about Ghairen?"

"Ghairen. We have been watching him, through the good counsel of our friend Iraguila Ust." The shiffrey glanced up at the governess. Alivet thought she saw the shadow of a smile on the woman's face. "Ghairen has told you nothing less than the truth, Alivet."

"The truth?"

This was not what she had expected to hear, but the shiffrey continued, "He seeks to oust the Lords of Night, to drive them from Latent Emanation. He seeks to free your world of their sway, but he plans this so that Latent Emanation can come beneath the control of those who rule Hathes: the Soret. Ghairen has powerful allies, at the highest levels of Hathanassi society. You must stop him, if you are to save your world. Believe me, you are better off with the Lords of Night than Ghairen's masters. But if you can make the substance that Ghairen seeks, and use it wisely, then you can be rid of both."

"Why are you telling me this?" Alivet asked. "Why are you helping me? Surely you're taking a risk, if Ghairen is as powerful as you say."

"I am telling you so that you may avoid our fate. My people were glorious, once. We took the form in which you saw me, inside your mind. We were tall and beautiful and strong. We built cities: the ruins that you see around you now. We had technologies that rendered life gracious. Then the humans arrived, brought out of the darkness by those who wished us ill, and swept through us with poison and death. Our children were born crabbed and small, our cities were leveled. We were driven out to the barren hills or permitted to stay as domestic servants. This was over a thousand years ago. Since then, we have been as you see us now. But some of their kind have grown enlightened, and seek to help us. Iraguila is one such. We do not have the strength to save what remains of our people, but we may be able to help others. Thus I have told you what Ghairen is planning, in order that you and your world may not endure the same fate."

"What do you recommend that I do?"

"Find the substance for Ghairen. But when you have done so, you must take it and flee. Go back to your world through the portal. Administer the poison to the Lords of Night. Alert your people to the plans of the Poison Master. Make sure that he will be prevented from returning to your world. Then you will be free of both Ghairen and the Lords."

The shiffrey spoke earnestly. The stiff whiskers around her jaw trembled with agitation, and she wrapped her filthy rags more closely about herself. Alivet could not bring herself to be surprised. The news fit everything that she had suspected about Ghairen. Now that the curse of the poison was lifted, she could set about his downfall, but it was already beginning to occur to her that she might accomplish that of the Night Lords, too. What was that old expression, killing two birds with one stone?

Alivet scrambled to her feet. The headache caused by the shiffrey's invasion was retreating and she was eager to return and rest before morning. The thought crossed her mind that once they were away from the alchemist's domain, she might manage to evade Iraguila Ust and slip into the hinterlands of the city, but Iraguila and the shiffrey were her only allies, so unless she could find somewhere to hide, she could die from the cold. Besides, if Ghairen was as powerful as the alchemist said, then he would surely have her hunted down and she could rely on no support from anyone else. It might be better to remain in Ghairen's household, have him suspect nothing, and keep him under her own watchful eye. Alivet bowed to the shiffrey.

"Thank you," she breathed.

"Defeat Ghairen," the shiffrey replied, "and that will be all the repayment I ask."

Iraguila Ust tugged impatiently at Alivet's sleeve.

"We must go. Dawn is not far away; we must get back while it's still dark."

Alivet was quick to agree. As she bent to pass under the door of the ruin, she turned and looked back, wanting to say good-bye, but the shiffrey had already vanished into the shadows.

"Remember her," Iraguila said, softly. "She has done us a great favor."

Alivet, filled with new resolve, nodded. Iraguila led her back through the growth of the lower levels, but instead of returning to the heights, they passed out through a tall side door. Alivet was once more standing outside, under the cold night sky.

"We will return a different way," Iraguila informed her. "I do not wish to risk going back the way we came—it's too close to first light."

This time, she led Alivet to a dock running along the side

of the parc-verticale. There was a knot of people gathered on the dock and Alivet hung back.

"It's all right," Iraguila said quickly. "They are friends."

Each member of the group was hooded and robed, clad in sweeping dark-red garments. Before she could protest someone slipped a robe over Alivet's head and girdled her around with a mesh. It cut into her ribs, and it was, she reflected, a good thing that she had become accustomed to the corset. She could hardly see through the heavy folds of the hood.

"Where are we going?" she asked.

"Be quiet!" a voice hissed. It was not that of Iraguila Ust; Alivet could not even tell whether it was male or female. "We go to the cell, and then the temple."

This did not sound encouraging and Alivet was about to say so when she glanced around to see Iraguila's pale face floating in the depths of her hood.

"They will get us back into the poison clan's tower," Iraguila whispered. "Do as they say."

"But who are they?"

"They are Sanguinants," Iraguila said, as if this explained everything. "Our principal religious order: the Adorers of Blood. They are among those who travel to morning worship. This is why I do not wish to take the other route—there are too many people around at this hour."

"But we weren't all that long in the parc-verticale, surely?"

"You were under the will of the alchemist for three hours," Iraguila said, disapprovingly. "I grew quite cold and stiff waiting for the healing to be over. Now we must go. Do as the Sanguinants do. Say nothing."

Leaving Alivet to digest this startling information—for the healing had seemed to take only a short time—she strode away to where the Sanguinants were assembling. Alivet fell in behind them as they moved away: moving two by two, murmuring as they walked. Alivet kept her head down and tried to look pious. What did "Adorers of Blood" mean? Alivet decided that she would prefer not to know. There was a brief rocking motion as they stepped onto one of the barges and were whisked away. Alivet stood patiently, her hands folded in front of one another in the manner of the other Sanguinants.

Why were these people helping Iraguila Ust? Perhaps these were the people of conscience of whom the shiffrey alchemist had spoken. Maybe they objected to the injustices served upon others by Ghairen and his ilk. In any case, Alivet was disinclined to scorn their assistance. If Ghairen was planning to wrest her world from the Lords, she needed all the help she could muster.

The journey was brief. Soon, Alivet looked up to see that they were passing beneath a great metal portal, etched against the sky. Liquid poured from either side, forming cascades that hissed and frothed into the canal. The barge became unstable and rocked, but the Sanguinants remained rigidly upright. By dint of moving from one foot to another, Alivet managed to retain her balance, but her companion reached out a hand and helped to steady her. Alivet was grateful for this small show of sympathy. The wharves between which the barge was gliding were massive, carved from gleaming red stone. Rows of steps led up toward a series of platforms and Alivet saw that a group of several dozen people were gathered along the higher levels. The barge rocked to a halt.

Still moving two by two, the Sanguinants marched onto the wharf and up the steps, but before they had reached the crowd on the higher levels, a great booming note rang out across the city. Alivet looked up and in the growing light saw a figure with a curling horn. Once more the note sounded. The Sanguinants climbed higher, moving swiftly. Alivet heard their feet pattering like small hooves against the stone steps. As they reached the first platform, the horn roared out and Alivet's neighbor seized her by the arm and turned her around. Moving as one, the Sanguinants poured over the lip of the platform toward the tower. Alivet went with them, her eyes fixed firmly on her feet.

The crowd seemed expectant, even anxious. They shuffled closer toward the temple gate. A robed figure, whom Alivet realized to be Iraguila, seized her arm and propelled her forward. Angrily, Alivet pulled free. A wind arose, driving through the gate and across the platform. The crowd gave a strange, small cry. The wind smelled of frost and as it touched Alivet she raised her arms protectively against her face. When she lowered them, hoping no one had seen, the sleeves of her robes were white. Her face felt pinched. She tasted the snap of a tiny icicle between her teeth.

Then the wind died and the platform was as before. The Sanguinants gave a collective sigh, a mournful sound in the half light. Turning, Alivet saw a spark on the far horizon, between the towers. The sun was rolling over the edge of the world. Light flashed out to strike an answering note from the high gates above them, turning them red as blood.

"What was that?" she whispered in Iraguila's ear.

"The Sanguinants disdain the sun. Every morning, they pray that it will not rise."

Now that the sun was coming up, flooding the city of Ukesh with radiance, the Sanguinants were hurrying away as if they could not bear to be touched by the light. Alivet and Iraguila went with them, swept through another great gate and into a labyrinth of red corridors. The Sanguinants, in their crimson robes, reminded her of corpuscles, sailing down the veins of some vast organism. And what did that make her, the unwilling intruder? Was she a virus, a microbe come to infect the world of Hathes and heal it of its sickness? Or would she simply be swallowed by that societal entity: consumed and neutralized by a poison of Ghairen's devising?

It occurred to her that he might have infected her with something other than the mayjen poison, some other toxin lurking within her bloodstream ready to prey on her mind and strike her down. But surely the shiffrey alchemist would have said if that had been the case? After all, if she were to be deployed as the instrument of the shiffrey's vengeance, then they would want to keep her alive. But Alivet did not like the thought of being so used, even in such a noble cause. The shock of the shiffrey's revelation of the woes committed against them by humans was starting to wear off. If Iraguila thought that she could control Alivet, now that the debt of healing was repaid, then she would have to learn differently. Whatever the wrongs suffered by the shiffrey—and they were surely terrible—Alivet's main consideration had to be Latent Emanation and her sister.

What about Celana? her conscience reminded her. Alivet had come to feel sympathy for the girl, an unsought obligation that nagged at her like a toothache. Perhaps there would be something she could do for Celana, too.

"Here!" Iraguila said, in Alivet's ear. She pulled Alivet to one side. The corpuscular stream of Sanguinants flowed around them and was gone, leaving only three people in their wake.

"This is how we shall return to the Poisoners' Tower," Iraguila explained. "My friends have been summoned to see a resident: this is why we had to visit the alchemist last night, to fit in with their appointment. From the resident's quarters, the stairs lead to Ghairen's own apartment."

"Why have they been summoned?" Alivet asked.

"I do not know," Iraguila replied, evasively. Alivet was certain that this was untrue, but she did not want to argue with the governess. Perhaps to allay any suspicions Alivet might be entertaining, Iraguila explained.

"The Sanguinants see themselves as the blood that powers the city. They undertake a constant round of prayer and worship, from sunrise to sunset and then on to midnight, to keep the spiritual heart of the city beating. They also act as the city's enforcers, to purge social toxins from the bloodstream of Ukesh. The poison clans supply the means by which they do so."

"Ghairen is assisting the local assassins, then?"

"You might put it like that. But they are not here to see Ghairen. They are visiting another Master."

Alivet pulled the robe more closely over her hair, determined to keep her face out of the sight of any monitors. The

Sanguinants entered one of the elevators. Alivet cast covert glances in their direction as the elevator soared upward. One of them spoke in a rasping voice:

"Does this Master understand the situation, Raclaud?"

"Vareyn, I believe that he does. And if it should prove that he does not, then he must be made to understand."

The second voice was fat with anticipation: a gloating beneath the quiet words. Alivet decided that this was as close as she ever wanted to get to the Sanguinants. She was relieved when the elevator slowed to a halt and the two men stepped out into an opulent entrance hall. Iraguila, following, pulled Alivet behind a curtain.

"Keep quiet!"

Alivet did not need to be told. She heard a low mumble of voices, a brief conversation, and then footsteps receding down the hall. Iraguila took her through a nearby door and then they were out into the stairwell. Alivet took care to count the number of flights: the Sanguinants' appointment was seven flights below Ghairen's apartment. What that might say about the relative social status of the two, Alivet could not say.

Alivet held her breath as they stepped into Ghairen's hallway, but the place was silent, with an early-morning feel.

"Do you have your key?"

Alivet held out the bloodied splinter of glass. Iraguila inserted it into the lock.

"Here," she said, handing Alivet a twist of paper. "Take this if you feel tired today. Ghairen must suspect nothing."

"What is it?" Alivet asked.

"Quickly, now," was all that Iraguila would say. A moment later, Alivet was back in her bedroom, staring out over the red dawn light of Ukesh as though nothing had happened.

chapter III

TOWER OF THE POISONERS, HATHES

Alivet, unhooking the numerous fastenings of her garments in order to bathe, found that her fingers were trembling. She could not stop yawning: great gaping yawns that felt as though her face was splitting in half. This was a fine way to start a working day. Ghairen would surely notice her fatigue, especially if she fell asleep with her head among the crucibles.

Dressed in her shift, she sat down on the bed and examined the paper twist that Iraguila had given her. Unwrapping it, she found that it contained a pale powder. Experimentally, she licked her finger, then caught up a few grains and rubbed them over her gums. After a moment, her mouth grew numb. The powder was a stimulant, then, probably some kind of amphetamine like the powder extracted from the leaves of the hermetic plants, to give swiftness and speed of thought. They also made your teeth chatter for hours at a time.

Despite her fatigue, Alivet frowned. She did not approve of such drugs. There was no spiritual element to them; they were purely a crutch to help folk get through the day, and that was a good way to develop an addiction. If Ghairen asked, she would simply say that she had not slept and reproach him for giving her sufficient cause for insomnia. She wrapped the twist of paper and put it in a drawer by the bed. Then she bathed, dressed once more in her confining clothes, and left the room.

To her relief Ghairen was not present at breakfast. The only other occupants of the dining room were the shiffrey servant and Celana. Alivet regarded her with interest. The girl wore her usual sullen expression, but there was a glaze of tiredness in her eyes. Alivet entirely sympathized with that, but it did raise the question of why Celana was so weary this early in the morning. Maybe she'd been having night escapades of her own. Alivet suppressed a wry smile. No one in Ghairen's household seemed able to keep to their beds. There was a more sinister explanation, however, which Alivet did not feel up to contemplating.

"Good morning, Celana," she said, primly.

Celana glanced at her, but did not reply. Alivet found herself startled at the content of that glance. It contained a kind of wary desperation, as if the girl was longing to reach out, yet did not know how.

"Are you all right?" Alivet asked, in an undertone.

"Celana is a little tired this morning, aren't you, my dear?" Ghairen appeared in the doorway and a dozen curses ran through Alivet's mind. "She didn't sleep well last night."

At least he had given her an opening. Alivet put her head in her hands and rubbed her eyes.

"Neither did I."

"Indeed?" Ghairen's eyes widened. "And why was that?"

"Nightmares," Alivet said sourly. "Of death."

"We *are* a morbid little gathering this morning. Perhaps I should give you something this evening to help you sleep. We can't have you going all brooding on us, now can we?"

Ghairen was unusually arch today, Alivet reflected. She forced herself to smile.

"I'm sure it was nothing," she said. "I'll be fine tonight. It's just that I may be a little slow in our work."

"Don't be too slow," Ghairen said, and the avuncular benevolence was entirely absent now. "After all, we don't have a great deal of time."

"I'm well aware of that."

"May I be excused from my lessons today?" Celana asked abruptly.

"You may not. You must learn discipline, Celana. There will doubtless be times in your life when you will be hungry, thirsty, tired, or ill, and you can let none of these things stand in the way of your work. It is not an easy lesson, but best that you learn it now while you are still young. Consider Alivet, who has come here under the most difficult circumstances and yet is in the alchematorium every day, working with a will. Is that not so, Alivet?"

"I do what I have to do," Alivet said, "nothing more."

"As Celana must learn. Have you finished your breakfast? Then go to your governess. And tell her that I should like to see her later, before lunch. I need to discuss a matter with her."

When she heard this, Alivet's skin started to prickle. It suddenly seemed wholly possible that Ghairen knew of the previous night's adventures, and would take Iraguila to task for it. If that was the case, then she could not permit Iraguila to take sole responsibility. Her thoughts were racing and she forced herself to put a halt to her own paranoia. Wait and see. Perhaps it was something else entirely that Ghairen wanted to discuss with Iraguila, and it was only her own fears that were leading her to the worst possible conclusion. Yet she felt that everything Ghairen said to one person was aimed at another, that there were so many layers and complexities to his speech that one looked for the meaning behind the words and not the ostensible intent. She pushed her empty plate away and stood up.

"Let's get to work, then," she said.

Light-headed though she was from lack of sleep, the processes of the morning's preparations were soothing and familiar. Alivet went mechanically through her work, adding element upon element to the crucible, building up blocks of alchemical materials. A touch of flame here, the cooling water there, and then the transfer to the pelican vessel for the next stage. At least she had work in which to lose herself and was not merely a prisoner held immobile in a cell. That must be true torture, Alivet thought: to sit day after day with only the meaningless repetition of meals to break the monotony. Whereas in her present situation, the end was coming toward her at speed, whether it was life or death. And that death had at least been rendered more distant by the alchemist's intervention. The knowledge that she was no longer facing the threat of a toxic demise was an enormous weight off her mind.

Alivet did not feel that she was a coward. The thought of cringing away from death did not appeal to her: she had come too close to the world beyond during the course of the Searches not to know how best to suppress her fear. No, empty captivity, never knowing when the end might come, would be worse. She wondered whether this was how Inki felt, day after day in the palace of the Lords, yet presumably with work to keep her busy and tasks to accomplish.

Had Inki managed to carve out some kind of meaningful life for herself, despite the immense constraints imposed upon her? Alivet hoped that this was so, but the memory of her sister's empty eye socket continued to preoccupy her. And what about her aunt Elitta? With a surge of horror, Alivet realized that she had hardly given her aunt a thought since she had come into the clutches of the Poison Master. Had the anube passed on Alivet's message? Was Elitta now in the relative safety of the fens, or languishing in an Unpriest's cell?

As if he had read her mind, Ghairen put a hand on Alivet's shoulder as she bent over the smaller crucibles.

"You look exhausted, Alivet. Tell me about these nightmares. There might be a remedy for them."

"I told you," Alivet said. "I dreamed of death." And then something—perhaps no more than the momentum of her previous thoughts—compelled her to add, "And I dreamed of my sister."

"What did you dream?" Ghairen's voice was low, almost hypnotic.

"I saw her in the palace of the Lords of Night—she was as I glimpsed her a few days ago. Her eye was missing."

"I see. Well, that is a hallmark of those who have been touched by the Lords."

Alivet swung to face him. "I know that. And some of the Enbonded, once freed, lose their minds, or the power of speech. Many of them have only one eye. They are the lucky ones, the ones who make it out of Enbondment. But what does it mean? What happens to their eyes? Do you know? There is a rumor that the Lords make Unpriests of them and that is why they are allowed to leave servitude."

Ghairen looked genuinely troubled. "I have theories and hunches, not facts. To you, the Lords appear to be creatures of immense whimsicality, performing random acts for the sake of simple amusement. I have reason to believe that this is not the case—though it is possibly true of the Unpriests." He grimaced. "I don't like such people. They use their power irresponsibly, for their own ends."

Coming from someone who was allegedly planning to take over her world, Alivet found this a bit much, but of course she could not say so. She turned angrily back to the foaming crucible.

"You say that the Lords are not whimsical. What are they, then?"

"I told you before. They are corrupt. I think that there were once good reasons for everything that they do—for the Enbonding, for the restrictions imposed upon the population, even for the blinding. But now those reasons have atrophied into nothing more than custom and control."

"But what could the reasons possibly have been? Why should one race assume control over another for any reason other than power and enslavement?" Might as well hear how Ghairen would justify himself, Alivet thought.

"To assist them, perhaps? At least in the beginning. A form of benign dictatorship—or maybe not dictatorship at all but a genuine effort to help."

"Well, they've been going about it in a strange manner, then," Alivet snapped.

Ghairen smiled. "I told you—they have become corrupt."

"And so must be challenged?"

"And so must be changed, or sent elsewhere."

"Changed how?"

But Ghairen did not reply.

"Say we *could* send them somewhere else—back to where they come from. What then?" Alivet asked. She could not bring herself to look him directly in the eye, afraid that he would read her knowledge of his intentions. Instead, she bent low over the workbench to hide her face.

"Then your people will be free to follow whatever path they think best," Ghairen replied, smoothly. "How are you getting on with those preparations?"

"Well enough. The structure is holding. This combination of elements seems more stable than the last."

"I'm pleased to hear it. I will stop pestering you with chatter, then, and get on with my own work."

He turned to go. Alivet waited until he was out of the alchematorium, then went to sit down on the workbench. Fatigue hit her like a sudden blow. She would not sleep, she would only close her eyes for a moment . . .

She awoke to discover that the crucible had boiled dry. An acrid smoke was curling about the ceiling of the alchematorium and her eyes were red and watering. A thick residue remained, coating the crucible like rust. Alivet rose, feeling stiff and sluggish. She wondered what the time might be, but though she went to the window and drew aside the blind, the chilly light seemed unchanged. Sighing, Alivet picked up the crucible and examined the residue. It crumbled against the glass in a soft shower. It resembled dried blood, glittering with golden flecks.

The lessons that Alivet had been taught early on in her training, about wasting materials, and also about the role of serendipity in scientific investigation, returned to her now.

Carefully, she scraped the residue from the crucible and placed it in the Philosopher's Egg. Later, when she had finished the rest of the testing, she would draw up a schematic for the analysis of the residue. Chances were that it would prove to be of limited interest, but one never knew.

As she was finishing the last of the tests, the door of the alchematorium opened and Ghairen reappeared.

"Alivet? You're working very hard. I expected you at lunch—you must be hungry as well as tired."

Alivet forbore to remind him that she was locked in the alchematorium, and it depended on Ghairen himself as to what time she was summoned to her meals. She felt sure that he had indeed returned to the alchematorium and found her sleeping. Yet the red gaze was as guileless as ever.

"Thank you for your concern," she said, politely. Was that a flicker of amusement in his face? "Yes, I find that I am hungry. Perhaps I might take my lunch a little late?"

"Actually, it's already dinnertime."

"I seem to have let my work absorb me," Alivet remarked.

"Commendably diligent. Do you have much left to do?"

"No." It wasn't true: she had a world of tasks to finish and they were running out of time, but she felt too weary to proceed and if she carried out any more work today, she was bound to make mistakes.

Ghairen held the door open for her to leave. As she passed through he said, "Alivet? I am well aware of scientific methodology. There is a role for dreams within the practice."

Was he telling her that he had caught her sleeping and was prepared to forgive her for it? Well, she would take whatever ground he was prepared to concede.

"Dreams," said Alivet, pointedly, "are very important." She did not wait to see him smile.

chapter IV

Tower of the Poisoners, Hathes

Pleading fatigue once more, Alivet asked to be served her dinner in her room and Ghairen agreed. He seemed mildly disappointed, but Alivet dismissed this. He could hardly be longing for her company, after all. Now that the dullness brought on by her afternoon sleep had worn off, Alivet was making plans. As soon as the household was quiet, she intended to go exploring again. But the chance did not come.

She was washing her face in the basin when there was a soft knock at the door.

"Who is it?"

"It's me," Ghairen's voice said. The door opened slowly.

"Ghairen? What do you want?"

"Are you very tired?"

She hesitated a moment too long for conviction. "I'm all right."

"I realize that locking you into your room every night is hardly the act of a thoughtful host. I wondered whether you might like to join me for a drink."

"Here?"

"In my rooms."

It wasn't so much the prospect of a late-night drinking

session with Ghairen that appealed as it was the thought of seeing his rooms and perhaps gaining some further clue as to what was really going on. And if he believed her still to be under the influence of the mayjen toxin, he was unlikely to try to poison her again.

"Very well," Alivet said.

His eyes widened; she got the impression that he had been expecting her to decline. "Then come through," he said, gesturing toward the door.

Alivet, burning with curiosity, followed him across the hall. Ghairen unlocked the door with a small black device like a pin, which he then placed into a little case. It vanished into his pocket. Alivet took careful note as she stepped through the door. A faint light came from a source that she could not immediately identify. It took a moment before she realized that it was coming from the plants that lined one wall. They were ferns, and their fronds glowed with a soft inner radiance. Their light was sufficient to show her that the room was large, with bookcases along the opposite wall. The walls themselves were paneled, creating an impression of gloom. In the center of the room stood a divan, covered in black velvet. Before it was a table, on which lay a collection of glass globes. Soft rugs lay beneath Alivet's feet. This room was like the rest of the apartment: luxurious yet somber. In the far corner, close to a large and ornamental desk, was another door, and this was firmly shut.

Alivet went over to the table to look at the globes. Each one was exquisite, containing all manner of glass creatures. Anemones and sea horses were captured in aquamarine light; salamanders hissed from glass fire and a tiny serpent coiled between the fronds of a vitrified fern. When Alivet looked more closely, however, she saw that the creatures were real. She took a step back. There was something terrible about the glass globes; their occupants frozen at the moment of death.

"They belonged to Arylde," Ghairen murmured, lighting a lamp. "Come and sit down."

Alivet perched primly on the edge of the divan.

"Would you like some wine?"

Alivet hesitated. Caution told her to decline: it was all very well to drink at dinner, but here in this more intimate setting, the prospect made her wary. But it had been a long, grimy day and she heard herself say, "Thank you."

Ghairen poured a glass for her and one for himself.

"It's a reasonable vintage, I think." He held it up to the light; it was ruby golden in the glass.

"I'm not a connoisseur."

He smiled at her. "Neither am I."

Cautiously, Alivet sipped it. The wine tasted smoky and sweet, not particularly strong. But she knew from painful experience that appearances could be deceptive.

"How's Celana today?" she asked.

"As well as ever."

"And your other daughters?"

"Ryma is with her mother. Ladeiné has been studying."

Alivet despised herself for asking the next question.

"Do their mothers visit often?"

"No," Ghairen said, with a measured look. "I rarely see them. Both alliances were political. Ryma's mother is the daughter of a prominent member of the Soret. Ladeiné is the child of an heiress. Hathanassi law encourages brief contract marriages. My youngest daughters are the product of such."

"And your first wife?"

"I married her for love." Ghairen poured more wine, leaned back upon the divan. "Arylde Galu. She was one of the beauties of her generation." He fell silent.

"You must miss her," Alivet said inadequately.

His face was bleak. "Life is certainly quieter."

"And you never found out who poisoned her?"

"No. And what about you, Alivet? Do you leave a lover behind in Levanah?" He spoke with care, and it was only then that she realized he was already a little drunk.

"I don't have a lover. A few casual affairs, nothing more. My life has revolved around my work."

"Do you find it rewarding? Or merely necessary?"

"Both. But it's meant that I've had little time for love."

"What about Genever Thant?"

"He was my employer, not my lover. I hardly think I could have appealed to him."

Ghairen smiled again, with more than a shade of bitterness. "Don't underestimate the power young women can have over middle-aged men."

"I've always thought it was the other way round."

"Political power, yes. Economic, certainly. Sexual power? That's where shadows lie. That's where the tables can be turned."

He spoke idly, but she knew he was looking in her direction. She could feel his gaze boring into her. She took a quick sip of wine and choked.

"Are you all right?" Ghairen edged next to her and patted her on the back. The coughing subsided. Ghairen did not move away. "I get the impression you're not used to wine. Well, wiser to stick to drugs. As the old saying goes, 'Alcohol provokes fits of madness; opium provokes fits of wisdom.'"

"Maybe so," Alivet said sourly. "But they're still fits." She glanced at him. The mask was well in place once more: amusement, challenge, sexual confidence. He reached out and touched the back of his hand to her face. Then he said, very softly, "Come here."

"Ghairen, I don't think—" Her voice faltered. *That* hardly sounded convincing. Only days ago she had been prepared to strike Hilliet Kightly where it hurt for just such a proposal. Kightly had been repulsive, but essentially harmless. Unfortunately, Ghairen invoked a different set of parameters. He slid to his knees beside her and took her hands. Alivet froze.

"I told you about power," he murmured into her ear. "Which of us has power over the other? Do you want to find out?"

"I think it's already obvious," Alivet said. To her dismay her voice sounded high, and a little frantic. His breath was warm on her neck. Lightly, his fingers traced her hands.

"What if I were to tell you that I find it hard to breathe in your presence? That I can't stop looking at you? That all I can think about is touching you?" Very gently, he began to kiss her throat.

He was playing games again, she thought, staring grimly over Ghairen's shoulder, but it had become very difficult to think. And then he said, "Alivet. Look at me." She looked into his face and the mask was gone. She saw uncertainty, and longing, and need.

"Ari?"

Ghairen took her face in his hands and kissed her mouth. His eyes fluttered closed. He tasted of wine. She forgot about poison, about Celana. She felt as though she'd been ignited. He touched her breasts and gasped. Alivet pulled him back onto the divan, her fingers tangled in his silky hair. Through the roaring in her head, however, she did not forget the key in Ghairen's pocket. She slipped her hand into his robes and around his waist. Iraguila had told her that he wore armor: if this was so, he was not wearing it now. Her hand grazed a soft under-robe, then cool skin. Finally she found the pocket, arching her hips underneath him in a mixture of distraction and genuine response. Ghairen groaned. The key was in her hand, but then his full weight was on her and a determined hand was already pushing aside her skirts. Desire was transformed into sudden panic.

"No, stop, stop it!"

He was immediately still. He gave her a single, searching glance and sat up, breathing hard. "Alivet, I'm sorry. I thought—never mind. I didn't mean to push you so fast." His expression was rueful.

Alivet stood up shakily. The room was spinning and she put out a hand to steady herself. She was not sure if it was the wine, or something in that wine, or just Ghairen.

"It isn't that I don't want..."

"My timing could have been better," he murmured.

"I think I should go back to bed. Alone."

After a moment, Ghairen nodded. She could still read the need in his eyes. He rubbed his hands over his face. "I'll see you tomorrow."

chapter V

TOWER OF THE POISONERS, HATHES

A little later, as she inserted Ghairen's key into the lock of her bedroom door, Alivet thought: *All my weapons are small ones.* But even small weapons could be useful, if used in the right way. If her foray was successful and she did not get caught, she would undertake some further exploration of the apartment. All those locked doors, sealed secrets...

She stole quietly across the hallway and paused before Ghairen's door. If he caught her sidling into his room, at least she had an excuse: she would stammer apologies for her earlier flight, tell him she had stolen the key just in case...

And would you also give him what he wants? a voice asked inside her mind. The trouble was, Alivet thought, it wasn't only Ghairen's needs that were preoccupying her. The memory of him was so strong that he might as well have been standing beside her. She took a breath and opened the door.

The room was quiet and empty. The sight of the divan brought memories back with a rush. Trying to ignore them, Alivet stole across to the far side, and inserted the key into the lock of the next door. She peered through. This room was much smaller and the walls were also paneled. A bed stood on the far side of the room: Ghairen lay within it, sprawled on his back amid a sea of dark robes. One arm was flung upward and his face was turned toward her. In sleep, he looked solemn, even sad. She had to resist the urge to slide into bed beside him. *Think of poison*, the little inner voice suggested. *Think of murder.* Reluctantly, Alivet turned away.

The room itself was strangely austere. Alivet, if she had imagined Ghairen's bedroom at all, had pictured decadence, but this room was spare in its decoration. The only ornament was a figure standing in one corner: a carving the height of a man. As Alivet's eyes adjusted to the light she saw that it had four faces, looking out to every direction. It was very similar to the statue that they had seen beneath the Night Palace and Alivet's skin crawled. There were too many connections between Ghairen and the Lords of Night for comfort; the pull of desire became somewhat less.

The face turned to the room was male, but at one side Alivet could see a woman's flowing hair. It was impossible to say what the other faces might be: they lay in shadow, or behind the figure. Its arms were raised before it, the hands placed together. It was made of a glossy black stone and the dim light of the ferns touched gleaming specks within the statue, as if it contained mica. Now that she could see more clearly, Alivet noticed that the air around Ghairen's bed was also shimmering, like looking through a heat haze. Well, it stood to reason that he had some additional form of protection.

She stepped softly back through the bedroom door and into the main room. The desk was of the sort that rolled open. Very carefully, Alivet drew it down, grateful that she had had the foresight to wear her gloves. She did not like the prospect of leaving fingerprints over the surface of the desk, and who knew what traps Ghairen might have laid.

The desk was full of papers. Alivet leafed through them with interest, noting diagrams and alchemical formulas. It seemed that these were Ghairen's working notes. Afraid that they would rustle, she did not remove them from the desk, but reached to the back of the compartment, feeling for alchemical phials. She found nothing. So she began to examine the documents. She could just about see by the light of the ferns, but soon her eyes began to feel strained and the papers meant nothing to her. Just a few more moments...

At the very bottom of the desk lay a small, folded piece of paper. Alivet pulled it out and opened it up. It was yet another diagram: a sequence of oblongs and lines. As she was puzzling over this, there was a sound from the bedroom. Hastily, Alivet stuffed the paper into her pocket and closed the desk. There were footsteps coming across the bedroom floor, soft and purposeful. Alivet fled across the room, her flying feet muffled by the rugs. As she twitched the door open, she looked back, half hoping to see him standing there.

But it was Celana. She stood at the entrance to her father's bedroom, dressed in a night shift. She was staring directly at Alivet, who froze. Celana's mouth turned down, but she made no sound. Turning, she drifted back into the shadows like a ghost and the spell was broken. Alivet stumbled from Ghairen's rooms and into the hallway, where she closed the forbidden door as quietly as she could behind her.

Back in her own bedroom, she waited for a few minutes, but the hallway remained silent. She looked down at the key in her hand. Might as well use it now that she had it, though the thought of simply crawling into bed and going to sleep was most alluring. Alivet's fingers closed upon the key. One more little foray, she decided. This time, she would find out what lay behind the locked door on the other side of the hallway. Once more, Alivet ventured forth.

At first, the key seemed stiff in the lock, but then the door swung open. Alivet found herself in a narrow, dark passage. It smelled old: ancient material, musty with dust. The walls were paneled with metal; as she stepped through, she heard a faint humming and the walls began to glow. There was just enough light by which to see. Alivet hastened onward. The passage twisted and turned, a small maze in the heart of the Poisoners' Tower. She traversed a narrow flight of steps, up, and then down again. At last, afraid that she might lose her bearings, Alivet came upon two more doors: set opposite to one another, knee-high in the wall.

Arylde Galu. She was one of the beauties of her generation. I married her for love.

The room in which Ghairen slept had been so severe, with no trace of feminine comforts. Had Arylde slept there, too, or had she occupied her own room? Alivet thought of a shrine, whispering with echoes; of the glass globes. She thrust the key into the lock of the left-hand door and opened it.

Something loomed out of the darkness, tentacles coiling. Alivet stumbled back with a stifled cry. The thing sprang after her. She pushed it away. It fell into the cupboard and was still. After a moment, shaking, Alivet discerned the outlines of a cleaning device: the bag, the tubes, the brass wheels. She slammed the cupboard shut. Perhaps the second door would be more rewarding.

Again, the lock was stiff and the door stuck. No longer caring about long-dead wives, or the threat of discovery, Alivet gave it a single hard shove. It opened. She looked through, into her own room, seen from the other side. The passage led right through the apartment, presumably past the alchematorium above, then down again. The only mysterious woman in Ghairen's present world was, it seemed, herself.

ELABORATION

Sun, Moon, Mars, Mercury, Jupiter, Venus, Saturn, Trine, Sextile, Dragon's Head, Dragon's Tail: I charge you to guard this house from all spirits whatever, and guard it from all disorders, and from anything being taken wrongly, and give this family good health and wealth.

— Inscription on Elizabethan house in Burnley

Chapter I

Dee had spent the morning of that fateful day in conversation with a Mr. Clerkson, a man who served as an agent for scryers and mediums. Over the past few weeks, Clerkson had paraded a procession of likely fellows before Dee: roving scholars and runagates, chapmen and cozenors. After receiving the fifth such person, stinking and shifty, Dee had taken the agent aside.

"Look, it cannot be borne, this motley collection of piss-prophets and Kit Callots that you keep bringing before me. My wife has a tongue like a veritable shrew, but for once she has been complaining with good reason."

"They are all practiced men," protested Clerkson.

"Yes, but practiced in what? What good is a scrying-man to me if he can stammer no more than 'I see a dark man upon the road when the moon is new' or 'There is a devil in the wainscoting'? I need firm answers and a knowledge of the lore behind them. Besides, I do not want to have to lock up the silver every time such a person comes to the door."

"Your reasoning is sound," the agent admitted, with very poor grace.

"Then find me a man who knows what he is about."

"I shall do my best."

That morning, Clerkson had appeared at the gate with an expression of moon-faced smugness and a man at his side.

"This," said the agent, with the air of one who plucks a gold coin from the gutter, "is Edward Talbot."

Dee regarded the man. He was young, perhaps in his middle twenties, with chestnut hair of a fashionable cut. His color was high, suggesting a choleric disposition, and Dee was inclined to think that Clerkson had discounted his stern warnings and brought along some mere roaring boy. But Talbot's manner was curious: he muttered to himself beneath his breath as he looked about the garden. Puzzled, Dee listened.

"Oh yes, this is very fine, most fine indeed: here we have lavender, here white poppy and thyme, to be planted when the March moon is new. And here the little clover of the Trinity and gillyflower..."

He knew his herbs, Dee thought, but did he know anything else? There was a hectic ardor beneath the young man's manner that suggested madness, but this was no bad thing in a scryer, whose work was by its very nature prone to attract those who were touched by the moon. Dee had no quarrel with such Tom O'Bedlams, but he did have a problem with rogues and Talbot was wearing a strange garment akin to a cowl, which hid his ears. Dee would have liked a look at those ears, to see if *they* had been clipped for coining.

"Mr. Talbot," he said, firmly, and at once Talbot was all attention, like a dog that has been called to heel. "Shall we venture within? I should like to see you at your art."

Once they were inside the study, Dee ushered Clerkson out the door and told him to wait. Then he found a seat for the young Edward Talbot, who was gazing around the study with entranced fascination, and placed the obsidian mirror before him. Talbot's eyes grew wide.

"Black as night and solid as air," he said.

"Quite so," Dee said, crisply. "Let us see if you have as great a talent for seeing beyond the world's confines as you have for remarking upon the obvious."

Talbot gave a great laugh at this. Then, sobering, he stared into the mirror. He did not undertake any of the mystical incantations or curious passes so favored by Clerkson's usual clients, nor did he feign a trance. He simply looked.

"What do you see?" Dee asked, urgently.

"I see an archangel, four-faced, spinning upon a globe," Talbot replied. Dee found himself gripping the edges of the table.

"Does it speak?"

"It speaks," Talbot said. His gaze was as intent as ever, Dee noticed, but there was an odd glaze over his eyes, a kind of milky film with fire behind it. He had never seen such a thing before.

"It says," Talbot went on, and now his voice seemed subtly changed, "that to achieve your goal, you must consult both *Steganographia* and *The Book of Soyga*."

Dee sank into a nearby chair, his hands trembling. He now had both works in his possession, but there was no way that Talbot could be aware of this. Both were filled with Cabalistic invocations, with lists of spirit names, but he had wondered about the value of *The Book of Soyga*, which seemed incomplete.

"Is my *Book of Soyga* of any usefulness?" he asked.

"The book was revealed to Adam in paradise by the good angels of God," Talbot replied. "If properly construed, it reveals the language of the universe itself. But man has made little use of it, for though he possessed comprehension of its purpose, the knowledge has been lost."

"Lost?"

"Others have taken the high road to the stars, traveling through the small spaces of the universe across vast distances. I see them: dark-eyed men, with sallow complexions. The angel says that they came from the east, from Araby and Egypt. They have founded colonies and learned much."

"What does the language do?" Dee asked in a whisper.

"It opens a way between the worlds. Here, we are upon Malkuth—the Earth itself. The language will grant you passage to the other worlds: to Yesod, Hod, Netzach, and beyond. It does so by means of mathematical incantations—they are not mere spells, as a cunning witch might summon some spirit to run errands. The language of angels is the language of the universe; its words have the power to make or unmake reality."

"Do not all spells do this?"

"Spells are an imperfect copy of this fundamental tongue. The language of the universe enables those who understand it to unpick the fabric of reality, to weave and stitch the universe in a different way and travel between the cracks. Such a language will be given to you."

"You spoke of the spheres depicted by the Cabala. Is my Meta Incognita such a world?"

Talbot began to stammer, as though speaking in tongues. Dee reached out and gripped him by the wrist.

"Answer me!"

"Yes, it is such a world. It is the nearest world in this system—I do not know what the angel means, it calls the world an 'emanation.' I do not think that they perceive reality in the same way that we do. They speak of 'emanations' and 'membranes' to describe the spheres: they appear to see different levels of existences. But the world of Meta Incognita is the one that the Cabala calls Yesod. There are others within the system. The Eastern people have already made a civilization upon one of them, and I see others, too: strange folk, no longer men."

Talbot's eyes were now entirely opaque and as Dee watched in horror, a single tear of blood crept from the corner of the young man's left eye and snaked down his cheek.

"I can see too much," he cried. "I can see between worlds."

"Talbot, enough." Dee leaned forward and snatched the mirror away. "You will do yourself harm—no more."

Talbot blinked. The film was gone. He reached a hand to his cheek and stared at the red smear upon his fingers.

"It is hard to see so far," he said, wonderingly. "Human eyes are not the same as those of the angels. They are a different kind of creature altogether."

"You have done very well," Dee said. Against the more ruthless part of his nature he added, "But I cannot let you proceed if there is risk of injury."

Talbot shook his head. "I need practice in this new art, that is all. This is not like the usual manner of scrying."

"No," Dee agreed. "It most assuredly is not." And went down into the hall to tell Clerkson that his client would be hired.

That evening, the sky over London turned to a fiery crimson: the color of the garnets that folk used to banish melancholy and restore the spirits. But in this instance, the omens were wrong.

MORTLAKE, LONDON ⸺ WINTER 1582

Dee locked the door of the study behind him and sank into his chair. He so disliked these arguments; they upset him for days and they had become increasingly more frequent since the scryer had come into his life and household. The young man was a menace, no doubt about it, but unfortunately there could also be little doubt about his spiritual gifts. Dee needed him, and the man who had been calling himself Edward Talbot knew it.

Talbot had spent some months in Dee's household,

working on the tongue of the angels: the language that would, if used correctly, unravel and remake the universe itself. It had become a tempestuous relationship: Talbot was alternatively choleric and melancholic, spinning from one to the other like a child's top and mercilessly whipped by his moods. He was never sanguine and rarely phlegmatic; there was not enough moisture in him, to Dee's mind.

Dee took care to put such foods as whey and curds before his guest to induce phlegm, and kept him away from cabbage and spleen, but it did little good. He had always been thus, Talbot informed him, even as an infant. This surprised Dee, for as everyone knew, children were born phlegmatic and usually tended toward the sanguine as they grew older. Talbot was clearly an exceptional case and Dee wondered whether the heat and dryness in him corresponded in some manner to his facility for angelic converse. Whatever the reason, Talbot was an explosive presence in the household and Jane hated him.

Dee sighed. If Katherine had still lived, perhaps she would not have taken against Talbot, for she, too, had been melancholic. But his new wife, Jane, was young and brisk and prone to marvelous rages when she thought that someone might be trying to cozen her husband. And when Dee's suspicions about Talbot's conviction for forging had been proved correct, Jane had become incandescent with fury.

Dee could not help but appreciate her devotion, but it did not improve the atmosphere. When Talbot had stormed from the house, crying that he would not be treated thus, Dee had never expected to see the young man again. But in a matter of weeks, Talbot was back, all smiles and enthusiasm, and mentioning as a matter of passing interest that he had been traveling under an assumed name. His real one, it seemed, was Edward Kelley. Despite searching questions about the deception, the matter had never been satisfactorily explained.

Now the angry voices of Jane and Kelley could be heard all the way up here in the study, sizzling through the cracks in the floorboards like wasps. Dee looked around the study in despair: at the globes and maps, the parchments containing the half-completed annotations of the universal tongue, and sighed once more. He needed both Kelley and Jane. But there was a good chance that one of them might slay the other before the task of deciphering the universal language was complete. If a gate to another world had opened before Dee then, he would have sprung through it as though Herne's hounds were at his very heels and not looked back.

chapter II

TOWER OF THE POISONERS, HATHES

Alivet sat on the bed, cursing her own stupidity. The parchment lay in her lap. What would Ghairen do if he found it was gone? Would he even notice? She picked up the parchment and studied it. It was very old—she could see the cracks in its surface—but it had been protected with a flexible laminated film, doubtless to keep it from falling into pieces. The diagram that it depicted made little sense: an oval inside a triangle, with lines radiating from it. Struck by an idea, Alivet fetched the book called *Cabala* and leafed through it, but at first none of the diagrams seemed to match. But as she was flicking through the pages, she came across a familiar image. Astonished, Alivet let the book fall to her lap. The image was part of yet another diagram: a series of circles connected by lines, and this time, the image was the same as the one on the parchment. But this diagram had pictures.

The lowest circle contained an image of a woman's face, her hair billowing around it like the rays of the sun. From this circle, a line led directly upward to a second sphere, in which was shown a creature with an anube's face and four legs. From here, two more lines led out in opposite directions: one to a circle containing a thing very like a shiffrey, and the second to the image of a plant.

Light was beginning to dawn: both book and parchment alike depicted no random sequence of symbols, but a map of the worlds. The sphere with the anube was surely Latent Emanation, and the sphere with the shiffrey must be Hathes. In that case, could the circle with the woman's face denote the Origin? Yet it was the fifth sphere that had initially caught Alivet's attention, for in this circle was a man, bound to the shape of a cross. It was the same image as her pendant. Lettering stood beside it: *Tiphareth*. Alivet frowned. Was this the name of the man? Patiently, she pored over the next few pages of the book until she found the word again:

> *Tiphareth, also called the "Lesser Countenance," or Melekh: the King. Its order are the Malachim, the Messengers. Its image is that of the sacrificed god.*

Alivet pulled the pendant from her dress. The sacrificed god. Well, the man bound to the cross certainly looked dead. She puzzled over the pendant and the diagram for a little longer, until the words of the book began to blur before her eyes. Then, turning off the lamp, she climbed into bed and lay staring into the darkness.

Next morning, Ghairen unlocked the door, but did not come into Alivet's room. He said nothing about the missing key, nor did he make any reference to the previous evening. He looked both tired and haunted.

"Good morning," he said.

"Good morning." Alivet felt equally subdued.

"I hope you slept well?"

"Well enough. Thank you."

They looked at one another for a moment. Ghairen seemed about to say something else, but hesitated.

"I ought to get to work," Alivet said quickly, to conceal her discomfort.

He nodded. "I'll ask the maid to bring you tea."

Once in the alchematorium, Alivet took up the Philosopher's Egg containing the residue, then picked up the tall glass container and put it carefully inside the water-bath. She watched as the water began to heat up and tiny bubbles started to crystallize around the base of the egg. Looking through the transparent neck of the egg, she saw that the glistening residue had slid down the side to form a molten pool at the bottom. With these preparations under way, Alivet took an alembic from the equipment cupboard and filled it half full of antimony. She set this on a stand and lit a flame beneath it. It would be necessary for both substances to reach the liquid stage together. And then the familiar processes of the alchemical art would be carried out: dissolution, evaporation, crystallization, distillation, calcination, and many more. With the sensation of Ghairen's touch still sharp in her memory, she felt as though she had passed through a similar process herself.

Once the alchemical preparations were complete, she would see what kind of substance resulted. And if it appeared to be stable, she would test it. The antimony must be watched, however, for it had a lamentable tendency to ignite. Alivet sat down on a nearby stool, tucking her skirts under the workbench, and waited. She heard the door open behind her, but was too intent on watching the heating antimony to turn around.

"Ghairen?" she asked nervously. "Is that you?"

"No," a small voice said. "It's me."

Alivet glanced up, to see Celana standing in the entrance to the alchematorium. The girl reached out and pushed the door shut behind her.

"I saw you last night," Celana said, accusingly. "In my father's rooms. What were you doing there?"

"I was looking for anything that might help me get out of here," Alivet said. The girl had witnessed her in plain view, there was little to be gained by dissembling and it was certain that Celana would not believe any excuse that Alivet had to offer.

"I don't believe you," Celana said. "I think you were trying to kill him."

"How? He's a Fifth Grade Poison Master. He's almost certainly immune to anything I could cook up. Have you told him you saw me?"

"No. Not yet."

"Are you going to tell him?" *Ask a pointless question,* Alivet thought.

"That depends."

"On what?" Alivet glanced back at the antimony mixture, which was starting to bubble.

"On whether you promise to help me."

"Celana, why don't you come and sit down? You're making me edgy, hovering there in the doorway."

Celana did not move. She said, in an urgent whisper, "You have to help me get out of here. He killed my mother."

"Celana, I'm really sorry to hear about your mother," Alivet said inadequately, thinking: *Just what is the truth of this matter?* "But why have you come to me? I'm sure your governess would help you."

Miserably, Celana shook her head. "My father has sent her away. He spoke to me last night—he wouldn't let us talk to one another or say good-bye. He says that she is not a healthy influence."

"I see," Alivet said, dismayed. With Iraguila gone, she had lost her only ally in Ghairen's household, though a dubious ally at that. And what had Iraguila's dismissal to do with the night journey they had so recently taken? Had Ghairen learned of this?

"She promised to help me," Celana said. "We were going to escape—she knew of a place we could go, where we'd be safe. Somewhere my father would never find us. Then you came and Iraguila changed her plans."

That explained some of the resentment that the girl had appeared to feel for her, Alivet thought, noting that Celana had used the governess' real name. But there were still many unanswered questions.

"Your father told me that he was on my world for some time. Wouldn't that have been the ideal time for you to go? Iraguila knew ways out of the tower. You could have been long gone by the time your father returned from Latent Emanation."

"That was the plan," Celana muttered. "But then Iraguila discovered why my father was going away. She said that it was more important for her to stay here. She found out about my father's plot to overthrow the rulers of your world and she needed to find out more. She went to the drift-boat to do so. But now he's sent her away! I can't stay here for the rest of my life. You have to help me."

Agitated, Celana ran forward and grasped Alivet by the hand. But as she did so, her sleeve caught a leg of the heating tripod, which toppled. The alembic containing the mixture of antimony shattered, grazing Celana's hand and causing blood to spatter across the work surface. Molten antimony spilled out and a lick of flame touched Celana's trailing sleeve. Celana screamed. Alivet seized a cloth and, wrapping the girl in it, smothered the blaze. But a line of flame was already racing along the edge of the workbench.

Alivet reached for Celana, but the girl had stumbled across to the other side of the alchematorium. Covering her face, Alivet threw herself to the floor. The residue exploded, sending a tongue of fire high above her head. Gripping the edge of the workbench, and coughing from the sudden boiling cloud of smoke, Alivet hauled herself upright.

Celana was curled, unmoving, in a ball at the far side of the alchematorium. Alivet, her hands shaking, tore off her top-skirt, seized a container of the fire-resistant powder, and dusted it liberally over herself. Then, swiftly choosing a place where the flames were thinnest, she jumped through. The fire licked her hand as she passed through and the pain was so searing that she cried out. But she was past the fire now, on the other side of the alchematorium, and Celana was only a few feet away.

Ignoring the pain in her hand, Alivet hastily wrapped

Celana's trailing hair and face in the protected skirt, hauled the girl up from the floor, and put an arm around her waist. The sight of the flames leaping like a wall from one side of the alchematorium to the other nearly caused her to falter, but if she lingered they would both die. The smoke was suffocating. Averting her face, Alivet bolted through the firewall, rolling over and over with Celana beneath her to smother the small flames that had caught the hem of the girl's dress.

And then there were voices, and hands raising Celana up and away. Choking, Alivet lay on the floor, unable to move. Flames billowed over her head and were gone with a great hiss. She smelled a sharp, chemical odor. Then she was being held against Ghairen's robes as he whispered reassurance in her ear. She buried her face in his shoulder, unsure whether it was his closeness or her own narrow escape that was making her shiver, and for the moment, no longer caring.

chapter III

Tower of the Poisoners, Hathes

Alivet was somewhere stifling. Heat enveloped her, bathing her in perspiration. Alivet opened her eyes and a face swam above her, lizard eyes alight with curiosity.

"You're awake," a woman's voice said. "How are you feeling?"

"I don't know," Alivet said, and the woman laughed, low and not altogether kind.

"I *know* you," Alivet said, for it was the woman from her dream of the parc-verticale, with the striped, translucent skin.

"Of course you do. I have visited your dreams. My name is Gulzhur Elaniel. And you will be coming to see me very soon."

"How?" Alivet asked.

"Through your dreams, of course. How else?"

"But you're not real." Alivet was starting to wake up now. The woman's face was fading like a leaf in autumn.

"Come," Gulzhur Elaniel said, frowning, "you know better than that, Alivet. You know that the truth may be attained through dreams: the drugged visions that plants give you, or simply those that come to you at night, when you lie defenseless. Even in sleep, you seek out the truth. How much more eagerly will you seek it out when you are awake? I know about the

Search. I know the store your people place in the royal roads of the unconscious."

"Listen—" Alivet started to ask the woman how she knew about the Search, but then Gulzhur's glistening face was gone and she was awake.

"Alivet? Can you hear me?" She knew *that* voice. Ghairen was leaning over her. Her throat was raw and dry and her head throbbed like a drum. She was still fully dressed, wrapped in her own skirts as though mummified. She remembered clinging to him, shaking in his arms, and she felt the heat rush to her face.

"I can hear you. Don't *shout*." What was he doing here in her bedroom, so early in the morning? *Don't start thinking,* Alivet told herself.

"I'm sorry. I've been worried about you." A cool hand brushed her forehead. Memories of fire and blood came flooding back.

"Celana—is she all right?" Alivet doubled up, coughing.

"Yes, she's all right. Her arm is burned and she has a cut hand, and you both breathed in a lot of smoke, but otherwise you'll be fine."

"Has she told you what happened?" How much did Ghairen know? Alivet wondered.

"No. I gave her a sedative and put her to bed. What was she doing in the alchematorium?" Ghairen's glance was sharp.

"She just wanted to see what I was doing, I think," Alivet said. It was hardly a convincing explanation, but Ghairen appeared to accept it.

"I'll talk to her later," he said. "Are you well enough to get up? There's something I want to show you."

"What is it?"

"It's in the alchematorium."

She had not seen Ghairen in this mood before, a kind of suppressed excitement, almost fey. It was as though the fire had clarified her perceptions, pared her down to the essence of the world. The immutable processes of alchemy: *This is the phase of crystallization, where dreams start to become real.*

"Very well," Alivet said. "Show me."

She could smell the smoke even before she set foot in the alchematorium. The hallway stank of its sourness. Her throat ached. Ghairen hastened along beside her, his robes stirring up a drift of ash.

"Look at this," he said, and held open the door.

Alivet stepped through into the alchematorium. The fire had scorched the wall nearest to the door, coating it with a thick layer of soot. The room reeked of smoke and the smothering odor of the fire-powder, a cloyingly sweet smell. Alivet put her sleeve to her face. The remnants of the crucible that had contained the antimony mixture lay upon the workbench like shattered, frozen bubbles. But the workbench itself was glistening with a layer of frosted red snow. As Alivet stared, a shaft of sunlight arched through the window. The substance grew as bright as fire, as if touched by a taper, and Alivet cried out, momentarily blinded. She put a hand to her eyes. Red sparks flickered across the dark field of her palm. She turned to see that Ghairen, too, was shielding his face.

"*What is it?*"

"I was hoping you could tell me," Ghairen said.

Together, they drew the blinds down across the windows, but the substance still continued to spark and gleam. There was no need to use a lamp. The substance provided an illumination of its own, like a heap of garnets in firelight. Alivet took a spatula and scraped some of it up from the workbench. It was hard and brittle, a kind of crystalline grit.

"I've never seen anything like this before," she said.

"Neither have I. But you see how it behaves, Alivet? You see how it holds the light?"

Alivet nodded. "I think we may have found your carrier."

"But what caused it? Was it the antimony? What exactly was in that mixture?"

"The residue of the tabernanthe, and antimony. It's true that I was working toward a phase of crystallization, but I don't see how it could have produced something like this." But even as she spoke, Alivet was seeing the alembic shatter and Celana's blood running over the polished surface of the workbench.

"The blood," she said, aloud.

"What?"

"Celana cut herself when the alembic broke. Her hand was bleeding. It was her blood that reacted with the mixture, not anything I put in it. A drop of human blood, a sacrifice to the spirit of the plant."

"Have you heard of such a process taking place before?"

"No—the use of blood is forbidden in alchemy. It's one of the first principles. It's viewed as black science."

"It will need to be tested," Ghairen said. His face was a study in abstracted calculation, and Alivet, to her dismay, realized what was going through his mind. Would a small quantity of this unusual substance be enough to defeat the Lords, or would they need more? And if they needed more, who would be the one to supply the blood? Alivet feared for Celana and herself. She said quickly, "I'll test it."

"Are you sure?"

"I'm the one who has the experience with hallucinogens. Isn't that why you brought me here?"

Ghairen gave her a dubious look. "You're not in the best of health right now."

He seemed genuinely concerned for her welfare, but doubtless it was just that he wanted the best results from the test. Once again she pushed away the memory of that evening in Ghairen's bedroom, of his voice murmuring in her ear. He did not care about her, she told herself, but was simply trying to lull any suspicions that she might have; seduce her into complicity, or friendship, or more.

"I'll be fine," she said, quickly.

Ghairen was obliged to agree. He fetched the shiffrey servitor to clean the alchematorium while Alivet set about carefully removing the substance from the workbench. It would have to be in a suitable form for ingestion. Given its antimonic antecedents, Alivet thought that burning a very small amount in a brazier and inhaling the smoke might be the best method. But she did not want to do the test in the alchematorium, with its current atmosphere of acrid fumes. She said as much to Ghairen.

"You can undertake the test in your own room, or in mine, if you wish. It's quiet; you'll be undisturbed."

She made the mistake of looking into his face. His expression was carefully bland, but she knew she was not the only one with memories. It would be too tempting to forget about all this hallucinogenic scheming and just sink back down onto Ghairen's divan to lose herself in his arms. For some reason, however, the image made her think of Madimi Garland: a salutary shock.

"I'll use my room," Alivet said.

The coals of the brazier glowed in the darkness, almost as brightly as the substance that Alivet now carried inside an alembic: the powder formed of antimony, tabernanthe, blood, and pain. Ghairen was right, the substance absorbed light into itself and then released it, dispelling the shadows that clustered about the room. Now he sat beside her, watching anxiously.

It seemed that Celana had not yet woken from the sedative. Alivet had asked to visit the sleeping girl to check for herself that Celana was not badly hurt, but Ghairen had refused.

Alivet, however, had been insistent and at last the Poison Master, for the sake of peace, had allowed her through into Celana's room. It was similar to her own, rich and somber. A scatter of bronze leaves chased across the walls. Celana lay on the bed, dressed in her shift, with one arm bandaged. She breathed peacefully and Alivet did not have the heart to disturb her.

"You see?" Ghairen had said, with a touch of impatience. "Just as I told you."

"That's a relief," Alivet had replied. Indeed, it was nothing more than the truth; she would have been unable to concentrate on the test with the worry of Celana twinging at the back of her mind like a toothache.

The brazier was beginning to smolder, sending a thread of smoke up into the room and making Alivet's throat sore all over again. Perhaps it wasn't such a good idea to inhale the stuff, but it was too gritty to be soluble into a tincture and she did not like the idea of injecting the substance. She had seen too many fellow citizens succumb to the allure of the swamp poppy; the tiny needles with their intricate wooden handles littered the shores after festivals, but the opium brought little that was new to the Search, though it was true that it was a useful sedative.

So the brazier it was. Alivet stirred the coals with a metal rod, sending a shower of sparks fluttering up the sides. She made sure that the four feet of the brazier were firmly planted on the stone base that Ghairen had provided for the purpose. The last thing she wanted was to leap up in the grip of a trance and knock the thing over. One fire was already too many. A straight-backed chair stood next to the brazier. Settling herself upon it, Alivet took a pinch of the glittering red powder from the alembic with the tongs and scattered it over the coals.

Given the brightness of the powder, she was careful not to look at it directly and this proved wise. From the corner of her eye, she saw the coals flare up, catching the light. Ghairen gave her an encouraging smile. The room was suddenly as bright as day. Her own cowering shadow marched across the paneled walls. The flare died down to a more muted glow, and when Alivet glanced cautiously at the brazier she saw that the coals themselves were red and sparkling. Alivet took the water-jug and let a few drops fall into the heat. The brazier hissed like a serpent and a column of smoke reared up. Alivet leaned into it and breathed deeply. She repeated the procedure twice more, then sat back.

Her head was filled with fumes: she detected the iron scent of blood, but also a deep, bright sweetness. It was as though light had been transmuted into smell. Alivet closed her eyes.

Gradually, by degrees, her body became detached from her consciousness. Alivet left it and slipped sideways into the air. It was very easy to leave herself behind in this way, a far simpler matter than the endless unbuttoning required by her clothes. She looked back and saw her body still seated by the brazier: prim in the restrictive garments, eyes serenely closed, hands folded in her lap. Ghairen was leaning forward, studying her face, but making no move to touch her. Alivet turned away from her body and found that the room had disappeared.

Where the wall of the Poisoners' Tower had been, and the city of Ukesh beyond, she was now gazing out across a field of stars. It was the most beautiful sight she had ever seen: suns strung like rubies across the sea of night, great spinning clouds that were the webs in which those suns were born. A planet burned like fire behind her, but she had no time to look. Great presences swept by, their tails flickering between a thousand points of light. She was falling in the wake of an immense being, its gaze fixed on some impossible horizon. Comets blazed in its path and spun about its head like tendrils of fiery hair.

Alivet, her mouth open, knew that she was screaming, but there was no sound at all in this teeming vastness. A green world loomed below her, marbled with seas and mountains and plains, veiled in cloud. *I know that place!* She fell toward it—and then something hissed inside her head. Alivet turned and found she was looking into an immense double countenance: male on one side, female on the other. Its mouths were open, it was spitting with hatred. Alivet, after the first shock, recognized the mayjen: the spirit of the plant from which—or so the shiffrey alchemist had told her—Ghairen's poison had come.

"But you're gone!" cried Alivet, and the mayjen said with ringing triumph, "No, I was *given* to you."

It reached out a clawed hand and touched a finger to Alivet's shoulder. She was spun away with great force, turning and turning in the roaring field of stars . . .

. . . and was spat out into an unfamiliar room at a pair of striped feet.

part VIII

SEPARATION

At the far end of the earth is Bohemia
A fair and exotic dominion
Full of deep and mysterious rivers.

― KONSTANTIN BIEBL, *Protinozci*

chapter I

On one side of the cart sat Hendrick Niclaes, leader of the Family of Love, fidgeting nervously with the reins. On the other sat Count Nicholas Laski, clad in his customary scarlet garments and peering from the depths of his magnificent beard. In the back of the cart sat Edward Kelley, talking to himself. They were hardly the most inconspicuous coterie of alchemists ever to grace the Moravian countryside, Dee reflected sourly, but there was nothing for it.

For the hundredth time, he wished that he were back in the quiet solitude of the house at Mortlake, with Jane and the children playing in the garden and the waters of the Thames sending ripples across the ceiling. But was the house even there any longer? His brother-in-law's letter, received a day ago, had not been encouraging. What precisely had Fromonds meant by "ransacked"? It was the kind of alarming word that could signal any amount of chaos. Had Niclaes' Family members managed to rescue the most precious things: the globes and maps, the measuring instruments and alchemical vessels, or did they lie broken across the floor? Or were they even now gracing the rooms of one of Dee's rivals? At least Jane and the children were safe in Krakow. The scrying mirror was secure in the otherwise unreliable hands of Kelley, and the language of the universe resided firmly within Dee's own skull; at least they could not ransack that, not even if his enemies placed him upon the rack.

Do not fret, Dee told himself. *Niclaes and the Family are prepared for the journey; they will not turn back.* He remembered the conversation of the previous evening.

"We will go to this place, this Meta Incognita of yours," Niclaes had said, mouth set in resolve. "We are reaching the point where we have no choice. Mark my word upon it, Dee—persecution will grow. We have already been chased from the Low Countries, and London itself grows restless as a hound with fleas."

"There is always the New World," Dee had said, with a smile.

"Yes, America—but who is to say that the new world will prove more tolerant over time than the old? Besides, I have seen the world in your glass, shown by angels, and it is fair enough." He fell silent for a moment, doubtless recollecting the little image of the watery place with the great gate, guarded by Anubis.

"It is damp," said Dee, playing devil's advocate.

"So is Flanders, and in London the moistness of the days reaches my bones."

"And it is dangerous. When Kelley first began to study the Meta Incognita through the black glass, his eyes began to bleed. It seems that looking between worlds is hazardous. It is only through much diligent work in placing himself in trance that he is not now blinded. And what of the jackal-headed creatures that seem to haunt the fens of Meta Incognita? Do you not fear them as demons?"

"I feared so at first, but I prayed much on the matter. Also, I have spoken to Brother Edward, and your scryer has talked with the angels and informs me that they are as the beasts before the Fall, gentle and innocent. Besides, if they possess intelligence, who is to say that they shall not join our sect before God? We have welcomed Turks, after all."

Sometimes, Dee reflected, Niclaes was almost alarmingly open-minded. After that, the conversation had turned to practical details: how many folk, what materials, what seeds and animals they should take with them. And Dee had learned that Niclaes had made great roads already into the project, encouraging members of the Family to learn new and different skills. It was no longer a dream; it was an expedition. And the north-west passage across the universe itself did exist and would be traveled. Despite his worries about his house and books, Dee felt the now-familiar pang of excitement. In a few years, perhaps less, the journey would be made. The task they must now work upon involved the summoning: the opening of a gap between the world and the ship promised to them by the angels.

For the moment, they had the assistance of the flamboyant Count Laski. Dee was not entirely sure what he thought of the Count's trustworthiness, but he was becoming used to being uneasy when in the presence of his associates. He told himself that Laski was a friend of Niclaes', a fellow member of the Family of Love, and a committed alchemist. Had he not sponsored the first edition of Paracelsus' writings on the subject, and been welcomed to England as a prince should be? Moreover Laski had money—or said that he did—and would be able to provide Dee with all the alchemical equipment he needed to make the summoning. For that, however, they must travel to Prague.

The journey was already taking its toll on Dee. The road was little more than a rough track, mile upon mile, through pinewoods steaming with mist and cloud. August had brought drenching rains. What must it be like in the winter? Dee wondered. The Vistula River thundered beside the road, an alternating mass of foam and deep dark pools. Dampness filled the air and crept into Dee's bones. *If I live to see this new world,* he thought in despair, *I shall not live long upon it.*

Wistfully, he remembered his dreams of the flying machine, and to raise his spirits, he began to imagine everything that the Family of Love would be able to accomplish in the new world. There would be an alchemical college, free from persecution and academic sneering; flying craft would fill the skies; men would converse freely with angels and speak to one another across great distances. And others had gone before them, those ancient peoples of the East, to nearby worlds. What manner of people would they be? The angel had told Kelley that they were greatly learned. *It will all be well,* Dee told himself. *It must be well.*

After what seemed to Dee to be a veritable eternity, the cart rolled over a ridge and Prague lay below.

"A charming city," Laski proclaimed from the depths of his beard, as though bestowing some personal seal of approval upon the place.

"Gracious indeed," Dee concurred, and indeed, there was much to please him. He liked the narrow streets, the high turrets and fanciful plasterwork, which made it seem as though a multitude of fabulous beasts stalked the lanes, accompanied by skeletons and rams. The cart took them past inns with curious names: the Spider, the Vulture, the Blue Star.

For a moment, Dee could almost believe that they had already come to Meta Incognita, that it was years in the future with the city of the Family of Love already built and flourishing. Idly, he toyed with names for the new city. New Prague sounded a little prosaic. Celestia, perhaps? He must speak to Niclaes of the matter; naming a thing, Dee knew, brought it closer to reality, just as the crystallization phase of alchemy could be assisted by incantation.

The cart trundled into a wide square and rolled to a halt. Laski leaped down and helped Dee clamber from the high seat. The moistness of the air was doing nothing for his joints; it was just as well that they would be staying at the house of a physician. As they made their way across the square, Dee noted a plethora of characters, clad in costumes as fantastical as Laski's bloodred garments. Laski nudged him.

"See over there? Old Geronimo Scotta, especially known for his diabolical legerdemain. Arrived in town one day with three red carriages and forty horses. Now he flogs vitriol of Mars and stag-horn jelly from a market stall."

"And but for the grace of God and his angels," said Dee dryly, "there go I—a marketplace quack."

Laski snorted. "Nonsense. The very air is a salve to your labors. Wait until you see where we are staying."

Indeed, Dee was to find the physician's house most reassuring. The physician himself, a contact of Laski's, had inherited the property from his father, of whom Dee had heard.

"Simon Bakalar? A known alchemist in his day. And this was his house?" He gazed with admiration at the golden letters, the flowers and fruit and birds that decorated the walls. And inside, Laski and the physician took him to see the words that Bakalar had inscribed about his rooms:

This learning is precious, transient, delicate and rare. Our learning is a boy's game, and the toil of women. All you sons of this art, understand that none may reap the fruits of our elixir except by the introduction of the elemental stone, and if he seeks another path he will never enter or embrace it.

"Stern words," said Laski.

"But we do seek another path," Dee murmured.

Laski clapped him on the shoulder, making Dee wince. "And we shall achieve it."

At first, all went well. Dee's welcome at Rudolf's court was all that he could have hoped for, and the visionary work with Kelley was encouraging. The maps of the new world, attained by means of the black mirror, were progressing. In agreement with Kelley, Dee had decided that it would be too dangerous to commit details of Meta Incognita directly to paper, and so they had devised a code, using the alchemical language which Dee used with as much fluency as he did English. Kelley's first scrying session in Prague yielded a strange landscape, with great trees along an estuary; their roots rising up from the still, black water in a tangled mass. Between these roots flickered odd spirals of light, like diaphanous veils, from which Kelley recoiled in horror, saying that they were trying to draw his soul out through his mouth.

Dee duly noting down the vision, encoded: "A lake of black pitch, from which emerged a creature with a double head and a serpent's body." If anyone were to find these writings, they would take them for no more than an alchemical experiment: Dee's friendship with Elizabeth's spymaster Walsingham had taught him that it was best to hide a thing in plain view.

The next vision was different.

"Kelley?" Dee queried. "What do you see?"

"I see a man—or perhaps he is no man at all, but rather a devil. He has eyes like the very coals in the hearth and a smooth Egyptian face, rather pale. A subtle man, I should warrant. He has the smile of a courtier. There is a woman with him, or maybe a spirit. They are staring into an alchemical crucible. The picture is distant and very small, and it has a haze, unlike my usual visions. It is like a glimpse of the future, not of the present. Strange," Kelley murmured, frowning into the mirror. "It seems to me the girl has a look of you."

Dee was about to question him, but then the vision changed again. One moment Kelley was gazing into the placid surface of the mirror, the next, he was falling back onto the floor and crying out that they were consorting with devils.

"Edward!" Dee cried. He rushed to Kelley's side, but the young man was spitting and hissing as if possessed. "What is wrong?"

At last Kelley leaned back against the wall, white with shock and revulsion. "That I should so fall into a fit, like any counterfeit crank!"

"Yes, but what *happened*?"

"A spirit has come! A being in the form of a luminous woman, who told me that the angels with whom we have been consorting are corrupt."

"Wait," Dee told him. "I will call Niclaes and Laski. For this is something they should hear."

Kelley, exhausted by his experience, fell asleep with his head on his arms, but not before Dee had made him recount the experience to the others. While Kelley slept, they sat in the patterned alchemical room and discussed the matter.

"Spirits are unchancy beings," Laski said, with magnificent insouciance. "Everyone knows it. They come and they lie, deceivers all. It is the angels to whom we should be listening."

"I am not so certain." Niclaes counseled caution. "For ourselves, perhaps, it is part of the risk of the matter; we are alchemists all and we know such dangers. But we cannot gamble with other folks' souls. If we lead the Family to Meta Incognita and find that we are deceived . . ."

"And you, Dee," Laski said, when they had wrangled

the question between them for some time. "You have been most silent. What is your opinion?"

Dee looked at the three men before him: at the flashy Laski, the pensive Niclaes, and the sleeping Kelley, who, lost in tiredness and ill dreams, suddenly looked no older than a boy.

"Niclaes is right," Dee said wearily. "We cannot gamble with others' souls. I began this course, gathered together the expedition. I recall my old friend Richard Chancellor, now lost beneath the cold North Sea, and what he once said to me: that a captain would give his life for his crew, for any sailor. So must I risk my life; I cannot ask you to do the same. Our main task has been to find a way to take a great number of people to Meta Incognita, but expeditions have always been pioneered by the few. The mathematics of the universal language are almost in place. If we can open up the smallest passage to this new world, I will go there to see for myself if it is safe."

After a long moment, Niclaes said, "And if you, and then ourselves, should be deceived?"

"You know that the Queen's court runs on coded messages, sent between her spies? I shall devise a code to deceive the very angels. If I do not return, I shall find a way to send it, by means of the mirror."

chapter II

NETHES

Astonished, Alivet looked up. She was sprawling before the woman from her dream, the striped, translucent person who called herself Gulzhur Elaniel.

"So you're here at last," Elaniel said, evidently delighted. She crouched down to look into Alivet's eyes. Her black-and-silver hair fanned out across the floor. Elaniel smelled of fire, of ash, of death. Before she could stop her, Elaniel's tongue flickered out across Alivet's cheek. The woman pulled a face.

"You're *sour*. La! I didn't expect that."

"What did you expect?" Alivet took exception to being insulted, not to mention licked. "Where am I? How did I get here?" The floor was smooth beneath her hands. This was not a vision, created by a drug. This was real.

"I thought you'd be sweet. Like dew."

"Where *am* I?" Alivet scrambled to her feet and looked around her. The floor on which she stood was made of glass, translucent and gleaming. Alivet glimpsed movement: what appeared to be small silver fish, darting away through smoke. There were no walls: only columns made of some pale spongy substance. There was a powerful smell of burning.

"Why, you are at home with me," Elaniel said, surprised. She sat down cross-legged, and began combing her silky hair with her fingers. "You are on Nethes."

"*Nethes*? But I was experimenting with a drug."

"I know," Elaniel said, vaguely. "You've found your poison for the Lords, and the mayjen brought you here. But Nethes is much nicer than Hathes, you know. I'm sure you'll like it here."

"You don't understand." Alivet reached down and shook Elaniel's shoulder. The woman's skin felt hard and cool, more like a shell than warm flesh. "I have to get back. I have a task to accomplish. And what do you mean, the mayjen brought me?"

"Surely you understand these things? I thought your people were familiar with hallucinogenics and entheogens. I thought you realized that when you take such substances, it is not just a vision that you see, but parts of the universe's own fabric: the roads between worlds and suns, along which spirits travel. It was down such a road that you were carried here. Although," Elaniel added, with a frown, "it is not correct to call them 'spirits.' That is a primitive term and does not reflect scientific truth: that each element of the universe is alive and possesses its own consciousness. You must know this; you are an alchemist."

"I have to get back," Alivet said, desperately. Metaphysics or not, time was ticking onward like the movement of a waterclock.

"I'm sure your task can wait," Gulzhur Elaniel said. She sounded dreamy and detached, as though nothing was entirely real.

"No, it *cannot* wait."

Belying her vagueness, Elaniel's hand snaked round with alarming speed and caught hold of Alivet's wrist. The glowing eyes looked directly into her own.

"No, it is you who do not understand. I tell you, *it can wait*. Come with me."

Elaniel's gaze was hypnotic. Alivet tried to pull away, but could not. She felt like a small bird, gripped in the glance of a dangerous serpent. Her head spun with dismay, yet she found herself following Elaniel meekly between the pillars and into an adjoining chamber. Here, too, there were no walls, only a tangle of fleshy red stalks that coiled around one another to form an impenetrable barrier. But one of these stalk walls was broken by an opening, through which an uncertain light cast patterns across the floor.

"You will rest," Elaniel said with dripping sweetness. It was clearly not a suggestion. She reached out and ran a caressing palm down Alivet's face. Her hand was hot and dry. Alivet's head was filled with fog. She started to lie down upon a spongy protrusion covered in a kind of lichen. And then she heard a voice at the back of her mind. The voice was her own; it spoke in a whisper. It said: *It is only another drug. And of all things, you understand drugs, and how to conquer them. You must distance yourself from her, you must watch her pass over the surface of your mind as if she were nothing more than a dream. Do not feel fear, do not trouble yourself. Do not become engaged with her presence.*

"Thank you," Alivet murmured. "I think I will rest, perhaps. I'm very tired." She lay back and pretended to close her eyes, then curled on her side and made a small contented sound, all the while hiding in the back of her own consciousness like a seed. She listened to Elaniel's stealthy footsteps withdraw and opened her eyes just far enough to see the stalks part and let Elaniel through.

When she was sure that the woman was gone, Alivet jumped from the couch and ran to the opening between the stalks. A wilderness of stone stretched away from the house. Beyond, were sharp peaks of rock and a great dull world hanging above the horizon. Sparks of light like hot coals hung unmoving in the upper air. The smell of fire grew stronger and Alivet saw a mass of lichen roll across the stones, with flame trickling from it. It drifted past a pod the height of a man, formed of a glassy substance that reminded Alivet of Elaniel's own flesh. With a rush of sparks the pod caught alight and exploded, releasing black seeds into the air. Not a welcoming world, Alivet thought, but she was only a few feet from the ground. If she could climb through the opening, perhaps she could find a way of escape, but this world seemed so hot . . .

Alivet went back into the room and snatched up a handful of lichen. She dropped it through the opening and immediately it caught fire, releasing a sulphurous smoke. Escape became even less of an option. The very worlds corresponded to the humors, Alivet thought: Latent Emanation was wet and cold; Hathes cold and dry; Nethes hot and dry. Somewhere, there must be somewhere warm and wet on which humans could still live. Perhaps that was the world that Ghairen had called Malkuth.

Alivet slid down and leaned against the wall. She thought of Inki, of Celana: of all the people under the sway of the Lords of Night. She could not fail now. She would try to explore the place, see what Elaniel might be hiding. She had just reached the pillars, however, when something caught her by the ankles and dragged her into the room. Alivet fell heavily to the floor. Red tendrils had roped themselves around her boots. She pulled at them, but they tightened, and more crept out across the floor to wind themselves about her wrists. This was why Elaniel had been able to leave her here, then: the very plants were under her instructions.

Alivet, cursing, tore at the tendrils with her nails but it was no use. She was trapped, snared tight as a fly in a web. In addition to this, the room was growing hotter, filled with a heavy, dry warmth that made the sweat pour down Alivet's back beneath her restrictive garments. Fuming, she edged back against the wall so that she had something to lean against. She found herself thinking of Hathes with something approaching nostalgia. At least Hathes had been a cold world, unlike this drenching heat.

The tendrils remained around Alivet's ankles, so that she was held in a secure red noose. She struggled, but the grip of the tendrils grew even tighter. And now the growth that composed the opposite wall was beginning to move, snaking long vines across the floor. Alivet shuffled backward, fearing that the vines would wrap themselves around her until she lay embalmed in a living cocoon, but the tendrils stopped a short distance from her feet. Swiftly, they curled together and coiled upward.

It was a few moments before Alivet realized what was happening: the vines were knitting themselves into a cage around her. She struck out, but her wrists were swiftly secured. In a very short while, Alivet sat imprisoned within a conical mesh of tendrils. There were a few gaps in the cage, through which she could glimpse the room with the pillars, but she could not move her hands and feet in order to prise them apart. Grimly, she watched as the vines began to put forth tentative buds, as delicate as rolled parasols. Slowly, the first bud began to unfurl into a long golden flower like a lily. It was followed by others: Alivet was secured within a glorious bower that she had little inclination to appreciate.

The perfume of the lilies was heavy and narcotic. Alivet found her head nodding as she slumped back against the wall of the bower. She fought to stay awake, but as she struggled—following the mental tricks that she had been taught in order to pursue the Search—the petals of the flowers spread wider so that she could see past the fleshy stamens and down into their rosy hearts. The petals flexed: a stronger draught of perfume sailed forth to overwhelm her.

She woke to find Gulzhur Elaniel sitting cross-legged outside the bower, which had opened by a crack. Alivet's head felt like a seedpod: stuffed with wool and about to burst. The figure of Elaniel flashed now bright, now dark, as Alivet's vision pulsed to the pounding of her head.

"Let me go," she managed to say.

Through the gap in the bower, she saw Elaniel smile.

"But I only want to keep you safe. My dear Iraguila has told me of your penchant for adventuring; I should hate to see you hurt yourself. You might try to run away, and so burn, or become the prey of seedpods. You might fall foul of the lichen that entwines itself around the house. And then where would you be? No, here you are quite safe, quite secure. The lilies will give you marvelous dreams if you stop fighting them: simply relax and let them do their work. You have nothing to worry about anymore."

"You don't understand," Alivet said thickly, echoing her earlier words. "I have to go home. Back to Latent Emanation. I have to fight the Night Lords."

"But of course I could never let you do anything as dangerous as that," Gulzhur Elaniel said, and her eyes opened wide. "If I let you go, I would surely be sending you to your death. Why, when Iraguila first learned of Ghairen's plan, she was horrified. To use a young, innocent girl in such a manner? She resolved then that she must save you."

"But—Iraguila tried to help me," Alivet said. A fog seemed to seethe before her eyes, robbing her of sense. "She told me that both the Night Lords and the Poison Master could be overcome."

"Why, Iraguila has no interest in doing battle with the Lords of Night," Elaniel said. "She seeks only to limit the damage that Ghairen is trying to wreak. The Lords cannot be challenged, Alivet. They are the universe's own army, the gatekeepers. The order of all our worlds depends on them. I see that you understand nothing about them."

"Explain them to me, then," Alivet whispered. Her head was swimming and she was no longer sure if this was the effect of the perfume, or simply of confusion.

Elaniel clapped her hands, as if asked to tell a favorite story to a child. "It is quite simple. All of our people came to these worlds through a single gate, from the same place. Some, such as my people and the Hathanassi, came thousands of years ago. Some—your own folk—have been here for only a few hundred. Our ancestors all came from the world named 'Malkuth.' You know it as the Origin; to its people, it is called 'Earth' or simply 'the world.' It is a terrible place, wracked by plague and war—the lowest and worst place of all. But every so often a few people, wiser or more desperate from the rest, manage to break free of their bonds and find a way to summon the sentinels and pass through the gate to this part of the universe, where there are a cluster of inhabitable worlds."

"The sentinels?" Alivet asked, but she felt that she knew what Elaniel was going to say.

"You know them as the Lords of Night. They are those beings who guard these worlds, who permit us to pass from world to world when we are ready."

"How do we become 'ready'?"

"Those of us who live in the longer-established human worlds are wiser than you, most naturally," Elaniel said. She spoke kindly, condescendingly, as though Alivet were a child indeed. "We have evolved, physically. And we have evolved, too, through spiritual practice: we meditate, day by day, we pray, we make offerings to those who are yet higher than ourselves—to the Kherubim, the gatekeepers or sentinels, who guard us."

"You worship the Night Lords? They're *here*?" Alivet felt as though the floor had caved in beneath her, the breath forced from her lungs.

"We welcome them. They watch us, guard us, guide us. They protect us. They are our angels."

"How do you know they protect you?"

"Why, they tell us so." For an instant, a flicker of doubt passed over Elaniel's features, so swiftly that Alivet was not certain that she had imagined it.

"But on my world the Lords of Night do terrible things," Alivet protested. "They hold people captive as slaves; they are keeping my own sister. They have folk blinded as punishment, and their servants rule the populace as they please." But even as she spoke she thought of those folk who chose to remain unseeing of the Lords' true nature, who took favors from the Unpriests in exchange for their protection, who would hand over other humans to the Lords' creatures for their own gain. The Unpriests themselves were human. The thought gave her an entirely unwanted insight into the nature of Elaniel. She wondered what this woman might really be getting from the Lords.

Elaniel put her head on one side and smiled.

"Of course, the Kherubim welcome some of our own people to them. It is an honor to serve them. I'm sure your folk have misunderstood the situation. And certainly, the Kherubim wish only to help you." She paused, adding kindly, "It's difficult, perhaps, for those of a lower spiritual level to understand the motives of the higher."

Alivet did not understand what Elaniel meant by "spiritual," but she knew when she was being patronized. She took a deep breath to quell her rising rage and said, "You say that the Origin is a place called 'Earth.' Is it possible to travel there?"

"Why should you want to?"

"Let's say curiosity."

"If you could find your way back through a portal and a ship, perhaps," Gulzhur Elaniel said. "But you could have little reason to try. Best you stay here, and learn enlightenment over time, and tell us what you know of alchemy." A greedy light flickered in Elaniel's eyes: this, then, must be why Iraguila Ust had schemed to bring her here. Like Ghairen, the Nethenassi too must be in need of information. "I will take pleasure in teaching you the Hundred Hymns," Elaniel went on. "The Prayers of Praising and Lamentation. You do not belong in this level, and so cannot have free rein within it, but that does not mean that you are incapable of learning."

Her voice, filled with a drowsy sweetness, filled the air, just as the perfume of the lilies had done. Alivet found both to be intolerable. To make Elaniel go away, she said, as humbly as she could manage, "I will try to be worthy of your teaching. But I am very tired, and so—"

"Of course." Elaniel rose fluidly up from the floor. Alivet could see her peering down through the tendrils. "Please rest. I will return later, with food." She clapped her hands in delight.

I am supposed to be her pet, Alivet thought sourly. *Nothing more and nothing less. And when she is tired of me and I no longer amuse this 'higher being,' what will become of me then?* It was easy to envisage Elaniel forgetting to feed her. This time she had no sharp instruments to hand, no alchematorium resources, but there had to be *some* way of getting out of here . . .

Alivet settled herself as best she could and began to think.

chapter III

NETHES

B y the time that Gulzhur Elaniel glided back into the room, Alivet had formed the glimmerings of a plan, but she had no time to put it into practice. Elaniel touched the vine mesh, and it shrank away to create a wider net. Alivet could have got her head through the spaces, but nothing more. She looked up at Elaniel. The woman wore a long shift, of what Alivet initially thought to be velvet. Then she saw that the dress was made of lichen: held together by a web of vines and starred with flowers. Elaniel's beautiful face was dusted with golden pollen. She looked as serene as calm water. Alivet hated her.

"Some folk are coming," Elaniel informed her. "They wish to see you." She bent and peered through the mesh of Alivet's living cage. "I've told them a lot about you."

"Have you."

"Yes, and they are *longing* to see you, perhaps even to converse with you a little, if you are not too awed."

"I'll manage."

"Wonderful," Elaniel said. Softly, she clapped her hands. The cage in which Alivet was held began to rise, gliding smoothly into the air. Alivet looked up in alarm and saw that she was being lifted by a cable of vines, coiling into the mat of dry growth that formed the ceiling.

"What are you doing?" she cried.

"They will wish to see you. You can't expect my visitors to crouch on the floor."

Elaniel was now standing beneath Alivet. The cage elongated and stretched so that Alivet could stand up. She did so, her joints cracking with relief. Grasping the bars of her cage, she looked down. Elaniel smiled up at her and beyond she could see others entering the room. They, too, were clad in lichen and flowers. Their hair snaked down their backs. Their eyes were bright and they whispered behind their long hands. A pungent, smoldering odor filled the room. Alivet's skin began to crawl.

"You see? I told truth. She came here, this morning, transported bodily by the spirit of a drug—a visitor from the world of Yethes."

The Nethenassi surrounded Alivet's cage, pulling it down to tweak the bars aside. Their hands came through the mesh, plucking at Alivet's shift. She was sorely tempted to bite, but the hands were clawed and sharp.

"Stop it!" she snapped. "Leave me alone."

Murmuring, frowning, the Nethenassi withdrew.

"She is unsocial," one of them said.

"Yes, an animal."

"And you wish to teach her? Truly, Elaniel, you have a generous soul." They clustered around Gulzhur Elaniel, cooing and whispering, until Alivet felt quite nauseated. Not even Ari Ghairen had been so complacent—and that was an unwise thought, for she found herself missing Ghairen with a sharpness that surprised her. Perhaps if she kept silent and refused to look at them, they might leave her alone. She sat down on the floor of her cage with her back to the Nethenassi and stared grimly toward the window. She could hear the seedpods exploding, and the crackling of distant fires. The Nethenassi whispered and laughed. Gently, they rocked the cage so that it shook. Alivet paid no attention and closed her eyes so that she would not have to look at them. She thought about Latent Emanation, concentrating hard.

Whatever the truth of these labyrinthine machinations, she was convinced of one thing: if Elaniel and her friends approved of them, the Lords of Night intended nothing but harm. It seemed that Ghairen had been right after all: if they had once been perfect beings, they were surely now corrupt, and they corrupted those who touched them, like this bunch of sinister idiots.

If she could bring about the Lords' downfall, she would do so. If she could break out of this prison and find her way out of here, she would risk returning to Hathes if she could not find her own world. Even Ghairen was a better choice than these simpering folk, so convinced of their own righteousness. The Nethenassi, stuck in the honey of their own complacency; the people of Hathes, with their rigidly paranoid society and murderous antics; and her own community on Latent Emanation, who had invented little that was new for a hundred years and whose only form of inquiry remained the Search, which if Elaniel spoke the truth, was nothing more than a retrograde quest for a miserable world.

And Alivet thought: *All the worlds are stagnant. We have all become trapped and embedded, like flies in river amber. But how are we to transform and break free? How am I going to get out of here?* In the crucible of frustration and anger, however, her thoughts were beginning to crystallize. She had come via the drug. That meant that unless she could find another portal, like the one by which Ghairen had brought her to Hathes, she would have to use the drug and the roads by which its spirit traveled to take her home.

She opened her eyes to find that the rustling, twittering visitors had gone away. The bars of her cage had once more shrunk together, so that her view of the room beyond was filtered by tendrils. Hearing Elaniel returning, she lay hastily down on the cage floor and feigned sleep. Distantly, she heard Elaniel's coaxing, cajoling voice, but eventually it grew silent. Perhaps she really did doze, for when she once more looked up, the room had grown quiet and dark.

Now, then, was the time to try out her plan. It was, in essence, simple. The tabernanthe had taken her out onto the road of the unconscious, but the mayjen had kidnapped her. And from what the spirit of the mayjen had implied, it was not Ghairen who had poisoned her, but Iraguila and her shiffrey accomplice. The mayjen was not a proper poison at all, but a hallucinogen, planted like a dangerous seed in the depths of her being.

If a drug had brought her here, then a drug could take her back again. She needed new allies—one to deal with the mayjen, and the other to take her back between the worlds. This time, Alivet had every intention of going home.

Sitting cross-legged on the floor of the cage, Alivet reached out and prodded one of the furled blossoms. At first, for a dismayed moment, she thought the lily might remain tightly shut, but gradually it began to unwind, releasing its soporific perfume upon the air. Reacting to her activity, it was trying to put her to sleep, but rather than attempting to resist it, Alivet breathed deeply, inhaling the perfume until it filled her lungs. This time, however, she treated the narcotic scent as a potential friend, rather than an unwelcome invader. She remembered her long training as an apothecary, her experiences in the Search. She must seek to ally herself with the drug instead of fighting it. Persuasion, not attack: that must be the key. As the narcotic perfume sank farther into her veins, Alivet began softly to converse with the drug.

"You are welcome in me," she told it. "Let me learn from you. Teach me what you are."

Slowly, she felt the animating spirit of the narcotic begin to uncurl also, just like its attendant blossom. It felt fragile and strange, a barely conscious presence, and she realized that the narcotic's spirit, too, must spend most of its life in sleep. It was like talking to a dream, something half real. Deep inside her mind, she felt the presence of the mayjen beginning to uncurl, slithering from her subconscious; the enemy within. How could it not know what she was planning to do? It was inside her head, after all. That meant that at some point in the not-too-distant future, she would have to confront the mayjen, but for the moment, it could be ignored.

"Can you hear me?" Alivet murmured, inside her head. And after a long moment, a small, sweet voice said, "I hear you. Who are you, and what manner of thing?" It was the voice of the narcotic drug of the lilies.

"I am a human. Your corporeal self—the drug that houses your spirit—is inside my body. It is affecting me, making me sleepy."

"And then you can dream!" the spirit said, with a kind of exultation.

"I do not want to dream here," Alivet said, patiently. "It isn't the right place for me. I need a special place to dream."

She did not know if the spirit understood, but then it said, "Where is this place?"

"It lies outside this room. Indeed, it is outside this world. If you and I were to dream there, spirit, then our dreams would be marvelous. I could show you incredible things, inside my mind. We would work together. But not here."

"Can we go there?" The narcotic was intrigued.

"I can't. There are two other drug-spirits in me. One is my ally, the other is my enemy. My enemy is holding me prisoner. Help me to be free of it, and we will travel together."

"But I have been told to keep you here," the spirit said, puzzled. "Why should that be?"

"I do not know. Perhaps the person who told you did not realize that I could dream better elsewhere. I am sure she means things only for the best."

"Maybe that is so," the narcotic mused.

Inside Alivet's mind, the mayjen stirred suddenly, like a serpent that has caught sight of a bird.

"Who is that?" the narcotic asked.

"It is an enemy. Can you help me defeat it?"

"I have no weapons, no toxins. I am a drug of sleep, nothing more."

"Precisely," Alivet said. "Put the mayjen to sleep."

She could almost see the particles of the narcotic seeping deep into her brain: running down its channels, leaping across the connection points that linked thought to thought. She did not know if this would work. It was nothing more than a mimicry of the healers' art: to use a drug to fight a sickness, or to combat the effects of another drug.

Using the imaging techniques that she had been taught during her apothecarial training, Alivet sought to see what was happening inside her head. She glimpsed the mayjen, its snakelike tail whisking around the corners of her unconscious, hiding in deep wells of uncertainty, behind the spikes of paranoia and the lagunae of guilt. Alivet took a breath. The narcotic particles of the lily slipped after the mayjen, dispersing into a perfumed cloud which gradually grew to fill the chambers of her brain. Alivet felt herself sliding away, faster and faster down the slope to sleep. But now she could feel the tabernanthe, stirring. She glimpsed its face: it looked like Celana. Its eyes were huge and dark.

"No!" she cried to the tabernanthe. "I've got to stay awake—I have to direct you, tell you where to take me."

"Do not worry," the voice of the tabernanthe said, serenely. "I know where to go. I have cousins there."

Alivet's inner vision was beginning to dim. From the corner of her mind's eye she saw the figure that represented the mayjen sink down beneath the influence of the narcotic, curling its tail beneath it and folding its hands in sleep. It was defeated. But so was Alivet.

"And now I will take you home," the tabernanthe said.

"Wait!"—but it was too late. Alivet felt her body dissolve, transported into the space between the worlds—and then she was pulled abruptly back into the cage.

"Where are you going?" Gulzhur Elaniel said.

Alivet's eyes flew open. The woman stood in front of her,

smiling with terrible sweetness, but inside her, the drug was continuing to work, momentarily hindered by adrenaline.

"You," Elaniel said, "are not going anywhere." She lashed out and her fingers caught Alivet's arm, the long nails razor-sharp. Alivet struck out, catching Elaniel on the side of her face. She grasped the woman's silken hair and pulled. Elaniel emitted a high, eerie shriek. Vines fell from the ceiling, raveling into a noose. Alivet ducked. Tendrils rose up from the floor, clutching at her ankles. She kicked free and threw herself at Elaniel. The woman was howling, a long ululation that was like nothing Alivet had ever heard. It did not sound like anything from a human throat.

As her body made contact with Elaniel's, the cry abruptly stopped. Alivet had a glimpse of Elaniel's face beneath her, mouth open, hair streaming into a sudden abyss. The tabernanthe was taking them both between the worlds. Alivet glanced over her shoulder. Behind her was the room; a mass of twisting vines. Before her gaped the universe.

CONJUNCTION

But let that man with better sense advice
That of the world least part to us is read:
And daily how through hardy enterprise,
Many great Regions are discoveréd,
Which to late age were never mentionéd . . .

⌐ EDMUND SPENSER, *The Faerie Queene*

chapter I

PRAGUE ⤳ 1584

D ee stood in the center of the chamber, dressed in a long plain robe. At the desk sat Kelley with the mirror before him, already deep in trance. It was close to midnight. Kneeling, Dee drew a rough chalk circle about himself, then set about inscribing the calculations that would open the gap between the worlds. A skein of mathematical incantations, interspersed with sigils, began to cover the floor around the circle: the language of the universe, designed to unweave reality and open gaps between. From the direction of the desk Kelley said softly, "It comes."

"The angel? Ask if it can come through."

"It says, not yet. The calculations are not yet complete. The formula must be finished, to rend the veil that remains between dimensions."

Dee scribbled furiously, drawing each formula to its logical conclusion. As he did so, he became aware that the air about him was growing brighter, as though the sun had come forth at midnight and was creeping across the sill.

"It comes," Kelley repeated, and now Dee sensed the

presence of the angel at his shoulder. His hand flew above the boards, inscribing formulae, and as he reached the very last equation, the world around him changed and tore. A small hole appeared in the air, through which a cold wind streamed. As Dee stared, the hole widened and became a rent, ragged and drifting. The angel stood behind it, and Dee realized that the being's previous appearances had been nothing more than a shadow of this one. The angel's four-faced presence was intensely physical; it struck him like a blow.

"Come through, then," the angel's ringing voices instructed him.

Dee paused, uncertain. The angel seemed huge and solid, but he could sense movement all around it.

"Your calculations are imperfect. The portal is not stable. Step through," the angel commanded. Dee took a tottering step forward and, after a moment of pure fear, threw himself through the rent in the air.

The chalk circle, the room, and Kelley himself were all gone. Dee stood in an echoing chamber that hummed like a hive of bees. The angel towered above him.

"Where is this?"

"This is the ship."

Dee looked uncertainly around him. The place in which they stood was more like an empty hull; he could see the great metal ribs of the thing arching over his head, but there was no sign of furniture or fittings, no sea chests or cargo. But why should an angel need such things? A still small voice inside his mind said: *Why would angels need a ship at all?* But of course they did not; it was surely for the convenience of humans only, who could not travel the roads of the stars as the angels surely did.

"It is spare and plain," the angel said, revolving so that he was faced with its female side. Dee wondered if it had heard his thoughts. "The journey will not take long, but it is hard on humankind." With that, the angel touched Dee on the cheek and he felt himself crumple to the floor.

He woke to find himself in the same place, curled on the metal floor of the ship like a child. He was sore and stiff, and the humming note of the ship ran through him as though he was a bell that had been struck. His head splitting, Dee clambered to his feet. The angel was nowhere to be seen. A dim pallor was cast down from a row of lights in the roof. This must be the hold of the ship rather than the ship itself, Dee thought. At least if all went well, there would be room for the Family, who by now numbered some eight hundred people.

As Dee stared up into the metal arches of the ship, the angel came back, stepping out of nowhere.

"We have arrived."

"We are there?" Dee echoed, stupidly. It seemed so swift, so improbable.

"Follow me."

Dee stumbled behind the angel to a doorway, which opened as they drew close. Pale sunlight streamed in, casting Dee's shadow behind him, but the angel, he observed, cast no shadow. It drew back, until it stood behind the door.

"Go," it said. "Look. Be careful."

Dee hastened to the door and realized nearly too late why the angel had given its warning. They were hovering some fifty feet above a great expanse of river and marsh. A flock of birds akin to herons rocketed up from a reed bed and soared past the door. Below, in the shining water, Dee saw a school of fish flick their tails and vanish into the depths. A strange bulbous shadow cast the reed beds into darkness: it was a moment before Dee realized that it was the shadow of the ship itself. He leaned precariously out and squinted up. A great black hull, pitted with craters as if by the pox, stretched above him. The ship began to move, drifting over an area of land. The earth was dark red and looked fertile; there were few trees.

"It seems a rich land," Dee said over his shoulder, somewhat heartened.

"It will be yours."

"What of the jackal-headed men?"

"They keep to the deep delta. They will not trouble you here."

If the adventurers to the New World can deal with savages, Dee thought, *so, too, can we*. The air was fresh and sweet, smelling differently to that of Earth, and the light was different, too: paler, and seeming to come from another angle. He wondered if Kelley could see what he was seeing, through the window of the black mirror.

"When we come—if we come—can we bring beasts with us? The Family should like to raise cattle, for instance."

"We shall advise you."

"And now, may we make landfall? I should like to study this place, to see what manner of plants and creatures are here."

"The ship will not land."

Slowly, the door began to hiss shut before Dee's face.

"Wait! Please, I must see more—" But the door had closed. The ship shivered and hummed.

"The portal you opened will not stay open much longer. You must refine your calculations," the angel said.

"Will you help me?"

"I will."

This time, the angel did not immediately send Dee into unconsciousness. As it was reaching to touch his cheek, a note like a great bell sounded, deep within the ship. The angel spun around and vanished, leaving Dee rocking back on his heels.

"Where have you gone?" he called, but there was no reply. Dee walked slowly along the hold of the ship, staring up at the metal arches and laminated girders. When he had first stepped into the craft, an idea had struck him with heretical weight, and now he was free to give it a degree of attention. If he was honest with himself, Dee admitted, the notion had been biting at the heels of his imagination for some considerable time.

The idea was terrifying, but as Dee contemplated it, it fell seamlessly into place like the workings of one of Mercator's miraculous astrolabes. Dee was thinking: *What if these beings are not angels at all? What if they are simply other to ourselves, just as the savages of the Americas are other?* Nothing that Dee had read of the people in the colonies of the New World suggested that they possessed less wit than Englishman or Spaniard, whatever the clerics might say. It had long been Dee's opinion that the natives of the Americas simply pursued different knowledge, in a different way.

To these "angelic" beings, he reasoned, *it is likely that we are as savages: primitive and uncouth, possessing limited intellect and groping our way toward the light as a flower does toward the sun, but nonetheless worthy of attention.* And then the stale air of the hold seemed to stir and blow colder, for Dee thought: *These beings are as far above us as we are above the Indians, and see how we have treated the peoples of the Americas.* But there had been no sign from the angels, or whatever they might be, that their intentions were hostile, and they spoke of God with reverence. Yet what if that was nothing more than an evil lie?

The dim light pulsed and changed. Dee turned, to see the angel standing behind him. For a moment, it looked like something else entirely. It seemed to have a different shape, monstrous and contorted. Then the vision was gone and the angel was once more bland and four-visaged. Was that image no more than a mask, to hide horror?

"Tell me," Dee said, very softly. "What manner of being *are* you?"

He thought he saw a flicker in its eyes, but the angel did not reply. Instead, it reached out and he felt its cold fingers touch his cheek. When he next awoke, he was lying on the floor of the chamber in Prague, with Kelley and Niclaes hovering anxiously over him.

chapter II

HATHES

Elaniel's hand was locked around Alivet's wrist as they fell, and her touch burned. Alivet struck out, but failed to dislodge Elaniel's grip. Against the span of stars, Elaniel's serene face was stripped down to a mask: gaunt and bony like a leaf in autumn, her teeth sharp as thorns. She hissed, and Alivet saw a spiny tongue protrude. Elaniel spat at her and Alivet turned her head away, but she still felt the acid prickle of the woman's saliva spatter across her cheek.

Elaniel's tongue curled up inside her mouth, a worm within the bud. Before she could spit again, Alivet hauled her imprisoned wrist up to her mouth and gave Elaniel's hand a swift sharp bite. The hand opened; Elaniel shrieked. Alivet, still falling, kicked her away and watched her spin down toward the field of suns. Soon, she was no bigger than a lizard in a meadow of daisies, and then she was gone.

Alivet gasped, but her lungs took in no air. It was as though she were a child again, diving for frogs in the marsh and staying down too deep and too long. She spread her arms and dived down the silvery road that the drug was unraveling beneath her. The terrible cold gave way to a sultry blast of heat and Alivet fell through subconscious space to land heavily on the carpeted floor of her room in Ghairen's apartment.

The breath was knocked out of her. She lay retching on the stones, reveling in the sudden warmth. The room smelled of the smoke and hot coals from the brazier, with the familiarly acrid chemical tang of the air of Hathes. Alivet hauled herself shakily to her feet.

Ari Ghairen said from the shadows. "So, how was your trip? What of the tabernanthe?" He spoke lightly, but she could hear the relief in his voice. Alivet spun to face him. He looked the same as ever, precise and elegant in the voluminous dark robes, but when she looked into his eyes, she saw only the fear fading from them. And Alivet, noting her own foolishness with a distant amazement, flung herself upon him. He had brought her to these nightmare worlds under duress, had held her a virtual prisoner, doubtless had lied, but he was not Gulzhur Elaniel and at that moment this was all Alivet cared about. Ghairen's arms tightened around her. Into her ear, he murmured, "Are you all right? What happened to your face?"

"There was a woman. Elaniel. She held me captive on a world called Nethes. I got away. She spat at me."

"*Nethes?*" He held her away for a moment, to look at her, then drew her back. She felt no inclination to resist. "However did you get all the way to Nethes?"

"The drug took me. Not the tabernanthe. Something else." When she got a moment, Alivet thought, she would have plenty to say about Iraguila Ust, but it could wait. Ghairen frowned.

"We'll discuss this later. Her name was Elaniel? A Kherubim name, given to her by her masters, most probably. Yes, they are often filled with bitterness and bile. Your face is bleeding—if we don't treat it, it will scar."

"She said they were enlightened," Alivet said. She put her hand to her burned cheek and her fingertips came away touched with blood. Ghairen fetched a cloth and a salve, and gently began to treat the burns.

"Well, they are certainly a more advanced form of humanity in certain senses, but unfortunately their gifts entail that they often have a peculiar disdain for the lower forms, such as you and me. They spend hours of their days in poetry and meditation, and human flesh is served on their menus. They have entered into symbiosis with the plant life of their world; you'll have noted that vegetables are not long on sympathy. And now," Ghairen said, looking down at Alivet's hands as they rested upon his robe, "after your experiences with the people of Nethes and my erstwhile governess, you will not know what to think, or who to trust. Can I suggest the lesser evil of myself?"

Too tired to protest, Alivet nodded. She did not want him to let her go. The blood on her cheek had smudged his robe.

"Come and sit down. By the way, my daughter is up and about, but we have not seen Ust since her dismissal—which, I now realize, came rather too late."

Alivet looked up at that.

"You know who she is?"

"Ust is not her real name, nor did I have her father murdered. I looked into it, most carefully, when she first inquired about the post—occasionally these things slip one's mind, you know. I knew she wasn't who she claimed to be, but she laid a false trail behind her, posing as the daughter of a prominent politician, born out of wedlock. That's common enough here. Having found one concealed scandal, I didn't look for another. But it seems that Ust is a provocateur of the Lords of Night. I was deceived." He grimaced. "Not a pleasing confession to have to make."

"I can imagine."

"From the little that you have told me, it seems probable that she has been working with Elaniel. And I have also found evidence that she is connected to a religious group." He guided Alivet to the couch.

"The Sanguinants? She had friends among them, but I didn't know what they were."

"The Sanguinants are the religious order I mentioned to you—the remnants of our own manner of Unpriest class."

"You said they had been chastened . . . Maybe they want to bring the Lords back to Hathes, seek to regain power. The Nethenassi aren't the only ones to ally themselves with humanity's enemies. The Unpriests would hate to see the back of the Lords, and so would the Nine Families. No doubt it is the same with the Sanguinants."

Ghairen's gaze narrowed. "What else did Ust tell you?"

"That she wanted to help the shiffrey."

"I see. How much do you know about the shiffrey?"

"That they were once a noble people, living close to nature."

Ghairen snorted. "They certainly live close to nature. They've always been as you see them now. They hide in burrows and seize the young of rival clans in which to lay their eggs. They are very good at deception, at psychological manipulation. They can induce all manner of impressions and ideas in the minds of their prey."

"Why do you keep the shiffrey as servants, in that case? Aren't they dangerous?"

"The nerve-toxins and hallucinogens that they produce are useful. The maid is milked, on a regular basis, by a special machine. This denudes her of her poisons and keeps her placid. In return, believe me, she has a far nicer life than she'd be enjoying as a brood-daughter in a shiffrey burrow."

Alivet wondered about this, but said nothing. She was uncomfortably reminded of the Lords themselves: perhaps they, too, felt that humans had more pleasant lives under their rule than they would have done alone. But this was not a time for social analysis. Despite the salve her cheek felt as though it was about to peel from her face; waves of erratic pain caused her vision to blur.

"Now," she heard Ghairen say, "I need to know about the tabernanthe."

She said something, but the words made no sense.

"Alivet? Are you all right?" His voice was sharp with concern.

"Ghairen?"

"I'm here, Alivet."

She reached out. The high paneled walls darkened as pain pulsed through her. Alivet's head lolled back against the seat; she could not seem to keep it upright.

"She's poisoned me," she said. She did not know, now, whether she was talking about Ust or Elaniel.

"What did you say, Alivet?"

She echoed her fears, but though she thought she spoke clearly, she could see from the uncomprehending expression on his face that Ghairen had not understood her.

"You're not making sense, Alivet. Try not to speak. You can tell me later."

Alivet nodded. The chill of between-space had long since worn away and she was now feverish and hot. She could think only of poison. A voice said above her, anxiously, "Is she going to be all right?" She thought it was Celana.

Then Ghairen, speaking calmly enough, but with a hint of panic that she could not remember hearing in his voice before: "I don't know. Bring me the mennenope and the hathrey."

Hathrey is a stimulant for the heart, to be used only in cases of terrible illness. It simulates the power of the sun, drawing life into lifelessness. Gilbert's Herbal echoed through her head: the precise, dry voice of her instructor back home in Levanah.

"And then?"

She was sitting in front of the examiner; his eyeglasses pushed up onto his forehead as he stared at her. She noted, irrelevantly, that there was a hole in his earlobe where a ring had once been set.

"Mistress Dee? I asked you a question relating to the properties of mennenope."

"It thins the blood," Alivet said, slowly. "It drives certain toxins from the veins. But it can be dangerous, causing the lungs to falter and fail. It must be used in very small quantities."

"Good," the examiner said, and his face elongated and grew pale. His eyeglasses melted into bony sockets; his eyes were the color of the garnet stones that she had once found along the shore.

"You've passed the exam," Ari Ghairen said, and smiled.

chapter III

TOWER OF THE POISONERS, HATHES

A livet awoke to find Ghairen sitting by the side of the bed. She stared at him for a moment, wondering where she was and whether she was dreaming, and then she remembered. Ghairen's face had lost its habitual expression of avuncular concern. He looked gaunt and hungry, as though about to take a piece out of her. Her fingers tightened around the sheet, pulling it closer. But when he spoke, he sounded mild enough.

"How are you feeling, Alivet? Do you feel well enough to talk?"

"I think so."

"I'm sorry to press you so, but I have to know about the tabernanthe. Is it an ally or not?"

Alivet thought back to the face of the drug: its dark, serene eyes and the way that it had taken her so obligingly out onto the roads of the unconscious. "I think so. Yes. Yes, it's an ally."

"And you can persuade it to carry the light that will poison the Lords?"

"I think so."

"Then today we're going home."

"Home?" Alivet faltered.

"To Latent Emanation." Ghairen stood abruptly, in a rush of robes. "And once we're on the drift-boat, we'll take the tabernanthe up to the solar deck and you must convince it to absorb the rays of the sun, hold it as latent light. This is where it begins, Alivet."

The thought of going home was enough to make her throw back the bedclothes and reach for her clothes.

"I'll leave you to dress," Ghairen said.

"No! Wait a moment." She turned to face him. "Ghairen, listen," she began, and told him the story of her visit to the alchemist.

"She said she was healing me, removing the poison that Iraguila said you had given me. But she wasn't, was she? She was poisoning me herself, with the drug of the mayjen."

"Iraguila," Ghairen said, "seems to have been most enterprising."

"There's something I need to know, and rather than more plots and schemes, I'm just going to ask. Are you planning to have me killed at the end of all this?"

The garnet eyes looked straight into her own. Ghairen turned and sat down on the edge of the bed. "No. Why would I?"

"Because you might want an inconvenient witness out of the way when she had accomplished the task set for her?"

"I am a murderer, it's true. But I am not *gratuitous*, Alivet. I reasoned that your sister would be a good enough reason for you to help me." He hesitated. "Alivet—when the Lords are gone, it isn't death I have in mind to offer you." He reached out and took her hand between his own.

"What, then?" Alivet faltered. She leaned a little closer to him.

"I was going to offer you a job."

"I'll think about it," Alivet said, alarmed by how disappointed she felt. She hoped it was not revealed in her voice as she added briskly, "And I'd appreciate a health check. To make sure that there are no additional poisons in my system."

Like love, she thought, but she was not going to say that aloud.

An hour of tests later, Ghairen could find nothing.

"An interesting plan, to implant the mayjen. A spy in your head and a carrier to bring you to Elaniel." He slipped her sleeve down to cover her arm. Throughout the testing, his touch had been impersonal and sparing, as though he no longer entirely trusted himself in her presence.

"Why couldn't Iraguila have done that herself?" Alivet asked.

"I suspect she lacked the skill. The shiffrey shamen have a delicate relationship with the entheogens of this world, which we Hathanassi do not possess. We're much farther from our natural surroundings than you are."

"So there's nothing wrong with me?" Alivet asked.

"Nothing that I can find." With which Alivet was forced to be content.

She insisted on saying good-bye to Celana before they left. It was not an easy parting; the girl clasped Alivet's arm with white, desperate fingers.

"Don't leave me here," Celana whispered. Her arm was still swathed in bandages; she looked small and pale and somehow very reminiscent of Inkirietta.

"I have to," Alivet said sadly. "But you'll be safer here. Your father will be with me, after all."

"It's not my father I'm afraid of now. It's Iraguila." The girl's face crumpled. "My father told me what she did to you. I thought she was my friend. But she just used me. Like everyone else."

"I haven't been using you, Celana." As she spoke, Alivet remembered Celana's blood spilling out over the workbench, to make that glittering and unnatural drug. But that had been an accident, and no more of the girl's blood had gone into the mixture. Or had it? Celana was so pale...

Alivet took a deep breath.

"Celana—since the accident, your father hasn't hurt you in any way, has he?"

Celana shook her head.

"Has he ever actually hurt you? Or—done anything? Touched you in a way that he should not have?" Within the pockets of her skirts, her hands tensed into fists in anticipation of the girl's answer: not just dismay for Celana, but for herself. She could forgive Ghairen for many things, but not for that.

"No, never." Celana sounded startled, and mercifully indignant. "It's just that I've always been afraid of him, ever since my mother died. I knew she never loved him, and there were the contract-wives, after he married her." Celana paused. "She came from one of the music clans. She was so beautiful. She was always playing the kithera and she used to sing, too... Then, when we went to Loviti, she became sick. When Iraguila came here, she told me that it had been my father who had killed her—grown tired of her and wanted her gone. Iraguila said she had been my mother's friend, you see, that she came here to find out what had happened to her. She told me she had found proof of the murder, but that my father's allies were too powerful and we would never succeed in bringing charges. Was all that a lie?"

"I have no idea. But it doesn't entirely make sense, Celana. Couldn't your father have got a divorce?"

"Of course not. Such disgrace!"

Hathanassi customs, thought Alivet. "Why would he kill her, though? He told me he loved her."

Celana pondered this. "I don't know."

"Isn't it possible that your poor mother just died of natural causes?" She had never thought that she would be sitting here arguing Ghairen's case, Alivet thought.

"I suppose so. But Iraguila seemed so sure."

"How old were you then?"

"I was ten."

"I see," Alivet said, thoughtfully. Perhaps she had been taking Iraguila Ust's role as potential assassin too literally. For though the governess appeared to have left her enemy's daughter physically unharmed, she had poisoned her nevertheless: with words and ideas rather than chemical toxins. Surely and effectively, using Celana's motherless state as her instrument, she had turned Celana against her father. And now Celana was in the same position as herself: uncertain who to trust, the boundaries of her life shifting and changing.

"Listen," Alivet said, and then she told Celana about Inki.

"I'm so sorry," Celana said. Her mouth turned mournfully downward. "I see why you have to go home."

"I can't make you promises, Celana," Alivet said. "But if I can come back, I will."

Ghairen took her down through the tower, retracing the steps that they had taken on that first day, which now seemed months ago to Alivet. Here was the elevator with its brass trimmings, the mechanism whirring silently within the depths of the tower. Here was the echoing hallway, and the dock upon which the canal quietly lapped. Alivet could hear her footsteps clattering through the hallway, but Ghairen's feet made no sound, moving as noiselessly as a ghost.

"Where are we going?" Alivet asked, though she thought that she already knew the answer.

"We are returning to the portal. From there, we will go back to Latent Emanation. I've sent a message to an anube clan; they are the only ones I can trust now." Alivet saw Ghairen's fingers close tightly on the small case containing the poison.

Earlier, they had worked out how to carry it: placing as much of the powder as they could in a lead-lined phial and packing it down.

"What shall we call it?" Ghairen had asked. "I think it should have a name."

"We'll call it Blood Tabernanthe," Alivet said. She had thought of naming the substance "Celanem," but it seemed inappropriate to connect Ghairen's daughter with such a powerful new drug.

Now the dappled light of the metal river sent shards and ripples across Ghairen's face. "So we begin our campaign against the Lords of Night. It will be short, Alivet, and either it will be entirely successful or an utter failure."

"How optimistic are you?" Alivet asked before she could stop herself.

"I am a scientist," Ghairen said. "I weigh evidence when I get it."

"And on this occasion?"

"I've no idea."

The barge was gliding down the canal toward them. Alivet stepped over the side, and Ghairen cast off.

It seemed an eternity before they reached the gate tower. Alivet stepped out onto the familiar red marble stairs. The walls of the parc-verticale hung nearby, eerily translucent in the early-morning air. *Somewhere inside*, Alivet thought, *there is a shiffrey shaman living in a burrow, casting dark energies*. She hoped never to set foot inside the place again. Though it did contain some interesting plants . . .

She looked up to see the observation point of the gate tower spiraling above her head, a glass needle catching the light of the sun. She thought of injections and blood. Behind it, she could see the storm-cloud shadow of the drift-boat. A group of Hathanassi men stood nearby, looking askance at Ghairen.

"Who are they?" Alivet asked.

"Passengers, perhaps."

"To Latent Emanation?"

"No, to other places. Nethes, perhaps—there is some trade with the Nethenassi—or Tisach. Most probably the latter. The Tisachen are friendly, and their shadow-art is much in demand in wealthier circles."

Alivet frowned. "Is the orbit of Latent a regular stopping place for this ship, then?"

"No. I had to pay." Ghairen's fingers flickered in dismissal. "A great deal, in fact. But it's government money. If we can open up Latent to trade, as the Soret hopes to do, then you will see greater traffic in Latent's orbit. But for now, we are the only ones going to Latent Emanation."

"Ghairen, when we get there, are we going to go back through the same portal?"

"There are five portals on your world. Four are located in the Palaces of Night; the other one allows only entry, not departure. We'll be going back through that one. I don't want to end up in another Night Palace, not after last time."

Alivet, immediately interested, said, "Where is this portal?"

Ghairen grimaced. "In some swamp somewhere. The anubes patrol it regularly, in case of visitors. I am counting on it that they will be there."

Whatever might happen, Alivet thought, she was going home, away from this arid, dry world with its strange rivers and piercing air, its poisons and its schemes, and she was never coming back again.

But then a face rose up before the eye of her mind: pale and scared against the dark velvet pillow. Alivet blinked. It was as though she once more stood before the statue in Ghairen's room, or the anube's ancient chamber beneath the Palace of Night. Two faces were staring back at her from memory: Celana and Inkirietta, like two sides of a coin. One living as a prisoner in toxic luxury, and the other a mutilated servant of the Lords of Night. If she could, Alivet thought, she would save them both.

She and Ghairen walked between the crimson glass walls of the gate tower and up the stairway to the platform where the passage to the drift-boat lay.

"Have you still got the phial?" she asked Ghairen, anxiously.

He smiled at her. "Don't worry, Alivet. It's quite safe."

"What if Iraguila's around somewhere?" Alivet had been keeping an eye out for Ghairen's erstwhile governess ever since they had left the tower, but apart from the small congregation of passengers, the early-morning city seemed deserted.

"She is not. I have been keeping track of Iraguila ever

since her dismissal. She has gone to ground, it seems—quite literally, into a shiffrey burrow."

"And you're sure she's not here? I don't suddenly want a poisoned dart in my neck. And what about the others? The Sanguinants?"

"She has not returned to Ukesh. The Sanguinant temple has been closed: the Soret ordered a raid last night, on my recommendation. That's partly why the city's so quiet this morning."

Despite these reassurances, Alivet continued to keep a watchful eye upon the passengers. They joined the queue for the portal, standing impatiently in line as the passengers for the drift-boat were processed.

"Do you have papers for me?"

"Everything is in order, Alivet. If we're going to encounter problems, they'll be at the other end."

Now that the prospect of returning to Latent Emanation was finally becoming real, Alivet found that she was more nervous than ever. The thought of buying a shack in the fens and spending the rest of her life fishing from the veranda was extraordinarily appealing. Inki and Celana and her aunt could live there, too...

And Ghairen? She stole a glance at him. Entirely too urbane for life in a swamp. Alivet gave up her fantasy with a sigh. Besides, Inki was still Enbonded, Celana was traumatized, and Alivet's aunt was who knew where. Presumably the Unpriests had doubled their efforts to bring the fugitive Alivet to justice after the events in the Night Palace. The thought of her aunt's neat house ransacked and riven by Unpriests was a terrible one. *Once we defeat the Lords of Night,* Alivet told herself, *the Unpriests are going to be the first to go.*

Her shoulder blades remained itchy until she stepped through the link to the drift-boat and had once again taken a seat in the waiting area. She watched the patterned leaves entwine about her waist with a mixture of impatience and relief. Ghairen was distracted and uncharacteristically silent until the boat had risen past the atmosphere of Hathes. Then he rose to his feet.

"Time to go up to the solar deck. Bring the phial with you."

The solar deck was perched at the pinnacle of the ship; she could see the drift-boat's vast dark hull curving away below. Hathes hung against the star meadows, baleful as an eye. Into her ear Ghairen murmured, "You have no idea how much it's costing for us to stroll around up here. Usually it's reserved for the upper echelons alone."

"Won't people wonder what we're doing?"

"Doubtless. But they're unlikely to come over and make inquiries. I *am* a Fifth Grade poisoner, after all. Can you talk to the drug?" Ghairen asked.

"I'll try." Alivet took the small burner from her pocket and placed a pinch of the tabernanthe upon it. "I'll need a light."

"Here." Fire flickered across Ghairen's gloved hand. The tabernanthe began to smolder, smoke drifted upward. "You'd better sit down." He guided Alivet to a nearby seat. A group of passengers, enjoying the view, eyed her nervously. Alivet ignored them. With Ghairen's steadying arm around her shoulders, she closed her eyes and inhaled. And after a moment, it was there. She could see the face of the ally: inquiry in its great dark eyes.

"It is you," the tabernanthe said.

"Yes. Do you remember me?"

"You were with me, moments ago." A ripple passed over the ally's face, like water or heat. "Or was it years? I cannot remember."

"I need you to do something for me. Do you see this sun?"

"Of course."

"I need you to absorb some of its light into yourself, to take it and hold it. Can you do that?"

"Why must I?"

"To help the bloodlines from which you spring," Alivet said, holding her breath in case it was the wrong answer. She had never before worked with a drug that shared a common origin with humanity. The ally seemed to recede within her mind, as though glimpsed through the wrong end of a telescope. Then it was back.

"I will do as you ask," it said. Alivet opened the phial. The substance of the drug lay glistening within. She placed it in front of the viewing port. Gradually, as they watched, it grew brighter, until it shone with a light of its own. Alivet could hear muttering voices behind them.

"That's enough," Ghairen said, and closed the phial with a snap. Hathes receded, to become no greater than the head of a ruby pin. A veil slid across the viewing port. "Preparing for the journey," Ghairen said. "Nothing to see in No-Space. We should go back down."

They returned to the depths of the ship. Eventually, Alivet grew tired of the ragged frustrations of waiting. Making sure that the phial was safely stowed in her pocket, she found a dormitory capsule, hoping that when she awoke, the drift-boat would have reached her own world. That was one thing that could be said for the road of the unconscious: it might be less comfortable, but it was certainly quicker. She dozed, plagued by shapeless, disturbing dreams. When she woke again, it was to find Ghairen's hand on her shoulder.

"We've arrived," he said.

They made their way to the ship's portal. Again there was that brief, electrifying moment, then Alivet and Ghairen were stepping through into cool, dim air. A breath of salt breeze drifted through the room. Alivet ran toward open double doors and found that she was looking out across a great expanse of placid water. It was evening. A smear of sunlight remained on the far horizon and a marsh bird cried plaintively from the reeds. Water lapped at the edge of the doors. She could see steps leading down beneath the ripples. There was no other way out besides the portal and the doors.

"I can't see anyone."

"The anubes will come, Alivet. I told you, they patrol

regularly." But for all the confidence in Ghairen's words, he did not sound entirely sure of himself. They waited, sitting with their backs to the wall. Alivet could not stop fidgeting; Ghairen was unnaturally still. Eventually Alivet rose and went to the water's edge to wash her face. She did so cautiously, but it was good to be worrying about liches and water-children again, rather than unknown terrors. She stood to find Ghairen behind her. He took her by the shoulder and pointed into the growing twilight.

"Look. A boat is coming."

Alivet could see it now. It was a pilgrimage boat, like the one that had brought her to Shadow Town. It glided soundlessly through the reeds. There was a single anube standing in the prow with a pole.

"Will he take us all the way to the Night Palace?"

"He'll take us to the back gates. We'll have to get into the palace ourselves. We have a single day. The Lords hold their banquet tomorrow."

"How are we going to carry out the poisoning?"

"That is something that your sister can help us with."

"If she's still alive."

"If, indeed, she is still alive," Ghairen echoed after a pause. The pilgrimage boat knocked gently against the step and Alivet climbed in. The anube gave her a considering look and said, "We will go through the deep fens, the hintermarshes. You know that they are still looking for you, for the attempted murder of the aristocrat?"

"*Attempted* murder? The girl died," Alivet said, taken aback.

"It seems she has recovered."

"From death? You can't recover from that!"

The anube gave a smooth, rippling shrug. "I do not know the details, only rumor. All Levanah has been searched. The Unpriests seek apothecaries, healers, empirics—anyone whom they find it amusing to persecute."

"Has anyone been killed?" Alivet asked, dreading the answer.

"Many have been taken, from their homes in daytime or midnight. It is not known what has happened to them."

"Have you heard of a woman named Elitta? Do you know what has befallen her?"

"I do not."

The anube spun the pole, sending the boat out into the stream. The place of the portal fell behind. Alivet looked back to see it shimmering on the edges of the marsh: two pale pillars rising like bones out of the water. Ghairen sat hunched in the stern, saying nothing. Alivet slid along the boat to sit beside him.

"Ghairen, just tell me one thing. Was it you who poisoned Madimi Garland?"

"No. Why would I have done?"

"To force me into a vulnerable position?"

"You were already in a vulnerable enough position, because of Inki. I told you, Alivet. I don't go around poisoning everyone." She saw the glint of a smile in the twilight. "Waste of resources. Do you believe me?"

She wanted to. Perhaps it was time to change the subject.

"How long will it take before we get to the Night Palace?" Alivet asked the anube.

"It will be a while yet."

Alivet settled back against the side of the boat and closed her eyes, reassured by the familiar salt-weed odor of marsh and water, the rustling of rushes, the sudden hiss of dragonflies. *If we were free of the Lords and the Unpriests, think what we could do with such a world.* She was not used to such hopes; it was strange, to consider a future further than the next scrambling goal of survival.

As the boat glided on, Alivet began, for the first time, to consider what a world free of the Lords might be like. When Ghairen had initially raised the possibility, she had not thought very far beyond Inki's release, and the vague promise of a world where people could do what they pleased without fear of reprisal. Now she realized that they needed much more than that. The Unpriests and the Lords were not the sole source of woe in the world: think of fat Hilliet Kightly, snatching at her with greasy hands. If the Unpriests were deposed, there would be plenty of monsters-in-the-making to take their place. And was Ghairen himself one such monster? Hathes was no paradise, after all, and when he spoke so promisingly of opening up her world to the trade-routes, was he not hoping only for more people to poison, more clients for assassination?

We have been stagnating, Alivet thought, *mired in our fens*. Even the Search, that great quest for meaning, now seemed only to look backward, and Alivet now wondered whether this was not why the Unpriests had turned a literally blind eye toward it; that it kept the citizens of Levanah preoccupied and distracted from the future. It seemed now that the Origin was a world like any other, and from what she had seen of Hathes and Nethes, it appeared that Latent Emanation was to be preferred, even if it did allegedly lie farther down the ladder of human evolution. Given Gulzhur Elaniel, that would seem to be no bad thing. *It isn't where we come from that matters. It's where we're going.*

But where was that? *If we had our own drift-boat*, Alivet mused, *we, too, could go exploring. We could trade drugs and books and metals and ideas. Transformation is the true goal of alchemy, after all. Why should we not transform ourselves?* If the Lords could be disposed of, the people of Latent Emanation could have their own boat, assuming that Ghairen did not stand in her way. The shiffrey may have lied about some things, but perhaps not about all. She might have to deal with Ghairen when the time came, and she had no idea how to go about it. Her thoughts turned back to the drift-boat.

Dreams of an eight-year-old, escaping into flight...And she realized, too, that the appeal that the Search held for her was not so much the quest for a lost origin, it was the notion of traveling. Drugs or dreams or drift-boats; the means did not matter. A boat would need a captain, someone versed in the realms beyond the world. Well, Alivet had been beyond that world on two occasions now, which she was fairly sure was twice more than any of her fellow citizens. And a citizen of Hathes had offered her gainful employment.

"Ghairen?" she said aloud. "What qualifications do you need to fly a drift-boat?"

"It takes about three years, so I'm told. There's a tower on Hathes dedicated to the art, but not many job opportunities, given that there are only about nine of the things that anyone knows of. Why do you ask?"

"If the Lords were gone, we could take their boat."

"Thinking of traveling, Alivet?"

"I was thinking of trade. Can you hire people to crew these things?"

"You could try. Look. There's the causeway."

A narrow band of lamps bisected the twilight air, far ahead. The boat turned, snaking through the rushes. Far above Alivet's head, the bulbs of the rushes stirred in the boat's passage.

"Ghairen?" Alivet whispered. "Do the Lords set snares in these marshes? What if we run into one?"

"Of course. There are net traps and wires strung all through these reed beds. But they're known to the anubes. That's why we are taking this route."

The bulk of the Night Palace hung above them, petals of darkness that turned the surrounding sky into a deep, translucent indigo. An attern gave a desolate cry out across the marsh, making Alivet jump. The boat rocked.

"It's only a bird," Ghairen said, in warning.

"It startled me." Now that they had almost reached the palace, Alivet could no longer distance herself from her fears. What if Inki was already dead, thrown into the marsh like a kitten in a sack? As they glided up to the metal pilings that supported the vast structure of the palace, she found that she was holding her breath. She looked up at the platform, which towered hundreds of feet above the water. It reminded her of the architecture of Hathes: a frighteningly inhuman scale. Dim shapes rocked and bobbed in the water ahead and Alivet clutched at the side of the boat before she realized that they were the tethered craft of the Unpriests. The pilgrimage boat slid into a corner of shadow and stopped. It was so dark that Alivet could not see her hand in front of her face. Cold fingers touched her own, guiding her hand upward until she could feel metal.

"It's a ladder," Ghairen murmured into her ear.

"Where does it go? Up into the palace?"

"Yes, but it's a long climb."

"Then I'll need a knife."

"I'm planning to avoid the Unpriests. This is a reconnaissance, not a battle."

"It isn't for the Unpriests. It's for me."

After a bemused moment, Alivet felt something heavy being pressed into her hand. She touched the blade, assessing its length, then hacked off the hated skirt until the material swung around her knees.

"Good thing it's dark," Ghairen said, evidently realizing what she was doing.

"I'm keeping the knife. Just in case." Alivet tucked it into her belt and swung herself up onto the ladder. "I hope you have some idea of what to do once we reach the top."

"Yes. The ladder will bring us out into the food store. From there, we head for the kitchens."

"The kitchen? I suppose you have poisoning in mind?"

"Yes, but not immediately. Start climbing."

Alivet did so, feeling her way from rung to rung. She looked down once, but could see nothing except the faintest glimmer of light on water. Perhaps this was just as well, though if Hathes had given her anything, it was a head for heights. The metal was slick and difficult to hold. She tried not to think of falling. From this height, the water would swallow her like a stone, but that was another thing not worth thinking about. Alivet continued to climb and her fingers grew chilled and numb. Hathes seemed a thousand years away. The world contracted to damp air and colder metal and the rustling of Ghairen's robes as he followed her. She heard a whisper from the darkness.

"Mind your head. We're nearly at the top."

"How do you know?"

"I know how many rungs there are. I've been counting."

Just where had Ghairen gained his inside information? His knowledge had surely come from Inkirietta and the anubes. If either of them was to be used as any kind of decoy duck... Alivet reached above her head and discovered a flat metal panel. She gave it an experimental push. It was loose.

"Push it upward and to one side. But be careful." Ghairen's voice was sharp with anxiety. Alivet thought of Unpriests waiting above the hatchway like dragonfly larvae, ready to strike and snatch. "Here," Ghairen added. She reached down and felt something smooth being placed in her hand. "At the top of this device, there is a bulb. If anyone's there, press the bulb and turn your head away. Don't breathe in."

"And it will kill them?"

"I'm hoping no one's there."

Alivet shifted the spray to a more convenient position and pressed on the panel. It slid up. There was no movement in the darkness beyond. Cautiously, Alivet hauled herself through into an arctic space. She stood, shivering, as Ghairen came to stand beside her.

"Where are we?" She reached out. Her fingers met a block of something cold and smooth, like ice or glass, but the room smelled of nothing at all.

"In the food store. Darkness and evening, congealed into ice. The opposite of latent light. This is where the Enbonded can go—there is another room, beyond this point, behind a great metal door. In there, a different kind of food is kept: the dark energy on which the Lords must feast, every year or so, to maintain their structure. It's toxic to humans; it rots the bones."

"And one of those feasts will be tomorrow?"

"That's why we're here."

"How are we going to make them ingest the poison? Won't it be obvious to them?" Inside its phial, the blood tabernanthe surely glowed and gleamed; Alivet could not see how it would be possible to hide it in a realm of darkness. Perhaps if she kept it cold...

"You will need to consult its spirit. And we also need to find the kitchens."

Alivet heard the faint sound of a door opening, then felt Ghairen's hand around her wrist. They slipped through the door into a metal passageway, then up a flight of erratic steps that did not appear to have been designed for human feet. Another passageway, another door, and then Ghairen drew to a halt. He seemed in no hurry to let her go. Above the sudden pounding in her head, Alivet could hear a low susurrus of voices.

"The kitchens?"

"If my map is correct, yes."

He led her through into a nearby chamber, where there was a small opening high on a wall.

"Alivet, if I lift you up..."

Acutely conscious of her mutilated skirt, and Ghairen's hands around her waist, Alivet let herself be hoisted up until she could peer through the window. She was looking directly down into the kitchens, lit by a bank of great furnaces. Enbonded servants scurried to and fro, bearing platters of glass and ice. This must be the substance that she had seen in the stores, the raw material from which the delicacies of the Lords were made. Alivet remembered Madimi Garland, sipping a sorbet of night and sliding down into death, and a shiver ran through her. But from what the anube had said, the girl had not died after all...

"Alivet? What can you see?"

"There are a great many people down there. It's a busy kitchen."

"Can you see your sister?" Ghairen's tone was urgent, but Alivet had already been scanning the dim faces below.

"No."

"Are you sure?"

"Ghairen, she's nowhere to be seen."

"I'm going to let you down," Ghairen said, and brought her to the floor. She could see his face in the wan light that filtered through the window. He seemed even paler than usual.

"Where do you think Inki is?" Alivet whispered.

"If she isn't in her usual place in the kitchens, I'd imagine that she is in an Unpriest's cell."

Or dead. She could see it in his face. It was not an option she wanted to confront without hard evidence.

"Do you know where the cells are?"

"No. I know the part of the palace that Inki knows, and I also know the anube's tunnel and the portal location, but that's about it."

"Then our best chance of getting Inki out—of getting all of them out—is to defeat the Lords." She thought for a moment. "And *that* means I'll have to take Inki's place in the kitchens in order to carry out the poisoning, won't I?"

"Admirably succinct. It's likely to work. You'e twins, after all, and they won't have seen her for a while. You could say, in the guise of Inki, that the Unpriests let you go because they thought you might be needed for the banquet. Besides, the kitchen is a dark place and there are a great many apprentices. As long as no one gets a good look at you—"

"What about the eye? If I tie something around my head, perhaps?"

"And you'll have to keep that tattoo hidden."

"But if I pretend my hand's been injured, they might not let me work. They must have hygiene regulations. We'll just have to chance it."

With the knife Alivet slashed her clothes into rags until no one could have told what their provenance might have been. She ran the knife along her arm, wincing as a fine edge of blood appeared, and sopped it up with a length of her skirt. Ghairen tied the bloodied rag about her head and Alivet stripped the apothecary's rings from her hair. That hurt more than the cut, as though her self had been taken from her, but then it occurred to her that she would willingly give up more than her self if it would save her sister.

"Look after them," she said to Ghairen.

"I'll keep them safe." For once, he did not smile. "Inki's hair is shorter than yours."

"Cut it, then." She stood still while Ghairen hacked at the long plait with the knife. Then Alivet tangled her hair and said, "Well? Will I pass?"

"It's the best we can do. Find out what the plans are for the banquet, and start work on the poison. You'll probably need to keep it informed, as well. Talk to it, tell it what's happening."

"You do realize that I'm not a trained chef?"

"Why is the profession of apothecary held to be most suitable for women?"

"Because it's just like cooking," Alivet answered. This time, it was her turn to smile. "Ghairen, what will you be doing when I'm down there?"

"Watching you."

"If you went to look for Inki—"

"I'll see how the land lies," Ghairen told her. He handed her the phial of blood tabernanthe. "Alivet. Be careful." He leaned across and kissed her hard and quickly on the mouth. When Alivet found her voice, she heard herself say, "You, too." She kissed him in return. Then she went through the door.

 *Part* X

IGNITION

Stand still you ever-moving spheres of heaven,
That time may cease and midnight ever come.

— CHRISTOPHER MARLOWE,
The Tragicall History of Dr. Faustus

chapter I

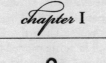

LONDON ∼ 1595

I t grows colder," Niclaes said, and shivered.

"Do you speak of the season, or the time?" Dee answered.

"Of both." Niclaes wrapped his arms about himself and drew closer to the fire. "There have been agents abroad, seeking word of the Family. The Queen grows older; she becomes like Saturn at the year's end."

"Seeking to devour her young?"

"There are plots everywhere she turns. Why should she not be afraid? And these young men she has around her—the sons of old men who knew her when she herself was a girl—they are like jackals around a great dying beast, awaiting the moment when they can sidle in and seize their pound of flesh."

"An unhappy metaphor. I doubt the Queen would be flattered by it."

"You and I foresaw these days, Dee. You foresaw it when you returned from Meta Incognita, and spoke to me of your grave doubts. I remember that we prayed."

"I remember that we prayed, too. And went on planning."

Niclaes sighed. "Yes, because the devil we know might

be worse than the devil we do not. We are being squeezed from England like a pip from a Seville orange."

"There are other choices," Dee said, quietly. "There have been other choices all this time."

"I know. But what are they? Back to the Low Countries, who have treated us worse than the English? Onward to the New World, which is being carved from pole to pole by dissenters and schemers? We might purchase a hundred years or so, but the New World will turn into the old soon enough. No, Dee, better that we take our chances in this Meta Incognita of ours."

"And what of your soul?"

"We have spoken of this already. I trust in the Inner Light, Dee. Even consorting with devils cannot blow it out. It is not a candle, small in the universal winds. It turns always toward God. I have come to see that, and to trust it." He glanced at Dee and though Niclaes was no longer a young man, his eyes shone in the light of the fire. "Are we ready? Is it time?"

"Almost. I have been consulting with the—angels." If Niclaes noticed the pause, he did not comment upon it. Dee continued, "I seek to sow necessary rumors. Edward Kelley's death will be announced in a month or so. I have spread the word that I shall be going north, to take up a post there. I have friends here who will let it slip that my wife and children are dead of the plague. In truth, they shall go into hiding, and I shall not be long after them. In the meantime, others will take on my name: just as the Merlin of ancient days was said not to be one man, but many. Dr. Dee will be seen in all manner of places in the years to come, except in the one place that matters. We will take the mirror with us. Meta Incognita will be lost to the Earth. No persecution will follow us; we will close the door and deal with whatever lies on the other side."

"I have," Niclaes said, "made similar arrangements."

"Then we are ready."

chapter II

PALACE OF NIGHT, LATENT EMANATION

T here were lamps set along the walls of the corridor that led to the kitchen, but the illumination that came from them was splintered and dim. Alivet hurried through thistledown light with the phial of tabernanthe clutched close to her heart, hoping not to turn a corner and come face-to-face with an Unpriest. The cover of the phial was cool against her skin. As she reached the door of the kitchen she hesitated. She could hear the roar of the furnaces, smell a thousand complex odors of blood and juices and darkness. Then she stepped through the door.

At first, no one seemed to see her. Alivet sidled along the wall toward the darkest corner of the kitchen, until she was brought short by a bellow of rage.

"You! Apprentice! Sneaking toward the candies, are we?"

A cadaverous bulk loomed above her. Alivet saw a tall man, his black apron covered with clots of something thick and sticky. She opened her mouth to mumble something and was immediately struck by an idea. She pointed to her tongue, made gagging sounds.

"Inkirietta?" The chef rocked back on his heels.

Dumbly, Alivet nodded. Everyone in the immediate

vicinity turned around and stared at her. She had rarely felt so exposed.

"What happened? Did they let you out? I thought they promised you thirty days. They must have grown tired of your constant sniping and complaining."

Alivet touched her tongue once more.

"Can't speak?" The chef gave a roar of laughter. "Well, that'll make a change. At least we'll be spared the sound of your voice from now on. Let's hope it's permanent, eh?"

Inkirietta, Alivet thought, *clearly, you have aggravated this man beyond reason. I'm proud of you.*

"Still, at least you're another pair of hands for the banquet. Take off those filthy rags and get started. There's a spare set of clothes in the storeroom."

Glad to get out of sight and earshot, Alivet found the store. She fastened the black dress, which seemed much too large, around herself and tucked what remained of her hair beneath the smoke-colored hat. In the mirror, her pinched, pale face, half covered by the bloodied bandage, seemed a picture of furtiveness. She went back into the kitchen and was impatiently motioned toward a corner.

"Over there. Start chopping. You know what to do."

Stepping around the corner of the table, Alivet picked up a knife and started to work. She glanced up once, to the little window high above the kitchen, but if Ghairen was still concealed there, she could not see him. It appeared that the ingredients for the banquet's desserts and pastries had been assembled the day before. Surreptitiously, Alivet watched her fellow apprentices to see what they did; it was a good thing that Inki had apparently been relegated to the basic tasks. There were many covert glances cast in Alivet's direction, which she ignored. She tried to look miserable and oppressed. It seemed to be working.

Over the course of the next few hours, Alivet began to get a feel for how the kitchen operated. The head chef jealously guarded the ration of candles; everyone else had to work in the red glow of the ovens or simply by touch. No one spoke.

A boy dropped a tray and was smacked across the cheek. Threats to call the Unpriests to deal with the offender came to nothing, but Alivet caught a glimpse of the child's face when the chef had finished with him and it was white and stark, too frightened to cry. Alivet swallowed her anger and deduced that it was not unknown for the Unpriests to be so summoned.

Opening the icebox, Alivet's neighbor took out a container and placed it on the table. She opened it carefully and handed it to Alivet.

"Here. It's the night essence. It's to go in the sorbets." In an undertone, the girl added, "Inki? Are you all right?" Her voice was full of pity and concern and Alivet could have hugged her. It seemed that Inki had at least one friend in the kitchens, and this gave her hope. She gave a dull nod. If the girl thought that her mind had been affected, she might take care to give Alivet more precise instructions about the preparation of the food.

The container, which was painful to the touch and numbed her fingers, was full of glassy dark ice, possibly from the seas near Latent Emanation's southern pole, a place that Alivet knew only from legend. Perhaps the anubes brought it in their pilgrimage boats. If that was so, she wondered how they kept it cold. The ice seemed to hold its own glow; it was almost green. With a sharp scalpel, Alivet touched the edge of the sheet of ice, so that it split and cracked into a nest of slivers. Following the directions of the girl beside her, Alivet arranged the shards of ice in the center of each of the sorbet dishes, then reached back inside the icebox for the ingredients of the sauce. The girl beside her touched the controls of the portable generator that stood at the end of the table, and a containment field crackled up around the workplace.

It seemed, from what Alivet's neighbor then told her, that a complex, subtle accompaniment was planned for the simple ice: a touch of fragrant Cepherian River darkness, gathered close to midnight, redolent of spiced smoke. Placing the darkness in a bowl, and careful to keep within the containment field, Alivet added a pinch of flavors as directed: twilight from Shadow Town, warm and clouded, with a hint of star anise. Then a touch of evening from the deep fens, water-clear and cool. Alivet stirred all of these elements nine times with an ebony spoon, then poured the swirl of darkness into a silver pan and lit the chilly flame beneath it. The darkness was half-solid, swirling around the end of the tongs, and Alivet marveled at it. But strange as it was, it was not so different from drug-making, after all.

She waited, frowning, as a drift of smoke began to rise from the sauce. Casting it in a spiral around the little columns of ice, Inki's friend clapped her hands imperiously for the serving staff to take it into the dining hall, where the Lords of Night were waiting. The staff carried special platters, about which the cold lightning of containment fields snapped and played. The head chef looked up, once, as the procession passed by, and gave a single grudging nod of approval.

Having dispensed with the appetizers, the responsibility for the meal passed on to the head chef for a time, while Alivet and Inki's friend busied themselves with the desserts. Alivet hoped to get the chance to take the phial from her pocket and slip it into the icebox, but the head chef had got some of the other apprentices out of his fevered way by sending them over to work in Alivet's corner. Frustrated, Alivet got on with her own tasks, still under the direction of Inki's friend. She prepared fondants of gloom, sorbets of shadows, and sherbets of dusk, each one gathered from the unseen corners of Latent Emanation. Finally Alivet wiped her weary hands on her apron and stepped back to admire her handiwork. Behind her, the booming voice of the head chef said, "Not bad. Perhaps there's some promise in you after all."

Alivet jumped like a tortured hare and gave a little cry.

"Found your tongue?" The head chef thrust his cadaverous face close to that of Alivet. "Nervous, are we? Been doing something you shouldn't? Been gobbing in the fondants again?"

Alivet bridled silently, but she wondered just what havoc

Inki had previously managed to wreak in the kitchens. As much as possible, Alivet hoped.

"Get over there, girl, when you've finished. I want some help in scrubbing the floors."

The head chef's head jerked in the direction of the apprentices and they scrambled after him as he ambled back toward the cold crimson glow of his own territory. Heart pounding, Alivet sidled into the corner, retrieved the phial from her pocket, and slid it underneath the floor of the icebox. The phial was still warm. It seemed to radiate its own heat, and Alivet was relieved when at last it was safely out of sight. Then she went to where the head chef was waiting and began to rinse the stone floor clean of blood, but she kept thinking about the poison lying in its casing of ice.

Once the kitchens were quiet, and everyone had left for the night, Alivet planned to rescue the phial containing the blood tabernanthe. She would speak to the ally, ask it how best it might be concealed. And then she would begin to cook: a special dish for the banquet of the Lords of Night. Over the course of the next few minutes, however, she realized with despair that it might be too late to even think about executing her plan. The Unpriests had arrived.

They slithered down the kitchen stairs, boot-heels clicking on the expensive tiles. Alivet risked a glance, and the nape of her neck grew cold. The people in this group were no ordinary Unpriests. Their long coats bore the Lords' own insignia, and there was a woman with them, dressed in black velvet breeches and a leather cuirass. A single dark pearl dangled from one ear, like a bead of jet. Her right eye was hidden behind a thick dark lens. Her head swiveled from side to side. The woman made Alivet feel hollow and numb, so she stared grimly down at the floor as the Unpriest passed. The language that she spoke was archaic, formal, and barely intelligible; she enunciated slowly, evidently for the benefit of the head chef who, as a mere servant, might not be expected to understand her.

"The Unchurch has had word that an attempt is to be made on the lives of the Lords of Night, by nonpersons, by dream-sellers, by ghosts. The servants must submit to be searched."

Alivet cursed silently. It had to be Gulzhur Elaniel, if she was still alive, or Ust and her Sanguinant friends; they must have sent a warning to the Lords.

"An attempt on—?" The head chef's thin face quivered in shock. "By whom?"

"I told you. Nonpersons. Those who deny darkness, who seek That which is Not."

"By what means?"

"Unknown," the Unpriest said stiffly, then conceded, "by myself, at least. The Lords, of course, know all, but in their dark wisdom they have not divulged the answer to one as lowly as myself and were I to know that answer, I would be no more likely to divulge it to *you*. Now. Prepare to be searched."

A brass tube began to spiral outward from her eye, glistening with oil. At the end of it was the round lens. The woman raised her head to the level of the head chef's face, and passed her gaze down his body from the crown of his head to his toes.

"Are you afraid, chef?"

To Alivet's surprise the chef said, "Yes. I am afraid. I have been afraid ever since I can remember."

A thin charcoal brow arched above the lens. The woman said, "Indeed? Of what?"

Boldly, the chef answered, "Of not matching the expectations of the Lords of Night. Of not meeting the standards that I myself set to serve them."

"You talk like an artist," the woman said, brows still raised.

"I *am* an artist, madam," the chef told her. Perhaps it was the bravery of sheer terror, Alivet thought, or perhaps the man had long since been touched by madness. "I am an artist of culinary color and its absence, a master of texture and shade, of monochrome uniformity. I drain the delicacies that I prepare of the touch of light and fire and brightness that is bestowed upon them by the flames on which they are conjured into being, so that the palates of the Lords of Night may not be seared for one moment by the tiniest spark of light."

The woman bowed her head in mocking acknowledgment. "Well, then, I am honored. But you must still be scrutinized."

She raised her head once more and the lens rotated along its appointed track. The woman put her head on one side, studied the chef.

"You absorb light, you say? You purify the foods of darkness?"

"I do."

"I had not thought that the life of a pastry chef would be so fraught with hazard. Take care that you visit the Unpriests more regularly, to purge your soul of traces of light as effectively as you purify the foods that you prepare."

Fascinated, Alivet nonetheless stared straight ahead, afraid of attracting undue attention, but she glimpsed from the corner of her eye the chef's cadaverous form, surrounded for a moment by black energy, an aura of unlight. One by one, the woman passed the device along the rows of apprentices: darkness crackled and snapped. At last she reached Alivet. She stared at her for a moment, and Alivet raised her reluctant gaze. She could see nothing in the Unpriest's face. One eye was entirely concealed behind the thick obsidian lens and the other looked dead.

She said, caressingly, "Stand straight. You seem alarmed, girl. Are you afraid?"

Alivet nodded. Something long and thin whipped from the tube that held the lens and lashed Alivet across the face. The impact spun her around and she sprawled backward, stunned. The Unpriest said, "I asked you a question."

"She cannot speak," the head chef hastened to say. "Your illustrious colleagues did something to her tongue. They were quite right, I must say. The girl has the mouth of a viper."

"Yes," the Unpriest said, consideringly. "Now that you mention it, I think I have seen her before in one of the cells. I did not realize she had been released, but there are so many of them . . . One loses track."

The Unpriest turned away. The rest of the kitchen was searched methodically, and Alivet's heart skipped and hopped as an investigation was made of her work area, including the little icebox. The Unpriest lingered as she examined the pastries and sorbets, and Alivet hid a bruised smile as she saw the stealthy fingers creep out and flick a piece of brittle icing into the Unpriest's mouth. But the phial of blood tabernanthe remained secure. The woman headed for the stairs with an angry flounce and Alivet inclined her head until the beetle-click of boot-heels betrayed her absence.

No one said a word after the Unpriests' visit, except for the head chef, who turned to Alivet and snapped, "You. Have you finished?"

Alivet shook her head, pointed to the floor, then to the work surface. She tried to emit a sense of quivering misery, which wasn't too difficult.

"Slow, aren't you?" The chef grinned. "Better finish what you have to do, then."

When he had gone, Inki's friend leaned over.

"Inki? Do you want me to stay and help you?" As she spoke, she stole a fearful glance toward the chef and Alivet realized that there would be a punishment awaiting the girl if she remained too friendly with the troublemaker. That fear suited Alivet's own purposes, however. She shook her head and gestured to the door.

One by one, the apprentices left the kitchen. Alivet hovered over her tasks, slicing and molding and freezing, until the head chef uttered a curt good night, along with instructions to lock up. Alivet listened carefully as the chef's footsteps pounded up the stairs and the door slammed behind him, then she ran to the icebox and took out the phial. She dropped it on the table and flicked open the lid, then stared for a moment at the sparkling crimson dust. *The color of blood*, Alivet thought. *The color of life*.

She separated a pinch of the substance and dropped it into the dim fire of a nearby stove. The tabernanthe smoked upward.

"Me again," she said, when the face of the ally once more appeared wonderingly before her.

"I hold light," the ally said. "But I am cold."

"I know. I need to hide your substance in something, so that the light does not show. How may I accomplish this?"

"Cut me with utmost fineness," the ally said. The effects of the smoke were wearing off; the ally's face was growing thin and translucent in her mind's eye. "Cut me thin." Then it was gone.

Working quickly, Alivet took her sharp knife and began to chop, her hand moving faster and faster with an apothecary's practiced speed until the tabernanthe was segmented into tiny lines, too fine to emit the contained, betraying light. Then Alivet began her final great work, the last work which, if all went well, she would ever perform in the palace of the Lords of Night. She started to place the substance into the sorbets. At last she passed her hand over the surface of the chopping block and found only a minute sugar sliver, glowing red like a splinter of glass. Alivet looked at the splinter for a moment, then she put it back into the phial and put the phial in her pocket. Finally, she slipped everything into the darkest recesses of the icebox, to wait there till morning. As she turned to leave, she fancied that when she next opened the door of the icebox, the box itself would have begun to glow.

Then she went back up the stairs, to the small chamber. At first, with a thud of her heart, she thought that Ghairen was gone or had been taken, but then she saw him standing like a ghost in the shadows.

"It went well?" he whispered. "I've been watching you."

"Well enough, I think."

"I saw the Unpriests. Was there any trouble?"

"No more than usual. They underestimate the Enbonded." Alivet gave a bitter smile. "Never trust mim-mouthed girls who keep silent, Ghairen."

"I'll remember that. But now it's to our advantage. I'll take you to the dormitory."

"No, I want to try to find Inki."

"If you're caught," Ghairen said forcefully, "as you might well be if the others notice you're gone, then we might as well throw everything we've worked for into that swamp. If she's dead, then nothing can help her. If she's alive, she can last another day."

"But—"

"Alivet, I think I have come to know you a little. You do not seem to make a habit of acting before you think. Don't do so now." His hand brushed her face.

Alivet could see the sense in this, but she did not like it. Reluctantly, she went to the dormitory with Ghairen. But as she stepped through the door, she realized that there might be a way to go in search of Inki after all. One that would not entail leaving her bed.

RESOLUTION

Also Travellers in the Night, and such as watch their Flocks . . . are wont to be compassed about with many strange apparitions . . . yet sometimes they make so great and deep impression into the Earth, that the place they are used to, being onely burnt 'round with extreme heat, no grass will grow up there . . . The inhabitants call this Night-sport of these Monsters, the Dance of Fayries.

— OLAUS MAGNUS,
De Gentibus Septentrionalibus,
Historia, 1658 translation

chapter I

YORKSHIRE ～ 1595

Together, faces hidden in their cloaks, Dee and his wife, Jane, left the safe house that the Family was using in York and headed for the moor. Dee had always regarded science as indoor work, but there were too many folk for even the greatest hall: a thousand and one men, women, and children, from the cities of London, Prague, and Amsterdam. Dee saw many faces for the first time; some, from their dress and manner, he recognized to be Jews. Two of the families were Spanish Moors: tall men, perhaps brothers, and children with dark, grave faces. Dee thought, *This is indeed a marvelous work, that unites so many different creeds. The Church should learn from the Family, not shut us out.*

It was cold on the moors and Dee shivered in spite of his thick cloak. He saw members of the Family exchanging small, conspiratorial smiles with the others. Here, at least, all were brothers and sisters, and Dee knew that whatever befell them during the course of this night, there would be no going back. They would be dead, or Beyond in Meta Incognita. And when they reached that world, Dee told himself, they would have the chance to make the world anew, and they would not waste it in greedy squabbling and murder as those who had ventured to the Colonies had done. They would take the best of the old and the best of the new and weld them into a seamless whole.

He thrust his doubts of the angels to the hidden chambers of his mind. *Whatever befalls us, wherever we go, we must never forget where we are from and what we leave behind. We carry it within our hearts: our love of God, our need for a better world, and we must never forget.*

He kissed Jane, saying, "I have preparations to make. Do not worry. I will see you later." God knows, she had made enough sacrifices for his sake. He pressed the crucifix that had been his mother's last gift to him into her hand and then he was striding up the hill toward Niclaes and Laski, who even now were lighting the great braziers, fashioned from gold and silver and bronze, that stood at the four quarters of the crowd. And as if they had been rehearsing for months, the gathering of the Family drew into the center of the circle.

Though there was no moon, it was a bright night. The milky stars spilled out across the moor and seemed to sparkle in the grass. Dee heard Kelley begin the chant, calling the names of the worlds Beyond: "Yesod, Hod, Netzach, Tiphareth..." Strange names, Dee thought, though they would be familiar to the Jews amongst the crowd. "Geburah, Chesed, Binah, Chokmah, Kether..." *We will not be going so far*, the angel had told him. *No human can look beyond Tiphareth and live.*

A wind was growing up across the moor, stirring Dee's cloak. The crowd murmured once in a single voice and then fell silent. Dee clutched at his cloak and the wool sparked and clung to his skin. He knelt beside the light of a brazier and began to write, inscribing the sigils of the language of the universe upon a parchment. He had indeed improved the calculations. As he wrote, the sigils and formulae spun away from the page and spiraled up into the air, to hang glowing above the grass.

Something was coming over the moor, blotting out the stars. People cried out, a man close to Dee lost his nerve and tried to bolt, but there was a line of light around the crowd, holding them in. The crowd surged toward the center. Dee looked briefly up, saw another Presence in the southern quarter, gliding up over the moor, then *something* was descending. Dee looked up, mouth agape. It was a great waterworn stone, or perhaps a bowl, its smooth sides gleaming in the starlight and striking bronze reflections from the lamps. It was the ship. A fourth angelic form appeared at the last quarter in the north and Dee felt his mind being wrenched out of all proportion. He looked down into stark madness.

Slowly, like the hand of God, the thing slid down from the sky.

chapter II

PALACE OF NIGHT, LATENT EMANATION

The apprentices slept on pallets in a cold, damp room above the kitchens. Most were asleep when Alivet entered—which, she reflected, was just as well. She found a spare pallet along the wall and curled up, telling herself that this was no more than another Search. This time, she would not burn the drug into smoke. She had another method in mind. Taking the phial from her pocket, she removed the splinter of sugared blood tabernanthe and put it in her mouth. It exploded like sherbet, an unnatural candy fizzing on the tongue. Alivet waited, feeling her mouth grow numb. At first there was no response from the universe around her. And then, very faintly, something answered.

"Who calls?" it said. Alivet had the impression of a great, swelling voice and she was seized with a sudden terror that someone might hear it.

"Hush," she whispered inside her mind. "Speak softly." The voice hummed in her veins, causing her heart to pound.

"Who calls?"

"I am Alivet. You know me."

She had the immediate impression of something vital and alive, a quick, glittering figure. Taken orally, the figure of the ally seemed to take a different form, but then it turned and she was looking into its dark gaze. Now, however, she found herself looking at the mental image of a tall figure, red as a ruby, the skin flayed away so that she could see the tracery of muscle and sinew. Gleaming hair poured down its back.

"You have disseminated my essence," it told her. "I wait to reconfigure."

"It won't be a long wait. In the meantime, I need your help, to find my sister." She stepped across the imaginary space and took the spirit by the hand. The spirit looked down dubiously at their linked fingers.

"Take me with you," Alivet whispered.

The next moment, they were gliding swiftly through halls and passages. She saw now that the Palace of Night was far vaster than she had imagined. They passed through halls in which suns glowed in firework clusters and stars poured like waterfalls down the walls. The possibility of finding Inki in this immensity of space seemed suddenly remote.

They came into a room where an armillary sphere sat upon a table, and as Alivet drew nearer, she saw that the jeweled planets were real: she could witness the glow of cities across their nightsides, count seas, and mountains. She wanted to stay and look, but the spirit swept her by. A second room, a second set of spheres.

"Look," the spirit said. "These are our worlds." The worlds of the Cabala hung in the lambent air, each separated by a veil of dust. Alivet saw a white and blue planet like a marble, then a dim azure ball that she knew to be Latent Emanation. Red Hathes, ash-gray Nethes, and a pale gleaming world which the spirit recognized as Tiphareth and whispered the name in her ear. Beyond Tiphareth, however, the worlds were lost in clouds.

"And that's the Origin," Alivet said in fascination, staring down at the little marbled world. It did not seem to be part of the same system, somehow: it wavered and changed as she peered at it and she saw that this world and her own were separated by an immense gulf, a jagged edge of night.

"That is where we come from," the spirit said, pointing to

the marbled world. "A world in another part of the universe, linked to these worlds by a gateway. I *remember*," the ally said, and Alivet knew that it spoke the truth. Memory, passed down in the human bloodline; stored in the genetic fibers of the species.

The spirit pointed at the floor, which seemed to be made of stone, or perhaps it was wood, or earth—Alivet could not tell. The Night Palace was too strange for her to take in; her mind was creating familiar images to cope with the inexplicable. But over the floor crept something like a flock of beetles. Alivet bent her head to look more closely and saw that they were none other than the Lords.

"When the first groups of humans came to these worlds," the spirit said, "from Babylon and Egypt, seeking the lands of the dead, all went well. The Lords themselves traveled freely between their dimension and this one—until the Lords became corrupt, ensnared in this more physical realm. Over time, even their appearance altered and they could no longer return to their own dimension. They sought to do as humans did, to keep slaves. But you were not stolen away by the Lords; you chose to come. A group of occultists, who had already found an opening to the crossing, chanced upon ancient technology. They summoned the Lords, brought them through to Earth, and then sealed the route behind them.

"But the one who did the summoning, who learned to speak the language of the universe—he was your ancestor, Alivet. I know this. I have the knowledge of all human blood. He was your many times great-grandfather: the magus mathematician Dr. John Dee."

"My *ancestor* brought us here?"

"He was responsible for the last group of humans who made the crossing between the stars. The descendants of their leaders are now the Nine Families. But Dee quarreled with them when they reached Latent: encouraged by the Lords, they sought power for themselves."

"It seems to me he still did us a great wrong," Alivet said.

"Perhaps. He did what he thought was right, at the time."

"And now I do what I believe to be right, also. But you can free us from the Lords, or so Ghairen believes. The latent light which you now hold will slay them, he says, or dispatch them back to their own dimension." She could feel her grip starting to slip as the blood tabernanthe faded from her bloodstream. The palace contracted around her, suns winking out like mayflies, moons fading from the skies of night. She stood for a moment in a small paneled room, and then it was gone and she was back on the pallet, stiff and cold and dreaming no longer. She had seen a universe of wonders, but she still hadn't found Inki.

Next day, silent in her corner of the kitchen, Alivet waited. She had slept in snatches, waking once with a shock, convinced that a Night Lord had been standing over her, but there was nothing there. Very early in the morning, when just a few of the apprentices were yawning their way to the washing area, Alivet had checked the small chamber above the kitchen. Ghairen was nowhere to be seen. The day had been spent in helping the chefs prepare an endless parade of dishes for the banquet, which even now was taking place within the depths of the Palace of Night.

Now Alivet watched as the dishes of the main course were carried upstairs. The head chef had excelled himself. The foods he had prepared were rarefied to their finest extreme: all blood and essence. Alivet did not like to think where such food came from, but she doubted that it had been produced by the meat-racks in the city. Wild things, she thought, reared in the deep swamps of the delta, hunted down. The notion reminded her uncomfortably of her aunt. The water-clock moved on. The seemingly endless parade of dishes was borne from view. At last it was time for dessert.

Alivet hovered anxiously as the sorbets, each one with its pool of night around the tabernanthe-incarnadined ice, were taken upstairs by the serving staff. She remembered the spirit of the blood tabernanthe: that red, vivid figure. *Have I done enough to help you?* she asked silently. *Will you free us from the Lords?*—but there was no reply. She could not just wait down here until all chaos broke loose; she had to know what was happening. Where was Ghairen? And where was Inki?

Alivet waited for a frozen moment until she was certain that the attention of the head chef was elsewhere, and then she slipped after the servers. Her footsteps rattled on the stairs, but no one looked up. Alivet followed the servers into the hall. Apart from a pair of Enbonded at the far end of the hallway, their numb gaze fixed on the great bronze doors, it was empty. Alivet hastened to the dining hall, her footsteps muffled by the carpet. The Enbonded were still looking toward the doors, but now Alivet could see that there was a tiny crack between the door frame and the wall. She sidled behind the wall curtains, put her eye to the crack, and waited.

Inside, it was almost dark. A faint phosphorescence illuminated the high, echoing vaults of the hall. Beneath, the shadowy presences of the Lords of Night dined on the last of the meat essences. There must have been a hundred of them. Each Lord was different, as if snatched from a variety of nightmares. Alivet could see the great arch of ammonite skulls; the twisting spines that curved like untrimmed fingernails. Their carapaces betrayed hints of indigo and jade, overlain with a veneer of darkness. She saw the roll and slide of their lambent eyes, trained to other dimensions, but now fixed purely upon the world around them. She thought of the blood tabernanthe. She thought: *You are nothing more than beetles under my heel.* Somehow, however, the notion was not convincing.

Human Enbonded moved among the Lords like automata. They were dressed as finely as the Unpriests themselves: in stiff, intricate folds of silk that swung as they walked. Their hair was hidden beneath bronze hoods, which coiled out behind them like rams' horns. They wore gloves, with artificial talons. The aesthetics of such formality were beyond her, unless one held the uncomfortable clothes and the weird hoods to be evidence of a refined, obscure sadism.

There was a susurrus of anticipation as the desserts were

passed around the hall by the silent serving staff, who then trooped away. Alivet, her hearing fine-tuned by anticipation, heard the tiny crack as the first silver spoon touched the first sorbet; then another, and then another. There was the grinding crunch of mandibles upon ice. Alivet took a trembling breath. The Lords, moving as one, each swallowed a single spoonful of blood tabernanthe. The world hung, suspended in time, like a globe upon an armillary sphere. She thought of the light of a sun, absorbed and hidden, ready for release. The memory of a crimson figure danced inside her mind. Alivet breathed out.

And the first Lord exploded.

The blood tabernanthe electrified every filament of the Lord's body before it flared up into a great column of brilliance. The metal doors of the dining room were blasted from their hinges and flew down the hallway like leaves. Alivet, thrown back against the wall, could see nothing but the shattered form of the Lord branded upon her retinas, but she could taste the light which streamed out from the dining hall: the hard, clear sunlight of mountain peaks; the roseate depths of sundown over ocean; the golden, glittering brightness at midsummer noon, and behind them all the taste of human blood and human memories.

She dimly saw that, exposed to light, a second Lord was transformed into a pillar of flame, then another, and then all of them. It had worked. The Lords were gone up in fire, snatched up by the poisonous drug so carefully concealed in darkness and ice by the skillful hands of Alivet. Were they dying, or becoming transformed? And into what? But she could not stay and witness her triumph; the brightness was too much to bear. Afraid for what remained of her sight, Alivet turned. Hands gripped her shoulders and Alivet struck out.

"Alivet! It's me," Ghairen said. His voice was ragged.

"Where's Inki? Did you find her?"

"I found the cells. I couldn't see your sister. Alivet, we've got to get out of here. The whole palace is beginning to fracture."

"No! I'm going to find Inki." Alivet wrenched free of Ghairen's protective hands. "Tell me where the cells are." She could hardly see. She reached out, groping, and found the wall curtains.

"Alivet, listen—" Ghairen sounded utterly exasperated, but Alivet did not care.

Where are the cells?

There was a splitting, rending sound, like an immense tree struck by lightning. Alivet blinked upward. A crack was running the length of the ceiling.

"All right!" she heard Ghairen say above the tumult. "We'll go together."

He took her hand and they stumbled down the hallway. Alivet's vision began to clear. The hall split down its length and the carpet rolled up like a tongue. Alivet was hurled against the wall. Ghairen pulled her back onto the shifting floor.

"Down the stairs."

A twisting spiral led down into the depths of the Night Palace. Alivet, by now almost entirely lost, caught sight of the dormitory through a gaping hole in the wall and realized that they were close to the stairs leading down to the kitchens. The metal panels peeled away from the wall like riverbirch bark and fell to the floor. Alivet fell. Ghairen pulled her upright. The wall to her left collapsed in a shower of shards; through the gap, she glimpsed the marshes beneath a green twilight sky.

"Why is it collapsing?" she shouted as they bolted down the stairs.

"Release of energy from the Lords' physical bodies. You were lucky not to have been killed—I went to the kitchen to find you and you weren't there."

"I wanted to see what would happen. Why didn't you tell me they'd explode like that?"

"I didn't know," Ghairen admitted. "I thought they might just dematerialize."

They had reached the bottom of the stairs. Alivet looked back to see that the walls of the staircase had now peeled away: the spiral led up into a shattered ruin. Sky poured through the broken roof of the Palace of Night.

"Where are the Lords now?"

"I don't know," Ghairen said. His foresight and planning seemed to go no further than the disintegration of the Lords. Perhaps he had never really believed that they would be successful.

"Where are the cells?"

"Down there." Ghairen pointed. Alivet looked down onto an iron walkway, running along a series of cages. Each cage was roughly the height of a man: an external skeleton of bars and straps. Blood gleamed in the seething light and for a brief moment Alivet seemed to see the red spirit of the tabernanthe, head raised in grief and exultation. She brushed past Ghairen and ran down the steps to the walkway.

"Inki? Where are you?"

The first cells were empty, but eyes looked out at her from the darker cells along the walkway.

"Inki?"

And a voice answered: "I'm down here."

Alivet looked down to see a sea of pale faces staring up through a grille in the walkway. One of them—one-eyed but defiant—was the face of her sister.

"Inkirietta!" Alivet fell to her knees and started pulling at the grille. Ghairen dropped beside her to help. Using the knife as a lever, they prised up the nails and lifted the grille. Between them, they hauled Inki through the gap. Alivet threw herself at her sister.

"Sister Inkirietta Dee," Ghairen said behind her. "Good to see you again."

"I knew you'd come," Inki said. "Both of you." The walkway shuddered once, like an animal straining against its chains. The empty cages broke away and fell from the walkway, splashing down into the marsh. Other prisoners, wan and dazed, were coming up through the gap to stand on what was now a fragile platform, jutting over the water. The remains of the palace, a huge and complex ruin, rose before them.

"Go through the walls!" Ghairen shouted. "Over there, toward the causeway."

Alivet turned. In the water below, dark thrashing shapes were beginning to congregate. Alivet drew Inki more tightly to her side and turned to follow the prisoners.

"Don't you want to say good-bye?" someone said. The voice was sibilant, and familiar. Alivet spun around. And there was Iraguila Ust, covered in ash and holding a needle to a prisoner's throat.

"Iraguila," Alivet said, and then she recognized the prisoner. It was then that she realized that Ghairen had not been the only one to watch and plan.

"Aunty!" Inki cried.

Alivet's aunt Elitta was smaller and older than she remembered, her gray hair disheveled and her clothes torn. She struggled, but Ust touched the needle to her throat and Elitta grew still.

"I don't want her," Ust hissed. Her face was distorted with fury. "I am a Sanguinant. I want the architects who brought down my masters. You first, and then him. Step forward."

Alivet looked cautiously around. She and Inki stood between Ghairen and Ust; if he tried one of his poison-at-a-distance tricks, it would miss the governess and fall on them. She stepped forward, within reach of the needle. Ust thrust Elitta away and lunged at Alivet's throat, but Alivet dodged. Grasping Ust's wrist, she seized the woman by the arm and bent it back, but as she did so, she lost her own footing on the trembling platform. Alivet and Ust fell over the side and into the marsh.

Ust was torn from her grasp the moment they hit the water and vanished beneath its churning surface. Alivet felt a rasping, suckered thing wrap itself around her like a vine. She, too, was pulled down, into a forest of weeds. The weeds clung, wrapping themselves around her arms and throat, and gripping her ankles in a razor embrace. A swirl of mud flew up to blind her.

She thought of the thing that had fallen from the anube's pole to seize the Unpriests and drag them down. She struck out with the knife, slashing at the weeds, and broke free. But even as she struck upward from the surface, the current seized her and took her down into deep water. Her lungs were bursting, but strangely, it reminded her of the Search. The depths were serene, light filtering dimly down. She thought that perhaps it would be best to go with it, let herself be carried out on the current, but then that small cold voice at the back of her mind, that served her so well during the Searches, said: *You are drowning. Swim!* And Alivet swam up, past a great jutting outcrop of rock, and into the air.

Just as she broke the surface, she was hauled back down. Rank water once more filled her mouth and this time she tasted blood. Iridescent light filled the water; she saw a great mouth and eyes like lamps, then the sudden vision of Iraguila's head, torn off at the neck. Iraguila looked startled, as if surprised behind a keyhole. Something wrenched at Alivet's ankle and she was gripped from behind by a sinuous, strong form. Her vision went black, she lashed out, but then she was dragged out of the water and over the side of a pilgrimage boat. The anube who had rescued her was close behind.

Alivet lay gasping on the boards like a beached fish. Far above her head, she saw a trio of anxious faces peering over the side of the platform. Ghairen's lips moved; he was calling to her but her ears were full of water and she could not hear him past the ringing in her head.

"I'm all right," she thought she said.

The shattered remains of the Night Palace filled the sky, an immense latticed ruin, lit by a ghostly column of light that twisted and turned and knitted itself into a shining coil. As Alivet watched, a tiny hole of nothingness broke open the air. The coil swept forward, questing like a serpent, then poured through the hole, which widened briefly to form a crack. Through it, Alivet glimpsed familiar forms: four-faced, spinning beings. One of them looked back and she met its eyes. She could not interpret what she saw there: elation, despair? But then the crack closed behind the host with an audible snap.

"The Lords have gone," the anube said, sounding no more than faintly interested. Perhaps the Lords had been seeking such openings all along, Alivet thought; minute cracks between dimensions through which they could escape, once freed of their corrupted physical form. And if a human looked through such a thing, would it be enough to blind them?

Alivet sat up. Fighting was taking place within the ruins. She saw a group of Enbonded, tiny as birds in the rigging of the wreckage, swarming down toward a group of Unpriests. There was the sudden flare of a webgun, followed by a rain of debris as the Enbonded retaliated. Alivet watched as the two groups flowed together. Unpriests and Enbonded fell from the platform like ripe fruit, to be swallowed by the marsh. Unhurriedly, the anube steered the boat toward what remained of the ladder, where three figures were already climbing down.

EPILOGUE

If mankind had to choose between a universe that ignored him and one that noticed him to do him harm, it might well choose the second. Our own age need not begin congratulating itself on its freedom from superstition till it defeats a more dangerous temptation to despair.

— E. M. W. TILLYARD,
The Elizabethan World Picture

Latent Emanation, Month of Ice

A livet's hands rested on old wood, bleached by salt and light. She looked out over the fens, tranquil now beneath the winter sun. A thin skin of ice frosted the water underneath the deck of the cabin, trapping the reeds. She could see the silvery form of a fish, idling in the cold water under the ice. This weather should please Ari Ghairen, Alivet thought. It would become as chilly as Hathes itself very soon, now that the Month of Dragonflies was past and the winter had begun. Certainly he seemed in no hurry to depart, now that he had sent for Celana. She would be arriving soon, on the next drift-boat to visit Latent Emanation.

Across the fens, far on the edge of the horizon, the shattered remains of the easternmost Palace of Night was just visible. Only a couple of days, and already it looked like the most ancient of ruins. The other three palaces remained; there was talk of moving the university into one of them, or perhaps a pleasure complex similar to Port Tree. Now that Latent Emanation would be welcoming visitors from elsewhere, there seemed plenty of scope.

Inside, Alivet could hear the voices of Inki and her aunt, arguing over the best way to prepare rush fennel. Inki, it appeared, had plans. There would be no question, she had said firmly, of Alivet sacrificing anything to take care of her; she was quite capable of looking after herself. She did not want to become an apprentice apothecary or go and live in Shadow Town, even if they could afford it, or any of the grand dreams that Alivet had entertained on her behalf. She would open a restaurant, she had told Alivet, in one of the now-vacant Night Palaces.

"After all," she had said, "it isn't as though I don't know my way around the kitchens."

And Alivet, standing openmouthed, had no option but to agree.

Behind her, the veranda door opened, letting out a breath of heat. Alivet turned, to see Ghairen.

"It's too warm in there," he said. "And I think I'm in the way."

"You're not in the way out here," Alivet told him, rather stiffly.

"Thank you, Alivet." He gave her a sidelong look of mock gratitude.

"Tell me something. Did you ever really believe we'd succeed?"

"I did not dare to think of such a thing. If I'd failed this time, the Soret would have had me assassinated."

"*Assassinated?*"

"That is why I couldn't wait another year. When the previous attempts ended in disaster, the Soret gave me an ultimatum."

"Why did they choose you, and not another Poison Master?"

"Because I am supposed to be one of the best. And also, I don't know if you remember my telling you this, but my daughter Ryma's mother is the child of a member of the Soret. There was some—ill feeling, when we separated. It has crossed my mind on more than one occasion that certain members of the ruling class might have wanted an excuse for me to fail." He frowned. "It wasn't so much the prospect of death that I minded, as the professional humiliation."

"But why didn't you tell me?"

"I didn't want to put you under any more pressure. If you knew that my head was destined for the block if we failed, then where would that have left you? Of course, I didn't know you thought *I* was to be your murderer."

So he had only been trying to protect her. All the mysteries, the secrets, for her own benefit. Did that mean that the incomplete seduction was less of an attempt to use her than something genuine, something real? Alivet found herself smiling. But if the Soret had so ruthless an approach to their own people, then did that make them any better than the Lords? What plans did they really have for Latent Emanation? Out of the frying pan, Alivet thought, and into what fire?

"Where do you think the Lords are now?" she asked.

"Back in their own dimension, I hope. They must have been so frustrated. Their home within view, through those minute rents between dimensions, and they could no longer reach it. Until the light in the tabernanthe blasted darkness apart."

"And that glimpse through the rift: the four-faced beings. Was that the Lords' true form, or just another way of perceiving them?"

"We'll never know." Ghairen's face was grim. "When I sent word to Celana, I told her to get rid of that statue in the bedroom. I know you saw it," he added, before she could interrupt. "You seem to have been most enterprising in your midnight wanderings."

"I had to be, given that you locked me in my room."

"It was for your own protection."

But if he had not suspected Ust until it was almost too late, who had he been protecting her from? Did he think Celana might have tried something unpleasant, during the course of her own "midnight wanderings"? Even if Ghairen was by no means the monster she had feared, and even if Celana's own terrors had been laid to rest, it was a further hint of a disturbing family dynamic. *If we should ever share a bed*, Alivet thought, *I think I will insist on one of those force-fields. Just in case.*

"Why was the statue even there?" she asked.

"A reminder. It's old. It came from a Sanguinant temple. At first, I used to lie there and look at it and make sure that I did not sleep too easily until the Lords were gone. Later, of course, it became unnecessary. I have not slept well since the Soret issued their ultimatum." He paused and she knew that he did not want to talk about the Lords anymore. "It's quiet out here. Very peaceful."

"More peaceful than the city, anyway." Alivet grimaced. "A bloodbath, I heard. People hunting down Unpriests, scores being settled . . ."

"Perhaps it's for the best. Latent can start again, with a clean slate. All revolutions are founded in blood."

"Inki told me that the Unpriests were those of the Enbonded who showed a particular loyalty to the Lords, who would plot and scheme and sacrifice their fellows."

"Even after they themselves had suffered—forced as punishment to peer into another dimension, blinded as a result. They used it as a badge of honor, I believe. People who have been abused seek power where they can get it."

"I can't mourn them too much."

"Unpriests aren't the only plotters, though. Just look at your former employer, Genever Thant."

Alivet stared at him. "What about Genever Thant?"

"I spent the morning making inquiries about Thant and the 'murder' victim. If my information is correct, Madimi Garland will be marrying him a week on Marsh Day."

"What?"

"Madimi Garland is not dead, just as the anube told us. You certainly did not kill her. It seems that on the night that I approached you in Port Tree, my plotting met someone else's. While you were out of the fume room, Genever Thant gave Madimi a dose of a poison called merope, used by the anubes in their spirit journeys. As I'm sure you know, it comes from the spotted toad of the fens. It has two stages. At first, it causes unconsciousness, and then, if a suitable catalyst is applied, it mimics death. And the catalyst is a substance found in the most common brand of smelling salts. When you held them under Madimi's nose, you plunged her into coma."

"But the apothecary found no trace of it, only a smear of darkness on the handkerchief." That must have been from the sorbet, Alivet realized. "And why would Genever poison his own client?"

"So that the blame would fall on you."

"Why should Genever seek to blame me? I never did anything to him." Alivet was conscious of a growing outrage. After all the trouble she had gone to in order to be a supportive assistant...

"I doubt whether it was personal. You were convenient and expendable, that's all. After you ran away, Genever went to the Unpriests and informed them that you had made an attempt on Madimi's life. I don't know what story he used to account for this, but whatever it was, they believed him. They also believed him when Genever told them that he could cure Madimi, who at that point was lying cold on a mortuary slab. The family gathered round, tragic and weeping; Genever scattered a few drops of an antidote upon the motionless girl and a few minutes later, like the heroine of a fairy story, she opened her eyes and sat up. I imagine it was extremely dramatic. In fact I'm thinking of offering Genever a position in the Tower of the Poison Clans, since he seems to have demonstrated such an aptitude for the art. Anyway, having achieved this miracle, I'm sure you can imagine the result. Madimi's family pressed gifts and money upon their savior, which Genever modestly turned down. That was probably enough to make an impressionable, traumatized, and exceedingly wealthy heiress fall in love with him. As I say, the wedding's on Marsh Day."

Alivet, after a dumbfounded moment, said, "I hope there's no longer a warrant out for my arrest?"

"With the Unpriests gone, I doubt it." He drew closer as

she stood by the veranda rail and Alivet found herself acutely aware of his presence, and of the sexual menace beneath the civilized facade.

"Alivet. Where do we go from here?"

"I think we should start making a list of exportable products, between Latent and Hathes. Then, secure the Lords' drift-boat, wherever it is. Procure cargo. And I intend to grow my hair." She was aware that she was babbling.

Ghairen sighed. "I had taken note of your single-mindedness. It was partly why I enlisted your help in the first place, so I suppose I've only myself to blame. I was *not* referring to our economic options, as I suspect you are aware." He took her by the shoulders and turned her to face him. "Was it what happened between us that night? Did I frighten you?"

"I scared myself. I haven't had much time for men. Only for drugs and my work."

"But now you have all the time you want," Ghairen said. He looked pensively down at her. "We work well together, it seems to me. The drug-maker and the Poison Master."

He has a point, she thought. Her heart sailed up at the thought of a life with him. It would never be dull. But she foresaw shoals and rapids ahead: there was the entire question of his work, after all. She did not want to be a party to assassination and murder. How far could love transform a man? Alchemy was surely easier.

"We complement one another," Ghairen went on. "And besides," he looked up, with a sharp red gaze and she caught her breath at what she read in his face, "it's more than that for me."

"Ari, I am an alchemist and an apothecary. You cannot rush an experiment, without unpredictable consequences. Alchemy so often results in nothing more than lead. Conjunction of the wrong substances can result in explosions, too."

"And conjunction of the right substances?"

"Then," Alivet said, and reached out to him, "if you're very lucky and very careful, sometimes you can get gold."

ABOUT THE AUTHOR

LIZ WILLIAMS is the daughter of a stage magician and a Gothic novelist, and currently lives in Brighton, England. She received a Ph.D. in philosophy of science from Cambridge, and her career since has ranged from reading tarot cards on Brighton pier to teaching in Central Asia. She has had short fiction published in *Asimov's*, *Interzone*, *The Third Alternative*, and *Visionary Tongue*, among other publications, and is coeditor of the recent anthology *Fabulous Brighton*. She is also the current secretary of the Milford UK SF Writers' Workshop. *The Poison Master* is her third novel. She is working on her fourth.

Be sure not to miss

NINE LAYERS OF SKY

the next exciting novel from

LIZ WILLIAMS

Coming in fall 2003 from
Bantam Spectra

Here's a special excerpt:

They had reached the border early that morning, leapfrogging the grim skein of industrial towns that strung from Almaty to Chimkent. The early part of the journey now seemed remote: a grimy memory that made Elena's skin crawl with remembered pollution. It had taken almost four hours to reach the Uzbek border, crawling all the way, with the powerful wipers of the Sherpa grinding the snow into a grey slush. The slush accumulated at the bottom of the windscreen, periodically slewing down the hood and turning to packed ice beneath the wheels.

Atyrom drove without speaking, occasionally groping on the dashboard for cigarettes. He smoked Marlboros, which Elena hated. Halfway to Chimkent his sister Gulnara, who was supposed to have given up smoking, broke down and reached for the lighter. Acrid smoke filled the van like the ghost of an American dream. The lack of conversation was compulsory, since Atyrom insisted on playing Uzbek rock at a level that could have woken the dead. It veered from maudlin ballads to aggressive nationalistic anthems that made Atyrom pound the steering column in erratic accompaniment.

Bleary with lack of sleep, Elena stared out across the pale and endless expanse of the steppe. In summer, the land was constantly changing under the light: alternately subtle and harsh, depending on the time of day. Sometimes, she and her sister would borrow her cousin's car and drive out to Lake Kapchugai to sit by the quiet water and watch the shadows lengthen across the steppe, the afternoon sun striping the land with colors that had not changed since prehistoric times: ocher and mauve and red. Now, in late February, the steppe remained featureless beneath the snow; they could have been driving over the moon. Shortly before seven in the morning, they reached the border and the tailback.

It was still snowing, and Elena could not see very far ahead. The rear lights of the truck in front of them glowed crimson, then died as the truck stopped. Atyrom gave a snort of irritation and switched off the engine. There was a sudden, shattering silence.

"How long do you think we'll be here?" Elena asked.

Atyrom glanced at her with manifest contempt. "How should I know?"

"You've done the trip before," Elena said, reasonably.

"It's different every time." Atyrom answered, dismissing the issue. He settled back against the seat rest and closed his eyes. Elena decided not to argue. Atyrom was doing her a favor, after all. If it had not been for his offer, she would have had to take the train down to Tashkent, lugging the heavy bag of black market clothes with her.

She turned to look at her friend. Gulnara was also asleep, curled on the back seat with her face squashed uncomfortably against the doorframe. Elena watched her for a moment before fishing in the glove compartment for diversion. There was nothing but a week-old copy of *Karavan*. Gloomily, she perused the for-sale advertisements and the lonely hearts, but there was nothing of interest to buy and she was not interested in romance with anyone. Not after Yuri.

The cosmodrome seemed suddenly very far away: another Elena; another life entirely. It was growing cold in the cabin of the van. It had been 15 below when they left Chimkent. She chafed her hands in the thick leather gloves and opened the door of the Sherpa. Atyrom muttered a brief protest as she stepped down. The cold hit her like a hammer, slamming its way into her lungs. Her eyes prickled and her cheeks started to burn. Squinting, Elena wound her scarf more securely around her face and trudged slowly up the line.

After a seemingly unending procession of trucks and vans, she turned the corner and saw the ramshackle customs post ahead. Blue lights sparkled eerily through the falling snow and unease settled in an icy lump in Elena's throat. She walked up the line toward a little knot of people; they were talking to someone in a Lada through the open door of the car. Elena made her way to the edge of the gathering. These were presumably the customs officials, but as everyone was bundled up under several layers of clothing it was difficult to tell. One man had the insignia of the Kazakhstan militzia. What were the police doing here? A pink-nosed face peered at her like a rabbit from a burrow. Elena glanced past him, to where the driver of the vehicle sat staring peacefully ahead.

"Won't he get cold like that?" Elena asked inanely.

The custom officer's face twitched with something that could have been a smile. "He's not likely to get any colder." And then Elena realized that the man was dead.

"Oh, my God," she said, stepping back and slipping a little on the icy surface of the road.

"Not the only one," the customs officer said, with a kind of gloomy satisfaction. He pointed to the customs post, where figures were loading a stretcher into an ambulance. "Frozen stiff. Happens a lot this time of year."

"Look," Elena said. "I don't want to sound callous, but how long is this going to take?" She had no intention of emulating the driver of the Lada.

The customs officer shrugged. "We're moving as fast as we can. But the road's blocked, just beyond the post. They're trying to clear it now. I suggest you go back to your vehicle."

Elena rubbed her face indecisively, but there was nothing that could be done for the driver, and the ambulance was there, anyway. Her cheeks felt raw and red, and her lips were already chapped. Ice crackled in her hair; she could see a frosty blonde fringe just above her eyes.

"All right," she said at last, and walked back along the line. She did not dare look through the icy windscreens of the other cars; she was afraid of what she might see.

Atyrom stared at her as she climbed back into the Sherpa. "Where have you been?"

Tersely, Elena explained, haunted by the memory of the dead man's silent, frozen face.

"Well, never mind," Atyrom said, with something that almost approached cheerfulness. "As long as it's not us, eh?"

Elena couldn't help agreeing with the general sentiment, but not with the way in which it was expressed. She mumbled something. Through the frosty windscreen, she could see the lights of the ambulance as it came back down the road. But just as it drew level with the truck in front, the truck driver chose that moment to open his door and leap out. The ambulance veered clear of the door and the driver slammed on the brakes. The wheels of the ambulance spun, hammering it against the door of the Sherpa.

There was a thunderous bang. The van shook and rattled, and Atyrom was flung sideways across Elena's lap. Gulnara screamed. Atyrom shouted with fury. Scrambling up, he wrestled with the door, punching and kicking until the damaged lock gave way and the door shot open.

Atyrom fell out of the van, still shouting. Elena hastily levered herself across into the driver's seat and followed. The ambulance was trundling slowly down the road, the azure lights wobbling on top. Atyrom stumbled after it, bawling insults and curses.

"Are you drunk, asshole? Look what you've done to my van!"

As quickly as she could, Elena caught up with him. Atyrom was panting with rage. He shook off Elena's restraining hand and bounded through the snow, taking long, floundering leaps like a hunting dog. Elena struggled after him. Catching up with the ambulance, Atyrom pulled open the door and dragged the driver out. Both men fell heavily into the snow.

"Hey!" Elena shouted. "Atyrom, stop! It was an accident. Leave him alone!"

Atyrom was not listening. He hauled the ambulance driver to his feet and shoved him against the side of the nearest vehicle. All down the line, men were coming out of their cars to join in the argument, and to her dismay Elena saw the dark-coated figure of the militzia man heading purposefully towards them from the direction of the customs post.

"Atyrom, for God's sake!" she called. "You'll get us arrested." Atyrom was shaking the driver, pushing him against the tarpaulin side of the truck.

"What about my van, you fucking bastard?"

Something fell out of the driver's pocket: something long and bright that Elena could not see clearly. Atyrom stared down at it for a startled moment, then gave a roar of rage and head-butted the driver. A thin spray of blood spattered out across the snow. The driver gave a wail of pain.

"Grave robber!" Atyrom shouted.

Elena reached the irate Uzbek and hauled him back by the arms. The ambulance driver slumped back against the side of the truck as the policeman panted up. Elena caught a glimpse of a young, bony face beneath the militzia hat: one of those Ukrainian countenances with cold eyes set too far apart. She pulled Atyrom aside as the policeman swung the butt of an ancient Kalashnikov at the Uzbek's head.

"Don't touch me!" Atyrom shouted, ducking. "Don't you fucking touch me! Look! Look!" Wrestling out of Elena's restraining grip, he pounced into the snow and thrust out a handful of dirty, glittering slush. The policeman stared. "Look what this bastard's stolen! Watches! Money! Teeth!"

Appalled, Elena saw that Atyrom was right. A single golden tooth rested on the snow in his gloved palm, its root still stained pink.

"Stealing out of the mouths of the dead!" Atyrom roared.

The ambulance driver, wiping blood from his face with his

sleeve, began to protest but the policeman snarled, "Shut up!" He swung the gun again. Elena reflexively ducked out of the way, but there was a hard, dull crack as the butt of the gun connected with the side of the driver's head.

The ambulance driver dropped as if pole-axed and lay still. The policeman crouched in the snow, the pale eyes glaring up at Atyrom. "Well, what do you say, then?" he remarked, quite calmly. "Half for you, half for me?"

Atyrom, evidently mollified, shrugged. "Ladna. Why not?"

Elena watched in horrified silence as the policeman began to pick through the driver's pockets and placed a motley collection into the Uzbek's waiting hands.

"What about him?" she said angrily, pointing to the driver, but no one seemed to hear. Elena knelt down in the snow and examined the man's head. The blood was already congealing, glazing like red frost across the driver's skin. Was he dead? Elena groped inside the man's sleeve. The skin felt cold and clammy. She could not feel a pulse.

There was a shout from somewhere up near the front of the line.

"Hey! We're moving!"

Atyrom hauled himself to his feet and began to hurry back in the direction of the Sherpa.

"Well, are you coming or what?" he said over his shoulder.

Elena pointed down at the ambulance driver. "What about him?"

"Leave him," the policeman said. He spat into the snow. "Filth."

"No! We can't just leave him." Elena said. "I think he's dead. And if he isn't, he soon will be in this temperature. And what about the ambulance?"

Atyrom looked momentarily puzzled. "So? If he's dead, there's nothing we can do about it. Are you coming or not? If not, I'll leave you behind."

Elena, rehearsing a dozen arguments, got to her feet, but as she rose she noticed something embedded in the snow, not far from the fallen driver. She bent to look more closely, and saw a small black sphere. Reaching down, she plucked it out of its icy bed.

The sphere was around the size of a golf ball and looked as frail as a sugar shell, yet it was unaccountably heavy. Its matte surface seemed to swallow light. Bewildered, Elena put it in her pocket and it weighed down her coat; she could feel it dragging the material as she hurried back to the Sherpa, but by the time she reached the vehicle she had forgotten all about it. With the light of battle in her eye, she climbed back into the damaged van and began to tell Atyrom precisely what she thought of him.

The argument—with Gulnara echoing Elena's every pronouncement—lasted all the way down the long road to Tashkent.

St. Petersburg ❧ 21st Century

Beyond the open door of the apartment block, the snow breathed a winter cold and lessened the ammoniac reek of the stairwell, so that Ilya Muryomets could smell his own blood. The hot, meaty odor filled the air, as though the whole world was bleeding rather than just one man.

Ilya's hand fumbled to his side; his shirt was sticky and stiff. He remembered, distantly, that the dealer had knifed him; the situation, so carefully engineered, had gone disastrously wrong.

Think, he whispered to himself. *You were a bogatyr, a hero, a son of the sun . . . think.* Then the soft clutch of heroin took him, shutting him off from both understanding and pain.

Ilya could no longer see clearly, but he could still hear. A confused blur of sound rushed around him: snatches of conversation across the city; the gulls crying over Sakhalin, thousands of miles away; a door shutting in icy Riga with a sudden decisive thud. All of these sounds became distilled as Ilya listened, resolving into the steady seep of his blood onto the concrete floor.

Ilya Muryomets' mouth curled in a rictus grin. The glittering winter light glared through the door of the hallway, sharpening the shadows within. He had to get outside, escape into winter before the rusalki came for him, but his feet moved down the stairs with a slowness that suddenly struck him as comical. He leaned back against the wall and shook with mirth, the breath whistling through his punctured lung like a ghost's laugh.

He realized then that someone was watching him. He turned with a start, but it was only Ludmila Murmanova from the upstairs apartment, clutching a bag of withered apples and gaping at him in undisguised horror. He wondered what she saw: a gaunt man with pale hair and paler eyes, like a wounded wolf.

Ilya's laughter wheezed dry. He wiped the blood from his mouth and murmured, "Oh . . . good day, Mrs. Murmanova. Been shopping?"

Ludmila Murmanova edged past him and fled up the stairs. The slam of her steel door echoed through the stairwell.

The noise stirred Ilya into motion and he staggered down the stairs and out into the winter afternoon. He wondered why he was even considering flight. He didn't have a chance, Ilya thought, as the sweet haze of the drug started to wear thin and reality—as cold as the day—began to intrude. He had never been able to escape the rusalki. His side was beginning to hurt now. His lungs burned and he could see his own fractured breath spilling out into the air.

Clutching his side, Ilya tried to run, but he managed only a few paces before the pain brought him to his knees in the snow. The world grew dark, then bright again. Ilya began to pant in panic, looking around.

Across the street, sheltered by the wall, stood a man. His gloved hands were folded in front of him; his face was broad and pale beneath a furred hat. His eyes were black, without visible whites, and they glistened like oil in the pasty folds of his face.

"Help me," Ilya Muryomets tried to say, but the words were a whisper. The snow was searing his hands. He struggled to rise, but out on the Neva the ice splintered like breaking glass. Ilya looked up and saw that it was already too late.

A rusalka was rising from the river. Numbly, Ilya watched as she slid over the bank of the Neva and started to comb the ice from her hair with bone-thin fingers. He thought for a moment that she might not have seen him. But his heartbeat was slowing in the impossible cold, echoing through the winter world like a bell, and when he raised his hand to touch his injured side the blood crackled beneath his fingers. It made almost no sound at all, but the rusalka heard it and her head went up like a hunting dog's. Beneath the glistening frost of her hair, her eyes were the color of water, but then, suddenly, he was seeing through the illusion.

He saw a small, pinched face beneath a fluttering flap of skin. Her hands were curled and clawed, with fingers spreading up from both sides of the wrist. She looked nothing like a human woman, but Ilya had learned long ago that the rusalki maintained a glamour to hide their true appearance.

The rusalka glanced from side to side with exaggerated slowness: she was playing with him. *They hear everything,* Ilya thought in despair. *If a single feather drifted down to the snow, she would hear it. She is like me.*

Slowly, the rusalka smiled with a mouth full of needles.

"No, no," Ilya heard himself whisper, over and over again, but the rusalka rose like a disjointed puppet and stalked towards him. Blood filled his mouth with a rush, and he spat into the snow. The rusalka, murmuring, crouched beside him on backward-bent knees and lifted up his chin so that he could look into her face.

It was the last thing he wanted to do. He could see through the rusalka's eyes; all the way to the back of the north wind, all the way to the end of the world. The rusalka bent her head so that the cold curtain of skin fell across his face and kissed him, freezing the blood on his lips and breathing arctic air into his mouth. He could feel the thin spine of her split tongue traveling down his throat, scouring it clean of blood and sealing the vent in the wall of his chest.

His lungs gave a convulsive heave. He knelt, gasping. The rusalka scooped up a handful of bloody snow and tasted it as though it were ice cream. A curious expression, of mingled greed and regret, crossed her face and then she sidled away, her image drawing the sunlight into itself until she was no more than a vivid shadow against the snow, and then was gone.

And Ilya raised his head and cried aloud, because she had healed him and he would live, and this was the last thing he wanted to do.

Some time after the rusalka had healed him, Ilya rose and brushed the snow from his frozen hands. When he looked across to the apartments, he saw that the stranger had gone. Uneasily, Ilya drew his coat closer about him and began to wander along the Neva, beside the eroded concrete fortresses of the tower blocks.

The rusalki were whistling a storm out of the north. Ilya could hear them as they hid deep in the forests around the Beloye Mor, beyond the Arctic Circle, singing up the wind. Patiently, he walked on, waiting for the storm to break. He felt as light and empty as air. The last time he had been so close to death had been ten years ago, up in the Altai, and that had been the last time, too, that he had seen a rusalki. He had been shot, during a deliberately clumsy and obvious escape from an internment camp, and he really thought, then, he had been successful in trying to die. His enemies, however, were eternally vigilant. He had watched with his dying sight as the rusalka slipped down out of the trees to whisper healing into his mouth, her fingers water-soft against his skin and a new moon rising through the bones of the birches. He had pleaded with her to have pity, but she had only smiled a cold drowned smile and made him live.

Since then the world had changed, and Ilya had lost his way within it. He did not understand these new times: a day when there were no more heroes but only the will of ordinary people. He had made and lost a fortune. If he wanted money these days, he had to work for it on the building sites or scaffolds of the city. It seemed to him that all heroes came to dust or blood or this half-life of his—enduring, like radiation. Yet he still took advantage of the advances of this scientific age: medicine to ease sickness, drugs to ease the soul. He would have to seek out a dealer soon—one of the runners who hung around Centralniye Station—and perhaps for a while he could pretend that he was nothing more than another casualty of the late twentieth century and not the last of the *bogatyri*.

There were no heroes any more, and men born in the twelfth century were not supposed to see the dawn of the twenty-first. There were not supposed to be supernatural creatures that fed off love and blood, though sometimes Ilya watched the fanciful programs on the television and wondered whether such ideas might be gaining in strength; whether there might be a clue in this now long-standing rationalism to his own plight. Genetic modification or black magic? Behind their glamour, it sometimes seemed the rusalki did not look so very unlike the small grey aliens that had become so popular nowadays. If one was to believe the TV, everyone in America seemed to be seeing them, and the thought made Ilya shudder.

He walked on through St. Petersburg, up the wide channel of Nogorny Prospekt. He could hear the storm now, sweeping down from the north, veering out over the Gulf of Finland. He stood still, listening with unnatural acuteness as the first wave of the storm drenched the city in a veil of ice. Thunder rolled overhead, cracking the frozen Neva with a sound like gunfire. Ilya stood quite still and let the storm break around him. Its passing left him deafened and cold through to the bone, but still unmercifully alive. It had been a warning, no more, from the forest's drowned witch-children, and when it was over Ilya sighed, then began trudging up towards the station.

The aftermath of the storm had left the city silent and deserted. The skies cleared to a pale haze and Ilya could see the crimson smear of sun far away to the west. *Time to get off the streets*, he thought. *Time to get drunk*.

There was a bar off Nogorny Prospekt which he sometimes frequented. Entering its dark environs, Ilya ordered a double vodka and felt it warm him all the way down to his heart. He put his hand inside his damp clothes, feeling furtively for the wound, but there was nothing. The storm had washed his clothes clean of blood. The rusalki were fastidious; they did not like to see the signs of a life lived hard.

Ilya drank in silence, for he had learned long ago to seal his tongue against the secrets that might otherwise be spilled. The bar was crowded. He thought, once, that he glimpsed the pasty-faced, black-eyed stranger who had been watching him by the river, but when he looked more closely, no one was there. He stayed in the bar until midnight, drinking hard, until the memory of who and what he had been had become numbed, and he could stumble back to what passed as home to sleep and dream.

KAZAKHSTAN/UZBEK BORDER ↦ 21ST CENTURY

Atyrom pawned the teeth as soon as they reached Tashkent, but by this time both Elena and Gulnara were too weary and disgusted to make further protests. They watched as Atyrom carefully counted his bounty out onto the pawnbroker's table. The teeth glittered as they fell, like the mockery of a smile. Atyrom glanced sourly at Elena and his sister, clearly expecting another barrage of criticism, but Elena, at least, had already decided that she had said everything she was going to.

"It'll pay for the damage to the van," Atyrom said for the twentieth time, as though reasoning with children. Gulnara muttered something sour and looked away. Elena thrust her hands further into the pockets of her overcoat and tucked her chin into her collar, though the room was stuffy in contrast to the bitterly cold outside.

The pawnbroker's office smelled of paraffin and despair, making Elena wrinkle her nose. Inside her right hand pocket, her fingers curled around the small, hard sphere. Although the thing had been in her possession for so short a time, she already found herself clutching it like a talisman. The little sphere felt hot and smooth, and Elena tucked it into her palm until her hand grew comfortingly warm. The thing seemed to beat with a pulse of its own, or perhaps it was only echoing her own agitated heart.

She had no reason to feel guilty, Elena told herself again. Atyrom had acted before either Elena or his sister had been able to stop him; it was not their fault. Then the pawnbroker gave a voracious grin at the sight of a fake Rolex watch and Elena's guilt flooded back, hot and fresh as blood across the snow.

Atyrom had emptied his pockets now and begun an earnest conversation with the pawnbroker; they were speaking Uzbek, which Elena was unable to follow. A woman wearing a shalwar kameez came in with a tray and three little glasses of sweet tea, then disappeared. Elena stared around the room, noting the detritus of lives: old shoes gathering dust, the entrails of a radio scattered across a crumpled newspaper. She tilted her head to read the headline. "Uzbekistan regains glory!" it read in Russian, with a pride that was now old, and wholly misplaced.

Elena's hand stole beneath her coat to the inner pocket where she still kept her Party card. She fingered the square of laminated plastic, thinking—with a familiar distant astonishment—of the events that had brought her here to a pawnbroker's back room. She'd studied philosophy at university along with astrophysics, and a memory of the Rektor flashed briefly before her mind's eye: face flushed with enthusiasm before a blackboard as he explained the differences between the Aristotelian notions of primary and efficient cause.

Elena allowed herself a brief, wry smile. The efficient cause of her presence here was a simple need for money: the only reason there was to accompany her friend Gulnara and a man she didn't like a thousand kilometers south before the end of winter, with a vanload full of black market clothes from the Emirates and a handful of Western videos. She was hoping for a hundred dollars—enough to pay the rent for another month and put the bulk of it into the box under the mattress. Elena smiled as she thought of the box. Every *tenge* they could spare went into it: Anna's waitressing wages, Elena's cleaning money, their mother's pension, and the results of occasional forays such as this one. The fund was growing too slowly, but if they were careful and no disasters like illness occurred, they should have enough by spring.

The familiar thoughts crowded into her head. *And then we're out of here. Moscow first, and then Canada. Yuri told me it was madness. What chance will I have of ever working in a space program again if I leave the country? But what's left here? I'd rather wait tables in Montreal than sit pining for an opportunity that might never come.*

Money was a good enough reason to do anything these days, Elena thought, then corrected herself as she watched Atyrom haggle with the pawnbroker. But not good enough to trade tragedy for a few miserable dollars. She wondered briefly how much the gold would fetch, and how a person would extract it from the teeth in the first place. Meditating on Aristotle seemed preferable.

So what was the primary cause of her present circumstances? Mikhail Gorbachev deciding nineteen years ago to drop his trousers and bend over in the direction of America? Mikhail Gorbachev being born? Elena knew, deep within her bones, that the architect of *perestroika* was the single reason why she was here now, sipping treacly tea in a dingy room in the back streets of Tashkent when she should have been sitting in her office at Baikonur watching rockets reach the bright skies above the Soviet Union.

She should have been what she had trained to be: an

astrophysicist. Or something other than a dealer in black market goods, anyway. At least Atyrom's videos weren't pornographic. It wasn't hard to see the funny side to the whole thing, but then, she'd always had a black sense of humor; she was Russian, after all.

Elena sighed, cradling the deceptive fragility of the little sphere, and waited for Atyrom to finish haggling.